Praise for Susan Palwick's
*ALL WORLDS ARE REAL*

"Susan Palwick is a master storyteller with a deep understanding of the human soul and an expansive imagination that charms (and sometimes alarms) me. Her stories will transport you to strange places and will introduce you to the people who inhabit them. And yes, all of those worlds and all of those people are very real. They linger in the imagination, as solid as the floor beneath you, as intriguing as the stranger you met at a party, and as startling as a human soul, captured in a lucite cube and sold at the gift shop in the tenth circle of hell."
—Pat Murphy, author of *The Falling Woman*

"The 15 inventive stories in the heartfelt second collection of speculative fiction from Palwick (*Mending the Moon*) are connected by themes of death and recovery . . . Palwick's mastery of vibrant, immersive storytelling is never in doubt. Readers will be thoroughly transported by these achingly beautiful tales."
—*Publishers Weekly*

"I don't just read a Susan Palwick story, I inhabit her characters. I experience their joys, doubts, sorrows, triumphs, and redemptions as if they were my own. Susan lays bare their hearts and, more importantly, their souls. I find the characters and their surroundings so convincing that as I read I know 'all worlds are real.' This collection includes many of my long-time favorite Susan Palwick stories and some brand new ones."
—Sheila Williams, editor of *Asimov's Science Fiction*

"Susan Palwick is an extraordinary writer. Each story is an unflinching and powerful glimpse into imagined worlds, crafted with tender compassion for the wounded souls that inhabit them."

—Ellen Klages author of *Passing Strange*

"Susan Palwick's vivid characterization and knife-edged prose draw the reader into situations they never imagined, partnering in adventure with oft-unsettling companions. Lost souls, true believers, and unwilling good Samaritans abound in *All Worlds are Real*, pulling you into worlds strange and thrilling, alien and yet familiar—and then leaving you in them, working to draw your own map home."

—A.M. Dellamonica, author of *Child of a Hidden Sea*

# ALL
# WORLDS
# ARE
# REAL

## SHORT
## FICTIONS

**Also by Susan Palwick:**

*Flying in Place*
*Shelter*
*The Necessary Beggar*
*Mending the Moon*
*The Fate of Mice*

# ALL WORLDS ARE REAL

## SHORT FICTIONS

SUSAN PALWICK

FAIRWOOD PRESS
Bonney Lake, WA

## ALL WORLDS ARE REAL:

### SHORT FICTIONS

A Fairwood Press Book

November 2019

Copyright © 2019 Susan Palwick

First Edition

Fairwood Press
21528 104th Street Court East
Bonney Lake, WA 98391
www.fairwoodpress.com

Cover and Book Design by Patrick Swenson

ISBN: 978-1-933846-84-2
First Fairwood Press Edition: November 2019
Printed in the United States of America

# CONTENTS

# INTRODUCTION

## JO WALTON

**T**WO KINDS OF people are likely to pick up this collection. The first kind know about Susan Palwick, and will have picked it up with cries of joy. Their only relationship with this introduction will be to race through it as fast as possible to get to the stories, especially the new ones. Some of them will be new even to the most enthusiastic Palwick fan, because a few of them have only appeared in obscure places and three of them are brand new for this volume. With this kind of reader, I share a conspiratorial smile. Yes, she *is* that good, isn't she? We share the knowledge that Palwick is an unobtrusive writer who nevertheless is writing stories of great significance and weight, worth grabbing as soon as we see them. We recognize that her work is important and want more of it. If you recognize yourself in this, you can safely skip the rest of this introduction and get on to the stories.

So I'm writing this for the second group of potential people who might pick up this book, people who aren't familiar with Palwick, but who are curious. There are a lot of books out there, a lot of writers and a lot of readers. Palwick hasn't yet made the big time. Why should you read this one?

All art is about the truths of the human heart, but science fiction and fantasy are more interesting because they can compare the truths of the alien heart, the monstrous heart, the ghost's heart, the cyborg heart. . . . So many possible hearts can have so many possible truths, can illuminate the human heart from many different directions. Palwick has been quietly writing this kind of science fiction and fantasy for decades, dropping one stunning short story or novel after another into the pool without any fuss. Some of them have cast ripples, and some, for one reason or another, have not cast as many as they should have. She is definitely not as well known as a writer this good ought to be at this point in her career, because attention is inexplicable and fickle and I just don't understand how it works, and being great, and having me jumping up and down saying "Look, look, she's so great, look over here!" clearly isn't enough to attract it.

And yet she has been consistently producing gems like the ones contained in this collection—not very fast, but steadily. These are stories doing what our genre does, about as well as it can be done. These are stories that ask "what if" questions of the human heart, stories about compassion and caring and neighborliness, about life and death and aliens and dogs and emergency rooms, about uploaded consciousness and literal ghosts in literal machines, and what that means. Palwick always makes me think, and makes me care, and makes me keep on reading. The easy comparison would be to Connie Willis or Neil Gaiman, but there's a depth and a groundedness to Palwick's work that makes her even better. These are important exciting stories that are fun to read, even when they're harrowing. I'm tempted to pick out favorites, but they're all so good!

Go read them. They can speak for themselves. You can thank me later.

# ALL
# WORLDS
# ARE
# REAL

*A family friend, who died several years back, had a child in prison. She told heart-wrenching stories about having to travel many hours to see him, and about her failed efforts to secure his transfer to a facility closer to where she lived. And of course, untold numbers of families have been separated by conditions—migration, political conflict—that make any visits impossible.*

# WINDOWS

**T**HE BUS SMELLS like plastic and urine, and the kid sitting next to Vangie has his music cranked up way too high. It's leaking out of his earbuds, giving her a headache. He's a big boy, sprawled out across his seat and into hers as if she's not there at all. She squeezes herself against the window, resting her head against the cool glass to try to ease the throbbing behind her eyes. Maybe the kid will get off at the next stop, in forty minutes or so. Maybe nobody else will get on to take his seat. The bus is completely full, and the waves of chatter and smell might have made Vangie sick even without the booming bass.

It's a ten-hour ride to see Graham; Vangie just hopes she'll get in this time. She can't shake her gut fear that everything's lined up too neatly, that something has to go wrong. More than once, she's spent the time and money to get down there—the time's no problem, but the money's not so easy, not with her monthly check as small as it is—to find the prison on lockdown, nobody in or out and God only knows what's going on inside. All you get are reports you can't trust, and you sit in the shabby town library Googling the news every two seconds until it's time to catch the bus back home, because you can't afford another night in a motel. Sometimes it's been days until Graham's been able to call out, until Vangie's been able to hear his voice again. She always accepts the collect charges, but they never talk long. Those calls cost.

Vangie's small overnight bag is under her feet. She's got her purse strap crossed over her body, and her arms crossed protectively over that, as if the kid next to her might snatch the bag and sprint to the front of the bus, diving out the door at seventy miles an hour. She knows this wouldn't happen even if she looked like someone worth robbing, even if what's in her purse had the slightest value to anybody except her and maybe Graham. He won't value it as much as she does. She doesn't see how he could. Every time she thinks about it she feels a great weight in her chest, a clot of grief and guilt and relief and love, and sometimes a tiny bit of pride creeps in there too—one of her kids got away, is getting away, even if it's too far— but she squashes that, always. No one else would think she deserved to feel proud. She doesn't think she deserves to feel proud. Pride is dangerous. So's luck, because it always turns, and there's already been too much this trip.

The kid next to her yawns and shifts, giving her an inch or two more room, and she takes it, grateful. It's getting dark, sunset a dull bruise to the west, obscured by clouds and by the dirty window, but at least she can see out, watch the gray highway rushing past. When she first started making this trip, three years ago, she promised herself she'd look out the window the whole time so she'd be able to tell Graham about it, but there's nothing next to the road but flat fields, corn and alfalfa. Sometimes a combine, but she can never make out people. She looked for cows the first few times, horses. No luck. She'll tell him about this sunset, though. She'll make it sound prettier than it is.

And when it gets completely dark she'll peer up through the window and try to make out stars. Sometimes she can see them. She can't remember if there's a moon tonight, but she'll look for that, too. Vangie feels like she has to look, because Graham can't. He doesn't get to see the night sky anymore.

Zel doesn't get to see anything else. She thought she was so lucky when she won the ticket, blind lottery, her name pulled out of the hat with all those other folks'. It still rips Vangie's heart open to remember how eager Zel was to leave all of them, leave everything forever. "I'm going to the stars!" she said, but all she's doing is living in a tin can, living and dying there, and they'll make babies out of her eggs who'll live the next leg, and babies out of their eggs who'll live the next, and finally there will be a planet at the end of it, that world the scientists found that's supposed to be as much like Earth as makes no never mind. Zel will never see it. She'll be long dead, her children's children will be long dead, by the time they get there. She'll never see sunset or alfalfa again.

As far as Vangie's concerned, she's got two kids in for life. She's just glad she can still visit one of them.

She's almost dozed off when the bus stops. The kid next to her gets off. Nobody else gets on. Nobody moves from their current seat to take that one. A shiver goes down Vangie's spine, and she crosses her fingers even as she's moving her bag onto the other seat, stretching out the way the kid did, sighing and feeling her muscles unknot because now maybe she can actually sleep the last few hours of the trip. More luck, too much luck, as much crazy luck this time as it took Zel to get that ticket. She won the generation-ship lottery right before Graham got caught moving more cocaine than anyone could claim for personal use, dumb bad luck, he hadn't noticed one of his taillights was out and got pulled over, third strike you're out. It's like Vangie and her kids only get so much luck, and Zel's heaping lottery serving—if you call that luck at all—meant Graham ran short. Vangie hopes she herself isn't hogging it now. The kids need it more than she does.

She knows there are people who'd say Graham doesn't deserve luck, say what happened to him was all about choice and not about luck at all, say he's scum for dealing drugs. Vangie wishes to God he hadn't gotten involved in the cocaine deal, but she wishes Zel hadn't won the lottery ticket, too. The world can think what it wants. Graham's her son. He's the only family she has left, and tomorrow's his birthday. And in her bag, infinitely precious, is a message from his sister. And if this impossible streak of luck holds, Vangie will actually get to deliver it to him on his birthday.

She gets dizzy just thinking about everything that's already had to go exactly right. Zel's end is tricky enough. The settlers—settlers! as if Zel will ever get to settle anywhere but inside that tin can!—don't get to send messages very often, because there are so many of them and they're all busy growing beans or doing things to each other's eggs and sperm or whatever they spend their time on up there. Vangie tries not to wonder about the babies. Whatever babies Zel has, Vangie will never get to hold them.

But anyway, they don't get to send messages very often. There's a schedule, as strict as the one dictating when prisoners can call out, and for how long. And the ones from the tin can have to travel a lot farther. There's a computer that tells the person sending the message when it will reach Earth. Right now it takes a couple of days, and a lot of messages don't even get through because they have to travel so far, bouncing off planets and satellites and space rocks and God knows what else. A lot of them just get lost.

So Zel just happened to get her slot last week sometime, or the week before that, and sent Graham's birthday video in time to reach Vangie's free e-mail account the week before Graham's birthday, which falls at the beginning of the month, right after Vangie's check comes in, which means she had the money to buy a thumb drive to put the file on, and also had the money for the bus ticket and the hotel down at the prison, because Graham's birthday falls on one of the weekend visiting days, and how often will that ever happen? It's amazing enough that the message actually came through. The trip will leave Vangie short on grocery money for the month, but she'll go to the food pantries and soup kitchens. She'll scrape by.

Of course she called ahead to the prison to see if they'd even let her show Graham the file. She hasn't watched it yet; she wants to see it with him. It's called "Happy birthday, Graham," so she knows what it's about. She and Graham will have to watch it on one of the prison computers, and she wanted to make sure she wouldn't have to pay: video visits are $100 an hour, another racket, like the collect phone calls. The prison's so crowded because there's no money, they always say, but it looks to Vangie like they're cleaning up.

More luck: because a prisoner just died in isolation and there's been a big flap about it, and they're worried about PR this week, her call got put through to the warden, and he promised her that she'd be able to use a prison laptop, no charge. Something about prisoners' rights to contact with family, and if your family's on a generation ship and your only possible contact's a video message that just traveled days to get to your mother's e-mail account, well then.

Vangie trusts this as far as she can throw the bus. The flap's died down now. Twenty to one there won't be any laptop. She doubts the warden will admit to taking her call, or even remember it.

The bus rocks her, that lulling rushing motion she's always loved, the feeling of going somewhere. She peers up through the window, but there are clouds now, and between them and the grime, she can't see stars. She pushes both of her seats back, and stretches out as much as she can, and sleeps.

It's a good thing she slept on the bus, because she can hardly sleep at all in her hotel room: a blasting TV on one side of her and raucous sex followed by a screaming fight in the other, and a lumpy mattress. Her own TV's broken, so she lies in the dark, staring up at the ceiling, reminding herself that Zel and Graham both have it much worse. Prison's even noisier than this, and much more crowded, and there's no checking out of the gen-ship.

She dozes off a little, finally, around three, but wakes up smack-dab at five, the way she's done her whole adult life. This means she gets close to first dibs on the hot water, which still runs out too quickly. A shower's a shower, though. The coffee at the diner across the street restores her even more, and the scrambled eggs are fluffy, just like she makes them herself.

She's first in line at the prison. "Evangeline Morris," she tells the guard, who looks like she's barely awake. "I'm supposed to be able to use one of your laptops. The warden said."

"Yes ma'am. I have that down here. They'll get it for you inside."

Marveling and suspicious—the PR flap must have lasted longer than usual—Vangie hands over her purse so another yawning guard can search it, and goes through the metal detector and reclaims her bag. There's a long line of other visitors behind her; she can feel the weight of them pressing on her back, pressing her through the doors into the visiting room.

The visiting room's a dull yellow cube dotted with tables and chairs. The two vending machines in the corner are always broken, and noise echoes off the walls. There's nothing resembling privacy, but if you have somebody in here, you take what you can get.

And there's Graham waiting for her, and someone else is with him, but Vangie doesn't care about that right now: she just reaches out for the hug she's allowed, one at the beginning of the visit and one at the end. She hugs Graham as hard as she can, as if she can force all her love for him through his skin, armor against his life here. "Happy birthday, baby."

"Mama." His voice is thick. She pulls back to look at him: he's thinner than he was last visit, and tears track his cheeks. "Mama, I brought the chaplain with me."

"What?" Her heart flutters. "What's wrong?" Graham's thinner than last time. "Are you—"

"Mama, the ship. You didn't hear? The news last night?"

"What? What news?" She was on the bus last night, in the hotel with the broken TV. No, she hasn't heard any news.

"The gen-ship. There was a fire. An explosion. They've lost contact. Nobody knows anything. Everybody's scared."

Vangie blinks. The chaplain reaches out to steady her, and she realizes she's swaying. Graham guides her into a chair. All that good luck: she knew something terrible had to happen. She swallows.

"I didn't hear anything." She didn't hear anybody talking about it at the diner, even. She was in a bubble, as isolated as any prisoner here, as isolated as the people on the gen-ship, dead or alive. "I— they don't know?"

Graham's sitting now, at the little table across from her. "Nobody knows anything yet. They're afraid it's bad."

The aftertaste of coffee is a bitter tang in her mouth, metallic as blood. The chaplain clears his throat. "Ma'am, I'm so sorry. I'd be happy to pray with you, or talk—"

She wants to send him away. If no one knows anything yet, maybe it's all fine. There are safety systems on the gen-ship. There've been fires in space before, haven't there? And everybody lived? Of course the news people are pushing fear. That's their drug, making everybody scared, as if life's not scary enough. News fear isn't real.

This chaplain's real, too real; he makes her nervous, and she wants him gone. But Graham brought him here. Graham's trying to do something for her. Graham, who may now be her only child, is trying to be a good and loving son. He doesn't have many ways to take care of her. She has to let him.

So she and Graham bow their heads, and the chaplain says a quick, bland prayer for safety and a good outcome and comfort for all the families here on earth, and squeezes her shoulder, and asks if she needs to talk.

"Thank you, reverend, but I need to talk to my son. I don't have long with him, as you know. It's his birthday."

"Happy birthday," the chaplain says softly, and leaves.

Graham wipes his eyes. The prayer seems to have moved him far more than it did her. "Mama, I don't know how we'll know if she's—"

"She's fine," Vangie says. She hears her own voice, too shrill, too loud. She recognizes that voice: it's how she talked when Graham was arrested, in the weeks before his sentencing when she had to hope that somehow everything would work out, that he'd get off.

Maybe everything will be fine, and if you say so loudly enough, maybe you'll believe it. "We don't know anything. Until we know for sure, she's fine. And she sent you something, Graham." She calls over a guard and asks for the laptop.

He brings it. This no longer surprises her. Her dread at the improbable run of luck is gone now, and she refuses to let any other dread replace it.

The guard clears his throat. "I need to stay here while you use it."

"Yes. We understand."

He turns on the machine, and Vangie, hands shaking only a little, inserts the thumb drive and opens the file. Somebody's set the laptop volume too high: there's a blast of music, the theme music for the gen-ship, like it's some kind of TV show, and then "Happy birthday, Graham!" fills the screen in flowery letters, and then there's Zel's face. Vangie hasn't seen it in months, except in photos. Zel's smiling. She looks healthy. Her hair's short, and she's wearing a white T-shirt; behind her, Vangie sees metal walls, a white corridor, people walking through it.

Vangie turns down the volume so Zel's voice will sound normal. "Hey, Graham! I hope Mama got this message to you in time for your birthday, but if not, happy belated. I only have about a minute, but I just wanted you to know that I miss both of you and think about you all the time. The ship's a little boring but not too bad. I'm still working with the plants. I like it." Zel holds up a tiny yellow jacket. "I crocheted this. One of my eggs took: I'm going to be a mom!" Her grin's huge now, the expression Vangie remembers from summer trips to the public pool, from the times Zel got to play with a neighbor's dog, from when she rushed over to tell Vangie she'd won a place on the ship. "So Mama, you're going to be a grandma, and Graham's going to be an uncle! And whatever the baby is, I'm naming it after one of you. It will be one of the first babies born here. I'm getting special food and everything, lots of vitamins. It's a big deal. Okay, that's my time. Love you both. Bye."

The message ends. The room's quieter than Vangie's ever heard it. She feels that pressure at her back and turns to find a crowd around the table: other inmates and visitors, other guards. The guy who manned the metal detector, the woman at the desk. The chaplain. Some of them are sniffling. They look stricken. They look alike, whatever they're wearing, uniforms or prison jumpsuits or street clothing.

They heard the music. They came to watch the message from the ship.

"We don't know anything yet," Vangie says. Her voice sounds like her own again. "Not for sure. And whatever's happening up there, we can't do anything about it. Today is my son Graham's birthday. Help me sing to him."

And they do. It's a ragged chorus gathered by shock and tragedy, wavering and off-key, and it won't last long, but it's here now. And Vangie knows that's luck, too.

*After the 1988 World Fantasy Convention in London, I took the train up to Edinburgh. My week wandering around the city included a walk up Arthur's Seat. I was happily hiking along when a voice next to me said, "Are you all right?" It was a policeman who'd seen me from the road that runs around the bottom of the park; he'd climbed up to make sure I was all right. He stayed with me until we met another group of hikers. It was clear to me, although he never exactly said so, that he was alarmed to see a woman in the park by herself. That encounter was the genesis of this story.*

# THE SHINING HILLS

**A**RE YOU ALL right?"

The voice, sharp and worried, shot out of the puddle of shadow to her left. Startled, she turned and found herself blinking at a cop, one of the ones who patrolled the park on foot. In the last light of dusk, she could just make out his half-frown, his badge, the hand resting on a nightstick. He reminded her of her father.

She shivered and pulled her sweatshirt more tightly around her. She should have brought warmer clothing, but she wasn't going to be here long. "I'm fine. Why wouldn't I be?" Her father would have said she was being rude, and foolish beside: you didn't talk back to cops, especially in foreign countries. She didn't care. Cops were cops.

"It's getting dark. Where are you going?"

None of your fucking business. Even she knew better than to say that. Anyway, couldn't he figure it out? She didn't answer, just gestured with her chin. When she glanced at the top of Arthur's Seat now, she couldn't make out the glowing lights she'd seen before. She wondered if the cop would have been able to see them even when they were there. Only the Chosen saw them, supposedly, which was why the non-Chosen thought anybody who saw them was crazy.

She hoped she hadn't missed her chance.

When you see them, don't look away. Follow them. If they vanish, they may be gone forever. There's no way to know if you'll get another chance. That's what everybody said. There were Chosen who were still here, stunned and yearning. Some of them killed themselves, and she didn't want to do that, but she wasn't sure what she'd do instead, since she'd come all the way here.

"Ach," the cop said, softly, and shook his head. "That's no place to be going, not at nightfall. You don't know what's up there."

Neither do you, she thought. And I know there were lights up there. Maybe they'd just been blocked by other people. Maybe they'd come back. She started walking again, but he hurried next to her. "Wait, please. Please, wait. I'm still here. I'm talking to you. What's your name?"

The lights hadn't come back; she couldn't even see the top of the Seat now, in the growing darkness. She could only see a few other people, far ahead of her. She wondered why the cop wasn't going after them. Frustrated, angry at herself for letting him distract her—although she supposed he'd just have followed her anyway, had she ignored his first greeting—she turned. "Niff."

"Niff?" She caught a flash of white teeth in the dusk, a smile. "That short for something?"

"Jennifer." Why was she even answering? But maybe he'd go away more quickly if she did.

"Niff. That's a good one. I've never heard that."

"Thanks," she said, throat tightening. She'd hated her name and all its standard nicknames as long as she could remember. Her brother Toby had hit on Niff, the one surprise hiding in those syllables, and it had stuck. Toby had always understood her, but he was gone now. War. IED. Not enough left to send home, not even his dogtags.

She turned back toward Arthur's Seat. Had she seen a brief blaze of light? She peered into the dimness, unsure, but started walking anyway, really more of a trot. The cop stayed next to her, an unwelcome growth.

"I'm Seamus. I prefer not to be called Shame." She didn't answer. He thought he was clever; he wasn't. She sped up. So did he. "Niff, what do you think you're going to find up there?"

He was faster than she was; he stood in front of her now, and she blinked, unsure how he'd gotten there. He could have been one of the fey himself. "Go pester somebody else," she told him.

"Not right now. Right now I'm pestering you."

"If I scream and say you were harassing me, what do you think would happen?"

His face in the fading light was grave. "If you scream, another cop will come. They know me. They're my friends." She shook her head and tried to go around him, but he blocked her. "Niff, listen to me. Just listen. I don't know if there's a faerie court on top of Arthur's Seat or not. I do know that people you don't want to meet have been going up there to waylay folks heading to the top to see faeries. Some of them shine lights to fool people. Robbery's the best you can expect."

"Nothing to rob." She'd spent all her money getting here. "The lights are real."

"Some of them are real. Others aren't. None of them, real or not, mean you any good."

She noted that he hadn't told her she was stupid to believe in them. He was pretending to keep an open mind, trying to win her trust. Again she tried to move around him; again he swung easily into her path. He made no move to touch her, just made it clear that they could do this dance for a long time. "Robbery's the best, I said. There are other things they can take, will take. You know about the bodies up there: everyone knows. Some say they're folks the fair folk rejected, say if they want you, they'll pull you into their world and you'll be safe and will never have to worry about rape or murder again, although don't ask me how anyone knows faeries don't have their own version of rape, or that they aren't just throwing people into stew pots."

She rolled her eyes. "They're vegetarians."

"And you know this how? The people who vanish don't come back: everyone knows that, too."

At least he wasn't trying to convince her they didn't exist, not that anybody could. Everyone knew people had vanished. Everyone had seen the lights, or knew someone who had seen lights, heard music, glimpsed gauzy forms with wings, flickering, here and then gone. Some said they weren't faeries but angels or demons or aliens. It didn't matter. Wherever people vanished to, they were somewhere else.

She thought the summoners were faeries, because she'd dreamed music, celtic-y, with harps and pipes. She didn't really know they were vegetarians; she just thought so. Nuts, flower salad. Berries. But she shouldn't have said anything. Dumb. Don't engage with assholes. "I'd like to go up there, please. I've done nothing wrong. You can't arrest me."

"Oh, Niff." He sounded very tired. "I'm not going to arrest you. When's the last time you had something to eat?"

Arthur's Seat wasn't very high, not really, but the path seemed longer now than it had before the sun set. She craned her head; she couldn't see the lights anymore, but if she started up, maybe they'd come back. "I'm nineteen. I'm legal. You can't stop me."

"In three hours the moon will be up," said Seamus the cop. "Full moon: you know that. That's why you came tonight, right?" She wondered how many other cops were in the park, trying to stop people heading up to Arthur's Seat on the night of the full moon. "You'll be able to see better then, if you still want to go. Let me buy you a burger, talk a bit. You still want to go up there afterwards, you're right. I can't stop you."


He took her to the Holyrood, one of the pubs closest to the Park. He hadn't expected her to say yes, and wondered why she had, but he was glad of it. Simple hunger, he supposed. She was American, that was clear enough, on a gap year before college maybe:

she'd be at school at this time of year, if she were studying. But then, plenty of college kids had run away to the Shining Hills too.

This time of year: late November, when it got dark before 4:00. Perfect for mysterious lights; bad for young women—or men, for that matter—wandering around the Park. In summer, especially Festival when it stayed light until ten and the city swelled to three times its normal size, Niff would have been much less easy to spot.

But kids had regularly washed up in Edinburgh even before the mysterious lights started. He'd been working Holyrood Park a long time, and he knew them from a mile away, just as the pimps and predators did: the lost ones, the runaways, headed up for a look-see. They gave off a sour smell that had less to do with food and hygiene—both usually in short supply—than with grief, desperation, despair. Some were on drugs, but not all; Niff wasn't, not that he could tell, and over the years he'd gotten good at telling.

The Holyrood was warm, crowded, renowned for its burgers. He wondered if Niff would order beer—he wouldn't have stopped her—but she didn't, asked for tea instead. "You really a pimp?" she asked, eyes narrowed, sitting across from him at the table. "Pimp dressed as a cop?"

"No, Niff. I'm really a cop." He was off-duty now and shouldn't have been in uniform, but he wasn't going to tell her that, and she hadn't asked about his lack of a partner. If she did, he'd tell her the radio on his shoulder kept him in touch with a partner, which indeed it did, when he was on duty. He walked the paths and trails and his partner drove the car around the Park down below. Sometimes Seamus patrolled down there too. If he heard a scream, he could make it up to the top in ten minutes.

Niff eyed him. She wore a nondescript faded sweatshirt and fingerless gloves, none of it warm enough for Edinburgh in November, although they'd had no snow yet. Well, sure she'd packed light. Planned to go somewhere warmer.

He wondered briefly why there were never stories about ice

fairies—or maybe there were, that kid's ballet—before Niff said, "You have a police budget to buy people burgers?"

He smiled. It was a smart question. "No. It's my own money. I won't say no to your repaying me, if you have any of your own." She looked away, and he said, "That's all right. I didn't think so." If she'd had money of her own she wouldn't have been hungry, wouldn't have agreed to come with him in the first place.

"So you're a cop who works with pimps?" Her eyes were still narrowed. "Being so careful not to touch me, taking me somewhere public. Trying to get me to trust you?"

He regarded her. Smart. "Has that happened to you?"

"No."

"Good. Because you're right: if that's what I were up to, I'd probably be going about it the same way. But I'm not. I'm worried about you—or anybody—hiking up to the Seat this time of day, that's all."

"You take them all out for burgers? What's your story?"

"Trade," he told her. "Your story for mine. But yours first, because I'm buying the burgers."

She told him. She didn't know why; she hadn't told anybody else except people online, the ones who gathered in the chat rooms to talk about the Shining Hills. The lights appeared in high places every six to eight months, but only in one place at a time, always somewhere with hills. Rome. Seattle. San Francisco. Edinburgh. They shone intermittently for a few weeks, and then they vanished, and some percentage of those who'd made the pilgrimage to see them vanished too: the Lucky, the people in the chat rooms said, and of course other people thought they were unlucky, doomed or damned. No one knew. All anyone knew was that wherever they were now, alive or dead, it wasn't here, and that was enough for Niff and the others like her.

She had never fit in, never felt like she belonged to her family—

mother dead of cancer five years ago, father distant ever since—never really felt like she belonged to the Earth. She'd always had strange feelings: heard snatches of song, flashes of odd color, been bored and baffled by the things other people found ordinary—football, baby showers, prom corsages—and smitten by the things no one else understood: the slant of moonlight through a window, the angle of a skyscraper rising into a flawlessly blue sky.

"None of that means you're a faerie," Seamus said. "You could just be an artist, Niff. Why not stay here and find out?"

She shook her head. If she did that, she might miss her chance. And there was nothing to stay here for, nothing, because Toby was dead. Toby was the only person here she'd ever really loved, the only person who'd understood her and never made fun of her, and he was gone, blown to bits.

Seamus was quiet when she told him this, quiet and attentive. He knew how to listen; she'd give him that. He didn't lecture like her father, like most of the other adults she knew. And, unlike her father—of whom he'd initially reminded her—he didn't seem lost. He wasn't bossing people around to give himself a job to do. He seemed rooted, at home.

"I'm sorry your brother died, Niff."

"Thank you."

"Do you think this is what he'd want, though? Do you think he'd want you to be gone, too, because he is?"

She shook her head. "You don't get it. I'm not *killing* myself. I'm just going somewhere else."

"You don't know. You don't know what will happen, even if you give the fakers up there a miss and get to whatever's real about it, if anything is."

That was true. She took the last bite of her burger, chewed and swallowed it. "Toby would understand."

Seamus gave her a level look, infinitely sad. "The dead always understand, don't they? Anything we want to do, they'll always approve."

"No. My mother wouldn't. She only cared about herself even before she got sick. But Toby would." She pushed back her empty plate and said, "Thank you for the hamburger. I have to go now."

"Ah," he said, and put out a hand. "Not yet. Not quite yet. We've still time before moonrise, and it's a trade, remember? You have to hear my story, too."

"You think I'm stupid," Niff said. "Or silly." She could hear the anger in her own voice, but it wasn't really directed at Seamus, this stranger: it was what she wanted to say to her father, to the endless therapists and counselors, to the other people her age who were too busy with school or hooking up or getting drunk to care about faerie. "You think I'm trying to avoid the real world."

"All worlds are real," Seamus said, and she looked at him, startled, feeling herself give a grudging nod of admiration. Not many people knew that.

"Yeah. They are. So why not go to that one?"

"Because it isn't yours, that's all. Look: you've heard about geographical cures, right? People taking vacations to get away from whatever's bothering them, but they can't."

"They bring it with them."

"They bring it with them. Suicide rates are higher in holiday towns, Niff, did you know that? Because unhappy people go to places where people go to be happy, because the places are supposed to make them happy, but it doesn't work. And when you're unhappy in a place like that, it's doubly terrible. There's nowhere else to go and no one to talk to. And that's true even when you're surrounded by other people. Look, if running off to bleeding faerieland would fix everything, I'd go myself. I'm not telling you to stay here because I want you to suffer, because I'm trying to keep you from something better. I'm not anti-pleasure. You can have all the drugs and sex you want, as far as I'm concerned. But I don't think faerieland's any better. I don't see how it can be. If they don't just eat you or put you in a zoo, it has to be the biggest jolt of loneliness and culture shock there is. And yeah, there would be other people there, presumably, a little expat community maybe. Why do that when you can find a community here?"

"You believe in it," Niff said, feeling her eyebrows rise. He wasn't faking, and he wasn't talking down to her.

"Yes, I do."

"Why?"

He turned away from her. In the dim light of the pub, she saw him swallow. "Because my daughter walked up a hill like that one five years ago and never came back down."

"No body?"

"No. No body."

She looked at her watch. Ninety minutes to moonrise. "All right. So tell me the story."


Audrey was fifteen when she walked up her hill. Hers was the Sparrow Hills in Moscow. She'd been there on a school trip—a music camp; she was a violinist—and the lights had come, and she'd followed them, although none of her classmates had. They'd all been warned by their teacher, but Audrey had crept out of the youth hostel in the middle of the night with her best friend Selena, who didn't see the lights but was curious, and wanted to keep an eye on Audrey.

Selena came back alone. She'd gotten almost all the way to the top with Audrey, she said, and then she tripped on a stone and fell, and when she got up again, Audrey was no longer there, and the air had an odd tingling sensation, the way it does right before lightning strikes, but Selena couldn't see anything except other people climbing the hill, passing her. She called for Audrey, and got no answer. She heard frantic cries, screams and shouts, ahead of her. Afraid to climb any higher, she turned back.

She killed herself six months later, hung herself in her parents' attic.

"I didn't blame her," Seamus said quietly. "No one blamed her," and Niff didn't know if he meant that he didn't blame her for losing Audrey or didn't blame her for killing herself. Maybe it was both. Maybe he couldn't tell them apart. "I can't listen to violin music anymore. None of it: not fiddle, not chamber music, not 'Twinkle Twinkle Little Star.' Anything on that instrument makes me too sad."

"What about your wife? Can she listen to violins?"

"I don't know. We split up after Audrey disappeared. That happens a lot, when bad things happen to children. Illness. Accident."

Faerie. "My mother's dead," Niff said. "So's my brother. My family's already split up. I doubt my father will even notice if I vanish."

Seamus' eyes narrowed. "I'm betting he will. If you're doing this to make him sit up and take notice, it's an awfully big gamble. And if you're right, you'll never know if it paid off."

Niff shrugged. "Maybe that would matter to me if I cared if he noticed." She pushed her plate back. "I'm going now. It's almost moonrise."

"All right."

"Are you coming with me?"

He looked startled. "Do you want me to?"

"You can if you want to, but you're not talking me out of it."

"All right," he said. His stomach twisted. He was afraid of the climb, but she wanted company; she was after all just a girl. And if any human evil was up there, he could maybe do something about it.

So he paid, and they left, and went out into the cool darkness, moon just rising, and began climbing the paths to the Seat. He used the torch on his belt to light the way until the moon came up more fully; then he switched it off. They didn't need it anymore.

As they went, others joined them, quiet bodies in the dark, climbing. No one spoke. A glow brighter than moonlight lit the path now. Seamus stopped twenty feet from it, and watched others walk in, two four six of them. A woman cried out behind him:

"Johnny, no! Stay with me! Stay!" Seamus half-turned, and in the light of the glow saw a woman holding a man her age, husband or brother or friend, saw him wrench away from her and race past Seamus and Niff. The woman keened, and Seamus remembered the screams Selena had heard. He watched Johnny approach the glow, a dark silhouette against it, and then vanish. Gone. Gone, like Audrey, like all the others.

Behind him, the woman was on the ground, sobbing. Someone helped her up and started walking her back down the hill.

Shaking, Seamus turned toward the light again, thinking that Niff would be gone, that she'd have vanished when he took his eyes off her. But she was still there, and for a dizzy moment he allowed himself to believe that she'd stay, that he'd saved her.

"Don't blame yourself, Seamus." She was watching him with something like pity. She reached out and almost touched his arm, but didn't. He knew her words for a great kindness. He couldn't answer. "Be happy for us. Think of us dancing." And then she moved forward until she too was gone, and he was left to remember those last words, how they had sounded clear and bright over the music. Pipes and flutes, not fiddle.

Seamus heard it too, the music. He'd always heard it: in dreams, in alley echoes, in the gurgle of water in the drain when he washed the dishes after his lonely dinners. He'd heard it his whole life. He'd never spoken of it to anyone, and Audrey had never told him she heard it too. He doubted anything would be different if she had.

He stood in the glow, leaning against its pull. He knew that if he walked into the dazzling brightness, he might wind up where his daughter was, might see her again, would anyway have solved some mystery.

Or died, or been eaten or dissolved. Better the devil you know.

The summons grew stronger the longer he stood there, with people streaming around him as if he were a tree, with the burger and beer cold and heavy in his stomach. He heard the faint, sweet music, smelled the flowers of that other land. He waited until the pull became nearly unbearable. Someday, maybe he wouldn't resist it.

Others had stopped. He knew some of them were predators, still and cautious now maybe because they'd seen his uniform. He couldn't arrest them if they weren't doing anything, couldn't tell them from heartsick friends and family.

He hoped Audrey was dancing somewhere, had reached the portal rather than falling to scum, human or otherwise.

Farewell, farewell.

The light blurred from tears; the music continued, endlessly enticing. How many of the others standing here heard it? "Sod off," Seamus said aloud, speaking to the glow and the lilting melody. He raised his voice, seeking a defiance he didn't feel. "I live here, don't I?" Then he turned away, back to the city and the dark, and began to descend the hill.

*My stories often begin with visual images. In this case, I was gazing out my bedroom window one autumn day and had a sudden, unexpected daydream about a tree with earrings and coffee cups as fruit. Of course I had to puzzle out what it meant.*

# ASH

PENNY TOLD HERSELF that the fire had been a blessing, a cleansing: all that junk she'd meant to sort through and discard, all the books she knew she'd never read, the letters and Christmas cards she'd never reread. Oh, she wasn't a hoarder; it hadn't been as bad as that. But she'd had file drawers that had gone unpurged for twenty years, because she'd tried to clean them out and been stopped dead in her tracks by things no one else would ever want that were simply too precious to discard: the short story she'd written in French and illustrated in colored pencil in eighth grade, with her teacher's ecstatic "A+! Merveilleuse!" in red marker; her long-dead mother's birth certificate; files of papers holding ideas for essays and articles she'd never write now that she'd retired from the university. And suddenly, everything had to be kept.

She'd thrown out plenty of other stuff: teaching files, old magazines (even the ones she'd meant to read and never had), her seminar papers from grad school. She needed to do more, but felt paralyzed.

And so the fire was a blessing. It happened when she was on vacation, visiting a friend in Seattle, the cats—thank goodness—safely boarded at the vet's. Some kind of short, the firefighters thought, wiring gone bad in the walls, although Penny could have sworn she'd turned everything off. Maybe shorts could happen anyway. She didn't know.

She left Seattle early. When she got back, there was only a stinking, charred heap where her house had been.

Insurance paid enough to entirely rebuild the old house, which had been much larger than she needed. Instead of replacing it, after she had the charred stuff carted away—she'd paid off the mortgage years ago and the lot was lovely, surrounded by mountains but still close to town—she had a tiny cottage built, much farther from the street than the old house. It was one story with a living room, one small bedroom, a full kitchen and bath, a wood stove for heat and solar panels for electric. Not counting her small front porch, just the right size for one rocking chair, the whole thing was 600 square feet. Her bedroom window no longer looked right out onto the neighbor's patio; her greater distance from the curb dampened traffic noise. It felt like a different world.

Penny settled down happily to a less encumbered life. All her books were on her Kindle now; none cluttered the house. She had the clothing she'd brought back from Seattle and a few necessities she'd bought, but she found herself happy with a very limited wardrobe. It wasn't like she needed nice clothing for work. The two cats would have preferred more room, but they were getting older now, too, and once she bought them a new cat condo, they claimed it as their perch and were content.

She missed amazingly little: some family photographs, a cherished set of dishes, her extensive jewelry collection, scattered in the soaked and smoldering ruins from which she'd salvaged almost nothing. She hadn't been able to bear to sift through that reeking blackness. Sometimes she woke at night with a start, aching from a dream of something she'd never see again; but always she told herself that she'd just seen it in her dream, hadn't she? All those things lived in her memory, where they were safest from the ravages of the world. She didn't need the physical objects.

And then, her first autumn in the new house, the tree outside began to bear fruit.

\*

The tree had been the only thing growing in her yard before the fire. Penny wasn't a gardener; she'd never had the skill or patience for it. She always forgot to water plants and didn't want to spend even the minimal time and money to put in a drip or sprinkler system. But a previous owner had planted this mountain ash, which grew quickly and tolerated drought, thriving even in the desert.

Penny liked the tree, which asked nothing of her and gave good shade. Sometimes in the old days she had sat under it, reading in a lawn chair. In late spring it decorated itself with clusters of white flowers. From late summer to late autumn, bunches of red berries drew enthusiastic attention from birds. By late October, the leaves turned yellow and orange, a pleasing palette, and then fell.

The tree had been some yards from the back of the old house. Penny had the new one built much closer to it, for shade; some of the branches almost reached the porch now. One warm August morning her first year there, she glanced outside to see a flash of silver and blue on the porch. Blinking, she put on slippers and went outside.

On the cedar planking of the porch rested an earring. She bent, her joints complaining only a little, and picked it up. It had been her mother's, a set of three hinged turquoise squares set in silver. She had thought it lost in the fire.

Throat tight—these had been her mother's favorite earrings, and Penny had worn them at her funeral—she sat in the rocking chair and cradled the earring in her palm. The earring must have been buried in the ashes and escaped being carted away. Maybe a ground squirrel had uncovered it and deposited it on her porch.

This seemed improbable even as she thought it. She sighed, scratched her head, and squinted up at the tree, rustling in the late-summer breeze that already carried cooler undertones, the promise of fall. On a branch near her dangled another turquoise and silver earring.

Penny stared. She stood. Straining on tiptoe, she reached for the earring; she had to tug to free it, although it came away cleanly. And now she saw, among the red berries the tree always bore, other things that shouldn't have been there: flashes of gold, the gleaming edge of a favorite coffee mug, a square of paper with blurry blotches she suspected would resolve into a photograph, like a Polaroid developing in the air.

She recognized all of them. She knew they weren't yet ripe, weren't ready to be harvested. She carried the earrings inside.

By late October, when the tree stopped producing fruit, the new house was fuller than it had been. A few especially cherished books, mostly from childhood—Tolkien and Lewis and Aiken, T. H. and E. B. White, Bradbury—graced a shelf in the living room. A cloissone box, a souvenir from the Victoria & Albert Museum gift store in London, sat on Penny's dresser, and inside it were several more pairs of earrings and also a particularly beloved silver bracelet. Framed family photos and small paintings by a cousin hung on the walls; the favorite coffee mug had been joined by two delicate Limoges bowls from her father's family.

The tree was fecund. Penny didn't keep everything it produced. Other books, the unread ones, went in the library's donation box. She tossed a flurry of letters and Christmas cards and went to Staples to shred old bank statements. Why had the tree thought she wanted those?

But trees couldn't think, could they? Perhaps it was only dumb luck that so many of the things it gave her were ones she wanted. She had a hazy idea that the tree was absorbing, through its roots, the ashes of her burned belongings, and reconstituting those small enough not to overwhelm it.

She was careful not to let the new things overwhelm the house. Losing so much had taught her to let go of what there was no room to keep. She was grateful for what she had.

Her belongings returned to her in improved, but not mint, condition. The books, still softened by age, had been healed of their coffee stains and cat-chewed covers. The jewelry was polished only to a soft glow, not a brilliant glare. The coffee mug no longer had the hairline crack she had fretted about, but no one would have taken it for brand-new. These were precious things in their prime, as Penny liked to believe she herself was, even with her arthritis and silver hair.

She wondered for a while if the tree's odd fruit would ripen and rot as ordinary fruit did, but as autumn wore into winter, and then early spring, everything stayed solid. It all appeared to be back for good.

She told no one what was happening: not the women in her knitting group, not university acquaintances she saw at concerts or in stores, not her friend in Seattle. She didn't want them to think she was delusional. She didn't want them to think she wasn't, didn't want the authorities to find out and send people to examine the tree, to dissect it and analyze it and try to plant copies of it somewhere else. She was perfectly content to accept what she couldn't understand.

The next summer, she sat on her porch and smiled at the tree, at its bright clusters of white flowers. She wondered what they'd turn into, come fall. She found herself mentally cataloging the contents of the old house, thinking of things she wanted back, speaking aloud to the tree to see if she could influence it.

"Tree, I had some tiny glass bottles. They sat in my bedroom window when I was a little girl; they made rainbows on the wall. In the house that burned, they made rainbows in the kitchen. They could make rainbows here, too, and they're very small. They shouldn't overtax you. Do you think I could have just one or two?

"Tree, if you could manage it, I'd be very grateful to get my red and yellow handknit socks back. They're the first pair I ever made, and they're so comfortable. I'm making some others now, but could you possibly see about those, too?

"Tree, I had a framed photograph of my father in his Coast Guard uniform. I really love the photos you've returned so far, especially the one of me with the kittens when I was a child and the one of my cousin Brenda with her husband; she died two years ago, and I miss her, so that's a comfort. But that picture was a lovely one of Dad, and it would mean the world to me to see it again."

She worried that she was growing greedy, but reassured herself by making long lists of all the things she hadn't asked for. She wondered if she should offer the tree something in return, but because she'd always had such terrible luck with plants, she was afraid that anything she might do would only hurt it instead. And anyway, she didn't know how this magic worked. She didn't want to blunder in and break it.

So she left the tree alone, except for her polite requests. She knit the new socks, thinking about those old ones, how warm they'd been and how soft. She treasured the photographs she had, telling herself that she'd be all right if she didn't get the Coast Guard shot back—her father so young and hopeful and handsome, his bad investments and bad back and hideous cancer still decades in the future—but yearning for it anyway. She stood at her kitchen sink, imagining the counter lit with the soft glow of sunlight through colored glass, trying to believe that her ability to picture the soft hues would sustain her.

That expectant summer was like waiting for Christmas in the wrong season. Every morning she sat on the porch and gazed up at the flowers, trying to guess from the shapes of the clusters what they might become. She concentrated on her three wishes, hoping they wouldn't overburden the tree. Even if it gave her just one of the things she'd asked for, she'd be happy.

But the tree gave her something else entirely.


It took longer, this year. Through August and September, the tree formed its usual berries, but crane her neck as she might, Penny didn't see them turning into anything else. Perhaps the previous year's odd fruit had been a one-time gift after the fire. She girded herself for disappointment, but still scanned the branches every time she went outside. She invented extra errands—oh, she'd forgotten to take this parcel to the Post Office, and it couldn't wait until tomorrow—so she'd be able to study the tree more often.

One windless morning in early October, she glanced up at the tree and saw a hint of movement, something that looked like fur. The fur was black and white, so it wasn't a squirrel, and surely skunks couldn't climb?

The patch was too high for her to reach. Looking up at it hurt her neck. She drove downtown to REI, that huge space full of high-tech camping and climbing and kayaking equipment, and made her way among muscular young shoppers dressed in hemp and Gore-Tex, and bought a pair of binoculars. When she got home, she leaned as far back as her rocking chair would go and trained her vision on the patch. It had grown larger while she was gone.

And it got larger every day, as the lump in Penny's throat grew larger, too. Here was a tail. Here were ears. And two weeks after she had first seen the patch, her most beloved of all past cats detached himself from the bark of the tree, and washed his ears with his paws, and climbed down into her arms. "Porridge," she said, stroking him as he purred.

Of course. She'd scattered his ashes in the yard.

He'd died terribly, in pain, throwing blood clots after routine dental surgery, but here he was in his prime, long-haired and glossy, mewing imperiously for cat food.

One of her current cats had known Porridge. One hadn't. Both hissed when she brought him inside; Porridge hissed back. Three cats in this tiny house would have been too many even if they'd gotten along, and for several weeks they didn't. On many evenings, as yowling and snarling filled the house, Penny considered staying in a hotel room, or finding another home for one or another of the cats. But she couldn't. She loved them; they were hers.

By a month after Porridge's resurrection, peace reigned in the house again, more or less. Each of the cats had staked out private turf—the bed, the sofa, the cat condo—and instead of fighting, they retreated to their high ground when they were annoyed. By Christmas, Porridge was once again grooming Muffin, the orange tabby, who'd been younger than Porridge in the previous house but now seemed older.

Penny fretted about the vet. Porridge was certainly overdue for shots, and she was desperately curious what an exam would uncover about his health. But the old Porridge had been microchipped, and the tree had already reconstituted metal objects. Her vet of many years had loved Porridge as much as Penny did, had wept with her when he died. She couldn't tell the vet that Porridge was alive again; Dr. Brun had sent his body to the crematorium. She might be able to say that she'd found a stray who looked just like Porridge—long-haired black and white cats weren't uncommon, after all—but then Dr. Brun would scan for a chip, and the number would come up in the registry, and Dr. Brun would know it was the same cat.

She took Porridge to a new vet. She said he was a stray she'd adopted from the pound. The new vet, a pleasant young man who looked no older than twelve, found the cat in perfect and unremarkable health. "This kitty could live forever!" he told her.

Penny thought about what else had been in the old house and watched her hands, resting on top of the carrying case, begin to tremble.


That winter, she watched Porridge obsessively, but as the vet had said, nothing was amiss. The cat ate, drank, slept, used the litter box, played with catnip mice, purred on her lap, and alternately chased and ignored the other cats. No one, she believed, would have been able to tell that he had grown from a tree.

She worked at not thinking about what might happen in the fall. On the winter solstice, when other people were getting ready to sing carols and unwrap presents, Penny went outside, shielding a lit candle from the wind, and spoke to the tree.

"Tree, thank you for all you've given me. Thank you for the jewelry and dishes. Thank you for the books and the photos and the artwork. Thank you, especially, for my beloved Porridge. Tree, you must be exhausted. You can rest now. Make nothing but your own fruit. I don't need anything else. I release you."

She felt silly. She feared this was presumptuous. She hadn't bound the tree, so how could she release it? The line sounded like something from a bad vampire movie. And anyway, it would probably do no good. She'd never had any sense that the tree heard her or paid attention to her wishes.

She went back inside and dangled a piece of string for Porridge.

The following summer was golden, extravagant. Her friends at the library and in her knitting group reported bumper crops of flowers, tomatoes, squash. They loaded Penny and each other down with the yield from their gardens. Meanwhile, the tree produced its usual bunches of white flowers, as if it had never given birth to crockery and a cat.

Everything would be fine, she told herself, stifling mingled dread and longing. It had to be fine.

And that fall, at first, everything did indeed seem fine. The tree produced its red berries; peer upward as she might, she saw nothing else. She began to relax. She sat on the porch, knitting socks, reading Victorian novels on her Kindle.

But then, in October, a bump appeared on the trunk of the tree, between two of the largest branches.

It was nothing, Penny told herself firmly. Nothing, or only an innocent something. Another coffee mug. Another painting.

For the next ten days, she didn't look at the tree. Eyes averted, she walked past it to her car. She spent longer than usual away from home; she made a road trip to buy yarn in California, another to visit a tiny town in eastern Nevada, just because it was pretty. She distracted herself.

But at the end of that time, unable to stop herself, she looked at the bump, which had grown and changed and become exactly what she had feared.

Hands.

Human hands.

Two human hands, clasped. One had broad knuckles and a scar from a childhood fishing accident. The other was smaller, more delicate.

Penny went inside and threw up her lunch. Then, shaking as one does after vomiting, she rinsed her mouth and washed her face and made herself some tea. No: it was too much. The hands weren't alive, couldn't be alive. Nothing else would follow them. The tree wasn't that big. How could it produce an entire human body, let alone two? Porridge, one small cat, had been last season's only fruit. It was too late in the season for this impossible, ghastly thing to happen. The tree would stop now. It had to.

It didn't.

The next morning, Penny went outside and saw that the hands had grown farther out of the trunk. The morning after that, the faint shapes of two more hands bulged beside them. And on the third morning, the first two hands had begun to move, the larger one caressing the smaller one in that movement Penny knew so well. Her father had always held her mother's hand that way, his fingers moving lovingly over the back, the palm, his thumb stroking her thumb. He had held her hand that way on winter evenings when they sat together on the couch. He'd held her hand that way when they strolled through stores, when they sat in restaurants, when they sunned themselves at the beach. He'd held her hand that way as he sat beside her hospital bed while she was dying of a sudden, mysterious infection.

Penny had never scattered her parents' ashes. She couldn't bear to. They'd remained in simple cardboard urns on the top shelf of her closet. They'd burned, again, when the house burned.

She stood staring at the hands. How she wanted to touch them!

How she wanted to feel her father's skin, her mother's pulse! These
were the two people she had loved most in the world, and who had
loved her. They were her first home, the one she still yearned for.
No one had ever made her feel as whole, as valuable, as cherished as
they did. They had been dead for ten years. She had never stopped
missing them. She never would.

She turned away from the hands. She went inside. The rest of
that day and all that endless night, she paced and wept and argued
with herself, trying to see some way to make this turn out well, happily, a good ending.

She couldn't.

How would three people, two of them married, live in this tiny
house?

They'd be younger than she was now. Either she'd have to survive their deaths again, a daughter's proper duty, or—more likely—
they'd have to survive hers. They had feared losing her more than
anything. She was their only child, their treasure. Some of their
friends had lost children, and Penny's parents had always shuddered, shaken their heads. "We couldn't go on if anything happened
to you."

Their deaths had been legally registered with the state, with
Social Security, with insurance companies and banks. They had no
existence anymore. She could spend the rest of her retirement money on fake IDs, she supposed, but then what? Her parents would
know who they were, as Porridge knew who he was. Her father had
been an attorney, her mother a nurse; they'd want to work again.
How could they, without proper diplomas and licenses? She believed both of them had been fingerprinted for various jobs. What
if those prints were still on file?

How could she support them while they tried to fit in? She'd
have to go back to work herself, with her savings spent on false
identities. The mere idea made every bone in her body ache.

How could she tell them what had happened?

Penny paced. She wept. She entertained and discarded wild

schemes; she plotted and prayed. But when dawn came, cold and gray, she knew what she had to do. She'd known it all along.

She made herself a hearty breakfast that tasted like bricks and charcoal, that sat like scorched iron in her stomach. She showered and dressed in jeans, sensible shoes, her favorite sweater.

When she left the house, she didn't look at the tree.

She drove to Home Depot and stood in that vast, echoing space until a polite young man in an orange employees' apron found her. "May I help you, ma'am?" A few aisles over, a child laughed.

Penny swallowed. "Yes, please. I need to buy an axe."

*A lot has changed since this story was first published in 2001. For one thing, marijuana is now legal in Nevada, and in many other places. But Welly's still one of my favorite characters, a deeply imperfect and wounded person doing his best in an incomprehensible situation.*

# CUCUMBER GRAVY

I WASN'T TOO happy when the knocking started on my door that morning. Nobody's welcome out here except UPS and customers, and I wasn't expecting any deliveries, and customers have to call first. New buyers have to be referred by people I know. That's a rule. I check references, too. I don't let anybody in who isn't vouched for, and even so, it's amazing I've never had cops out here. Some of my buyers ask why I didn't go legit when the medical-marijuana bill passed four years ago, but that's a no-brainer: I do not need the government crawling up my backside to regulate me, and I have a lot more customers this way, and I make a lot more money. Being legal would be nothing but a pain in the ass, even if I didn't have to worry about keeping people from finding out about the space cucumbers.

As it happened, my latest bunch of cucumbers was due to start singing any minute, which meant the last thing I needed was somebody in the house. That's another reason buyers have to call first: depending on what the cucumbers are up to, I tell people they have to wait, I can't see them today.

So when the knocking started, I thought, *shit, government,* and my stomach tied up in a knot. I'd have pretended I wasn't home, but you can get stranded motorists out here too, and the sooner you let them use your phone or whatever, the sooner they go away.

So when I heard that knock and looked out and didn't recognize who was there—some bearded guy pushing forty, about my age, in jeans and a plaid shirt and hiking boots, had tree-hugging liberal written all over him—I grabbed my gun and yelled through the door, "Who is it?" Since it was only one guy, that made cops less likely, but on the other hand his car was in front of the house, a nice little Toyota, which made mechanical failure less likely, too. Maybe he had to use the bathroom, in which case I'd tell him to use the desert. If he needed water I'd give him some, though. You always give people water, out here. You'd think people would know not to drive anywhere in this state without extra water in the car, but between the dumb college kids from Reno and the morons moving here from California, the average survival IQ in Nevada isn't what it should be. This guy was too old to be in college, so I pegged him as Californian. Local folks only drive in the desert with four-wheel drive.

"Mr. Whitwell Smith?" he yelled through the door. "Welly?"

"Yeah?" Only buyers call me Welly: It's a kind of code. I'm Whit to everybody else, not that I've talked to much of anybody else since Nancy Ann left. "Who wants to know?"

"My name's Jim Humphreys." The name didn't mean anything to me. "I'm a friend of Sam Mortimer's."

That name did. Sam used to be one of my best customers, out here once a month spending big money, until he suddenly stopped coming altogether about six months ago. No call, nothing. I'd been wondering what happened to him, not that it's any of my business. I'd almost started to think of Sam as a friend, I'd known him so long; we'd even gone skeet-shooting on my property a few times. "Yeah? You know Sam, you know you have to call before you come out here. Sam knows that."

"I've been trying to call for three days, Mr. Smith. Your phone's out of order."

Shit. That was the first I knew of it. I hadn't gotten any calls for three days, but that's not unusual: You never know when business is going to be slow, and nobody else calls me. But it could still be a trick. "You wait just a minute," I hollered through the door, and ran and picked up the phone. Dead. No dial tone. Nothing. Which meant I'd have to get telephone repair people out here, but that would have to wait until the latest batch of cucumbers was gone. In the meantime, I turned on my cell phone in case anybody was trying to reach me. I don't like the cell phone; I don't like having my conversations broadcast all over hell and gone for the government to spy on. But you have to have a cell phone for emergencies, just like you have to have water. If you miss a customer call, you could lose business.

"Okay," I hollered, back at the door. "Thank you for telling me about the telephone, but I can't see you today. We can make an appointment—"

"Mr. Smith, I drove seventy miles to get here, and this is an emergency. Please open the door."

Emergency? Nobody'd ever used that line on me before. My crop isn't addictive, which is one of the things I like about it. You don't get strung-out dopeheads at your door who'd murder their own mothers for their next fix. Who needs that kind of trouble?

I checked my watch. The cucumbers were due to start singing in about thirty minutes, but sometimes they go off early. I'm never sure exactly when they've gotten here, which makes the timing tricky, and that means I wasn't about to open the door. "If it's an emergency, call 911, Mr. Humphreys. I'm not in that line of work."

"Welly, please. Sam's very sick. He has cancer. He had surgery four months ago and now he's having chemo and it's making him sicker than a dog, and the prescription stuff isn't working for him. He says it isn't strong enough. He says yours is the best. He sent me out here with two hundred and fifty dollars to buy some. Please don't send me back to that poor man empty-handed."

"Huh," I said. I wasn't surprised the government couldn't grow good plants. They were probably growing oregano and charging pot prices for it; you can't trust those people as far as you can throw them. I started with the best stock when I got into business fifteen years ago, and I've been refining it since then. Genetics was my favorite part of biology in high school.

I looked at my watch again. I could run and get a quarter bag and shove it through the door and pull this Humphreys' cash in, and it would all be over in ten seconds. And if the cucumbers started up and he heard them, I'd tell him it was the TV. "You wait there," I called out. "I'll be right back."

I ran and got a quarter bag and a paper lunch sack, and put the gun on a shelf near the door, where I could grab it fast if I had to, but Humphreys couldn't reach inside and get it, and then I opened the door a crack, as far as the chain would allow. "Here," I said. I held up the quarter bag so he could see it, and dropped it in the lunch sack. "You pass the money through, you get this."

He held up a sheaf of bills and slipped them through. All singles and fives, Jesus, what had Sam been thinking? Come to think of it, a quarter bag wouldn't get him very far, not given Sam's smoking habits, but I was guessing he didn't have much money left over, after the cancer. He'd probably been saving up since the chemo started, the poor bastard, and insurance wouldn't pay for mine. I wondered if I should give him some extra for free—he'd been a very good customer for a long time—but in the meantime, I started counting the bills. Old habits.

While I was counting, Humphreys said drily, "Sam said you let him come into the house." I could hear him more clearly now, with the door open, and something about his voice nagged at me. He had a little bit of an accent, English or Aussie maybe. Where had I heard a voice like that lately?

"I know Sam," I said. "No offense." I finished counting—it was all there—and then I handed the bag through. As I did, I got a good look at Humphreys' face for the first time, and two things happened at once.

The first thing was that I recognized him from TV. You just don't see many preachers with Aussie accents feeding bag ladies on the news, especially when the preacher has one deformed ear, the right one, all ugly and lumpy and crumpled up like a cauliflower. I hadn't picked up on the ear before because I'd only gotten a side view of him when I looked out the window.

The second thing was that the cucumbers starting singing, all three of them at once: Wails and whistles and grunts, like a cross between a porno soundtrack and an orchestra of teakettles.

Humphreys' eyes widened. "What—"

"It's the TV," I said, and tried to slam the door, but I couldn't because he'd wedged his foot in there, and he was staring behind me, goggle-eyed. When I turned to look over my shoulder, I saw that one of the cucumbers had staggered out of the den, away from its friends and the nice warm heaters, and was hopping in pathetic circles around my living room, which makes it the first time in almost ten years that a cucumber's moved from where I put it once it got into the house.

I was about to have a very bad day.

The space cucumbers started coming here a few months after Nancy Ann ran off. I don't know why they picked this place—it's just a ranch house out in the middle of nowhere, halfway between Reno and Gerlach, with nothing to look at but sagebrush and lizards and alkali dust, so flat that the mountains on the horizon seem like a mirage—and I never have figured out how they keep from attracting the attention of the air base in Stead. Those bastards are government, and I figure they have to have instruments that can tell if you throw a penny in the air, and the cucumbers have to come in some kind of ship, or come down through the atmosphere, anyway. And you see those air base planes and 'copters doing maneuvers out here all the time, so I don't know why they've never picked up on what's going on. I guess the cucumbers are smarter than they are. It's not hard to be smarter than the government.

I call them space cucumbers because they look like a sea cucumber I saw once—or at least, they look more like that than like anything else. My parents took me on a trip to San Diego when I was a kid, and we went to the aquarium there. They had all kinds of animals, scary ones like sharks and smart ones like dolphins and whales who did tricks, but for some reason, the one I always remembered best was the sea cucumber. It was lying in a tank of water, in this kind of petting zoo they had, and you could reach in and touch it. It was brown and very, very soft, and if somebody had grabbed it and started cutting it into pieces, it couldn't have fought back. It didn't swim or do tricks. It didn't do anything. It just sat there. The aquarium lady said it ate by filtering tiny bits of food out of the water. It was a really boring animal, and I never have known why it made such an impression on me. Probably because I couldn't figure out how a creature like that could survive in the ocean with sharks and lobsters and stingrays. "I guess sharks don't think they taste good," the aquarium lady said, but you could tell she didn't know either. That cucumber was a mystery.

Which is what mine are, too. They show up two or three at a time, every five or six weeks. I just open the door in the morning and there they are, waiting on my welcome mat. They're much bigger than the sea cucumber in San Diego, about three feet tall and as thick around as a flagpole, and I can't touch them because they're wrapped in something like plastic. Like really thick shrink wrap. Or maybe that's their skin, but I don't think so: I think it's some kind of spacesuit, and the animal's the thing inside, the brown blobby cylindrical thing that hops along on nine stubby little legs, all clustered at the bottom of the cylinder, like tentacles. Hopping isn't easy for them, you can tell—I don't think it's how they normally move around, wherever they come from—so I usually pick them up to carry them inside. Wherever they're from, they've come a long way to get here, and I figure if there's anything I can do to make it easier for them, why not? They're always exactly air temperature, or the shrink wrap is, and they're not as heavy as you'd expect from their size. I can just stick them under my arm, like pieces of firewood.

When the first ones came I was terrified, of course. The cucumbers would have been weird whenever they showed up, but Nancy Ann had just left, and I was out of my mind with grief and anger, smoking entirely too much of my own crop just to get to sleep at night. I felt like I was going crazy, and having space cucumbers on my welcome mat didn't help. I didn't know what they were or what they wanted. I didn't know if they were going to kill me or take over the planet or poison the water supply, and I couldn't ask anybody because that would have gotten the government involved, and even if I trusted the government I couldn't have people tramping around my house and finding the plants and grow lights and sprinklers in the basement. I have one hell of a professional setup down there: no way I could argue personal use, even if possession weren't still a felony for anybody without an approved medical condition.

The first time they showed up and hopped into the house, I just went weak in the knees and started babbling at them, trying to figure out what they wanted, trying to find some way to communicate. Didn't work, of course. If they can talk or understand me when I talk, I haven't found any way to tell, not in all these years. Maybe the singing's some kind of language, like what whales have, but if so I haven't figured it out yet, and they never respond in any way I can tell when I say things to them. That first visit, they all hopped over to my wood stove and stood around it, shaking, and the entire forty-eight hours until they started singing, I don't think I slept a wink. I didn't know what they were going to do. I didn't dare shoot them because I didn't want to give them an excuse to destroy the planet, and anyway I could tell even then they had some kind of suit on, and if I broke through it and whatever they were made of came out, who knew what kind of plague I'd start? I never have breached one of those suits.

They didn't do anything that first time, of course, not until they started singing. When the noise started, I got into a duck-and-cover position under my coffee table because I thought they were going to attack me. And then when nothing happened and the singing stopped, I just crouched there, waiting, until about half an hour later the first one liquefied on me, and then within half an hour after that, the other two had gone gravy, too.

You know those gravy packets that come with some kinds of TV dinners? The plastic pouches you throw into boiling water and then pull out of the pot with tongs, so you can cut them open to pour the gravy out? I guess some people use microwaves, but I think boiling water works better. Anyway, that's what the cucumbers look like when they liquefy: giant gravy pouches. There's a big sploosh, and then all of a sudden where there used to be something that looked like an animal, there's just brown mush. If you pick up the suit then, it's like holding a bag of thick brown water, and frankly it's pretty disgusting. The first time I saw it, I nearly got sick, and then I got even more scared, wondering what would happen next.

Nothing happened. Nothing's ever happened, after they go gravy. I think they're dead, then. As near as I can tell, they come here to die. Why they'd come here, I have no idea. Don't think I haven't thought about it, but I've never come up with any idea that makes sense. The first few times it happened, I thought they'd just crashed here or gotten stranded, like motorists without water, and Earth had killed them somehow, or I had. But it's been happening every five or six weeks for ten years, so now I think they come here deliberately. Maybe this is some kind of pilgrimage for them; maybe my house was built on some kind of alien shrine, like Area 51. I just don't know. And I could be wrong, anyway. Maybe they aren't dead at all. Maybe if I opened one of the suits up, they'd come back to life.

For a while I kept some of the cucumber-gravy bags stacked out where the newest ones could see them when they showed up; I thought maybe they'd show me somehow what to do with them. They never responded at all. It was like the gravy packets weren't even there. Don't ask me what kind of animal doesn't recognize its own dead. Then I kept some of those first packets down in the basement, to see if they'd change over time, but they didn't. The suits keep whatever's inside from decomposing more, I guess.

Now I bury them. I've got forty acres here. I don't know what I'll do when my land gets filled in. Go out into the desert, I guess, and try to find places where people won't see me, places that aren't likely to get developed. Who knows what would happen if a backhoe sliced through one of those suits? None of the ones I've buried have ever gotten dug up by coyotes. I guess the cucumbers, dead or alive, are as invisible to coyotes as they are to the government. And as far as I know, the government hasn't seen me digging, either. I don't dig any time I can see or hear planes or 'copters, not that that's any guarantee.

For a while at the beginning I thought maybe the cucumbers really were invisible, thought I was having hallucinations, losing it over Nancy Ann. I drove into Reno a bunch of times to use the Internet at the library—I won't have a computer here because I don't trust the government not to spy on what I'm looking up—and did research, trying to find out if anyone else was reporting space aliens who looked like sea cucumbers. Nothing. I keep checking, every six months or so, but if other people are getting visits, I've never found any sign of it. I've read about crop circles and UFO abductions and all kinds of damnfool things, but never anything about singing cucumbers in plastic suits who turn into mush.

After a few visits, I wasn't scared of them anymore. They're nothing if not predictable. Every five or six weeks I wake up and open the door and find a couple or three on my welcome mat. I've never seen any bright lights in the middle of the night, or heard anything; I just open the door and there they are. And they hop into the house, and forty-eight hours later, give or take an hour, they start singing. They sing for three to seven minutes, and within an hour after that, they go gravy.

Sometimes I wonder what my life would be like if they'd never started coming. Would I still be living here? Would I have taken all the money I've made and moved to Hawaii, the way Nancy Ann and I always planned? Would I have taken that trip around the world I dreamed about when I was a kid? As it is, three or four times a year I take off for a week or two, always right after the latest cucumbers have gone gravy. I go someplace fancy, someplace that might as well be a different planet—New York or New Orleans or Bermuda—and I live it up. Good hotels, good food, high-class hookers. Those women like me. I tip well, and I treat them like human beings. They don't have to worry that I'll get ugly on them, and I don't have to worry that they'll break my heart. Works out for everybody. I could use Nevada hookers too, of course, the legal ones, and sometimes I do, but it feels less like a vacation that way.

I enjoy those trips. But I always come back home, because I always know another batch of cucumbers will be landing on my welcome mat.

I've learned what they like over the years, or I think I have. They like heat: They shake and shiver less the closer they are to the wood stove, or something else warm. I don't like having them in my living room for anyone to see, so early on I covered up the windows in the den and got some heavy-duty space heaters in there, the most powerful ones I could find at Home Depot. I figure the cucumbers wouldn't move close to things that made them shake less unless shaking less meant they were comfortable or happy, so I started paying attention to what else makes them shake. I feel itchy when they shake; it's like watching someone about to sneeze. They're happier on soft things than on the floor, so I used to cover the floor of the den with pillows, but then one time I had an old black-and-white polka-dot beanbag chair and the cucumber sitting on that shook less than the ones on the pillows did. I experimented, moving them around—I felt fine picking them up by then—and all of them seemed to like the beanbag chair better, although some of them shook a little more on it than others did. They seem to have individual tastes, although I can't tell them apart to look at them.

So I went to Wal-Mart—no sense buying fancy when budget will do—and bought a bunch of beanbag chairs. One of them was a really ugly day-glo pink, and I found out the cucumbers liked that better than the other colors, so I went back to Wal-Mart, but they were out of pink ones. They had day-glo orange and yellow and green, so I got those. The cucumbers love those day-glo beanbags. They seem to have different favorite colors, so when they get here I have to spend some time moving them around to see which one likes which color. But all of them like the day-glo chairs better than anything else.

The walls are another thing. Most of my house is decorated with *Penthouse* Pets and some *Playboy* pictures. That started as revenge after Nancy Ann left, but I kept doing it, because it makes me happy. Those women are even more beautiful than the hookers I hire, who can't always arrange perfect lighting. But the cucumbers hate those pictures. Once I held one up to my favorite *Penthouse* Pet, as a kind of joke, and that cuke started shaking like it was about to explode. I tried it with a few others: same thing. Maybe they think naked humans look repulsive, the way lots of people would think the cucumbers themselves do.

So I drove to the Reno library and got out a bunch of art books and started showing them pictures. They don't have eyes that I can tell, but if you hold a picture up to any place along the middle of the cucumber, it will respond. French painters, that's how they voted. Especially Matisse and Monet. So now I've got Matisse and Monet posters all over the walls of the den. I think those pictures are about as exciting as watching paint dry, and they seriously clash with the day-glo beanbags, not that I'm Martha Stewart. But when I put the cucumbers in that room now, they hardly shake at all.

Of course, there's always the chance I'm wrong about all of it. If there's anything I've learned, it's that you can't trust appearances, even in your own species. I loved Nancy Ann, and I thought she loved me. She was as beautiful as a *Penthouse* Pet, and she was smart and funny and taught me how to cook. I loved her even after she got religion; I loved her even after she started telling me that I was going to go to hell for cursing and growing pot and reading *Penthouse*, even when she said I was possessed by the devil. I figured she was saying all those mean things because she loved me too and didn't want me to go to hell, and even though I didn't believe in hell and never have, I tried to make her happy. I didn't shut down my business, of course, because we needed the money if we were going to move to Hawaii, which was what Nancy Ann wanted. She had expensive tastes, anyway: Diamonds and perfume and a new sports car every couple of years. She cut down on some of that stuff after she got religion, I'll give her that. She said showiness was the sin of pride. Since she seemed serious about it, I tried to curse less, and I canceled my *Penthouse* subscription for a while, and I even went to church with her a couple of times, to hear the Reverend Jebediah Wilkins bellow about Jesus and Satan and hellfire and how we had to *tithe* to the *Lord* if we wanted to be *saved*, hallelujah, while people nodded and moaned and said, "Oh yes, tell it brother," all around us.

That church was the scariest thing I've ever seen, much worse than space cucumbers could ever be. But I tried to love Nancy Ann through all of it, I really did. And I thought she was trying to love me too. And then one day I came home from a trip to town, where I'd just bought her some of her favorite perfume, because it was her birthday and she deserved something nice on her birthday, even if it would have been pride any other time. And I found all her things gone and a note on the kitchen table saying she wouldn't be back, because she'd found true love with Jebediah Wilkins. She said she'd be praying for me, oh yes she would, praying that I'd change my sinful ways before the Lord struck me down and I burned in hellfire forever.

So naturally I was not happy to have a preacher at my front door, staring at a space cucumber staggering in circles around my living room. The one time I've got unwanted company, and that's when the cucumbers have to go and do something different. I wish I could say I handled the whole thing calmly, but I didn't. I flat-out panicked. I'm not sure I've ever moved that fast before; I got the chain off the door and grabbed Humphreys and yanked him inside, and grabbed my gun off the shelf and aimed it at him. "The safety's still on," I said, raising my voice over the cucumbers' singing, "but if you do anything funny, it won't be, I'll blow your head off, I swear to God—"

Humphreys held his hands up and tried to say something, but it came out as a squeak. He was shaking worse than the cucumbers ever have, and I knew the cucumber behind me was too, although I couldn't turn around to look, because I had to keep an eye on Humphreys. Don't ask me what I thought he was going to do: go to the government, or start raving about Satan and try to burn my house down. All I knew was that I couldn't let him leave, once he'd seen the cucumber, and I'd never killed a man before and didn't want to, but I had no idea how else I was going to get out of this one, except that Sam was expecting Humphreys back with the crop and if Humphreys didn't come back Sam would call the police and—

You can see how clearly I was thinking. About all I could figure was that I was doomed. I couldn't see any way out that didn't involve a jail cell or worse.

Humphreys found his voice, then. "Please," he said. "Welly, don't shoot me. I don't—I don't —"

It occurred to me right then that if I could get that cucumber back into the den, where it belonged, maybe I could convince him he'd just been seeing things. And he'd just bought a quarter bag from me, which made him a criminal too. He wouldn't want his flock to know about that, except Sam. Preachers may be hypocrites, but most of them try to hide it. I had some leverage here.

I started calming down. The cucumber in the living room stopped singing, too, so it was a little easier to think. "Sit down," I said. "Right there. With your back to the wall." He did, just slid down that wall with his hands still up, and I said, "If you don't move, you'll be fine. Got it?" He nodded, his eyes still big, but he was watching me and the gun, not the cucumber. "Close your eyes," I said, and he did—he was still shaking, you'd better believe it—and I backed up, keeping the gun on him, and scooped that crazy lost cucumber back under my arm so I could take it back into the den.

But it picked that very instant to go *sploosh*, and Humphreys' eyes flew open at the extra noise—I guess he couldn't help it—and he saw that bag of cucumber gravy, and he turned green and gulped and whatever he'd had to eat that day came back up, all over his lap and my carpet. While he was heaving I backed up quick and opened the door to the den and tossed the gravy bag inside, and slammed the door shut again. I don't know if Humphreys saw that or not; he was busy reviewing the contents of his stomach. When he'd finished losing his breakfast he looked up at me, his face wet the way it gets after you've thrown up, and said, "I'm sorry. I really am sorry. I'll clean it up. If you bring me some soap and water and some rags—"

"Never mind that," I said. "I'll clean it up myself. You just get out of here, Reverend. You get out of here and bring Sam his medicine. You didn't see anything unusual, you hear me?"

He shook his head. "What *was* that?"

"It wasn't anything." One of the other cucumbers stopped singing, and I said, "You haven't seen or heard anything. Go on home, now." He just looked at me. The third cucumber shut up, so the house was very quiet, all of a sudden. I still had the gun trained on Humphreys; the safety was still on. I clicked it off and said, "Reverend, you need to go home now."

He swallowed. He'd stopped shaking. When he spoke again, his voice was a lot calmer than it had been before. "Mr. Smith, I've been in front of guns before. The worst you can do to me is kill me. I have to know one thing: That—that creature I didn't see, is it dangerous?"

"Something you didn't see can't be dangerous, Reverend. Go home."

He shook his head again. "I wish that were true, but it's not.

What we pretend not to see is what harms us. And if anyone's in danger—"

"Nobody's in danger but you, Reverend." I was starting to panic again. This guy wasn't going to let himself be convinced that the cucumber had just been his imagination. "As far as I know, the creature you didn't see isn't dangerous to anybody. Now go home!"

He just looked at me. He looked very sad. "If it's not dangerous, then why did you kill it?"

I lost it, then. Everything piled into my head in that one instant: how Nancy Ann had told me I was evil and how she'd left me even though I tried to make her happy, and all the work I'd done over the years to try to keep those cucumbers comfortable, to keep them from shaking. Jim Humphreys didn't understand a single goddamn thing. "I didn't kill it! It just died! That's what they do! They die! That's how they die! They've been coming here to die for ten years and you don't know a single thing about it, but you think you know everything, don't you? You think those creatures are the minions of Satan and you think I'm going to hell for taking care of them and for having pictures of naked women on the walls and for selling pot, and you think you can come in here and—"

"Welly!" he said. He sounded like I'd hit him over the head with one of those beanbag chairs. "Welly, if I thought you were going to hell for selling marijuana, why would I have come here to buy some for Sam?"

"How do I know? So you could preach to me about it! So you could preach to Sam and tell him he's going to hell! He probably confessed that he'd been smoking because he's dying and scared for his soul, because you people have your hooks in him just like you got them into my wife. I bet you smoke yourself, don't you? I bet you stand up every Sunday and preach about how drugs are a sin and everybody has to give you their money so they'll be saved, and then you come out here and spend that money on pot for yourself. All those fives and singles came from the collection plate, didn't they? Little old ladies giving you their last dollar and then you turn around and spend it on—"

"It's Sam's money," Jim Humphreys said. "The marijuana's for him, Welly. You can call and ask him. I have a phone in the car."

"I'm not done!" I said. "You just listen to me." It felt awfully good to yell at him like that, to have a man on the floor in front of me and to be able to point a gun at him and tell him exactly what I thought of him and have him not be able to do anything about it. It felt better than anything had felt in a long time. "I know about you people! Don't think I don't! I know how you ministers act in the pulpit, trying to scare ordinary folks who are just trying to get by and do the best they can, and then you turn around and you run off with people's wives after you've had the goddamned fucking nerve to make all that noise about the devil! Your kind think they're better than the rest of the world, don't they? Don't they, Reverend? You think you can tell me everything about who I am and how I should live my life, like you've got God in your pocket. Your people think that all they have to do to be saved is to put somebody else down—"

"My people," said Jim Humphreys, very quietly, "believe in welcoming all strangers as Christ." I squinted at him, because I couldn't believe how calm he was, and he said, "Even strangers who aren't human. I don't think I need to tell you anything about that, Welly. I think you've been welcoming strangers as Christ for—what did you say? Ten years? And if you're doing a better job with them than you're doing with me, well, that's because you think I'm not a stranger. You think you know who I am. But you're wrong, Welly. I'm a stranger, too."

I was ashamed, then, of how good I'd felt when I was yelling at him. And then I got angry again because he'd made me ashamed, which was what Nancy Ann and Jebediah had always tried to do. "High and mighty, aren't you? I bet you think I'm the scum of the earth—"

"I think you're scared," he said. "I think that if I were in your place, I'd be scared too. And I think it must be awfully hard, having to watch things die like that for ten years, without being able to talk to anybody about it."

I got a lump in my throat when he said that. It shocked me, because I hadn't cried since Nancy Ann left, and I was damned if I was going to start in front of this preacher. "It's not like that," I said. "It's not like I know them. They all look the same and they all die the same way, and I don't know how to talk to them. This is where they come and I do the best for them I can, but I don't get attached, Reverend. So don't get all sentimental."

He smiled, sitting there on the floor in his own puke. "All right. I won't. But would you mind if I cleaned up the floor here?"

Kicking him out hadn't worked. I might as well let him clean up his own mess. "Go on," I said, and used the gun to wave him into the kitchen. "Bucket and rags are under the sink." I watched while he filled the bucket with soapy water and carried it back into the living room and knelt down and cleaned up the mess. He did a good job; he was careful about it. When he was done he took everything back into the kitchen and rinsed it all out, and then he put a little clean water in the bucket and turned around and looked at me.

"Welly, I'd like to—may I visit your guests? May I see them?"

What the hell. He knew too much already; I wasn't going to get anywhere by trying to keep it from him. And I was starting to be curious about what he'd think of them, frankly. And I guess I wanted him to see that I wasn't just killing them. He'd struck a nerve there I didn't even know I had.

I looked at my watch. We had twenty-five minutes before the others went gravy, max, if they hadn't already. I didn't know what had gotten into the one who ran into the living room. Maybe it was crazy or extra sick, or maybe the cucumbers were about to start pulling new tricks on me, in which case I couldn't count on anything. "I don't know if the others are still alive," I said. "They may have gone gr—they may have died while we were out here. When they sing like that, it means they're going to die pretty soon. So they may look like that other one, now. I'm just warning you."

"Thank you," he said. "I think I'll be fine now." So I took him into the den. It was way too hot in there, with the space heaters, but that's how the cucumbers like it. I still had the gun with me, just in case Humphreys tried to pull something. The other two cucumbers were still solid. I'd never taken a gun into the den before and I was a little worried about how they'd respond, if they'd start shaking again, but they didn't even seem to notice.

Jim Humphreys had a plan, you could tell. He didn't pay attention to anything in that room except those two solid cucumbers. He got down on his knees right away and started muttering and waving his hands over the water in the bucket. Then he dipped his hand in the water and used it to make a sign of the cross on each cucumber—which was awfully brave, really, since it had taken me months to be comfortable touching them, but I guess he'd seen that I was okay after picking that other one up—and mumbled some more. "Look at you," I said. I didn't know whether to be impressed or disgusted. "You talk about welcoming all strangers as Christ and here you are trying to do an exorcism—"

He looked up at me, looking shocked. "Oh, no!" Then he looked a little sheepish. "Emergency baptisms. Although it's somewhat the same thing." He rocked back on his heels and stood up and said, "Now what?"

I shrugged. "Now nothing. Now they have"—I checked my watch—"maybe fifteen minutes left."

He looked at his watch, too. "May I wait here with them? Would that be all right?"

"I don't see why not," I said. He nodded and sat down on the floor, and I sat on the polka-dot beanbag chair. "All right, Reverend. You tell me this. If all strangers are Christ already, why do they have to be baptized?"

Humphreys smiled. "You should be a theologian. That's a good question. Mainly because it's what I know how to do, and it makes me feel better."

"Huh! You think it'll do them any good?"

"I have no idea. I don't see how it can hurt them." He looked around the room, then, up at the walls, and raised his eyebrows. "Matisse?"

"They like Matisse. Or I think they do. Don't ask me, Reverend. I don't know a damn thing. I do this and I do that, and I find chairs I think they like, and I say they're dying, but I could be wrong about all of it. They're not from around here. They're not dogs or cats; they're not the same kind of animal we are at all. I try to keep them still and happy, but maybe when they're still that means they're in pain. Maybe I've been torturing them all this time without meaning to. Maybe they're invading Earth and I'm the one making it possible, and in another ten years all these dead aliens are going to come back to life and take over the world."

He listened to me, his face still and serious. "Yes. It's hard, isn't it, not knowing if we're doing the right thing? I don't think any of us ever know, not really. We do the best we can, and we pray to do more good than harm, but we have to trust God to see it all, and to sort it all out, and to forgive us when we go wrong."

I looked away from him. "I don't believe in God. No offense."

"None taken, Welly."

"Good. What happened to your ear? I saw you on TV, feeding those bag ladies. That's how I knew who you were, when I saw your ear."

"It's a birth defect. My family didn't have enough money for plastic surgery." He shrugged. "I used to keep my hair long to hide it, but it doesn't bother me anymore. It's a help in my work, frankly. People bring their scars to church. They bring the wounds they want healed, but they're ashamed of them, too. If they can see mine, that makes it easier."

"I'll just bet," I said. Nancy Ann had a little scar on the inside of her left thigh, high up. It was a birthmark, too, like Humphreys' ear. It didn't take Jebediah very long to see that one, did it?

The second cucumber went *sploosh*, just then, and Humphreys and I both jumped a little. Humphreys didn't puke this time; he got back on his knees and made another sign of the cross and muttered some more. When he was done I picked up that gravy bag and put it in the corner with the other one, the one I'd tossed back into the den from the living room, and then Humphreys and I sat back down to wait for the third cucumber to go gravy. Five minutes, now.

"Why do you suppose they come here?" he asked me.

"Damned if I know. Maybe they're sick and their people send them away so they won't infect everybody else. Maybe they're dead already when they get here, and Earth's their eternal reward. Now that's scary, isn't it? Maybe when we die we're all going to land on some alien's doorstep, and we just have to hope they'll have comfortable chairs for us and find out what kind of art we like." My heaven will have Lay-Z-Boy recliners and *Penthouse* Pets, but I wasn't going to tell Humphreys that.

He smiled. "In my father's house are many mansions."

"What?" But the last cucumber went *sploosh*, so I never did find out what Humphreys had been talking about. He did his little praying routine again, and I piled the third cucumber in the corner with the other two.

He looked at the gravy bags, and then at me. "How do you— what do you do with them? Afterwards?"

"I bury them. I've got these things all over my property."

He nodded. "Do you need help?"

"If you're as good with a shovel as you are with a pail, I could use the help, Reverend. Thank you."

So we piled the gravy bags into my pickup, and I threw a tarp over them and loaded up a couple of shovels, and then I drove out to the next gravesite. I've been keeping track of where the cucumbers are, so I can pick a fresh place each time. I brought the gun with me, but that was in case we ran into snakes or something: I wasn't worried about Humphreys anymore, not that way.

He was good with a shovel, strong and fast. He hadn't always been a preacher, you could tell. He'd done manual labor someplace. Watching him dig, I started to get curious. When we stopped to take a break, I said, "So when were you in front of guns before?"

"In Africa." He wiped the sweat off his face. "In Zaire, back during the eighties. A group of us were rebuilding a church. Mobutu's thugs had burned it down because the clergy were speaking out against the government. And the soldiers came when we were rebuilding, and they lined us up against a wall and threatened to shoot us all. I still don't know why they didn't. They killed plenty of other people, before and after that." His eyes got far away, then, and he said, "All the people I worked with there—they're all dead now."

"That's not right," I said.

"No." He started digging again, and I let him. I know how working with your hands can help, when you're upset about something. I re-roofed the house all by myself, after Nancy Ann left.

We got the cucumbers neatly buried, one to a grave, and Humphreys said a little prayer over each one, and then we got back into the truck to go back into the house. I was worried. I had to figure out what to do about him, and it would have been easier if he'd been easier to hate. "Reverend," I said, "you were right before. I'm scared about what will happen if people find out about what's been going on out here."

"I'm not going to tell them," he said. "This is under the seal of clerical confidentiality, Welly. I take that very seriously."

I didn't know if I could believe him or not. I wanted to, but that's not the same thing. "I just hope I can trust you, Reverend."

"I hope you'll learn that you can. I can't expect you to, yet. You've only known me a few hours. Earning trust takes longer than that."

I grunted. That was a better answer than a lot of other people would have given. "Well, listen, you let me know when Sam dies."

"He may not die, not for a long time. We have to hope the chemo will work. We have to hope he'll be healed. But if he dies, certainly, I'll call you." Humphreys smiled. "He'll be having a church service, I have to warn you."

"Call me anyway." We were back at the house. I stopped the truck and said, "You left that bag inside, didn't you?"

"Yes, I did."

"Wait here. I'll get it for you. I'll be right back out."

The paper lunch sack was still sitting in the hallway, next to where Humphreys had gotten sick. It was wet from the soapy water he'd used. I threw the old sack away and got a fresh one, and then for good measure I threw another eighth into the plastic bag. I knew Sam would notice, and that kind of gesture's good for business, if you don't do it very often. I guess it was my way of gambling that he'd stay alive. And if he mentioned it to Humphreys, maybe the Reverend would be more likely to keep his mouth shut.

I took the sack back out and handed it to Humphreys. "I have something for you, too," he said, and gave me his business card. "Call me if you ever want to talk, about anything at all. You can call me any time. Both my home number and the church number are on there."

"Kind of you," I said, although I was thinking, *when hell freezes over*. "Thank you, Reverend."

"You're welcome, Welly." He held out his hand, and I shook it, and then he got back into his car and drove away. I watched his car until it disappeared, and then I went back into the house. I almost threw the business card away, but something made me toss it into one of my kitchen drawers instead. Don't ask me what. It wasn't like I planned on calling him. It was just a superstitious thing, maybe like what he'd said about the emergency baptisms. Having his business card probably wasn't going to help me, but it couldn't hurt, either.

I was hot, from all that digging. I opened the fridge and got out a beer and drank it down in one gulp. Then I got my cell phone and took it into the living room, and sat back in my recliner and started dialing the phone company.

*I started writing this story in 1988 and didn't sell it until over two decades later, after any number of revisions. Lhosi is a diminutive character dealing with a staggering weight of systemic oppression, genocide, and colonialism. Throughout human history, many people have suffered injustices massive enough to swallow entire cultures whole. Some of them used art to bear witness. This story is dedicated to them, especially the ones whose names we will never know.*

# HHASALIN

**M**ASTER AND MISTRESS didn't take Lhosi with them when they left the house to play tennis. She hadn't expected them to, and would have politely declined had they invited her, but she still wished they'd asked. They were gone to their game, and Sharina and Jakob were off on some equally strenuous excursion with friends, and that left Lhosi in the house alone. She didn't like being alone. She never had, not since her earliest days at the orphanage. There had been other shapers at the orphanage, of course; she had never really been alone. But so many of them had been sad, unwilling to play or to talk—except to curse the humans—that she had often felt alone. Most of them had been too sad even to shape.

Lhosi preferred the humans, the cooks and doctors. They were never unkind, whatever the others like her said. The humans gave her as much food as she wanted, and played games with her, and praised her cleverness. She had rejoiced when Master and Mistress took her home from the orphanage, because now she'd always be with humans.

Master and Mistress had chosen her because she was so clever, because she could speak their language and delighted in their numbers, which she added with ease, and also because the children, who had been just her size then—"Shari's a tall six and Jakob's a short

eight," Mistress had said—had been charmed with her and with the
air she shaped for them: figurines of fat little animals who perched
among the furniture, tiny cups perfect for serving tea, bright flower
buttons for Sharina's sundress. When Lhosi first came, Mistress
hadn't been able to get Jakob to do any of his chores, but if Lhosi
promised to shape a shovel or a ship or a gun for him, he'd do as
he was told.

That didn't last long. She'd had much more energy then; now
it was difficult for her to shape even a bead or a breadcrumb, no
matter how much she ate beforehand, and of course shaped things
couldn't do anything but sit there. The others had told stories, in
the orphanage, tales about how, long ago, before the humans came,
the shapers had been able to make things that moved, intricate creations of gears and pulleys. Lhosi didn't believe the stories, fantastical fairy tales. She had never seen anyone shape a moving thing. The
shapers were just jealous of the humans, who were so much cleverer
than they.

Shapestone was beautiful, perfectly smooth and lustrous. It
couldn't be broken or drilled or reshaped once a shaper had pulled it
from the air. This skill had served the shapers well, when they made
the old cities, shaped stone by stone over eons, but it had cost them,
too, sapped their strength: and there was no need for shapestone
now that the humans had come, with their metal and plastic and
glass, all of their wonderful machines.

When Lhosi first came to the house, Jakob and Sharina had
often asked her how she shaped things, but she couldn't explain. It
was as natural as to her breathing. One simply imagined the thing,
and reached with one's thoughts into the surrounding air to find
it, and there it would be, glittering and heavy, graceful or lumpish,
depending on the skill of the shaper. Some were better at it than
others, of course, and for all of them, even the strongest, it was tiring work. Lhosi's own gifts were modest: she had only ever made
small things, trinkets.

*Little things like you*, Aska had told Lhosi in their own tongue, back at the orphanage. *You're just a toy to them.* That was after the trial visit, when Lhosi had returned in triumph to pack up her few things and leave for good. *They'll tire of you, and then you'll wish you'd stayed.* Aska had been Lhosi's bunkmate. Every night Aska cried herself to sleep, remembering the death of her parents, and Lhosi, who couldn't remember her parents at all, told herself sadly that Aska was just jealous. Aska wasn't clever with sums, and would never learn to speak as humans did, and wasn't even very good at shaping, producing only cracked, deformed pebbles. She would never leave the orphanage. That was why Aska said what she did. No one could really wish to stay there.

And yet on days like this, when Lhosi was left alone, she sometimes worried about the things Aska had said. On days like this, she found herself dreaming about Hhasalin, the city in the south: the thriving city of her people, who had shaped it over centuries. Mistress had told her about Hhasalin—"Oh, it's beautiful, Lhosi"— and had promised that they'd all go there to visit someday, when Master and Mistress could make the time. "It's a long trip, you see; it's very far away. That's why you came here from the orphanage, instead of going there."

Lhosi had left the orphanage three years ago in the summer, when everything was bursting with life and nothing felt impossible. It was autumn now, the season of death, and Sharina and Jakob were far larger than she was; she came barely to Jakob's shoulder and only to Shari's chin, although she had been alive twice as long as Shari and was, by her own people's reckoning, fully grown.

The children had quickly become bored with Lhosi's gift, because the toys their parents gave them were much lovelier and more involving. Lately they had been bored with Lhosi, too. No one in the house needed anything Lhosi could shape, and so she had left off making things, keeping her energy for her frail body; but that meant that everything she did here was something a human could do better. For all her cleverness with sums, she was slower even at her beloved numbers than she had been when she arrived. Master and Mistress gave her the household accounts, but she knew that was only kindness. They could have handled the accounts much more quickly with one of their machines. More and more, all four of the humans left her alone in the house, as they had today.

She forced herself to turn away from the window, to stop staring out at the pathway Master and Mistress had taken to the car. She was alone in the house, and a beautiful house it was, and she should enjoy it: why, when she had first gotten here, just wandering through the huge, sunlit rooms had made her giddy with happiness. *Moping will not endear you to them*, she told herself. Her thoughts were, as always, in her own speech. She caught herself wondering where Aska was now, and put the thought aside with a shiver of dread. There had been too many deaths at the orphanage, and Aska had been ill when Lhosi left.

"Overcrowding and bad food," Master and Mistress had said sadly, shaking their heads.

"No," Lhosi answered, puzzled. "It wasn't crowded at all. Aska and I had a compartment to ourselves, although it was small, and we always had enough to eat. Why, three humans cooked for everyone there, as much as we wanted. You could ask them for food even when it wasn't mealtime, and they'd give it to you. The food was delicious."

But everyone had been too sad there. Every night in her sleep, Aska had cried out for her parents, and every morning when she woke, she cried again. *I will die here. I will die.* Aska had shaped her ugly pebbles and wept. *We could make things that moved once. They stole that from us.*

It was just a story. No shaper had ever made a moving thing, and the humans didn't need shapestone. They were kind creatures, generous to Lhosi even though they were so much stronger and smarter than she was. They played games with her, and stroked her fur, and praised how easily she had learned human language. Lhosi was glad to leave the orphanage, glad when Dr. Gronnell praised her own health and strength.

She didn't feel strong today. She barely had the energy to go upstairs to her room to lie down for a nap. She had decorated the room with her shapework: a row of funny animals on the windowsill, a vase on the desk. But today, lying on the bed, she turned her head away from the window, with its profile of small beasts. She couldn't throw them away. She'd made them. But she hadn't been able to take any pleasure in them since her visit to the Art Museum. Had that only been last week? She had never been there before, never seen the huge, graceful human sculptures with their sweeping curves and lazily moving parts. Of course the children no longer wanted her own tiny creations. Why would anyone want them?

She remembered how quiet Aska had been at the orphanage, when Lhosi shaped a curved bowl like a flower and Aska could only make a gritty lump. At the time, Lhosi had felt smug, triumphant. Now she felt ashamed. She shouldn't have made Aska feel that way.

Where was Aska now? Had she survived? Was she living with humans, like Lhosi, or had she made the journey to Hhasalin?

Stop it, Lhosi told herself, trying to shake off her gloom. It was just because it was autumn, the weather turning colder, the trees dying. Autumn always made her sad, and often clumsy, too, and remembering those times did nothing to cheer her.


Just a year ago, Master and Mistress had taken her to the tennis courts and tried to teach her to play. They gave her one of Shari's old rackets, but it was still too heavy for her, and she couldn't hit the ball, even after patient coaching from Master and Mistress and their two friends. She had strained and sweated in the crisp, sap-scented afternoon—an afternoon much like this one—missing ball after ball tossed gently at her racket. At last they gave up and began their own game, and Lhosi stood on the sidelines and watched them, filled with admiration and regret.

"Never mind," they told her later, "you tried very hard." And that winter, last winter, after the first snowfall, they took her skiing with them. It was a special treat, because the children were visiting their grandparents and didn't need Lhosi's care. Master and Mistress took her all the way to the wilderness which lay beyond the northern ruins, three hours from the human city. She didn't like the ruins, because her people had once lived there, Aska's parents and maybe her own, too; but she knew the humans were as sad about this city's death as she was.

"There was an epidemic," Dr. Gronnell had told her soberly. "We tried to help them, but far too many died, anyway." Lhosi nodded, remembering stories from the orphanage, terrifying tales of the tall humans moving among the dead and dying. Aska and many of the others thought the humans had caused the sickness, willed it. Lhosi knew this could not be true. The humans had been there to help, as they always did, but the ruins still made her sad.

Before Master and Mistress took her skiing, they had asked her if she wanted them to skirt around the empty, silent city. The shape-stone towers that must have taken so long to build were empty now, the streets deserted. These ruins did not even have a name.

"Of course not," she said bravely. "That would make the trip much too long. I'll just keep my eyes closed while we drive through it."

And she did, and the forest was worth everything. The clean white powder and the silence of the trees awed her; she could have stood still and looked at the tracery of black branches against gray sky forever, but she couldn't match Master and Mistress's effortless gliding. They sped past her again and again, chasing each other, laughing, while she slipped and struggled and fell.

At last Master picked her up and carried her, covered with snow and chilled to the bone, to the backseat of the hovercar. She shivered all the way home, despite the two dense, scratchy blankets Mistress piled on top of her. "Plucky little thing," Mistress said. "There, we went too fast for you, didn't we? I'm so sorry. You'll be all right once we get home."

But Lhosi hadn't been all right. She'd taken to bed with aches and a fever, feeling far too wretched to do any cleaning or read to the children, too weak to shape even a grain of sand. Sharina had brought her candy she was too queasy to eat, and Mistress, kind Mistress, had spent hours by her bedside, stroking her thinning fur. That was when she'd told Lhosi about Hhasalin. "There are thousands of your people there, Lhosi, all strong and happy."

"And warm?" Lhosi said, wondering why no one at the orphanage had ever mentioned this place. And yet when she closed her eyes, it seemed to her that she could see the city, full of trees and flowers, and feel the fragrant breeze. There must be a river there, and many birds.

"And warm," Mistress answered, tucking the blanket more tightly under Lhosi's chin. Lhosi could tell from her voice that she was smiling. "We'll take you there when you're older, so that you can choose a mate and start your own family."

Lhosi, in her weakened state, began to cry, obscurely afraid. "I want to stay with this family! I want to stay with you and Master, and Sharina and Jakob—"

"Shhhh, love. And so you will. And so you will, as long as you wish."

The day after that, Dr. Gronnell had come, but he had no medicine to offer for Lhosi's fever. "A virus," he said, gently stroking her forehead with his cool, massive hand, and Lhosi grew afraid, remembering Aska's illness.

"Is it—you said, an epidemic—"

"No, no. Don't be afraid. This is like a cold in humans, but a little worse. Just stay in bed until you're all better, Lhosi; drink warm things, and eat nourishing foods, and don't pretend to be stronger than you are. Why in the name of heaven did they take you skiing with them?"

"To show me how beautiful the forest is," she said, and Dr. Gronnell smiled.

"Yes," he said. "This is a lovely world, isn't it? But many things are beautiful. You should protect yourself from the ones that make you sick."

Afterwards she heard him speaking sharply to Master and Mistress in the other room, although she couldn't make out most of the words. She stayed in bed as he had asked and gradually grew strong enough to move about again, although it took many more long, weary weeks: weeks stretching into months as winter mellowed into spring, which ripened in its turn into summer. They had all been so careful of her through that time, although Jakob pouted because she got more treats than he did. "It's not fair," he said, "you're not even a *person*," and Mistress overheard him and flew into one of her rare rages, telling Jakob he would never have any treats again; and Master spanked him, while Jakob howled; and Sharina told him he was a little monster; and Jakob, looking miserable, brought her treats every day after that, although Lhosi tried to lighten his burden by teaching him games with beads and string, because she had no energy for shaping. He played the games dutifully, but she knew he'd rather have been outside.

He was just a child, she told herself. The children of her own people could be cruel, too; she had been cruel to Aska, when they were both children. And Jakob's remorse was real.

Yes, they had all been kind during her illness. But Dr. Gronnell must have forbidden sports, because one afternoon last week, when the children were off playing with friends, Mistress had taken Lhosi to the Art Museum. "I thought you'd like it," she said, "because you make things of your own."

Lhosi loved it. In high, airy rooms filled with warmth and light she ran from canvas to canvas, sculpture to sculpture, overwhelmed with color and shape and texture. Never had she felt so alive, not even before her illness. "Look," she said, tugging at Mistress's woven sleeve with long thin fingers, "look at this painting, see how they arranged those circles over there, see, that's the sun shedding heat, and those shapes, why, they must be birds, look how they're flying away from the world, and that statue, see, that's the flock of birds huddled in the cold, even though it's not by the same artist."

"Really?" Mistress asked, smiling. "Do you see all that? Well, I'm afraid it just looks like blobs of paint and stone to me, but I'm not very smart about these things. I'll just sit on this bench over here, Lhosi; you look as long as you like."

Lhosi looked for hours. At first she kept running back to the bench to try to tell Mistress about the wonderful things she had discovered, but Mistess, with her bag of sweets and her miniature television, was engrossed in the antics of bright moving figures no larger than gnats. "In the next room," Lhosi said, "there's a sculpture of the ship on the ocean, and the waves, oh! such curves as you've never seen, better than life because they're frozen and you can study them, you can almost feel the spray, do come see, Mistress—"

But Mistress frowned slightly from under her headset. "It's all right, Lhosi; I've seen the ocean. Maybe we'll take you there next summer, when we go to the city in the south. Go on: look at things. I'm fine."

After a while, Lhosi stopped trying to share what she had found and simply made her way from gallery to gallery, floor to floor, torn by the conflicting urges to stare at each piece as long as possible and to hurry, hurry, so she wouldn't miss whatever marvels were in the next room. She saw a bright metal mobile, as wide as the space which contained it, shifting slowly in sunlight; she saw elaborate models of buildings, an entire car polished bright as a jewel, carved wooden furniture as intricate and fragile as snowflakes. She saw ornate costumes Sharina would have loved.

Everything she saw elated her, but the sculpture filled her with a longing so intense it became pain. Needing air, she stumbled through an open door into a walled garden and found herself surrounded by yet more sculpture: shapestone, her own stuff, but these made her own work look as clumsy as Aska's. That graceful, gleaming tracery could be the branches of the forest, but those thin, elongated crystal trees grew nowhere Lhosi had ever been; here was a small scaled animal with large eyes; here was a series of domestic tableaux. A bowl of greenish fruit, a rumpled bed with a towel hanging from the end, shoes and sweaters scattered on a closet floor—

Lhosi blinked, frightened; the household sculptures made her feel the same stab of grief she'd endured as she tried to swing the tennis racket, as she struggled on unwieldy skis through the forest and watched Master and Mistress flying past her. Looking up at the bowl of fruit, she realized she felt that same grief whenever she had to stand on a chair to chop food at the kitchen table, or wash dishes, or reach the vase on the sideboard to arrange the black irises she had gathered from the garden—

These statues had been shaped by someone small, like she was. Well, of course: all her people were small. But this work, unlike the scaled animal, was about living in the human world, where things were too big. The bowl of fruit sat on a table far taller than the artist, and Lhosi marveled at the energy it had taken to shape such a towering thing. The shoes were huge and misshapen. The bed was larger than anyone could ever make properly, and it had just been left that way, rumpled, uncared for, the way Jakob and Sharina always left things, almost as if they were taunting Lhosi by making her wrestle with objects which they, even though they were not yet fully grown, could have handled much more easily—

No. Lhosi bit her lip, tasting sweet salt, and covered her eyes with her hands. Sharina and Jakob were good children, despite their moments of thoughtlessness, and she enjoyed caring for them. She liked to cook and didn't mind cleaning, and she enjoyed the elegant order of the numbers in the accounts, and didn't Master and Mistress always protest that she was doing too much? Hadn't they cared for her all those months when she was sick, and didn't she owe them something for taking her home from the orphanage where too many people died, where everyone was so sad, where even Aska, her friend, spoke only bitterness?

Master and Mistress had given her a private bedroom and let her share their meals and tried to teach her tennis; how else could she repay them for their kindness? She wasn't a fit partner in their games. As much as she longed to become golden and tall like they were, she would always be short and weak, her pale fur drab, patchy. But she could help with the things she was good at, with sums and chores and reading to the children. Even if she could no longer shape things that interested them—even if she would never be able to shape sculptures like these, which must have taken strength and concentration she could barely even imagine—still she had a place.

"We all have different abilities," Master had told her once as he unscrewed the lid of a jar which had defeated her. She clung to those words as she turned away from the statues. She wouldn't look at them again. They were evil, ugly things, despite their skill; little wonder so few people sought them out! She couldn't imagine why they were in the museum at all.

A yellow-suited guard looked out into the garden from the door. "Fifteen minutes to closing," he said. Lhosi nodded and tried to speak, but her throat felt as if it had been sewn shut. How long had she been here? Mistress must be furious.

"Do you like them?" the guard asked, nodding at the sculptures. Lhosi didn't want to talk to him, but he was blocking the way back in. "Me, I think Aranshai's better than Mrinah or Benniron, but that's an unpopular view. Most people like the nature studies better than the household scenes." He laughed. "You know, cute animals and trees—but even Mrinah and Benniron are awfully good. I don't think any of them have gotten the attention they deserve."

He smiled at her. She wanted to ask him to move, but she didn't know how. He was so tall, so tall, with a smooth tan just like Master's and Mistress's; he must ski and play tennis all the time when he wasn't at the museum, and he worked here, he belonged here, he knew so much about the art: more than she did, although her own people had made it. Shame swamped her.

She had to talk to him. He was waiting for her to say something, and Mistress was waiting for her on the bench. "They're very well done," she said, "but there's no grace to them. They're too real."

It was a stupid thing to say. Now the guard knew that Lhosi wasn't clever at all; he'd wonder why anyone had brought her home from the orphanage. Surely he would let her go now, get out of her way. But instead he nodded as if she'd said something intelligent. "You must prefer the abstracts, then. Many people find the Representational School tiresome." He paused, then, and added shyly, "Do you shape?"

His voice had grown diffident, almost deferential. But no, she must be imagining that; all she could really hear was the pounding of her own pulse. "Not like these," she said. "Never like these!" She realized that she both longed for the skill of these shapers and was disgusted by how it had been used. She swallowed, desperate to go home and busy herself with the account books, with the sweet oblivion of numbers, which never lied and never caused her pain. "Little things," she told the guard. "Tiny shapes in my spare time, when I'm not working—silly animals, eggcups—please, will you excuse me? It's very late, and someone's waiting for me."

"I'm sorry I kept you," he said, suddenly sounding confused and very young—as young as Jakob or Sharina when they had bad dreams—and she ran past him, past the shapestone monstrosities, back inside and through airy rooms filled with light and paintings of the sun, down stairways hung with banners, until at last she reached the bench where Mistress was waiting, scanning the other patrons, her bag packed and slung over her arm.

"I'm sorry," Lhosi said, fighting for breath, "I lost track of the time until a guard reminded me. How long I've made you sit here!"

"It's all right," Mistress said. "Really it is, Lhosi. It's just that the children are at school waiting to be driven to their dance lessons—"

"Oh," Lhosi said, "I'm so sorry." She'd completely forgotten that the children had their lessons today. "There was a place with some statues which disturbed me terribly, and it took me the longest time to figure out why, and then the guard—"

"I'm sorry you didn't like it," Mistress said with a sigh, and Lhosi began to tremble.

"But I did," she said as they hurried out of the museum, "I did like it, I loved it, there was just the one room—everything else was so beautiful, Mistress! It moved me more than I can tell you, and it was so kind of you to bring me. I hope I can come back. May I come with the children sometime?"

"I think they'd be bored," Mistress said. "They aren't old enough for museums."

"Do you think so? I saw plenty of children there younger than Sharina and Jakob."

"Yes—and misbehaving too, most of them. Children need activity. I hope Shari and Jake won't be late for their lessons."

They were late, and cranky about it. Jakob, in the front seat with his mother, fretted that he wouldn't get the recital part of the soldier boy if he didn't arrive in time. "You and your stupid tennis games," he said. "You're always late!"

"Never mind," Mistress said firmly. "Lhosi and I were at the Art Museum, and she had a wonderful time. She deserves to enjoy herself once in a while too, you know."

"She enjoys herself all the time. That's all she does. She lies in bed and plays baby games with beads and string—"

"Jakob!" Mistress said. "Lhosi works very hard. You lie in bed too, when you're sick. Now stop it! You can't always expect everyone to do your bidding."

The games had been for Jakob. Sitting in the backseat next to Sharina, Lhosi suddenly felt as if she were standing in front of the Aranshai shapework again, feeling bitter and used and insignificant. *Mistress is defending you,* she told herself. *She didn't have to take you there at all. And Jakob is mean to his sister and his parents, too, when he doesn't get his way.*

"Lhosi," Sharina asked, touching her arm, "what did you see? At the musuem?"

"Wonderful things," Lhosi answered quietly. Dear, sweet Shari.

"Paintings of the sea, and portraits of the most beautiful people in the world, and statues shaped from stone as polished as glass. And costumes, Shari, gorgeous dresses and capes—"

Jakob turned and made a face. "It sounds boring."

"They had a car too, Jakob." Why did she always struggle to mollify him? *You're just a toy*, Aska said in her head, and she went on, hating herself. "And drawings and models of buildings, like the ones you make—"

"Grown-ups make crayon buildings?" Jakob sounded incredulous.

"Grown-ups design buildings," Mistress said. "They draw them on paper, and sometimes they make models to give people a better idea of what the building will look like. But you need training to do that. You need to be good at math. How did your math test go, Jakob?"

"It went fine." He sounded sullen. He hated sums, refused to sit still through Lhosi's efforts to coach him. "Can I make some buildings for the museum?"

"Maybe when you're grown up," Mistress said. "If you're very, very good at making buildings then. But it's a very serious place, Jakob, and it's not for children."

"If you wanted to look at the buildings and the car for a little while, we could go there and then leave if you didn't like the rest," Lhosi said. "Sharina could look at the costumes. I saw other children there. Would you like to go sometime?"

But no one answered, because they'd reached the dance school, and Sharina and Jakob piled out of the car. Jakob didn't get his soldier-boy part; but Sharina won an even better role, as the brave mother mouse who saves her hungry family by stirring and stirring the cat's milk until it turns to cheese. All the talk at dinner that evening was of the recital, of fittings and rehearsals and opening night. Lhosi offered warm congratulations, but no one wanted to hear about the Art Museum. Master, Mistress, and Sharina kept bubbling about the dancing mouse, and Jacob kept sulking. Once he leaned over to Lhosi, while the others were talking, and hissed at her, "It's *your* fault. I'd have been the soldier boy if I'd gotten there on time!"

It would do no good to remind him that Sharina practiced far more faithfully than he did, and had been just as late for the lesson. "Try to be happy for your sister," Lhosi said.

"What?" Mistress said. "Lhosi, what did Jake just say to you?"

"He didn't say anything," Lhosi said. She got up, trying not to think of the towering shapestone closet, and lugged the dishes to the kitchen before going to her room. The first thing she saw was her little animals, lined up on the windowsill. She balled her fists to keep from knocking them to the floor. They wouldn't shatter as they ought: they'd only make noise and disturb the humans. "Cute animals," the guard had said with a laugh. Cute animals were small and easily frightened. They could be dismissed. They threatened no one and meant nothing.

Lhosi heard laughter from the dining room, quick snatches of conversation. If she rested for a week and ate as much as her stomach could hold, would she have the strength to shape something like one of the sculptures she'd seen today? Something huge and towering, something that would show the humans what it felt like to be small? Would they be proud of her then? Would the dinner chatter be about her accomplishment? Would everyone crowd around her lovingly, or only desert her in discomfort, as the garden with the sculptures had been deserted?

*Silliness*, she told herself. She was pouting like Jakob, resentful at not getting enough attention. And yet she found herself wondering yet again where Aska was now, Aska and all the others. When was the last time Lhosi had seen another shaper? In the orphanage she had preferred the company of humans, who praised her cleverness and didn't cry about what they'd lost. She hadn't wanted to be sad, in the orphanage; since then, she seemed to have grown sad anyway.

\*

*Because it's autumn*, she scolded herself now, in the silent house and her silent room: airy and vast, with white curtains and a large soft bed and a large closet. *Because you can't play tennis.* Her closet was as large as the shapestone one, but far neater. Her things took almost no room at all.

She'd rest and eat; she'd shape something serious, something beautiful to soothe herself with. Perhaps if she took her shaping as seriously as Master and Mistress took their sports, as the children took their recitals, she'd be better at it.

But she couldn't shape anything today, not even a speck of sand. She started as she always did, closing her eyes and relaxing, extending her mind to embrace the air around her and the elements within it. She could feel them there, heavy and gleaming, insubstantial as yet, waiting to be gathered and given form.

But when she reached for them, they eluded her grasp like glittering fish in a pond, slipping away from her; and soon she felt herself slipping, too, losing her sense of what surrounded her, everything solid fading into mist.

She stopped trying to shape. She opened her eyes and stared out the window instead, and found herself dreaming again of Hhasalin. Mistress spoke of it so often, but no one else ever did. There was an atlas in one of the bookcases on the landing, just outside Lhosi's room. Mistress had never shown her Hhasalin on a map. If Lhosi looked now, would she find it? It would be so easy to look.

And yet she discovered, suddenly, with a tightening of her heart, that she did not want to. What was this? Surely Mistress would not lie to her.

Back downstairs, she decided, giving herself a shake. Back down to the books, to the numbers, always comforting in their order. With a sigh of relief, she turned toward the door and then heard laughter, higher-pitched than Master's and Mistress's, on the path outside: the children were back, although she'd expected them to be gone all day. But here they were, and returning to her window she saw two friends—a brother and sister—and the friends' mother with them, too. Lhosi, obscurely ashamed, hurried out to greet Sharina and Jakob and the guests.

The four children tumbled into the house in a confusion of voices and stray leaves and toys. Sharina had a yo-yo and Jakob had a hoop. Their friends' names buzzed past Lhosi in a blur; she tried to greet the mother properly, but Jakob was tugging on her hand.

"We aren't home for long," he said. "We came to get you, Lhosi! We're going to—"

"I'll stay home with you," Sharina said. "I brought some clay home from school. Will you teach me to shape it, Lhosi?"

Shari and Jake's friends were running up and down the stairs. Lhosi looked helplessly at the mother, who was flipping through a clothing magazine she'd found on the hall table. But it wasn't her place to tell this woman how to discipline her children, and Jakob was still plucking at her. "Lhosi, we're going to—"

Sharina pulled at Lhosi's other hand. "Teach me to shape things, Lhosi! I want to make animals like you do!"

"We're going to the Science Museum!" Jakob shouted, his eyes gleaming. "We'll take you with us!"

"The children thought you might like it," the mother said, looking up from her magazine for a moment. "They insisted we swing by and pick you up."

"Jakob insisted," Shari yelled, "and he's wrong! It's the Art Museum she likes, Jakob, you know that! Lhosi, I'll go with you to the Art Musuem."

"But what's this other one?" Lhosi asked, puzzled and flattered; Jakob so rarely thought to include her in his interests, especially when he was busy with his friends. Maybe he'd gotten over his anger about the recital, finally, and this was his way of telling her he was sorry. "I'd like to see this other museum, too."

"You'll hate it," Sharina said, sounding very certain and very much like her mother. "I hate it. It doesn't have anything interesting at all. It's boring. Lhosi, please, let me stay here with you—"

"I'd like to see Jakob's museum," Lhosi said, "and you can't stay here by yourself, Sharina. Children? Won't you be tired, if you keep doing that?" The young guests were sliding down the bannister now.

"I don't want to go there," said Sharina, who was normally such a tractable child. "I want to look at the art."

"We can look at art another day," Lhosi said firmly, and Jakob treated her to the sweetest smile she'd seen in months.

"But Lhosi, you won't like it, I know you won't—"

"Come on!" Jakob shouted. "Let's go! Let's go let's go let's go!" And then he and the other two children were out the door, and the mother had put down the magazine with a sigh to follow them.

Lhosi set off after them. "Come on, Shari. We'll find something at the Science Museum you'll like, I promise."

In the car, Lhosi sat on Shari's lap and tried to find out why the girl was so upset. Every time she asked, though, Jakob cut in and said, "Because she's a baby, that's why!"

"I'm not the baby! You are! Lhosi—"

"Stop fighting," Lhosi said. The other two children were fighting too, over some toy; their mother, wearing a headset, didn't seem to hear anything. "Shari, isn't there anything in the Science Museum you like?"

"The minerals," Sharina said immediately. "They're jewels, Lhosi, they're so pretty, they sparkle so. They're too expensive for anyone to buy, but if you went to look at them you could shape statues of them for me, just little ones, and then I'd feel like I owned some."

"Well then, we'll go see them. Do you feel better now?"

"Maybe. Can we look at the minerals first?"

"No fair!" Jakob said. "You're always first! I want to be first!"

"We'll go through the museum in order," Lhosi said, "and that way we'll see everything, if that's all right with your friends." But the other children were still squabbling, and the mother was still listening to music.

This museum contained microscopes and meteorites, telescopes and topsoil, bodies and bones and beetles. Very little of it was beautiful, but all of it was interesting and impressive, and Lhosi felt honored to be there: as if at last she was being allowed to share important things, the things that determined the way the world worked, the same things the children studied so assiduously at school. She had heard Jakob talk about atoms, and here was a model of one, silver tubes with red and blue balls on the ends. Here were photographs of the stars and the surface of the moons and the other planets where humans lived; here was a film of a red, wrinkled baby being born; here was a diagram explaining the physics of tennis balls. In truth, she appeared to be far more interested in the exhibits than anyone else; Jakob kept racing ahead and Sharina kept trying to pull her back, and the other children and their mother had vanished somewhere. Lhosi supposed they would all find each other again at the entrance; for now, her job was to keep track of Shari and Jake.

She had already begun to grow tired when they turned a corner and found themselves in a hallway with rooms to either side. Left or right?

"The minerals are that way," Shari said, pointing left. "Lhosi, they're so pretty."

"You only want pretty things," Jakob called scornfully over his shoulder. He was already heading right. "*I* want to look at the Ancient Animals."

"No, Jakob! We've been doing what you want all day! I want to see the minerals!"

"She knows what rocks look like," Jakob said. "The Ancient Animals are much more interesting. Lhosi, come on."

"You're mean," Sharina said. "Mean! Lhosi, he's horrible, don't go with him—"

"We have to stay together," Lhosi said. "What are the Ancient Animals?"

"Monsters," said Sharina. "They're—"

"Oh, Shari, they are not monsters! They're animals that were alive a long time ago. You'd like them, Lhosi."

"No she wouldn't! She wouldn't! Jakob, I'll tell Mother—"

"We can see both," Lhosi said. "There's still plenty of time until closing. Sharina, are you scared of these things? Here, hold my hand. If they're dead they can't hurt you."

"Yes, they can. Lhosi, please don't go there."

"Why, child? What can they do to us?"

"Make us sad," Sharina said. "Make us sad because they're dead."

"Crybaby!" Jakob called in glee. "Crybaby, crybaby, misty-moisty Mother Mouse! That's all you are! Well, I'm going!"

And he ran off, and because Lhosi couldn't let him wander by himself—what would Master and Mistress say if something happened to him?—she set off in pursuit, Sharina dragging at her hand. "Shari, stop," Lhosi said, and shook herself free. She spotted Jakob in front of a huge skeleton of some sea-creature, but when he saw her he ran off again; he paused in front of a model of an odd furred animal with webbed feet and a single twisting horn, but was on his way before Lhosi reached him.

"Let him go," Sharina said, crying, behind her. "Just wait here. Don't follow him any more, Lhosi. It's a game—"

"I can't let him get lost, Shari."

"He won't!"

"Come on: he can't have gone much farther. That's the end of the exhibit up there."

They found him standing triumphantly in a small corridor hung with photographs. Odd, Lhosi thought wearily; he didn't usually like pictures. Well, it was a game to torment his sister. "Come on, Jakob. We're going home."

"All right," he said, smiling now. Sharina, whimpering, tugged at Lhosi's hand. Hot and tired, Lhosi glanced incuriously up at the photographs, which were scaled—like everything here—for tall people.

"Don't look," Sharina said, but it was too late. Lhosi blinked at the photograph in front of her: a city. A shaper city; it had to be, because there were the shapers. They stood in ranks, wearing strange helmets. They looked out from walls and parapets while odd things with gears and wings flew through the air toward a phalanx of humans holding guns.

She shook her head. What was this? *Shaper defense*, the placard read. *The shapestone weapons seen here are typical of the ones used to repel human incursions into shaper territory after the first landing.*

What? Shari was saying something, but the words faded into a blur, mere noise. Lhosi bent over a diagram of one of the weapons in the photograph. It was a lethal thing, all cogs and needles. The placard said that the cogs turned to drive the engine; it said the needles had burrowed into human flesh, twisting.

Moving parts.

Lhosi blinked again, shook her head, turned to the next photograph: shapers lying on cots, tall humans moving among them. She knew this image. It was the tale from the orphanage, the horror story Aska and the others had told at night.

She had begun to shiver; the room shook around her. She was surprised she could still read the placard. *The virus intended to suppress the shaping ability instead only blunted it, while also producing epidemic and disastrous illness.*

Shari was crying. Lhosi couldn't make herself turn to comfort the girl. Instead, as the room danced around her, she looked at the last photograph: a group of thin, pale figures with patchy fur. *Tragedy*, said the caption underneath, and *nearing extinction* and *gifted race*, and then a list of names: Takibon, Allargia, Mrinah, Aranshai.

Aranshai. Jakob was giggling, but it was the nervous giggle of a child who's done something horrible. "Do you shape?" the guard at the Art Museum had asked. He must have thought she knew.

"Mother and Father said we'd have to tell you sometime." Jakob looked down at his shoes. He'd stopped giggling. "They said you'd have to know. They did."

"Not like this," Sharina said. "Not so soon. Oh, *Jakob!*"

*Because of a dance recital*, Lhosi thought. *Because of a toy soldier*. "Never mind," she said, and fought to stay upright. Dr. Gronnell had told her about the epidemic, but not that the infection was deliberate, a weapon. "Never mind. Shari, we need to find your friends. We need to tell their mother that I want to go home now."

But when she tried to walk, the floor swung and swooped, and her limbs became as unresponsive to her will as they'd been on the tennis court, and all the pictures faded to black.

When she woke up, fighting her way out of a long tunnel, she was in her soft bed and Dr. Gronnell was leaning over her. "I'm sorry," he said. "Oh, Lhosi, that dreadful little boy, I'm so sorry—"

She shook her head. Her throat ached. "He showed me the truth. It was the truth, wasn't it?"

Dr. Gronnell looked away. "Yes," he said. "I'm sorry."

Of course it had been the truth; that was why Sharina had been so upset. Aska and all the others at the orphanage had told the truth too, and Lhosi wondered now how they had known—tales passed down in the dark, it must have been—and how Aska must have felt, watching her go off with the humans. *They are killing us. We will die here.* Grief stabbed her. Was Aska dead now?

"How many of us are left?"

He bowed his head. "Not enough, Lhosi. We're doing everything we can to help. We're preserving DNA; we're trying to clone some of you. There are breeding programs. If you get stronger, maybe —"

He looked away and said, "The virus wasn't supposed to hurt you. It was just supposed to stop the shaping, so you wouldn't hurt us."

"With our moving weapons," she said. "Because you came here and weren't wanted. But you took what you wanted, didn't you? Our planet. Our cities. Us."

He turned back to face her. He looked ashamed, like Jakob

when he'd been scolded. Lhosi went on, merciless. "You tried to take away what made us ourselves. You tried to make us like you, creatures who couldn't shape. But we weren't like you because we were smaller and weaker and not as smart with metal and plastic, and that was even better, wasn't it?"

"Some of you are immune," Dr. Gronnell said. "In all of you the shaping was blunted, but some of you are immune from the other effects. In some of you the virus doesn't progress."

She remembered the needles. "Am I immune?"

She saw him swallow. "We thought you were, Lhosi."

"Until I got sick," she said. "Until I stayed sick. Last winter."

"Yes. I told them to tell you."

She closed her eyes and saw flowers. "Mistress told me there was a city in the south, a thriving city of my people. Hhasalin, she called it. She promised they'd take me there. She said I could find a mate and start a family. But there isn't any city, is there? Or if there was, it's gone. Ruins, like the one in the north."

"No city," he said quietly, sadly. "And even if there were, it wouldn't have helped, moving you somewhere else. Not medically. And not socially; you'd lost your family when you were so young, and you'd always been close to humans—"

"Yes," she said, opening her eyes. She remembered swinging the tennis racket with aching arms, remembered slipping and sliding on cold skis. "I've spent my life trying to be something I'm not. How long, Dr. Gronnell?"

"For you? I don't know. Years, maybe. Maybe less than that."

"Why did you allow me to live here at all? Why didn't you keep me in a lab to protect me, if my DNA's so precious?"

"That would have been cruel," he said, sounding pained. "The adoptive families were screened very carefully. We wanted you to be happy."

"Happy," she said, and saw him flinch.

She heard him take a breath. "Everyone who knew Aranshai says he was very bitter before he died." His voice was as hesitant as

Lhosi had ever heard it. "Well, of course he was. But that's a kind of strength. I think you have to learn to hate us, Lhosi. If you don't already."

Did she? She didn't know. She had chosen humans when she was very young, had tried to become one of them, had mourned her failure; could she hate them without hating herself? And if she hated them, who was left to love? Even Aska had faded to a vague blur, the laughing cooks' faces much clearer.

"I'm sorry," Dr. Gronnell said. He rubbed his eyes and stood up. "I have to go now. Rest and eat well. Shari called her parents; they're coming home. The other family will stay until they arrive. You can call me if you have questions, Lhosi. Anytime."

"Thank you," she said, out of habit, and he left. Lhosi lay in bed, listening to the birdsong outside, to breezes stirring through the house. She could hear the children playing in the garden, as boisterous as ever. Once Sharina crept into the room, but when Lhosi pretended to be asleep, the girl went away. Where were Master and Mistress?

At last Lhosi got up and walked unsteadily to the windowsill, where her tiny shaped animals sat in a neat row. Never had they looked uglier to her. She thought of Aranshai's vast shapings, the closet and the bed. How much energy they must have taken! Had he already been sick, when he made them?

Dusk was falling; the children's thin voices rang through the house. They were playing a counting game, and Lhosi realized that she had no more use for numbers, which went on forever.

She stood without moving until she heard Master and Mistress coming up the walk. When she looked out her window she saw them, dressed in the absurdly stylized costumes of the game, clutching their rackets and hurrying toward the house. They had their future: it played with circles and infinities, with hoops and sticks, and was cruel to anyone who kept it from its desires.

The shapers had defended themselves with weapons, and so the humans had used weapons of their own: tiny ones, living and lethal. But remembering how she had felt in the Art Museum, Lhosi knew that art, too, could be a weapon. It could tell stories. It could make people feel pain, and guilt, and sorrow.

She closed her eyes, reaching. What would she shape if she could? What large thing would she make?

Hhasalin. The city Mistress had invented, or anyway part of it, a model of it. Lhosi would make it real. She would reach into the air and find her city, a shaper city, with her kind laughing and playing, planting flowers and tending their young. She would shape the city that had never existed, that never could exist. She would shape a city without humans, a city with no need of weapons.

She did not have the strength, of course. She would never be able to finish it. How would she even begin?

But she did begin, finding what she needed in the air, gathering it, depleting herself. She began to shape walls and towers, block by block, and as she did she imagined the crowds she would shape, too, the tiny figures. She would shape gardens and markets and vast outdoor galleries, all of them thronged with her kind, old people and young couples, families with children. She would shape them vibrant and smiling, living peacefully in a place where everything was the right size for them.

She kept at her work through dinner, through Jakob's punishment by his parents, through Master and Mistress's attempts to talk and confess and apologize and explain. She had no time for interruptions and no sympathy for excuses. Her muscles trembled with her effort, and Mistress backed out of the room and returned with bowls of food. Lhosi opened her eyes only to devour the stuff before going back into her shapetrance. She stood surrounded by a low, growing wall of shapestone, and whenever she stopped, shaking with exhaustion, she forced herself to rally. *This is for Aska*, she told herself, and reached again and again into the shining air.

*Anyone who's read much of my work knows that faith is one of my favorite subjects. I call myself "a proud member of the Christian Left"—I'm Episocopalian, if anyone cares—and I'm fascinated by how belief functions on the margins, especially for people who've been stigmatized or written off by those who consider themselves respectable. The margins are where the Christ of my tradition spent his time, and I've always said that if he came back tomorrow, he'd be crucified again in two minutes for hanging out with the wrong people. That said, the apocalypse in this story may or may not fit the definitions offered by Christian communities (which don't even agree with each other on the subject). The characters certainly have differing opinions about that. What do you think?*

# SANCTUARY

'D JUST FINISHED putting new eyebolts in the St. Andrew's cross in the Red Room—I hadn't installed the old ones, and they'd turned into pipe cleaners—when the angels came fluttering in, mewling and bumping into things. One of them veered into a wall, ricocheted, and got caught in the black leather bondage sling; the other smacked its shin into the cross and went down with a howl. They're ugly things, the angels, like fat giant babies with stubby chicken wings. They can't fly any better than most chickens can; they flap up a few feet, maybe manage to stay up for a few yards or so, and then whomp onto the floor, or into something else. They can't steer, and Cyn has to keep changing their diapers because she can't housetrain them, and they eat too much. They need lots of energy to stay up in the air at all, I guess. Cyn tried to teach them to walk when they first got here, but it didn't work. They can't talk, either. I don't think they understand anything we say.

The angels are one of the stranger things that showed up after the Rapture, and frankly, they're a gigantic pain. Most people want nothing to do with them, especially with food being so scarce. You'd think there'd be enough food for everybody now, since so many people were taken, but the distribution systems went all to hell, especially in the cities, and nearly anything that wasn't canned spoiled, and a few armed groups grabbed most of the canned stuff and hoarded it. There've been gang wars over canned corn, and who can manage home production? If Cyn hadn't been interested in gardening and sent for some seeds before the Rapture, and if Dimity hadn't turned out to be a Finder, we'd all be doomed.

A few people tried to eat angels, early on, and got so sick they nearly died, which explains why there are any of the creatures still around at all. They'd be extinct if they were edible. But Cyn won't turn anyone away, especially anyone who's hurting. She was like that even before everything went haywire—look at what she named the dungeon, after all—and she's ten times more so now. Carl thinks it's her Curse. The Curse of Community, he calls it, but I'm not so sure; I think it's just Cyn being Cyn. If it is a Curse, it's blessing too, although I guess that's true of most of them. At any rate, when Dimity found the two angels on the street, beaten into bloody pulps and left for dead, of course Cyn took them in and nursed them back to health. They've been crashing into the furniture ever since.

Jack threw a fit about the angels once, basically told Cyn that he couldn't stand the creepy things and didn't see how any of the rest of us could, either, but she didn't budge. "Well then, goodbye, Jack. You can walk away if you want to, but I'm not kicking the angels out. We've all been shut out, right? We all know what that feels like. I'll be damned if I'm doing it to anybody else."

"If you weren't already damned," Jack said, pleasantly enough, "you wouldn't still be down here, would you?"

I was repainting the upstairs walls that time, Carl helping me. Back when the world was still normal, I helped Cyn take this abandoned industrial loft on the waterfront and turn it into Mistress Cynthia's Sanctuary. I know every inch of sheetrock and wiring and plumbing in the building. These days, we're never sure when the laws of physics are going to quit on us, but so far, the stuff I Fix has stayed fixed. Nails I drive into place don't suddenly turn into caterpillars and wiggle away; when I toss something into the air it comes back down instead of floating up like a balloon. Because I built the St. Andrew's Cross, it hasn't gone funny on us the way the eyebolts did. Don't ask me why I even bothered replacing the eyebolts: it's not like we're using the equipment these days. Pipe cleaners where eyebolts should be offend my sense of order, I guess.

Cyn says I make things behave, but it's never worked with Jack. The very first day he got here, when she was introducing all of us, she told him, "This is Lazslo. He's our Fixer."

"Fixer? Never heard of one of those."

"If he touches something, it won't change into something else. It comes in handy, believe me."

Jack stared at me. "That's because he can't fix his own face, right?"

It didn't bother me that much—I got used to people being mean a long time ago—but I thought Carl was going to kill him on the spot. "What do you suppose that asshole's Curse is?" he asked me after Cyn had taken Jack outside to show him the garden. "I never heard of anybody called a Hurter, myself, but I think we just found one."

"Oh, he was probably that way before," I said. Like Cyn, except in the opposite direction. Of course it turned out that Jack's something rarer and much more valuable, but we didn't find out about that for a while. He wanted to be sure of us before he let us know, I guess, and I can't blame him, especially given what the Sanctuary must have looked like to him at first. Awful things happen to Aquifers: people lock them up, put guards around them, torture them to get water, kidnap them, you name it. And Jack came at the end of the rainy season, anyhow, when we could still depend on our water traps. A few weeks later, when water started being a problem again, he was happy to help out, although Carl always maintains that one reason Jack's so cruel is that he figures we'll never ask him to leave.

Carl and I could hear everything Jack and Cyn said, the day Jack complained about the angels; he and Cyn were downstairs, but the conversation carried up to the loft. It's where Cyn and Dimity sleep, since Cyn wants to be able to hear if anybody's trying to get in. I still don't know where the paint came from. Dimity must have

Found it someplace, an old warehouse or something maybe.

Carl wiped his face on the sleeve of his sundress—it was a hot day, and the air up there was stifling, even with the windows open to thin the paint fumes—and whispered at me, "Never mind the angels! Why won't she kick Jack out?"

I kept my voice as low as his, and carefully kept my eyes on the patch of wall in front of me. I knew the cartoons above Carl's head wouldn't be pretty right now. Broadcasting must be part blessing too, but it's hard to see how. That's one of the more common Curses, but all it does is turn people into open books, which was never a very safe thing to be and hasn't gotten any better. "She won't kick anyone out, Carl. You know that."

I felt him shaking his head. "That bastard's trouble. I wish he'd leave."

"He won't leave," I said. "He may be trouble and he may be mean, but he's not dumb. He's got a good situation here, and he knows it."

Carl shoved his roller into the paintpan at my feet, a lot harder than he had to. He's a lefty, and I saw the wedding band gleaming on his third finger. I don't think he'll ever take it off. "How can he tell her she's damned, then? How can he—"

"Because he thinks he is too, Carl. Come on: you know that. To him it's a fact, about himself and about us, about anybody who's left. He's stating the obvious, is all." This was a very old argument, so I already knew what Carl was going to say next.

"Do you really think—"

"No," I said. "You know I don't. And I know you don't. But we're a minority, and we're not going to change Cyn's mind about anything. Or Jack's. So leave it alone."

He rolled a new layer of paint onto his section of the wall—I'd mixed the paint myself to keep it from turning into, I don't know, leaves or cellophane—and said, "I just wish she'd love herself half as much as the rest of us love her."

That was old, too. "Even Jack?" I asked mildly, and Carl scowled.

I think Jack does love Cyn, in his fashion, or at least honor her, but Carl's never agreed with me on that, and never will. I can make paint and eyebolts behave, but not people. Anything alive moves around too much.

That's one of the few nice things about the angels; they don't fight you when you're trying to help them. So when the one went down with a banged leg, I grabbed the First Aid kit next to the door—there's one in every session room—and knelt down, making cooing noises the way you would to a kid, or a pet. "There there," I said, and swabbed the angel's scraped leg with some alcohol, which of course made it whine even more. "There there. You'll be fine, little friend. You don't need to use that thing to walk, anyway." The angel was still keening, so for good measure I dragged it into my lap and put a Bandaid on the scrape. Kids like Bandaids, don't they? Maybe angels do too. "There there. All better now, eh?"

Whimper, whimper. And the one caught in the sling was making meeping noises, so I went over and freed its foot from the sling, but that didn't seem to help. It bumped down on the floor and sat there, squealing. It got a rhythm going with its friend across the room, and then they both started fluttering their wings and waving their stubby little arms around. Wheep, wheep, wheep!

"What's wrong?" I said. "What is it?" I couldn't smell that they needed their diapers changed, and we'd all had a nice big breakfast that morning—although Dim was out scrounging again—so I didn't think they were hungry.

"What's going on?" asked Carl from the door. He was wearing a slinky gown, all sequins and seed pearls. In the air above his head hung a birthday cake with candles on it, and a smiling Cyn blowing them out.

It's hard for me to look at flames, even on birthday candles. But that's my problem, not Carl's, so I tried to be nice. "Lovely outfit, but really, don't you need some heels with that? And how do you know it's Cyn's birthday?"

Carl laughed. "Thanks. Dim Found the dress for me. You know

I don't do heels: bad for my back. And it's not Cyn's birthday; it's the anniversary of when she opened the dungeon." Carl would know that. He was one of her most loyal clients, before. He gestured at the angels. "What's wrong with them?"

I shrugged. I was worried—they'd never acted like this before—but I didn't want him to know that. "Dunno. Maybe Cyn'll know. Where is she?"

"Napping upstairs, I think. Not for long, though, with that noise."

I heard footsteps behind Carl. Of course it was Jack. He glanced at Carl, said stonily, "That dress makes your ass look fat," which was both nasty and nonsense—Carl used to run marathons, and he's built like a greyhound—and then said to me, "Can't you shut those things up?"

"I'm trying," I said.

"They're probably screaming because they have to look at you."

"Well, they never screamed from looking at me before," I said, and checked Carl's cartoon: a floating red haze of rage.

Jack had seen it too, of course. "Something eating you, Carla?"

"Bad manners," Carl said. His cartoon had changed into a block of ice. "Jack, if you don't like it here, why don't you leave?"

Jack grinned, looking feral and crazy. "You going to make me, faggot?"

"No," Carl said, "because that's what you want." His ice block was growing cracks, though. Jack looked at them, squinting above Carl's head, and laughed.

"You aren't going to do it because you're a coward, Carla, because you're a pretty-boy pansy-assed—"

"That's enough, Jack." It was Cyn. Her voice was very quiet, and she sounded very tired. She was wearing old sweats, her feet bare and her dreadlocks looking as disheveled as dreads ever look. "Carl's not a coward. He's a grown-up, and he's much too sane and strong to let you push him into doing something stupid. Isn't that right, Carl?"

Carl was only looking at her now; the cartoon was a bank of white roses, and his voice was as quiet as hers, with only the merest hint of irony. "As you wish, mistress." Cyn saved Carl's life, and he knows it.

"Good." She walked into the room and knelt down next to one of the angels. It was crying harder now, its sibling too, the two of them howling and hiccupping. "What is it, baby? What's the matter?"

"You know they can't answer you," Jack said. His voice was tight, and when I looked at him I realized with a jolt that he was scared, really scared, his hands clenched and his face pale.

"That's true," Cyn said. "So what do you think wrong's with them, Jack?"

"They're minions of the devil, aren't they? Fallen angels? So if they're carrying on like this that means—the Antichrist's nearby, doesn't it? We're all going to be punished? What else could it mean?"

"Plenty of things," Cyn said mildly. "It could mean they have indigestion. It could mean they have diaper rash." I didn't believe any of that, and I didn't think Cyn did. I hoped she didn't believe Jack's explanation, either, but I couldn't be sure. Carl had his block of ice back, except that it was a berg now.

"I'm home," Dimity called from the reception area, and we all turned away from the angels to see what she'd Found. She shouldered into the room, her backpack and messenger bag bulging. "Got some potatoes. Got some cheese, think it's still good. A bag of apples turned into marbles on me and a sixpack of coke just evaporated, cans and everything, Laszlo, you'd better touch this stuff to make sure it stays put, here—" She tore the messenger bag open and started tossing me potatoes. She wouldn't meet anybody's eyes, and she was talking way too fast, and she hadn't asked us why the angels were howling.

"Dimity," Cyn said, "what's going on out there?"

Dimity took a deep breath. "Mob. Not far away. Illinois and 16th. Ugly. Getting bigger."

"Well," I said, holding a potato in each hand. "There's your Antichrist."

Cyn looked at the angels, and I knew she was thinking the same thing I was. We were both pretty sure a mob had beaten them up, trying to win another chance from God by destroying the Fallen. After the Rapture all kinds of people converted who'd never had any use for religion before, and most of those creeds were way ugly. If the angels knew a mob was nearby, no wonder they were wailing. "What's the mob after, Dim?"

"Don't know."

"You're lying," Cyn said. She and Dimity have been lovers for twelve years, but even I could tell that Dim wasn't telling the truth. "Why are you lying? What's out there?"

Dimity blew air out through her nose, hard. "We can't get involved in this."

"Involved in what?" Cyn stood up now and went to give Dimity a hug. "What's out there? You're a Finder. Whatever it is, you Found it, didn't you? And you didn't bring it home, because you were scared."

"Damn straight," Dimity said.

"If you don't tell me," Cyn said, "I'll go looking for it myself. You know I will."

"Shit," Jack said. "Why're you like that? Can't leave well enough alone? What makes you go looking for—"

"Same thing made her take you in," Carl said, "and you know it. Jack, shut up."

Jack shut up, for once. Cyn ignored both of them. "Dimity? Talk to me. What's out there?"

Dimity closed her eyes and sagged into Cyn's arms. "Kid. Not really a kid, a young guy. Twenties maybe. Broadcaster like Carl. He's—sick, I think. Breathing, but unconscious."

"Why's the mob after him, Dim?"

"We don't want to get involved in this."

"Where is he, Dim?"

"We don't—"

"You wouldn't be telling me any of this if he weren't close enough for me to find easily. Laszlo, will you come outside with me?"

I cleared my throat. I don't like going outside, and Cyn knows it. If I hadn't been at Cyn's when the Rapture happened, that chilly December day nine months ago, I'd be dead now. I wouldn't last two minutes on the streets, not the way I look. "If there's a mob—"

"If the mob were that close, we'd hear it. Laszlo, come on."

"All right, all right." Dimity's voice was gray. "I'll tell you. He's right outside the building. In the gutter."

"Let me get shoes on," Cyn said. "We'll go out through the garden."

There are three ways to get into the building: a strong front door with a deadbolt, an even stronger back door with a thicker deadbolt, and a side door that leads into a garden with its own padlocked entrance, which leads into an alley, which leads to another padlocked gate. Back when this place was a thriving business, Cyn had to make sure that clients could walk in and out without anyone seeing them. If you were in a session room, you had to call out to reception before you opened the door, to make sure nobody was out there who wanted to stay incognito. If you were waiting in the reception area and clients showed up at the front door, you went into the garden until they'd gone through: the pain freaks and the fetishists and the cross-dressers, the couples renting space to do stuff they couldn't do at home, the folks showing up for classes in bondage and play piercing and kinky first aid, complete with CPR certification. Believe me, that was a much nicer crowd than whatever mob pummeled the angels.

Now the garden's really a garden. Cyn made me touch every single seed before it went into the ground, so the radishes wouldn't turn into rocks and the zucchini into xylophones. We walked carefully through the rows, careful not to trample anything; the garden and what Dim brings home give us just barely enough to live on.

It was even hotter than it had been the day Carl and I painted the loft, and I had a funny feeling in the pit of my stomach. Dimity doesn't rattle easily. I could smell low tide, the wind coming off the Bay. Cyn got the gates unlocked and relocked behind us—as if any of it would stand against a mob—and then we were on the street.

It was quiet out there, the cracked sidewalk littered with junk: broken bottles, scraps of paper, the bleached skeleton of a dead elephant that had been an SUV once. The poor beast had been killed for food and stripped of everything but its bones, and I was amazed nobody had taken those to turn into weapons.

Sure enough, there was somebody lying in the gutter. We walked over to get a better look, and I heard the hiss of Cyn's indrawn breath.

Twenties, like Dim had said: long blond hair, blond beard, and I knew that if those eyes opened, they'd be baby blue. Fairest skin you ever saw. His shirt and jeans had been white once; so had his scuffed cowboy boots. He was Broadcasting a golden glow, just slightly brighter than the hazy sunshine we stood in, and words unscrolled above his head, illuminated like an old manuscript. *I am the Way, the Truth and the Life. No one comes to the Father, except through me.*

I looked away, feeling sick. Dimity was right: we couldn't afford to take this one in. He'd be more trouble than Jack had ever been. I found myself straining to listen, to hear the humming of the mob, but all I could hear was Cyn's ragged breath.

"Cyn—"

"We'll have to carry him inside," she said hoarsely.

"Cyn, I don't—"

"Do you want to take his head or his feet? Take his head: it will be easier for me to put his feet down and manage the locks. Laszlo, hurry!"

I did what she told me to. There was no point doing anything else. Cyn could no more have left that kid lying in the gutter than she could have grown wings and flown to heaven.

\*

He was heavier than he looked, and we trampled a cabbage plant getting him back through the garden. But finally we were back inside and got him stretched out on the couch in the reception area. Cyn propped his feet higher than his head so maybe he'd come to, and started chafing his hands while the others gathered around to watch. I'd seen Dim hug herself and shiver the minute we came in. Carl's cartoon went from a white flash of astonishment to a question mark, and from there to a quick caricature of a fat pre-Rapture televangelist raking in cash: then it went gray. He's not very good at cloaking, but he can when he really wants to. It didn't matter. I already knew what he thought.

We could still hear the angels howling from behind the closed door of the Red Room. "I locked them in there," Dimity said to Cyn's raised eyebrow. "I didn't know what else to do."

"That's not very nice, Dim. Let them out."

"But—"

"Do it. I want to see how they respond to—our visitor."

Dim shrugged, and did it. The angels came fluttering and bumping out, still caterwauling, and went careening down the hall to the very end, into the White Room. The White Room's Victorian, all lace and canes and riding crops. That was Dimity's bailiwick when the house was open for business; Mistress Cynthia wore black leather and stilettos and wielded the whips, and The Lady Dimity in her corset punished overgrown schoolboys.

"They don't seem interested in our visitor at all," Carl said drily.

Jack grunted, his eyes narrowed. I could smell the fear on him, the sharp tang of sweat. "Or they're scared and trying to get away. As far as they can, down to that room—"

"They could be trying to get away from the mob," I said. "If the mob's heading down the street, the White Room would be farthest from that, too.

Dimity shuddered. "Bad news, either way."

Cyn was still chafing the kid's hands; the kid still hadn't responded. The scroll above his head now said, *Come to me, all ye that are heavy laden.* Cyn said, "We'll hear the mob as soon as it's close enough to be any danger. Relax."

"Not over the angels, we won't." Jack's voice was tight. "Can't you get them to shut up? Dope them or something—"

"No," Cyn said.

"Yes," Dimity said. "They're driving me nuts. I'll give them some booze, Cyn; it'll probably knock them right out. Maybe you can think through that noise, but no one else can." Liquor's a very scarce commodity these days; we were down to one bottle of Johnnie Walker. But nobody objected. The angels really were putting all of us on edge.

I checked Carl: still holding gray. But the minute Dimity left he said to Cyn, very gently, "This can't possibly be—who he thinks he is. You know that, right?"

"Why not?" she asked. She hadn't taken her eyes off the kid's face since we'd gotten back inside. "Why can't it?" I heard an angel coughing and spluttering; Dimity must have given it some Johnnie Walker. Then the other one started. I hoped she wasn't going to poison them. There was no way to know how they'd react to alcohol.

Carl hesitated, looking pained, his cartoon a swirl of jumbled colors. "Because—"

"Because He wouldn't be down here," Jack said harshly. "He's up in heaven with the people who got to leave. He's up in heaven with the people who are saved and we're down here with the freaks and the fags and the monsters, of which *that*"—jabbing his finger at the kid—"has to be Exhibit A, if you ask me, because it's sacrilege to worship anybody except God or to build false idols or to take the Lord's Name in vain, now isn't it?"

It was the longest speech Jack had ever made. I wondered if he'd been religious before, or if after the Rapture he'd started clutching at concepts he barely understood, the way so many other people had.

Carl cleared his throat. "Well, there's another possibility. I don't think he's a monster, but I don't think he's a messiah, either. For one thing, he doesn't exactly look Semitic." He gave us a small smile—really more of a grimace—and said, "I think he's either psychotic or on drugs, or both, and having delusions." I would have been able to tell how carefully Carl was choosing his words even if his cartoon hadn't been an image from a minesweeper game. "It happened all the time, before. Cyn, you know it did. The homeless shelters and the mental hospitals were full of people who thought they were Jesus or Mohammed or the Virgin Mary."

The angels were quiet, finally; the Johnnie Walker had either killed them or put them to sleep. "Well," Cyn said into the silence, "maybe some of them were. You ever go to church, Jack? Before?" She knew Carl hadn't gone to church. Carl was Jewish, although he'd only gone to synagogue on High Holy Days, with his wife and kids and parents. "We went to a lot of churches when I was little. Moved around a lot, because my daddy kept thinking life would be better somewhere else. Every new town we went to, Mama dragged us to a new church. Some of them were really scary, talked about how God hated sinners and how anybody who did anything wrong would burn in hellfire, and how Jesus would judge everybody on the Last Day. And some of them were really nice, and talked about how Jesus loved people and just wanted to help them. And at my very favorite nice church, they said that everybody was Jesus, and that we had to find the Christ in all our neighbors, and that we were helping Jesus whenever we helped—how did they put it? The least of these. The freaks and the fags and the monsters, Jack."

Jack's back had stiffened. "You think Jesus loves—"

"If there's a Jesus, I think he loves everybody. And if there's a Jesus, I don't think he'd be up there with the saints. I think he'd be down here, where people still need him."

Jack's laugh was incredulous. "It's after Judgment Day, sister. We've run out of time."

"I believe in a God of second chances," Cyn said. She was still holding the kid's hands, although she wasn't rubbing them anymore, and I looked down at my shoes so I wouldn't have to look at her rapt face, gazing into his. I'd never heard that story about Cyn's childhood. The only story I'd heard was the one about how her parents caught her in bed with another girl when she was sixteen and told her that she was no child of theirs, that she wasn't welcome under their roof anymore. Her father piled everything she owned in the middle of the front yard and burned it. When she told me that story I started shaking, picturing the flames, and Cyn touched my arm and said, "Laszlo, I'm sorry. We both had our families burned away, didn't we? I shouldn't have reminded you."

"How long did you go to that church?" I asked now. "Your favorite one?"

Cyn laughed. "Oh, only about five minutes, until Mama realized what they were saying and yanked us out of there. But I've never forgotten it."

"Your Mama was right," Jack said, and Carl made a hissing noise between his teeth. He knew the other story, too. He knew that Cyn's mother had told her she was possessed by the Devil and refused to kiss her goodbye. Cyn had hitchhiked to the next state, where her aunt and uncle lived, and stayed with them until her uncle climbed into her bed one night. She got out of there and got a fake ID and started tending bar at strip joints. That's how she met Dimity, who was dancing her way through a grad degree in English lit. Eventually the two of them figured out that BDSM attracted more money and better people than stripping; they started doing private sessions, and then scraped together enough cash to open the Sanctuary. They had help. A lot of men, some wealthy, were grateful to Cyn for giving them more acceptance than they'd ever gotten anywhere else. That was what she'd learned from her parents: how to be more loving than they were.

Dimity told me once, a few years before the Rapture, that Cyn still had nightmares sometimes, just like I did, that she'd call out "Mama!" in her sleep and wake up crying. Dimity could never get her to talk about those dreams.

I heard footsteps in the hall, and looked up to find that Dim had rejoined us. "Well?" she asked. "Have we figured anything out?"

"We've figured out that he's either the Christ or the anti-Christ or crazy," Carl said. His cartoon was one of those wind-up monkeys, the kind with a drum, staggering in circles, which meant he was exhausted. Cyn still hadn't looked away from the kid. "Useful, huh?"

"Very useful. So now what?"

Carl shrugged. "I guess we wait for him to wake up."

Dim crouched down and peered at the kid, making a face. "What do you suppose is wrong with him?"

Carl shrugged again. "Who the hell knows? If he's mentally ill, maybe he sensed danger from the mob and went catatonic. If he's an addict, maybe he got a bad batch of something. Does it matter?"

"Sitting ducks," Jack said. "I say we put him back out on the street."

"Over Cyn's dead body," I said, very quietly. Cyn gave no sign that she'd heard any of us; she was lost in the scrolling words above the kid's head. *The one who enters by the gate is the shepherd of the sheep.*

This dreamer had entered by two gates; we'd carried him in ourselves. I wondered if he knew that, somewhere in his subconscious, and was choosing the words deliberately. But then the text changed to *Ten bridesmaids took their lamps and went to meet the bridegroom*, and I decided he had a random-phrase generator going in there.

"Okay, well," Dimity said, "listen up. While you guys wait here with our, uh, dreamer, I'm going to go see if I can get a better idea what that mob's up to."

"Isn't that dangerous?" Carl asked. His cartoon showed a dark,

seething mass punctuated by flickering lights, and I wondered—
not for the first time—exactly what had happened to him between
the night of the Rapture and the next evening, when he showed
up here, gasping and incoherent, in sweat-soaked running clothes.

"Probably. But if the mob's up to anything bad, being here
could be just as dangerous. At least this way I'll get a better idea of
what's going on."

"Don't let them see you," Carl said.

"Of course not. I'm not stupid. Cyn, I'll be back as soon as I
know something."

"Be careful," Cyn murmured, but she didn't even look up when
Dimity left.

"I'm hungry," Carl said when the door closed behind Dim.
"Anybody else hungry?"

Cyn and Jack didn't answer. Both of them were still staring at
the kid; Cyn sat cross-legged next to the couch, one of the kid's
hands in both of hers, and Jack had hunkered down next to a wall,
squinting at both of them and chewing his lip.

"I could eat," I said. I didn't want to leave the room, not with
Jack looking like that.

We hadn't learned much about Jack in the five months he'd
been at Cyn's; he wouldn't talk about where he was during the Rapture or what he did before or whom he'd lost. All we knew was that
he was wandering the streets, starving, when he saw Dimity duck
into the front door and decided to knock to see if he could come
in, too. And of course Cyn said he could. He ate damn near all the
food Dim had just brought home with her, stuffing his face so fast
I was amazed he didn't throw it all back up. When he was finally
done eating, he looked at me and looked at Carl—who was wearing a sweater and plaid skirt that day—and glanced into the Red
Room, with its cross and stocks and iron hanging cage, and said,
"What the fuck *is* this place?"

Jack can work, I'll give him that. When Cyn told him he had to help out to earn his keep, he said that was only fair and offered to cook. Carl and I weren't comfortable giving him access to all the food, but it turns out he's a good cook. He takes pride in it, and he does amazing things with the unlikely stuff Dimity brings home. He chops vegetables faster than anyone I've ever seen. I guess we should have known he was an Aquifer even before the dry season started; Aquifers can't make much water, most of them, but they purify what's already there, which helps explain why Jack's food always tasted so good and why we stopped getting sick when he came. There are things even boiling won't get rid of. He weeds the garden, too, and if we need anything heavy moved, Jack's the man for the job. As much as he clearly despises all of us, except maybe Cyn, he never complains about working. And if he's mean, he's also honest. Since that first day, he's never tried to take more than his share.

I had my theories about Jack, but I'd never asked. None of my business.

"Well," Carl said, "I'm going to go mash up some potatoes and cheese. Anybody else want some, besides Laszlo?"

"Sure," Jack said. "Thanks." It was the first time he'd ever thanked Carl for anything, but I wasn't sure it was such a good sign: it meant he was so distracted by the kid that he'd forgotten his old feud. Then Carl left the room and Jack muttered, "Girly needs to learn to cook, anyway," and I felt a little better.

Carl came back a minute later, waving a large orange sponge. "Scratch that," he said. "Just potatoes. Laszlo, you forgot to Fix the cheese."

"We can use it to clean the bathroom," I said. At least the cheese had turned into something useful.

"Baked potatoes, then." Glowing embers appeared in the air over his head, and I looked away, feeling the scar tissue on my face tighten. I knew Carl didn't mean it; he's not always conscious of what he's Broadcasting. And like I said, it's my problem, not anybody else's. "I'll go get the grill heated up and put them on." We keep coals banked in the grill all the time. We still have some matches and a butane lighter, but they're scarce and valuable, and we can't afford to use them every time we need to cook. At least there's never any shortage of fuel, not with all the abandoned buildings.

I checked the kid's scroll. *What did you go out into the wilderness to look at?* Definitely a random-phrase generator. "Do you think we should try to wake him up?"

"*No,*" Jack said. "Wake up a devil? You have no idea what you're messing with, do you? Keep it asleep!"

"Let him be," Cyn said. "His breathing's good and he's got some rapid-eye movement; he'll come up when he needs to."

"Fine by me," I said. "I was just asking."

Carl came back, carrying a folding chair and a cushion, and sat next to me. "Okay, the potatoes'll be done in half an hour or so. Sorry for the wait."

"Sorry about the cheese," I said.

"Anything happening here?"

"Not a blessed thing," I said, and Jack grunted.

"You've got that right."

"I looked in on the angels," Carl said. "They're still asleep."

"I hope they won't have hangovers," I said, and Jack let out a sharp bark.

"That's a good one. Those things are bad enough when they aren't barfing."

We all sat there for a while, quiet, gathered around that shining kid like he was a television set. Watching those phrases unfolding in the air above his head, I felt my eyes wanting to close, and I pinched myself to stay awake. Cyn still sat cross-legged; Jack had his elbows propped on his knees. Carl's face was impassive, his cartoon a flowing moebius strip. I knew that meant he was meditating.

Finally Jack looked over at the two of us and said, "Can I ask you a question?"

"Sure," I said, trying to remember when Jack had ever asked a question instead of making an insulting pronouncement.

"Not you," Jack said. "Carla. The fairy," and Carl stiffened, his moebius strip scattering into a million shimmering particles.

"What's your question, Jack?"

"You're still down here because you wear dresses, right? So how can you keep doing it? Don't you know it's wrong? Or you figure it doesn't matter anymore, you can just roll in sin?"

"That's four questions," Carl said. The moebius strip was back, writhing like a snake. Carl was working very hard at keeping his temper. "Or maybe it really is just one. Jack, I don't know why I'm still down here. I don't know why anyone is. I don't think it has anything to do with what I wear. To tell you the truth, I don't think it has anything to do with God, either. I don't know what happened that day; I don't think anybody knows. People call it the Rapture because that's the story that fits it best."

"All those people went flying into the air," Jack said tightly. "Just like the Bible said would happen. And you don't think—"

"Look, I didn't see anybody fly into the air, okay? I was at work and all of a sudden there was this—this *ripple*, and when it was over practically everybody else was gone. Some people saw folks getting sucked into the air and some saw them growing wings or bursting into flames or exploding or melting or—Jack, everybody saw something different. Which means that nobody understands what happened and we're all making sense of it the best we can, fitting it into stories we already know, okay?"

Jack stared at him. "You wore dresses at work?"

"No, of course I didn't wear dresses at work."

"Where did you work?"

Carl sighed. His moebius strip spun, throwing off sparks. "I was a lawyer, Jack."

"A *lawyer*?" Jack looked incredulous. "What kind of lawyer?"

"A corporate lawyer."

Jack sniffed. "Corporate? Fancy. So you wouldn't have touched scum like me, right?"

"Right." The moebius strip had slowed down a little and stopped smoking. Well, I thought, there's part of my theory about Jack confirmed.

Jack didn't seem to realize what he'd just given away. "Okay, so why do you wear that wedding ring?"

"Because I was—I am—married."

"To a woman?"

"Yes."

"She's gone." It wasn't a question, and Carl nodded, his face tight. "Did she know you wore dresses?"

"Yes, she did. And she knew I came here for sessions with Cyn. And she didn't want to do any of that herself but she loved me anyway, Jack, and I loved her, and cross-dressing doesn't make someone gay, just for your information. I had a wonderful marriage. I was lucky. A lot of the guys who came here had horrible marriages. They had to lie to their wives, or thought they did. That would have killed me."

Jack eyed him. "Your wife was okay with you fucking another woman?"

"No," Carl said, his voice as taut as piano wire, "she wouldn't have been okay with that. Cyn didn't fuck her clients, Jack: she flogged them. There's a difference."

Jack shook his head. "I don't get it."

"I know you don't. Nobody's asking you to. The fact that you don't understand something doesn't make it a sin or a crime or—"

"You have kids?"

I looked away, then. I couldn't stand to look at Carl. He'd had two kids, a boy and a girl, seven and nine. He adored them. He used to show me and Cyn and Dimity pictures of them, school pictures and birthday pictures, pictures taken on vacations and at the park. The boy was an impish redhead with freckles, and the girl was dark and serious, with curly brown hair like Carl's. The night after the Rapture, when Carl came staggering in here, Cyn threw a blanket around him and hugged him and said, "Carl, where's your family?

Where are Donna and the children? Carl? Please tell me what happened."

"Gone," he'd said, and begun to weep in huge gasps. "They're gone. How will I live?"

"You'll live here," she'd said. We'd never asked him any questions about his family since then, and he'd never said anything. Nothing, not a word. And in all these months, none of Carl's cartoons had shown his wife and children. I knew he had to be thinking about them, but it was happening somewhere so deep down that none of us could see.

"I have kids," Carl said in a whisper. Cyn was still staring at the visitor—*Who do you say that I am?*, which at least was appropriate—but I could tell somehow, from the back of her head, that she was finally listening to us, too.

"Your turn," I told Jack. "Fair's fair. Carl's answered his twenty questions, so why don't you tell us a little about yourself, Jack? Where were you during the Rapture? And why do you suppose you're still down here, since you're such an expert on how everyone else should act?"

"I know I'm a sinner," Jack said fiercely. "I know I've done wrong. I'm trying not to do wrong anymore. I'm just asking questions. I've purified your water and I haven't hurt any of you or stolen your food or—"

"Words can hurt people," I said, "but thank you not for stealing the food. Those are prison tattoos on your arms, aren't they? Is that where you were, Jack? Sitting on a bunk in a little cell with one lightbulb and a bolted-down toilet—"

"We were in the exercise yard," Jack said flatly. "We had an hour there a day. And then—people started flying up into the air. It happened to people in the cells, too. I guess they floated up right through the ceiling, I don't know how that worked, but when I went inside to get my stuff—one of the guards, he was still there and had his keys and he let everybody else out, let us take our stuff, let us all go free—anyway, most of the cells were empty." He stopped.

No one said anything, and after a minute he cleared his throat and went on, talking too fast. "I'm not going to tell you what I did. That doesn't matter anymore. It just matters how I act now. I know why I got left behind. I agreed to hurt somebody, the day before the Rapture. I hadn't done it yet, but I was planning to do it. That's why. I never believed in God or Jesus or the Judgment before or I wouldn't have done what I did, either before I went there or after. Now I believe. When you see people flying through the air, you believe."

Bully for you, I thought. I wondered if Jack knew that Carl was Jewish. It might be better if he didn't have that information. There'd been lynchings, after the Rapture: of Jews and gays and punks, of teenage girls with bare midriffs and of clumsy angels, anybody who didn't fit somebody else's notion of holiness. All those people terrified of their own sin and taking it out on somebody else. I hoped Carl's wife and children were gone wherever the enraptured went and hadn't been lynched. There was no way for me to know, maybe no way for Carl to know. If he rushed home from work and no one was there, if he searched his wife's workplace and his children's school and didn't find them, he'd never know for sure. He'd only know for sure if he found their bodies, bloody and abandoned like the angels had been. He had to hope they'd been taken, that they were safe.

If he hadn't known for sure, surely he'd have kept searching. Did he know they were dead, then?

Cyn sighed, a soft sad sound, and we all three looked at her. She was still looking at the kid, who was still out cold. *The Kingdom of God is like a mustard seed.* I wondered what a mustard seed would turn into if you didn't Fix it. Into a grain of sand? Hadn't somebody said there were kingdoms in a grain of sand, too?

"Jack," Cyn said, "did it all make sense to you? Who got taken, who didn't? All those other guys who'd done things: some of them flew into the air and some stayed down here. You agreed to hurt somebody. Who asked you to do that? Somebody in a gang? Did he stay, too?"

"It's not my place to question God—"

"So he left," Cyn said. "The person who asked you to do the bad thing you think got you stranded here, the thing you hadn't even done yet." I wondered if he'd raped Jack, or threatened to. It would explain a lot. "And that guy got to go to Heaven? Does that make sense? Who else went, Jack? Did you like all of them? Did you think they were good people?"

"Some were, some weren't. That's what I thought. God knows better than me. I don't understand—"

"Then why are you saying you do? Jack, nobody understands. Not one of us. I think you're right. I think God knows better than we do, and I think all of this makes some kind of sense we can't see. But if you don't understand about those guys you knew, you don't understand about any of us, either. Not me or Carl or Laszlo or—"

"I know the Rapture happened!" Jack was sweating again, the veins in his face bulging. I glanced at Carl, but he was cloaked, his eyes lowered and his hands tightly clenched in his lap. I wondered if he were praying. "I know the Bible says—"

"I know some things the Bible says too," Cyn said. "I know the Bible says the first shall be last and the last shall be first, and that means maybe we're not doomed, Jack, because nobody here was exactly first before the Rapture."

"The rich lawyer?" Jack spat the words. "Lawyers and pharisees and you and your girlfriend getting rich off—"

"Dim and I have never been rich, Jack. We got by. The building would be in better shape if we'd been rich; Laszlo wouldn't have to keep doing repair work. Laszlo was a knockabout handyman, Jack. He just got by, too." Which is putting it kindly: not many people would hire me, no matter how good my work was. "Pharisees were priests. You see any of those here? And Carl was a lawyer, yes, but he hadn't made partner yet, and he had two kids, and this is San Francisco, which was damned expensive back when money still meant anything."

Carl was still cloaking, but he was also crying, two tears tracking down his cheeks. I'd never seen him cloak this long, and I couldn't imagine what it must have been taking out of him. "I'm going to go check those potatoes," he said quietly. "I think we should all eat something."

"Ah, shit," Jack said, but he sounded defeated now, instead of angry. Carl got up and headed to the kitchen. Down the hall, the angels had begun to moan, a droning sound like an air raid siren.

"I'll go check on our little cherubs," I said. I wasn't afraid to leave Jack alone with Cyn and the dreamer anymore. He looked too tired to do anything, at least for the moment. I figured the angels were coming to, and I didn't know if they'd be scared if they woke up alone, maybe feeling sick. If I'd been in that position, I'd have wanted some company.

But when I stepped into the White Room I got more scared, because the angels weren't coming to. They were out cold, flat on their backs and still unconscious, reeking of whiskey and dirty diapers but making that noise anyway. I didn't know what that meant. I was afraid it meant that whatever they were scared of was so close they were sending up Maydays even in their sleep.

I heard noise from the reception area and high-tailed it back down the hall, wondering if the dreamer had come to. But it was Dim coming in the door, her face dead white and her hair spilling out from underneath her cap. "Bad," she said. "It's bad. Where's Carl? Everybody has to hear this. Carl! Get out here!"

"Two seconds," he called, but he showed up quicker than that, holding a platter with steaming potatoes. "Here, we don't have butter but—"

"Never mind that," Dim said. "Listen to me! Cyn, stop staring at that kid and pay attention. The mob's farther away than they were, but not for long. They're searching, and they're big, and they've got fire." I must have winced, because Cyn reached out and touched my hand. "I snooped around the edges and eavesdropped. I was hoping they were just out for any kind of blood and something might distract them, but they know what they're looking for.

They know that somebody's been going around claiming all kinds of things, claiming he can heal, claiming he's Christ, Broadcasting a goddamn halo, and they're vowing death to the idolater."

"Did they see you?" Cyn asked sharply. "Did they follow—"

"No! It doesn't matter. Listen—"

"Then we're fine. If they didn't follow you here, then—"

"Cyn," Dim said desperately, "he's a Broadcaster. Don't you understand?" We must all have stared at her blankly, because she said, "All right, everybody out. Out into the garden for a minute. Cyn, leave him there, he'll be fine, just come outside! Come on, now!" She herded us all outside, into the garden and the fading daylight. "There," she said, pointing. "Look. Look up. Look at the roof. The sunlight must have hidden it today, but that won't work after dark. Do you understand now?"

We all looked up. The dreamer's glow was coming right through the roof of the building, a beacon for the mob.

"He has to go," Jack said. We were back inside. "He can't stay here. We have to put him back out on the street."

"If we put him back outside," Cyn said, "they'll kill him."

"If we don't, they'll kill all of us."

"Cyn," Carl said, "he's right." The flame-punctuated darkness seethed above his head again, and I felt panic rising in my gut, felt myself back in the burning car, pounding at the door to get out and listening to my parents' screaming from the front seat. "They'll kill all of us, and they'll torch the building for good measure."

Dimity reached out and caught Cyn's hand, pleading. "Cyn, please listen to them. They're right. When have Carl and Jack agreed about anything? It's because they're right. Don't you—"

"I can't do it," Cyn said simply. "I have to live with myself. How can I do that? How can I put him out there to die?"

"If you don't do it," Jack said, "we'll all die."

"Fuck." Dimity turned to Carl. "You're a Broadcaster. Is there any way to stop it? Can you block it with, I don't know, steel or wool or water or—"

"Mine doesn't go away when I put a hat on," Carl said, "but that's mine. I can't Broadcast as far as he can, anyway. Mine's not going through the roof, is it? Dim, we're all different. You want to try putting hats on him, go right ahead. But it's going through the roof, so why would a hat stop it?"

"A pot, maybe, something metal, put it over his head—"

I shook my head, my mouth as dry as ash. "There's some metal in the roof, Dim. Metal trusses. I really don't think—"

"Okay." Dim knelt down next to the couch, propped the kid up against one arm, and started slapping him. "Then we've got to wake him up and get him to start cloaking, that's all. Come on, you fucker: come to! Open your eyes! Laszlo, get me some ice—no, I've got a better idea. Help me carry him to the medical room, okay?"

Carl and I exchanged a glance. His cartoon showed the dreamer in gynecological stirrups. "Dimity," Cyn said, "what are you talking about?"

"Neurologists use pain to bring people out of comas. A doctor told me that once after my grandmother had a stroke. If somebody's out and you hurt them, sometimes they'll come to. Self-defense. The doctor said they're really mean to people in comas: they twist their nipples and press down on their eyeballs really hard and—"

"Shit," Jack said. "You can kick him in the balls, but he'd just pass out again. And he'd still be in the building while you were torturing him. You just miss torturing people, don't you? I say we put him back out on the street, let the mob have him, keep ourselves safe. You want to torture somebody, work on Carla here."

"We're not doing any of that," Cyn said. She was standing next to the couch, paler than I'd ever seen her, but her voice was perfectly steady. "We're not killing him and we're not hurting him and we're not letting anybody else do either of those things, either."

"Then what are we doing?" Carl said. "Cyn? I admire your principles, but I'd feel better about this if you had a plan."

"I—" Cyn closed her mouth, opened it again, put both hands on either side of her face and squeezed, as if the right answer would come squirting out like an orange seed. "I don't know. We'll keep him here. We'll—we'll—okay, Dim, you can try to wake him up but do it nicely, don't hurt him, and Carl, Laszlo, you can try putting different things on his head, that wasn't a bad question Dim asked, maybe—"

I'd never heard her sound so helpless. "You don't have a clue," Jack said, and I'd never heard him sound so gentle. "Look, Cynthia, if there's a mob after him we don't have that much time. You know that. And even if we managed to wake him up, he might not be able to cloak. Some Broadcasters can't. It's hard even for people who can, right?" He actually looked at Carl, who nodded. Carl's cartoon was a mutilated body. I looked quickly and looked away, wondering if it was something he'd seen or just something he'd imagined. "I know you're trying to be nice, but you don't owe him anything. You've known everybody else here, even me, a lot longer. And what you need to do to save us—"

"Caiphas," Cyn said dully.

Jack shook his head. "What?"

"The guy in the Bible. It's expedient that one man should die for the good of the people." She shivered and said, "We're in the same story, aren't we?"

"Cyn," Carl said, "I don't know who this kid is, but he's not Jesus, okay? He's not Christ. He just thinks he is. He's—"

"If the little church was right, we're all Christ. I don't care. I can't kill him. I couldn't kill anybody."

"Then you'll kill all of us," Dim said, looking up from shaking the kid back and forth.

"Listen to your wife, would you?" Jack had begun to pace, his hands jammed in his pockets. "We need to put him back out on the street. Everyone knows it but you. And we don't have much time. Are the rest of you going to help me?"

Cyn squinted at him. "What are you talking about?"

"You're not that big, Cynthia. One or two of us could hold you down or put you in that cage thing while the others carried—"

Cyn made a shocked noise, a sound of utter disgust. Jack's face was grim, desperate; Dimity wouldn't look at any of us, and I wouldn't look at Carl. "Anyone who dared to do that," Cyn said, her voice thick, "would no longer be my friend and would no longer be welcome here. Anyone here who loves me will not even think about doing that."

Well, I thought, remembering my conversation with Carl, I guess I was wrong. I guess there are ways to get ourselves kicked out, after all.

"Do you think maybe the mob knows what it's doing?" Jack was furious now. "Do you think maybe they wouldn't be after him unless—"

"Mobs never know what they're doing."

"He's a blasphemer, Cynthia! God didn't leave the good people down here! Jesus isn't down here anymore! This, this thing can't possibly be—"

"And even if he is," Dimity said, "which I don't think either, even if he is, he has to die, Cyn, right? If that's the story we're in, that's how it ends. He dies to save us."

"If we were saved we wouldn't be here," Jack said, still pacing.

"Second chances." Cyn was still shivering. "If God hasn't saved us, maybe it's time to save God. Maybe that's how we can undo all this. I don't know. It doesn't matter. All I know is that I can't let him die."

"It's almost dark," Carl said quietly. The angels were still moaning. They sounded a little louder to me, but it was hard to tell, because everything sounded louder. "We don't have very long."

"No, we don't." Jack had stopped pacing, finally. "So who's going to give me a hand? Come on. I'm trying to help all of you! I could just run away, couldn't I? I don't have to stay here at all, and there goes your water. You've been decent to me, so I'm trying to be decent back. Who'll help?"

"Shit," Dim said, and began slapping the kid across the face again. "Come on, come on, wake up!"

No one else moved. It came to me in a flash that Jack was a coward, that he was even more scared of being on the streets by himself than he was of facing the mob with us. No one would knowingly kill an Aquifer—they're far too valuable—but they get hunted and captured, imprisoned sometimes. There are all kinds of stories. "Well?" Jack said.

Carl cleared his throat. "No," he said. "I'm not helping you." Then he turned and walked away, down the hall, into the Purple Room, where he sleeps.

"Laszlo," Cyn said, and motioned for me to follow Carl. "Find out if he's all right, would you?"

I didn't think any of us were all right, or likely to be, but I did what she'd asked, because I didn't know what else to do. When I knocked, Carl said, "Come in," and when I opened the door on faux antiques and flocked velvet wallpaper—the Purple Room's very New Orleans bordello—I found him tying the laces of his running shoes. He was wearing the same sweats he'd been in the night he showed up here. Dim had washed them for him, but I'd never expected to see them again.

The evening gown was in a heap on the floor. Carl's cartoon showed three figures, a woman and two children, walking away, only their backs visible. One of the children had red hair. The other had dark curls. The woman was a slim brunette.

I swallowed. "Carl, what are you doing?"

"Leaving," he said. "This is madness. Jack's right about what has to happen, but I can't do that to Cyn. I can't hurt her that way and I can't stay here and I don't know what else to do. Laszlo, the building's mostly wood: you know that. It's going to go up like a torch, and all of you with it. I doubt very much that Jack could possibly produce enough water to make a difference."

I closed my eyes, the old panic rising again. He was right, of course. The angels were going to explode like little pipe bombs with all that booze in them. I pictured them popping in a reek of charred flesh, the stink I'd lived with for most of my life, the smell that's never left my nostrils. "Carl—"

"You're all going to die."

I opened my eyes. The three figures in his cartoon were getting smaller, smaller. I worked at keeping my voice calm. "Everyone's going to die. That's the only thing that's always been true, and there's no sign it's changed. Carl—"

"I'll climb over the back fence. I'm not going to go out the front way, onto the street. I'll be careful."

"Carl, they're looking for a Broadcaster."

"His Broadcasts and mine—" He gave his shoelaces a final vicious tug. "—could hardly be more different. Laszlo, if anything's left tomorrow, I'll come back. I will. I'd never abandon Cyn if she were still alive. You know that. But staying here is suicide. Will you come with me? While there's still time?" They were tiny now, his three cartoon figures. They were going to vanish any second.

"I can't," I said, and as I said it I knew it was true, and not just because the streets are dangerous.

I slept through the Rapture. I'd just finished putting some new pipe in the bathroom, and it had taken longer than I expected. It was late when I tightened the last fitting, so Cyn let me crash in a sleeping bag in the loft. I went to sleep in a normal world and woke up in the middle of chaos, the chaos where we've lived ever since, but I've never felt like I missed anything. It doesn't matter that I slept through the Rapture, because I'd already lived through my own, the car accident that killed my parents when I was fifteen and put me in a burn unit for six months and left me looking like this, even after all the rehab and multiple skin grafts and the reconstructive surgery that made it easier for me to eat and talk, but didn't make me look any more human.

For years after the accident, I wished that I'd died too. The doctors kept telling me how lucky I was that I'd kept my vision, but I didn't think I was lucky. The only thing worse than seeing people's reactions when they looked at me was looking at myself. I dreaded mirrors as much as I dreaded flame. Every night I prayed to die in my sleep, prayed to wake up in heaven with my parents. Most nights, I dreamed about doing just that, except that in the dreams, my parents always ran away screaming when they saw me.

When I was little, I had a cousin who'd been born with a harelip. The plastic surgeons had repaired it, but he still didn't look quite right. My mother hated visiting that part of the family; she couldn't bear even being in the same room with "that ugly little boy," as she put it. I liked my cousin. He had a terrific collection of toy cars, and he knew everything about baseball. But my mother couldn't see past the scar. She always told me how good-looking I was, how popular I'd be with the girls when I got older.

I was very popular with girls, before the accident. Afterwards, none of them would come near me, and I couldn't have done anything even if they had. The reconstructive surgery hadn't been able to restore penile function. I was lucky I could still urinate without a catheter. Small blessings.

When I told Cyn all this, not long after I met her, she said, very quietly, "That sucks. And you don't deserve it. I'm so sorry, Laszlo." Cyn was the only person I'd ever met who didn't flinch the first time she looked at me, when I showed up at the Sanctuary to put in some new windows. She looked me straight in the face, just like I was a normal person, and held out her hand and said, "Hi, I'm Cynthia. Let me show you where you'll be working," and that was that. My own little piece of heaven.

I started spending more and more time at Cyn's, doing whatever I could to help out. I kept my little room in a dingy boardinghouse, with my hot plate and books and TV, and I kept my other clients, but the Sanctuary was home. Carl and Dimity didn't flinch when I met them either, but I figured that was because Cyn had told them what to expect.

I couldn't just leave her. I couldn't run away from the only heaven I'd ever found.

I knew that Carl wouldn't have either, if he'd thought there was anything else he could do. "Carl, I'm sorry. About your family. I never—saw you think about them before."

He looked at me, his face the color of bone. "No, I don't suppose you have. I had to shut it out, Laszlo. So I wouldn't lose my mind. I had to shut out how I got home from work that day and there were three plates on the kitchen counter with half-made sandwiches on them, and a pot of soup boiling to nothing on the stove, and in Katy's room the TV was still on and in Joshua's room there was a pile of comic books next to the bed. Both kids were sick that day. Donna had stayed home with them. They were all three together; there was no sign that anyone else had been in the house. So at least I know a mob didn't get them."

Small blessings, I thought, just as his cartoon figures dwindled into nothing. The angels were definitely louder now. "Carl—"

But now that he'd started talking, he couldn't stop. "I'd had a fight with Donna that morning before I left for work. Both kids had heard it, and Katy had started to cry, and all day I'd been thinking how shitty I felt, how I was going to tell them all I was sorry. It was a fight over nothing. Donna had withdrawn fifty bucks from the cash machine and forgotten to tell me about it, so the checkbook hadn't balanced, and I blew up at her because I was having a bad week at the office. And that was the last conversation we ever had. I don't know where she and the children are now, if they're safe or even alive." He looked at me and said, "I didn't get to say goodbye. And I'm not going to say goodbye now either. I can't bear it. I'm too much of a coward."

"You're not a coward, Carl."

"I'll go out the back way. Lock the door behind me. Tell Cyn why I left. Tell her I'll be back tomorrow. If there is a tomorrow."

"All right," I said. "I will. Good luck. Be careful."

He held up a hand, a kind of salute, and then in a rush he was out of the room and out the back door, his head down. I knew he'd keep his promise. I knew he'd come back, if there was anything left. I locked the door behind him, and then I went back to the front room. Not much had changed. The dreamer was still on the couch. Dim was trying to rouse him by doing something complicated and painful to his feet, and Cyn was putting things on his head—a cooking pot, a wooden cutting board, a velvet cape—none of which reduced the glow one iota. The dreamer's scroll now read, *The light is with you for a little longer. Walk while you have the light, so that the darkness may not overtake you*, which made me wonder about my random-phrase theory. Jack was pacing again. "Carl's gone," I said, and they all looked at me as if I were speaking another language, and I told them what had happened.

No one said anything. All of them went back to what they'd been doing, as if they'd been hypnotized. And then we began to hear, very softly, a humming from out on the street. And then the angels started to scream.

Things happened very fast, then. Dimity bleated and leapt at the kid's face and started slapping him again, and Cyn tried to pull Dimity away and Jack ran towards the three of them, and everybody was yelling and there was a flurry of arms and a howl, whose I couldn't tell, and then Cyn started screaming even more loudly than the angels while Dimity tried to quiet her and the dreamer's glow flickered and faded and went out like somebody had turned a switch, and there was Jack standing with a kitchen knife in his hand, and everything was covered with blood. Cyn flew at him and started pounding at him with her fists and Dimity tried to hold her back and Jack, I swear, was crying. "He had to die, he had to die, if he hadn't died we all would have died, I could have run like Carl but I stayed here, I did it to protect you, it was what had to happen! I got left here so I could do this instead of killing that guy in jail but this is better, I helped people, I helped all of you, God knows that, that's what He needed me to do and even if I'm in hell at least I did one good thing—"

The angels were still screaming. The mob was still humming.

And I stood there and I watched that wretched little group around the couch and I knew that Jack had truly tried to do something brave and good, and I knew just as clearly that he hadn't done anything at all. The mob had seen the glow. They'd seen it go out, but they knew where it had come from. And they had torches. And the building was still mostly wood.

I knew what I had to do. I went out through the garden door, grabbing the keys hanging on the wall. None of the others even noticed me leave: they were too busy yelling at each other, while the corpse with its slashed neck bled out onto the floor. Carl would have noticed. Was he far enough away now to be safe? I couldn't know. I'd never know. Dim had been right about how the story had to end. I was only sorry it would hurt Cyn. I found myself thinking about the building, worrying about whether there was anything I hadn't Fixed yet, but they'd find another Fixer. It would be all right.

I slipped out through the gate, onto the street. The mob was thirty or forty strong, and by the light of their torches I saw that they'd dismantled the elephant skeleton, the bone clubs gleaming in their hands. I had to hope that they were mainly out for blood, that a kill would satiate them. They didn't even hear me over their own noise, and they were too busy craning their heads at the top of the building to notice me. I was as extraneous to them as I'd been to the ones inside. I could have gotten clear away, like Carl.

Instead I walked as far away as I dared, to put some distance between me and the mob. Then I turned, crouching, keeping my head down so they wouldn't get too good a look at my face. "I am the Way and the Life!" I shouted, and when they turned on me with a vast roar I started running, fueled by my fear of the fire. I prayed as I ran, although I stopped believing in God the day my parents died. I prayed for Cyn and Dimity and Jack and Carl. I prayed for the dreamer. I prayed that by the time the mob caught me and brought me down, they'd be too far from the Sanctuary, and too tired from the chase, to retrace their bloody footsteps.

*This is another of my image-driven stories; for many months before I wrote it, I was haunted by a vision of a robot carrying a young woman out of a blast site. Who was she? Where had she come from, and where was she going?*

# CITY OF ENEMIES

**S**CANNING FOR INFRARED signatures, the search-and-rescue robot found the young woman at dusk in a pile of smoking rubble outside the city. She was unconscious, cheek pillowed on one filthy hand, a tangle of long dark hair obscuring her face. The robot, a tower of twinkling lights and sensors atop sturdy treads, used its wonderful machinery to scan her for pathogens, for implanted weapons and surveillance tech, and found none. It did find injuries: a broken arm, long bleeding cuts. The robot bandaged the wounds, drew blood, determined that the patient was dehydrated and probably in shock. It administered antibiotics and fluids.

There were bodies nearby, and parts of bodies. The robot ignored them. Its priority was the living. It had been programmed for heroism and compassion, for tenderness. Its designers, who viewed storytelling as medicine, had coded it with tales about quests and orphans, dark forests, enchanted princesses. But the robot only told stories to people who could hear them, and its ministrations had not woken the patient. It extended its long flexible arms, well able to rend and tear but also softly padded, and scooped up the young woman, already tethered to it by IVs. It cradled her to its blinking carapace and carried her home.

*

Inru wasn't supposed to be alive at all. Later she found out she'd been lying in the rubble for almost a full day. She'd been thrown clear of most of the destruction by the bomb blast: lucky, that, and nothing her handlers could have foreseen. Some people who'd been rescued by robots had nightmares later, classic PTSD; they startled at trucks and fled in terror from trash compactors, but the memories that distressed Inru weren't of the robot.

Supposedly a traveler in search of plums, she'd strolled into the market outside the city just before the bomb went off. It wasn't her bomb. But the robot found her, and dumb metal beast that it was, didn't know the difference between Inru's people and the ones who had made it. She was a person; she gave off heat that showed up on infrared; she was injured, and therefore needed treatment. The robot brought her into the city, where she woke from a drugged sleep, like a fish rising from deep water, with her arm in a cast. She was alive, in a clean white place. Two men and a woman, in starched uniforms the color of newly budded trees, frowned down at her.

They spoke, their words both liquid and precise. Inru didn't understand anything they said. She wouldn't have answered even if she had.

A woman in a slightly darker uniform brought her water, and later a tray with sweet warm pudding, some soup, a patty of minced meat. Inru ate hungrily, greedily. Her handlers would have said the stuff was poison, all the more dangerous for being so hard to resist, but all her body knew was fierce hunger. She had never tasted food like this.

She slept. Perhaps the food had been drugged, but when she woke, she felt more clear-headed. She was in a clean bed, wearing a gown that smelled of soap. Her cast was as white as the serene walls. She heard distant noise, city sounds—people calling, dogs barking, traffic—but saw only cloudless blue sky through the window. Maybe the tip of a tree, when she shifted, but shifting hurt, and in that pain she recognized the throbbing at the base of her skull that had dogged her for weeks now, that she had walked into the market yearning to escape.

She was in the City of Enemies. She still carried her bomb within her. She did not know why it had not detonated; she did not know, now, if it ever would. She did not know why the robot hadn't detected it; they were supposed to discover such things. Had the doctors found it? They must have; but if they had, surely she would not still be alive, and if they hadn't, trying to tell them would be unwise at best.

She was fifteen years old, lying on clean sheets with sweet pudding in her belly and sunlight pooling on her skin. She wanted to live.

Before, she had known she wanted to live, but she had also known that wanting to live—like dreams of inhabiting a grand house in some far-off country, or drinking clean water that came out of pipes when you turned a handle, or never being hungry—wasn't for the likes of her. Other people got to desire those things. Other people, in some world she could barely imagine, got to have them.

When she'd strolled into the market, before the bomb that wasn't hers detonated, she had hoped to eat a plum before she died. She'd eaten a plum once, when she was five, in her grandmother's house. The next week, the bombs came, dropped from airplanes. They killed her grandmother, her parents, her little brother. Inru had been outside when the bombs came. She'd hid behind some rocks. She was bruised, shredded from debris—her legs would always be scarred—but alive.

The people who found Inru in that wreckage told her that it was her job to avenge her family. They fed her, clothed her, taught her what the world was, a stark place of friends and enemies. They told her a story about a brave girl, Princess Erlani, who became a warrior, willing to do impossible things—scale mountains, go weeks without sleep, fight monsters—to protect her country and avenge her dead. The most dangerous monsters were the ones who looked like Princess Erlani and her kin, who seemed kind; they were the betrayers who turned on everyone who trusted them. After many perilous adventures, when she lay in an arctic waste certain she would die, Princess Erlani was taken in by the monsters. They fed her and healed her. They tricked her, and for a little while all seemed lost: but then she recognized their true nature and killed all of them in a magnificent fireball, sacrificing herself. The monsters were wiped forever from the earth. Princess Erlani lived on in legend, so celebrated that she became a star in the sky.

Inru's first rescuers told her that she was Princess Erlani's descendent, that this was her destiny. They took her outside at night and showed her a constant star shining in the north. They told her that one day she could be a star in the heavens, too. The cluster of stars near Erlani would become a constellation, Erlani's Army.

First, however, it was Inru's destiny to have babies on earth. Military men came to her at night and sweated and grunted on top of her. She closed her eyes, enduring the pain, knowing this was part of her duty. One of them was kind to her; he brought her sweets and flowers and tried to be gentle, tried to give her pleasure as well as taking it. He rubbed her legs when her scars ached. His name was Malor. One day he told her that he had been called to battle. He never returned.

She had three babies, two alive. Her living babies were taken from her as soon as they were born. She never knew if they were Malor's, but she told herself they were.

The boy would be a soldier, like his father. Maybe he would have better luck. Maybe he would live. The girl would make more babies before receiving the highest honor, of bearing a bomb and becoming part of Erlani's Army. When the third baby, who would have been another boy, was born dead, the people who had rescued Inru decided that it was time for her to be promoted. The day after the stillbirth, they implanted the bomb in the base of her skull.

Her first rescuers had told her that the people who dropped the bombs, who killed her family, were evil. That was easy enough to believe then, but her second rescuers didn't seem evil. They had given her pudding and clean sheets. They had tended her. Inru knew that the story of Princess Erlani was designed to warn her against such seeming kindness, against trusting anyone. Nonetheless, she did not want to die, even if meant becoming a star.

Yearning for family—not for her own babies but to be a baby herself again, for her mother and father—she sat at her window and watched the life of the city, with its bicycles and balloons, parents strolling by with toddlers, street sweepers and bulging buses which periodically disgorged passengers in front of the place they were keeping her. She wasn't a prisoner; she could walk through the door of her room, wander down the hall into gardens and a cafe where she drank sweet tea, another wonder, but she had nowhere to go. She had never left the front gates.

The search-and-rescue robot came to visit her. On a screen on its huge gleaming carapace, it showed her a film of how it had saved her. It displayed words in many languages. She knew they were words, but she couldn't read. Then the robot began to speak, its voice warm and reassuring, the voice of a kind uncle. It said many things she couldn't understand; when she could understand, because it had begun to speak her language, she nodded.

"I am called Rumble," said the robot in her language. "You are not from here."

She didn't answer that. Afraid, she huddled into her window seat.

"We will not make you leave," said the robot. "You pose no danger." She closed her eyes, knowing she couldn't tell anyone about the bomb. "Why did you come here?"

"I wanted a plum," she said. "From the market."

That wasn't an answer, but the robot said, "I will bring you a plum. What else do you want?"

"I want to live," she said.

Rumble went away. He came back with a plum, and with a nurse who also spoke Inru's langauge, although haltingly and strangely, who asked her gently where she was from and how she had wound up in the place where the robot found her. She didn't answer. She couldn't answer without saying too much, telling them things that would make them fear her, maybe torture her. Her first rescuers had assured her that she would be tortured were she taken alive, but that hadn't happened yet, unless pudding and sweet tea were torture.

The nurse went away. Rumble stayed, and told her a long tale about a brave orphan seeking safety. His soothing voice lulled Inru to sleep. When she woke up, Rumble was gone, but someone else was waiting outside. He entered the room when he saw her sit up. He was from her own land. She knew it the moment she saw him, and saw that he knew it too. He stood in her doorway; they appraised each other. Both were thin and quick, with long shining hair, hers loose and his braided. "You are one of the bomb women," he said at last, in her own speech. He had clearly spoken it his entire life.

She raised her chin. "And who are you?"

"My name is Fawlak. May I come in?"

She supposed it was kind of him to ask. "If you must," she said. Who knew what the rescuers would do to him, if he did not?

He entered. "Why hasn't your bomb gone off? Why didn't the robot find it?"

She regarded him and scratched her nose. She wondered those things too. "Perhaps there is no bomb. Perhaps it was a faulty bomb. Perhaps they have disabled it, or it was disabled by the bomb that didn't kill me."

He frowned. "Or perhaps it has yet to go off."

Inru shrugged. "I think that if it were still working, the robot would have found it." She hadn't told him her name. She hadn't told any of them her name. They never called her anything, just spoke to her in kind tones. "We are always waiting for bombs, all of us, are we not?"

He sighed and squatted in front of her, his elbows on his knees. "What am I to call you, and what am I to tell them?"

"Call me nothing, and tell them I told you nothing. Maybe there is nothing to tell."

"There is always something to tell."

"Then tell me your own tale. How did you come to be here?"

He was, he told her, a motherless soldier, and when he said it she found herself wishing, fiercely, that her own child would wind up in a city like this, where everything was clean and the food was good.

She didn't tell him she had a son.

Fawlak had been taken prisoner after a battle in which he'd been badly wounded. They had healed him, he said, and given him books. A kind woman he wished was his mother had taught him to read. They had told him he could stay here, because he was just a child.

That had been ten years ago. He was no longer a child. He worked in a library, a place where books lived. He never wanted to go back to their own city again. "They'll let you stay," he said. "They're kind."

She spoke, now. "Their bombs killed my family. I remember that. You never had a family to lose."

"Our people have done terrible things—"

"And their people have, too. Their bombs crushed our house, crushed my mother and father and grandmother inside it. And my little brother, who was just a baby. I was outside playing. I hid behind some rocks when the bombs came, and then I ran to the ruins of the house on my bleeding legs, and all I saw of my family was a red mist leaking through the wreckage." She raised her chin, daring him to contradict her. "All people do terrible things."

"I am sorry," Fawlak said. "Would you like to learn to read?"

All people did terrible things. But some of them had books, and pudding. Inru wondered if Fawlak had been taught the story of Princess Erlani, or a story like it. She did not ask, because she feared the answer. She looked away from him, out the window, where a woman in a bright red coat was walking a very small white dog. "I will stay here if I can," she said.

She stayed. She learned to speak their language, although it never came easily to her. Neither did reading, but she loved to cook. Such fine food here: brilliantly colored fruits and vegetables, subtle spices, fresh fish from the sea. Robots did most of the cooking—robots much less intelligent than Rumble, skilled only at chopping and stirring and sautéing in hot oil—but cooking by people was especially prized. She found a job in a restaurant that charged outrageous prices for what she made, and with the money they paid her she rented a tiny apartment above some shops, across from the hospital.

People here had too much money. Some of them were kind, yes, but many were only soft. Inru herself grew softer, more padded, but she reminded herself to stay hard, inside. The arm that had been broken still hurt, sometimes, especially when the rains came, and her legs often ached. She never forgot what she had lost.

She and Fawlak were friends. She danced at his wedding and sewed a baby blanket for his first child. Once a week, she ate dinner with his family, always bringing something she'd made, some special dish from home: goat meat with figs and cheese, flaky pastry with olives. But she was not truly close to anyone, neither Fawlak nor the others who worked in her kitchen, and certainly not the customers who ate at the restaurant.

She had been close to her parents, to her grandmother, to her baby brother. She knew what happened when you got close to people. The bombs came, and they died. Inru might still have a bomb in her head. How could she allow herself to be close to anyone?

She was fondest of the robots. There were two in her kitchen, but they told no stories. From the window of her apartment, sometimes she saw rescue robots bringing the wounded from the battlefield to the hospital, and sometimes she went to the hospital and sought out Rumble, who always recognized her. She liked to eat her lunch in the hospital herb garden, fragrant and shaded, while Rumble, in his soft liquid voice, told her stories about brave children and monsters who granted wishes to those who were kind to them.

He never told her the story of Princess Erlani. One day she asked him if he knew it. "I do not," he said. "Will you tell it to me?"

The sun shone on the garden, and bees labored, buzzing, among the flowers. In this moment, she felt safe here. She told him the story.

Rumble said, "That story makes me very sad. May I tell you another one?"

"Tomorrow," she said, "or next week. I have to get back to my kitchen."

She came back three days later. Rumble was waiting. He told her a story about a brave girl, Princess Inru, who became a warrior, willing to do impossible things—scale mountains, go weeks without sleep, fight monsters—to protect her country and avenge her dead. The most dangerous monsters were the ones who looked like Princess Inru and her murdered kin, who told her that she was one of theirs and that there was no one she could trust. After many perilous adventures, when she lay unconscious and broken in a blast site, Princess Inru was taken in by strangers. They fed her and healed her. She wanted to love them, but would not allow herself for fear they would trick her. One day she met a motherless child, and loved her, and realized that if she was a trustworthy parent to this child, others could be trusted too. She opened her heart, and fell in love, and had children of her own. Her children had children, a legacy on the sweet good earth rather than in the cold, distant sky.

Rumble's story frightened Inru. It made her angry. She had not told him about her babies, and she had no intention of falling in love. Who could love her? She had been broken in too many places, and she might still carry a bomb.

"I do not want to see you any more," she told the robot. "You are not my friend."

"That makes me sad, Inru."

"You cannot be sad. You are just a robot. Sad is only a word you are using."

Rumble reached into a compartment in his carapace and brought out a button on an elastic band. "Here. This is for you. If you press the button, I will come, and I will help you if I can. You can wear this on your wrist, or in your hair."

"I will not wear it," Inru said, and when she got home, she tossed the thing in a basket next to her bed.

Her only real friend was Fawlak now, but she stayed alive. That was what she had wanted when she came here. She kept eating, kept cooking, strolled through the beautiful gardens on the outskirts of the city. There were days when she forgot about the failed or flawed or delayed bomb in her skull, but never for long. There were too many other bombs in the news, still. The city where she lived now kept bombing the city where she had lived then, creating other orphans who would, in time, become soldiers, or have babies until they were made into bombs.

Three years after she awoke in the hospital, there was an explosion on the outskirts of the city. If the bomber had gotten farther inside, many people would have died. The city began building a wall, with heavily guarded gates. The wall ran quite close to where Inru lived, and cast shadows in places where there had previously been sunlight. People from Inru's first city were no longer allowed entrance, and she became increasingly conscious of strangers staring at her on the street. At her restaurant, she was asked to stay in the kitchen, not to show herself to customers; some diners had left when they saw her and realized where she was from. They didn't trust her. They thought she was dangerous.

Well, maybe she was. She didn't know. Fawlak told her he was treated the same way. "It will die down," he said. "It's just panic. Once there's been peace for a while, things will be calm again."

"When will there be peace?" Inru asked.

"Our old home never would have taken in anyone from here. They wouldn't have given them what this place has given us. You know that."

She did know that. Inru watched as the robots continued to bring wounded to the hospital. She listened to the news stories decrying the inhumanity of her old home. No one talked about the inhumanity here. Instead, everyone extolled the cleanliness and beauty and culture of this place, under such constant threat by barbarians.

Barbarians. Inru remembered the men who had grunted and sweated on top of her; some of them had been barbarians, yes, but Malor had not. Every story was complicated.

One night Inru heard banging on her door. It was Fawlak's wife, sobbing. "Some people stoned him. They called him a savage. He told them he was a librarian, someone who loves books, that he is grateful to this place. They said that was just words."

Just words. It was what Inru had said to Rumble. Her heart was a cold stone in her chest. "Is he alive?"

"Yes. He is in the hospital. A robot rescued him."

"I will go there with you," Inru said, "but give me a minute to get ready." She put on her boots and her thickest cloak, the one that covered her hair and made her most difficult to recognize as an outsider. She dug in the basket by her bed until she found Rumble's button, and put it on her wrist. Maybe, like the bomb in her head, it wouldn't work or had never been meant to work; but it was some comfort to think that if she was attacked, she had a way to call for help.

Nothing happened on the way to the hospital. Fawlak lay in a bed like the one where Inru had woken up. His eyes were swollen shut from bruises; he moaned in pain. Anger and hatred clotted Inru's blood and clenched her jaw. Savages. How dare they call other people names? She wished, now, that the bomb in her head were real. She wished she knew how to make it go off. She would find the people who had hurt Fawlak and she would, she would—A red space behind her eyes began to throb, and she thought, quite suddenly, hatred is a bomb. It was a silly, facile idea, a slogan for children. But the throbbing stopped, and her vision cleared. "Fawlak," she said, "I am here. You will be all right. They will heal you, and you will go back to your books." She didn't know if she believed that, but she believed that it was what he would have told her.

She went to the hospital every day to visit him. They sat in the herb garden and drank tea. He grew better, stronger. He was still his kind, gentle self, but his eyes had been irreparably damaged. He could no longer read. "Maybe someday," he told Inru. "That is what the doctors say. Until then, the robots read to me."

Inru wondered if the people who attacked him had focused on his eyes because they knew he was a librarian. He should not have told them that. He should not have told them anything. There was no point talking to such people. She tucked her hands into her armpits. If anything happened to her hands, she would no longer be able to cook. If she was attacked, she would tell them nothing. She would give them no information they could use against her. She constructed a hard shell: she spoke to Fawlak, to his wife and child, and to the other people who worked in her kitchen, but to no one else. At night she looked out the window by her bed and saw the cluster of northern stars, Erlani's Army, and remembered: trust no one. Maybe hatred was indeed a bomb, but any appearance of kindness was still a trick.

Very early one morning, ten months after the attack on Fawlak, a blast shook Inru's windows and startled her awake in her narrow bed. She heard herself calling for her parents, her grandmother, her baby brother. She found herself squeezing her eyes shut, and in the redness behind her eyelids she saw the bloody mist that had mixed with the dust from the bombing.

Shaking, she got up. The blast had been close. From her window she saw a gap in the new wall, and even as sirens began wailing, she saw a small figure climbing through it.

Inru threw on clothing, her cloak and boots. She slid Rumble's button onto her wrist. The bracing morning air numbed her skin. She walked quickly, and soon enough she saw the child who had climbed through the wall. No one else was out, although the sirens were still howling and soldiers would be here soon. A succession of confused thoughts skipped through Inru's head. She had to protect the child. She had to protect those the child might hurt. If the soldiers saw her with the child, they would think she had been a spy all along.

The girl looked to be eight or ten, too young to have babies, still a baby herself. Inru spoke in her childhood language. "Do you know why you were sent here?"

The girl looked up at her, clearly bewildered. "They said there wasn't enough food for me. They said they would send me here so people could care for me. They said they would find a way for me to get inside." Her voice was high and thin, a bird's piping. Inru remembered herself as such a child, and her entire body ached.

"Did you make the wall blow up?"

"No. A soldier brought me. He was going to make a door for me, he said. He gave me something that made me fall asleep, but we were far away then. When I woke up he wasn't there, and then I heard the boom."

"When were you born?"

The child named a date nine years ago. Inru did not ask, "Do you know who your mother was?" because she knew the answer would be no. She remembered her mother's soup, her grandmother's bread, and ached for this child who had never known family.

"They said there's something wrong with me," the girl said. "They said I can't have babies."

Inru did not say, "You could be my daughter." She did not say, "Is there a bomb in your head?" because she knew there must be. She said, "Would you like to see flowers? They smell especially lovely in the rain."

The girl's face brightened. "Yes."

"Let's go, then." Inru had known she was a bomb; she thought this girl did not know. If they could reach the gardens before the bomb went off—if there was a bomb—fewer people would die. The gardens would not be crowded today, because of the rain.

She took the child's hand, cold and bony in hers, and they began to stroll. No one else was out, because of the blast. Inru imagined the buildings full of huddled, frightened people. Everyone would be staying away from their windows, but she and the girl could be in danger if anyone spotted them. Inru pushed the button on her wrist to summon Rumble, and soon she heard the humming of his treads on the pavement. "Hello, Inru," he said. He towered above her and the child. "I am glad you called me."

The little girl looked up at him in fear, and Inru said, "This is my friend. His name is Rumble. He protects people like us, and he tells stories." She could not ask Rumble to scan the child for bombs. That would only frighten her. Instead Inru said, "Would you like to hear a story as we walk?"

"Yes," said the girl.

Inru swallowed. "Do you know the story of Princess Erlani?"

"No," said the child. Of course, they had changed the story. This girl did not remember loving anyone she had to avenge.

"Rumble tells the best stories," Inru said. "Rumble will tell you a wonderful story."

"I think," Rumble said, "that you should tell this story, Inru." She looked at him, at his blinking carapace. There was a red light there she had never seen before. She wondered if it meant he had detected a bomb.

"The first story I learned? The one I told you?"

"No. Not that one. And not the one I told you, either. Your own."

She looked down at her feet, at the child's smaller feet next to them. She thought now that when Rumble had changed the story, making her so angry, he had been trying to give her a gift. Now he was asking her to do the same. She swallowed. "What is your name, child?"

"Oomia."

"Once upon a time," said Inru, "there was a brave princess who came from a place that didn't care about children. They tore children away from their parents, and then they turned the children into weapons. The princess had been a weapon too, once."

Inru took a breath. If the robot hadn't known that she was a bomb, he did now, but he said nothing. "Then what?" asked Oomia.

"The princess who had been a weapon learned that anyone can be a weapon, and that anyone can be a healer, and that everyone is wounded."

"This story is boring. Is something going to happen?"

Rumble was better at telling stories than Inru was, but he had asked her to try. "One day," she said, "the princess met a girl who was a weapon, who had come to the City of Enemies to explode, to kill as many people as possible. The princess began walking the child to the gardens, full of beautiful flowers, where fewer people would die if the bomb went off."

Oomia frowned. "Is that me? I don't want to die."

She had done what she had known she should not do; she had frightened the girl. "No," Inru said, "I don't either. Maybe you won't. I didn't. My bomb never went off. But if yours does, we will be together, and we will be someplace where there aren't many other people. I'm sorry it's not a better story, Oomia. I haven't had much practice, and it's hard to tell a story when you don't know what comes next."

She remembered Rumble's retelling of Princess Erlani. *One day she met a motherless child, and loved her, and realized that if she was a trustworthy parent to this child, others could be trusted too. She opened her heart, and fell in love, and had children of her own, and she lived on through their children.*

Her grip on Oomia's hand tightened. If I live, she told herself, if we live through this, maybe I will do that. Maybe I will begin to let people in. Maybe someone will be able to love me even though my legs are scarred and I cannot read very well and I wake screaming from dreams of my murdered family. Maybe I will have more babies, and maybe this time I will get to keep them.

She told herself that she had never known what was going to happen to her. Everything that had happened, good and bad, had been a surprise. She told herself that this moment was no different. She took another step on her throbbing legs, and another. She and Rumble and the child kept walking towards the gardens, towards that brightness in the rain.

*When I visited my sister one summer, we browsed a number of gift shops in "world-famous Intercourse, Pennsylvania." One of the stores sold animals enclosed in lucite: beetles, butterflies, even bats. Many of them were beautiful, but we left quickly. Later, we agreed that the sight of all those dead, trapped creatures had made us ineffably sad. What had their lives been like before they were encased in plastic?*

# LUCITE

**T**HE TENTH CIRCLE of Hell is a gift shop. Andrew, tired and dispirited, wanders among the predictable displays: T-shirts and refrigerator magnets, bottles of fire-and-brimstone hot sauce, racks of postcards and cheap costume jewelry and coffee mugs. They have thirty minutes to shop before the tour bus, filled with a group of sullen church youth groups and subdued adults, takes them back home. "Midway through my life, I became lost in a dark wood." Andrew knew how the poem started even before their guide, a pot-bellied minor imp with no resemblance to Virgil, gave them his droning lecture at the beginning of the tour. Abandon all hope ye who enter here, and that will be $99.95 plus tax. At least they get to recover their hope when they leave. Andrew, for his part, is very much hoping for a hearty salad and a beer this evening. He plans to avoid cooked meat for a while.

The gift shop sells many different translations of Dante's Inferno. Andrew sidesteps the bookshelves and finds himself facing a back wall displaying framed insects. Butterflies and beetles, he thinks, and wonders what they're doing here—cockroaches and stinging midges would be more like it—and moves closer to examine them.

They aren't butterflies or beetles, not quite. They have too many legs or not enough, eyes in odd places, tiny mouths with teeth. The larger ones are framed, but a number of small ones inhabit lucite blocks, some designed as paperweights and some as keychains. "The souls of the damned," reads a display card, listing prices ranging from $7.95 for the keychains to $150 for some of the larger souls with brightly colored wings.

Andrew's stomach clenches. The damned have already sold their souls, one way or another, although Andrew isn't sure he knows anyone who hasn't. How can they be sold again? And aren't those the souls he's been watching for the last five hours as they endured their various torments?

Tacky fridge magnets are one thing. This is different, much more personal. It bothers Andrew as much as anything he's seen today.

He feels a hot breeze blow past his cheek and turns to find the minor imp watching him. "Properly speaking, these are just the shells of the souls, no more inhabited than any shell you pick up on the beach. The actual souls you've seen, suffering for their sins. They're the meat of the matter. These have no actual value, but they're pretty. The really big ones, the grand ones, they're in storage. These are the minor souls."

No value, but still fetching anywhere from eight to several hundred dollars. Andrew feels his face tightening. The imp gives him an odd half-smile, almost of sympathy, and says, "They're among our best-selling items. Where else here can you find beauty?"

Andrew doesn't answer. He turns back to the display, eager to be rid of the imp, who has evoked low-level panic in him throughout the tour. "It's a myth that the Devil himself makes the deals, and collects on them," the imp told them. "Some of you know that from reading *The Screwtape Letters*. Really, another species of human vanity. None of you is that important. A servant like me is much more likely to be the one doing the job."

Andrew finds himself reaching for one of the paperweights. The soul captured within it is yellow and orange, the colors of sunlight and butterflies and popsicles. He maneuvers around the minor imp—who, sneering, refuses to move for him—and carries his purchase to the register, which accepts cash in the currency of every nation, as well as an impressive variety of credit and debit cards.

Andrew pays cash, handing over $15.00 to another minor imp, this one bored and sluggish.

"What happens to the money?"

"Beg pardon?" The imp raises a lumpish eyebrow and then yawns, affording Andrew a view of a pale, pulsing gullet that will show up in his nightmares for weeks.

"The money. What do you do with it? What does money mean here?"

The imp considers him, head cocked, and then shrugs. "Oh, it doesn't mean anything to us. It means something to you. This place is about taking what you hold dear—or should—and giving you something in exchange that's worthless. Haven't you learned that yet?" He—she? it?—puts the lucite block in a paper bag, along with a square of cardboard, and shoves it at Andrew. "Here you go. Enjoy. Maybe we'll be seeing you again?"

Andrew takes the bag and realizes that he's shaking.

Back home—where he immediately opens all the windows to flood his house with the smell of cut grass and the sound of birdsong, all the sweetness of summer—he removes his purchase from the bag and puts it on his desk. Looking at it brings an odd heaviness to his limbs. It really is beautiful, something like a moth and something like a hummingbird, with feathery antennae and delicate clawed feet and lacy, fiery wings. Crumpling the bag to toss it, he feels resistance, and reaches in to remove the piece of cardboard. A receipt of some sort, surely, or a coupon for a second visit to Inferno at discount rates; those were in plentiful supply throughout the tour, although no one was taking them.

But no. It's an information card. "Soul #99,364,271,482: Herbert Jonathan McManus, 1940-2012. Sold in 1965 for box seat at baseball stadium."

Andrew blinks. He anchors the card under the paperweight and goes into the kitchen to make dinner. As he chops onions and sautes frozen shrimp, he finds himself trying to imagine what could have driven McManus' choice. The desire to impress an employer, or a woman? Surely no one can love baseball that much. But he would have been twenty-five in 1965. He would have been a young man, and the young—as Andrew has just dimly begun to discern, being only a little past that threshold himself—cannot imagine ever dying.

Andrew eats his dinner and then settles down to watch TV, but he's restless, unable to concentrate. He flips channels and finds everything vacuous. He turns off the TV, goes back into the kitchen, reaches for the ice cream in the freezer, and then pauses. He bought the ice cream because he's on vacation, a week off his IT job. He bought the ice cream even though his doctor's been telling him his cholesterol is too high.

He suddenly no longer wants ice cream. He leaves it unopened and returns to his bedroom, where Herbert McManus' soul glows softly in the dim sunset light from the window. Andrew sits at his desk, elbows braced on the wood, and gazes at the paperweight. He wonders if Herbert McManus had any idea what his soul looked like. He wonders what his own looks like.

He goes to his computer, powers it up, and types "Herbert Jonathan McManus 1940-2012" into the search box. Here's a very brief obituary: "Herbert Jonathan McManus, aged 72, died of heart failure last Saturday in Babbling Brook Nursing Home in Whirligig, Pennsylvania."

That's it. There's no mention of friends, family, career, no mention of where the man was born or educated. No mention of baseball, even.

But Whirligig is only two hours from here. What, Andrew wonders, are the odds of his drawing so near a neighbor from his blind grab at the lucite cubes? He shivers in the warm breeze from the window, and remembers the minor imp. Had his choice been free, or determined in advance, or somehow coerced?

He wonders if he saw McManus on the tour, but there were so many damned, their features contorted by eternities of agony. They blended into one another, a vast suffering mass, nearly devoid of individuality. Or maybe the individuality was there, and Andrew just didn't have the courage to look for it.

He goes back to his desk and contemplates the lucite block. When he touches it, it feels cool, inert. Dante says that it's a sin to feel pity for the damned, but Andrew, even with the minor imp Google at his command, doesn't know enough about McManus even to pity him.

He wants to pity McManus, or at least understand him. He wants to break the rules. He wants this one unimportant soul, so easily dismissed by the minor imp, to matter to someone.

He puts the lucite block on his bedside table, gets into his pajamas, and goes to sleep. If he's going to drive to Whirligig tomorrow, he needs to be rested.


He's up early the next morning, which dawns cool and clear. He drives to his local Starbucks for a latte and an almond croissant, and then hits the road, his GPS guiding him with its soothing mechanical voice, female and British-accented. Part of the route is highway dominated by belching trucks, but at last he exits into peaceful farmland dotted with cows and sheep and Amish buggies, all of it like something out of a Norman Rockwell painting. He glances at the seat beside him, where the lucite block sits unwrapped, but it looks just like it did at home. Somehow he had an idea that as it neared Herbert McManus' last earthly residence, it would brighten or darken, change somehow.

He finds the nursing home with no trouble. It's old and drab, and when he goes inside—the lucite tucked into the oversized pocket of a sweater he wore for exactly this purpose—his nose itches from the smell of disinfectant.

He's about to lie. He doesn't lie often, and he's not very good at it. He wonders what will happen if he gets caught. He doesn't see how anything can happen; he isn't committing a crime. He's scared anyway. He swallows.

"May I help you?" A tired looking woman in a rumpled uniform, wearing a nametag that says "Donna," comes out of an office and smiles at him.

Andrew clears his throat. "Yes, I—I recently learned that an old friend of my father's died. A childhood friend of my dad's, none of us had seen him in years, but the obituary said he died here and I wondered if I could talk to someone who knew him. My father died a few years back"—this is true—"and, well, I'm looking for connections. Herbert McManus? I'd like to give my condolences to his family, if I can. I couldn't find any information about them. He died a few years ago, so I don't know if anyone here even remembers him."

Her face has softened. "I remember Herbie, yes. I didn't know him well. One of our aides spent more time with him than I did; let me see if she can talk to you." She turns and flags down a woman pushing a pail on wheels. "Angie? Can you ask Rosalita to come up front here, please? There's someone who wants to meet her."

Rosalita is short and squat, with an unremarkable face. Donna shows her and Andrew to a small room with card tables, all unoccupied. "Can I get you some tea or coffee?" she asks Andrew, and he asks for water before giving Rosalita the same speech he gave Donna. He hopes Rosalita knows more about Herbert, but also hopes she doesn't know enough to detect his deceit.

"Your daddy knew Herbie when he was little!" She clucks and shakes her head. "And you're here because of the obituary, such a shame. No one ever visited him. He didn't have any family that we heard about, and it takes his dying to get someone to come here? You know, I wish we could publish a list of the names of all the folks who are here, put it in the newspaper—put it on billboards!—and say, 'if you know any of these people, come visit, because they need you.' But we can't. Privacy laws. There's too much privacy, if you ask me."

Andrew nods, and thinks about his small, neat house. Too much privacy. "Tell me what Herbie was like."

"Oh, honey, by the time we got him, he wasn't like much of anything. Alzheimer's. But he was a sweet man, always said please and thank you. Sometimes he had nightmares and I'd go in and hold his hand, and he'd hang onto it for dear life. He was with us for a year before he died. Around here, that's a long time. I guess that's part of why I was so fond of him, but I can't really explain it. You just get a feeling about people, you know?"

Andrew takes a sip of the water Donna brought him. He tastes ash and brimstone. "He never talked about the past?"

"Oh, no. That was gone."

"What did he do all day?"

She shrugs. "Looked out the window—he liked flowers, you know, and the leaves when they turned in the fall—watched TV sometimes. I don't think he had any idea what anything on TV meant, unless there was music. He loved music, but most of them do, the Alzheimer's patients. Big Band stuff, Elvis, Buddy Holly: whatever they listened to when they were young."

"Did he ever watch baseball?" Andrew reaches into his pocket to touch the lucite cube, which contains a soul the color of flowers and autumn leaves, and gathers courage for a lie. "He loved baseball. He and my father played pickup games when they were kids, and he played ball for his high school. He dreamed of the majors, Dad said, but he wasn't good enough."

Rosalita brightens. "Really? I never knew that. He never had any reaction to baseball that I saw, but who knows what was going on inside? There was a thing he did sometimes, looked like he was throwing something. I thought maybe he'd been a fisherman and was imagining casting a line, but maybe it was a baseball, you know?"

"Maybe," Andrew says.

Rosalita reaches out and puts a hand on his. "Listen, his bed's empty at the moment. It won't be for long, but the person who was just there left us last night, and his roommate's in the dayroom patting the therapy dogs. Thank God for those dogs! Do you want to see his room?"

"Yes, I'd like that very much."

"It's not great," she warns him as they walk down the corridor. "But I guess you know that. These places never are. But he had the bed next to the window, and that's something. It looks out on our little garden, and some trees."

"Flowers and autumn leaves," Andrew says, and runs a finger along the smooth surface of the lucite.

Today all they see from the window is green. They stand looking out, the two of them, their backs to the drab room with its stripped bed near the window and its small set of trinkets arranged around the other bed, near the door: some family photos, some old-man clothing hanging in the closet, a teddy bear, a lap-blanket crocheted, Rosalita explained, by volunteers who make things for the residents but never deliver them themselves.

The green is lovely, soothing, the color of hope and new life. Andrew tries to remember if there was anything green in Inferno at all, but no, it was all black and gray and red, even in the circle of avarice. "I'm glad he had the bed next to the window," he says.

Rosalita nods. "Those are the good beds. Tell me more about him, since I can't tell you much. And tell me about your daddy." She touches his hand again. "I'm sorry for your loss."

"Thank you." Andrew hadn't been close to his father; he isn't close to anyone. Too much privacy. In truth, he knows little more about his father than he and Rosalita do about Herbert McManus, barely enough to fill a square of cardboard. But he combines things he knows are true with things he wants to be true, and finds himself telling a story. His grandfather died in WWII when his father was a child, and his grandmother worked at a diner where Herbert's daddy was a cook. The two became friends over pieces of pie—Herbie favored chocolate cream, while Andrew's father Jim preferred cherry—and games played in the empty lot behind the diner. After a while, other boys began to gather there too, enough for two scruffy baseball teams, and—

He's just about to launch into a story about how a professional baseball scout who had stopped at the diner for ice-cream saw one of the games and encouraged the boys (pure Hollywood, pure cornball, why would anyone believe such a thing?) when Donna pokes her head into the room. "Rosalita, I'm sorry to interrupt, but Maisie needs you down the hall."

Rosalita, who's been listening and smiling, snaps to. "Yes, of course." She reaches out to squeeze Andrew's arm, says, "I need to get back to work. It was so nice to meet you. Thank you for telling me about Herbie and your father."

"You're welcome," Andrew says. He leaves the room after her; he has no right to be there, not really. No right to be here at all. He leaves quickly, shoulders hunched, but then finds himself circling around the building. He wants to see the gardens and trees without any glass in the way.

There's a bench. He sits and takes the lucite block out of his pocket. It does seem brighter now, but that must be just a trick of the light, because it's not alive anymore. He almost holds the lucite up anyway, as if to show Herbert McManus trees and flowers, but then puts it back into his pocket.

His grandfather really was killed in WWII; his grandmother really did work in a diner, where her only child spent countless hours doing homework, helping to count forks, playing games with sugar packets. There was pie, sometimes, but no baseball. Andrew's father was no better at friendship than he himself is.

He thinks about Herbert McManus, who sold his soul for a box seat at the game, and who decades later, when he remembered nothing else, still made a motion with his arm that might or might not have been like throwing a baseball. Did he want the seat to impress friends, or people he wanted to be friends with?

There's no way to know. It's all lost. Andrew sits on the bench for a while longer, idly watching squirrels and birds. Then he gets back into his car and drives back home. His neat little house feels very empty. He eases the lucite block out of his pocket and puts it back on his desk, fixes and eats a sandwich and salad, and once again skips the ice cream.

He signed up for the Inferno tour on a whim, because he'd enjoyed a college Dante course. The class had been one of his rare forays into the humanities; back then, he'd been vaguely thinking about designing a computer game based on the Divine Comedy, but he found himself unexpectedly engaged by the poetry. And on a week's vacation, why not visit the real thing? The tour was something to do, something interesting.

But the minor imp chilled Andrew from his first words. "You're all here for a reason. Some of you don't even recognize it yet. I'd tell you to pay attention, but you humans aren't very good at that." The imp laughed, not a villain's movie cackle but an amused grandfatherly chuckle, and Andrew felt his gorge rising.

Sitting at his kitchen table, he remembers the gift shop, remembers thinking that he wasn't sure he knew anyone whose soul wasn't already paid for. It's a very small sample, admittedly: the other tech geeks at his job, all of whom seem to have traded their souls for ones and zeros; the very few women he's unsuccessfully dated over the years, most of whom were slaves to work or chemicals; his father, deadened by useless regret.

Has Andrew sold his soul already, to the safety of loneliness? Is it possible to sell your soul without knowing it? He wishes he'd thought to ask the minor imp that question, although the desire isn't strong enough to make him want to take another tour.

Restless, he gets up, goes to the window, and then walks outside to sit on his front step. He's a cliche. His father, his dates, his coworkers, the minor imp, Herbert McManus, Rosalita: they're all cliches. The story he told Rosalita is a cliche. His pondering their fate and his own is a cliche.

He recognizes this as the sin of despair. It occurs to him that what isn't a cliche—the thing he couldn't have known to expect, couldn't have imagined—is McManus' soul, that startling creature trapped in cheap plastic.

He gets up, goes back inside, fishes a pad out of a drawer and finds some colored pencils he once used to rough out a chart for a client. He sits at his desk for a long time, the paper blank in front of him. His mind's blank, too. He hasn't drawn anything since grade school, and he wasn't especially good at it then.

But he begins. He closes his eyes when he chooses the pencils, and lets the pencils wander, and begins to relax. Soon enough he's produced a crude sketch of a small, odd beast, part squirrel and part mouse, with brightly liquid eyes and a horse's mane. It's turquoise and emerald green and gold. With each minute he works on it, he loves it more, yearns more fiercely for it or something like it to exist. As he finishes the drawing, he feels a somersaulting in his chest, a movement both energetic and inquisitive, and in its lucite cube Herbert McManus' soul catches the sunset and flares brilliantly, a memory of flame.

*Between ten years of volunteering in an ER and two semesters as a social-work student at a psychiatric hospital, I've talked to a lot of people with severe mental illness. Some of them had very visible side-effects from longterm antipsychotic medication. Others lamented that their diagnoses kept anyone from believing anything they said. Many of them were smart and funny; almost all of them were lonely.*

# HODGE

T'S ALL A hodge-podge, a jumble, a pile of puzzle pieces. Here are the pieces: Nellene, her parents, her doctors. The hospital, the courts. The shadows.

The dog.

Nellene calls the dog Hodge-podge because he looks like an assemblage of broken-down parts, something cobbled together from a scrapyard. His head's too big for his body and he only has three legs and there are weird blotches on him where he has no fur, just scaly skin. He looks old, not that Nellene's a great judge of dog ages, or of anything at all right now: she can't think clearly when she's off her meds, and when she's on them, her head aches and gravity's three times what it should be.

"All medication has side effects," the doctor told her. He didn't tell her that if she takes these pills for very long, she could wind up with permanent side effects, shakes and jerks and weird spasms. A patient named Barry told her that, legs juddering and eyes rolling as he stuck his tongue out at her, fighting to get the words out around it.

"Get off it as soon as you can," he told her. "Wish I had. You know what people think."

People think people who have what Nellene and Barry have are dangerous. During Nellene's week in the hospital, when the only thing to do was stare at TV or draw with crayons or go to the stupid groups the social workers run, Nellene sat through a group on stigma. The social worker, a tall woman with blowsy hair and a chirpy voice, talked about the pros and cons of choosing to disclose your diagnosis.

Barry doesn't get to choose. Anyone who knows what the meds can do knows what he has. Anyone who doesn't just thinks he's weird, and keeps away anyway.

The chirpy social worker liked to talk about the importance of social support, too. Family. Friends. Pets! Nellene's parents are her only family, and they've warned her that she can't keep living at home unless she takes her meds and stays out of the hospital. Nellene's friendships don't tend to survive her crises, the times when the shadows are at their worst, and the prospect of having to make friends all over again is exhausting, one of the hardest things about getting out of the hospital. The last time she got out, she didn't even bother trying to make friends, which may be why she had to go back in again so quickly, the shadows and shapes flowing around her, whispering threats and insults that made her huddle into a knot of terror. When things get really bad, the shadows congregate so thickly that she can't see any way past them, can't move, just curls in on herself to try to withstand them, the inexorable agents of suffocating doom and bone-deep terror for which she has no adequate words.

She was in the library when it happened, this last time. She tries to spend as much time as she can away from home, so her parents won't know how bad things get. Her mistake in the first place was telling them about the shadows, hoping they'd be able to guide her the way they'd guided her through other difficulties: learning to tie her shoes, mastering multiplication, making it through her last semester of college. Nellene's parents are effortlessly normal, and want her to be too. "Oh, that's normal, honey." Trouble with shoelaces is normal, and so is trouble with math and trouble in college classes. But when she told them about the shadows and the hissing, they froze. Relentlessly normal young women get married and have babies, and they'd been hinting about that before the voices started. Nellene's twenty-five, after all. She came home after college but never even met anyone to date.

So she quickly fell into leaving the house during the day, telling her parents she was job hunting at the library. She didn't tell them how she found quiet corners and curled up there and rocked, or wandered through the lovely quiet stacks of books. When the shadows ganged up on her this time, the cops scraped her off the library floor and took her to the hospital, where the doctors gave her their drugs.

This was Nellene's third time in the hospital. She knows there's no point in saying no to the drugs, because that only works for so long before the doctors go to court and get papers allowing them to medicate her whether she wants it or not, and if she just agrees quickly she'll get out faster, and anyway, yes, the meds make the dread go away, although they also give Nellene a constant throbbing headache and make gravity much heavier than it should be.

This time, she took the meds quickly. She thinks the doctors don't trust her because she's been before. They told her that if she comes back again, she could lose the ability to make decisions for herself at all. They can do that. They can ask the court to appoint someone, the state, as her guardian, especially if her parents don't want her anymore, which they won't if she has to go back to the hospital a fourth time.

She's not going to keep taking the meds, not after what happened to Barry. She may be crazy, but she's not stupid. But that means she has to stay out of the hospital without the meds, because becoming a ward of the state sounds like a very bad idea. She's pretty sure that would mean all meds, all the time.

This time, one of the doctors told her about an injection they can give her. Enough meds for three months, all in one shot. "Doesn't that sound wonderful?" he said, smiling at her with too many teeth. "That way you don't have to remember to take your pills! Patients love these shots!"

"I hate shots," she tells him, and indeed she does, always has. "I'll take the pills."

She swears she will take the pills, promises she will take the pills, vows fiercely, when the chirpy social worker interviews her about discharge, to follow her aftercare instructions to the letter. This boils down to taking the pills.

She has no intention of taking the pills, because if people know what she is, they'll hate and fear her—her own parents are ready to give up on her, aren't they?—and if she starts jerking and twitching and spasming, everyone will know, or at least too many people, and even the ones who don't know will be afraid of her.

She just has to learn to live with the shadows. She has to learn not to be afraid. She has to learn to say "I'm fine" and sound like she means it, because that's the answer people want. She can't tell them that shadows are crowding in on her, whispering that her blood is pure poison and that the air she exhales can make people drop dead, another reason she can't have friends, and that even earthworms are smarter and more worthy of existence than she is. If she tells anyone all that—she hasn't even told the doctors any of it—they'll know she's crazy, and then they'll never believe anything she says again, because everyone knows that crazy people never tell the truth.

She leaves the hospital. She stops taking the pills. Every morning, she tells her parents that she's going out to look for a job, and then she goes to the library.

She feels better, for a little while. The headaches go away. Gravity goes back to normal. She even reads some job ads.

But, of course, the shadows come back. Or, rather, become harder to ignore, since they never really left. The bus from home drops her at a park across the street from the library; she has to cross the park on a path lined with trees.

Day 1 post-pills: just trees.

Day 2: Mostly trees, but the rustling of their leaves is louder.

Day 3: The leaves might be hissing at her, but Nellene can drown it out.

Day 4: The leaves are whispering insults—ssstupid, ussseless, disssgusssting—and the shadows cast by the trees move without wind, just on the edge of her vision.

Day 5: The shadows keep reaching for her, but she can evade them if she takes very quick, small steps in a zig-zag pattern; the whispers have freed themselves of the leaves to float on the wind and tangle in Nellene's hair. The mothers with their strollers on the path are staring at her and turning abruptly to wheel their children in the other direction.

Day 6: The whispers are shrieks now. Nellene covers her ears to drown them out, although it doesn't help, and fights to keep breathing as she feels the shadows pressing at her on both sides of the path.

Day 7: The shadows have blocked the path entirely, and the shrieks are screams, and Nellene crouches on the ground, arms around her knees, rocking. She's so scared and she can't get up and she can't take the path and the police will have to scrape her up again and put her in an ambulance and take her to the hospital where the doctors will know she didn't take the pills and give her the shot and gravity will weigh her down and she'll start twitching and drooling and spasming and all the mothers will know, they'll know, they'll run away from her forever and so will everyone else and she's doomed doomed stupid useless disgusting doomed and—

Something's walking through the shadows. Something's coming, making a sound like a toy train, a wheezing huff. Nellene squints. It's a dog. It's the ugliest dog she's ever seen, hopping along on three legs, chuffing, peering at her, and now the dog's come right up to her and stands in front of her. The dog growls, but its tail is wagging.

Nellene reaches out a hand, as much to determine if the dog is real as anything. The dog barks, once, a sound like all the doors in all the psych wards in the world slamming at once. Then the dog smells her hand, and licks her fingers, and stops growling. It's not wearing a collar. It looks like it hasn't eaten for a long time. It emits an explosively foul fart, comes a little closer, and yawns in her face, its breath a gust of reeking vileness.

Hodge.

Hodge follows her home. Her parents aren't happy. Her mother says, "You were supposed to get a job, not a dog! I don't like dogs!"

Her father says, "I don't like this dog. Why in the world do you want this dog?"

"He wants me," she tells her parents. Saying it takes a lot of energy. "He needs help. No one else wants him. They run away." That takes even more energy. She doesn't think they'll understand that she's Hodge, or Hodge is her—both of them broken, motley, revolting to everyone around them—except that Hodge can walk through shadows without apparent fear, but she can't tell her parents about that because then they'll know she isn't taking her pills and they'll know the shadows are back and they'll put her in the hospital again and tell her she can't come home, and she'll have to get the shot instead of the pills, because the doctors will hold her down or take her to court to give it to her, and then she'll start shaking and spasming and everyone will run away forever.

She keeps Hodge. He sheds fur and stench all over the house, the combination of his breath and his gas putrid and stultifying. He spends hours cleaning his crotch in the middle of the living room, splayed out in front of her parents' twin TV chairs, huffing and chuffing as they try to watch Masterpiece Theater. Nellene's mother lets Nellene borrow her credit card, "only to buy necessities for the dog," even though she doesn't like Hodge, and Nellene buys a collar and leash and takes him on long ambling walks through the neighborhood. Or he takes her, rather, dragging her down new streets, in unexpected directions. She can't take him to the library, so they spend hours wandering the city, resting sometimes on benches, and yes the shadows are there and screaming, always, but if Nellene focuses on Hodge—who is the most substantial thing she has ever had or known, more solid even than her terror—if she follows Hodge, he can lead her through them.

People still avoid her. Even people with other dogs avoid her. Hodge doesn't like other dogs, and they don't like him. But they avoid her because of what they see, not because of what they can't see, and somehow that's a little better.

Hodge doesn't avoid her. When she sits on a bench to rest, Hodge leans against her ankles or tries to clamber onto her lap. Hodge tries to lick her face, although she has to push him away because he smells so awful. She feels guilty, pushing him away, but she also fears she'll faint if she takes too direct a hit of his stench.

She uses her mother's credit card to buy food for him, and special dog shampoo to wash him with, although that doesn't help much. She and her mother agree that she should take him to a doctor for dental work and a checkup, and Nellene starts to do this, but when the doctor arrives with a needle to give Hodge she panics, flees, dragging him with her, because she has always been afraid of needles and she is even more afraid now because what if the needle was really for her, filled with the medicine that will make her twitch and spasm? She flees the animal hospital, knowing she can't tell her mother what she's afraid of and dreading what will happen when her mother sees no bill from the animal hospital on the monthly statement. Will they charge her for running away? Will they charge her with running away? Will they call the house? She has to think of a lie to tell. She can't think. The leaves scream more loudly than ever and the shadows reach for her and fear coils in every cell of her body, but she makes it to the park because she is holding Hodge's leash and Hodge is so big, so messy, so demanding. So solid, and so oblivious to shadows.

She sits on a bench with Hodge. He needs a doctor and she has failed him and she is drowning in guilt but he still tries to lick her face and she wants to reward him but she can't spend her mother's money on that, only on regular dog food, because rewards aren't necessities. She finds paper and a pen in her purse and makes a sign that says "my dog needs treats can you help" and she fishes a plastic cup out of a trashcan and people put money in there, and

Nellene tries to say "thank you" even when she can't actually tell if someone has put money in or if the shadows are making the noise to mock her or if there are people there at all. She sits there through many days, feeding Hodge his normal food for breakfast and coming to the park to beg for treats, and sometimes she sits and says "thank you thank you thank you" over and over to be safe, except that makes her look weird and she hears laughing and she can't tell if the shadows are laughing or people are laughing or both, probably both, probably everyone in the world is laughing at her and she stops saying thank you but then she's afraid she's offending someone by not saying it because she can't tell if there's more money in the cup than there was a minute ago and she sits and shakes and Hodge

Hodge

Hodge climbs on her lap with his awful breath and chuffs at her and tries to lick her face, and she can think clearly again for a minute.

A kid on a skateboard steals her cup with the money. She doesn't use the cup anymore. Someone gives her a ten and she stuffs it in a pocket and the same kid or another kid comes by and tries to hassle her for the money and Hodge

Hodge

Hodge gets between her and the kid and growls and barks and snarls and the kid leaves and Hodge flops back onto her lap again. She scratches his ears. Later she throws the ten away by accident, and she wishes she had a treat to give Hodge but she keeps losing the money or having it stolen and good dogs get treats but hers doesn't because she's

ssstupid ussselesss disssgussting

and good dogs also go to doctors but she can't take him there because of the needles and thinking about that makes her moan, rocking, hating herself—she's on another park bench now—but Hodge climbs into her lap and tries to lick her face again and stays on her, warm and heavy and solid, until it's time to go home because it's getting dark and they get up and the shadows are terrible terrible but Hodge pulls her through them. She closes her eyes and lets Hodge lead her even when it means she trips over things and falls and someone offers to help but she's too scared and Hodge barks and nudges her and she gets up and squints, keeping her eyes open just enough not to fall again, and Hodge pulls her home and her parents say "Why are you bleeding?" and "Why did you ruin your coat?" and "Weren't you going to take him to the vet last week?"

It goes on like that for a while, a while. She tries to be brave and she goes to PetSmart and stands in front of their vet counter and says "Help help" while she clutches Hodge's leash (the other fancy vet would think she's a bad person for running away and then coming here, she is a bad person, ssstupid ussseless disssgusting), and someone comes out and says "May I help you?" and she flees, turns and runs, almost but not quite stumbling because if she talks to them they'll call the police, they'll put her in the hospital and the doctors will give her the shot and she'll start twitching and spasming and why does it matter, maybe it doesn't matter because everyone hates her anyway and maybe she should just let them except

Hodge

Hodge

Hodge couldn't come with her to the hospital and she's afraid of what her parents would do, afraid that if she went into the hospital and came out again he'd be gone, gone, even if her mother has lent Nellene the credit card for him, and the doctors would have given her the shot and she'd start twitching and spasming and she'd want to die, and she would die, without Hodge to lead her through the shadows. She doesn't want to die now, she wants to live even with the shadows and the whispers because there are still things she likes, flowers and the sun on her face and

Hodge.

She doesn't go to the hospital. She doesn't die.

Hodge dies.

It's not dramatic or noisy or heroic. She wakes up one morning and he's lifeless on the floor beside her bed; she knows instantly from the dull glaze in his staring eyes, from his utter stillness, but she reaches to touch him anyway because maybe it's a lie maybe it's a trick of the shadows maybe

No. He's dead.

She gets up. She doesn't cry although there's a huge black hole in her chest and she knows it's her fault because she never took him to the doctor and the doctor could have saved him and soon the credit-card statement will come even if the animal hospital hasn't called, and her mother will know it's Nellene's fault that Hodge died, everything's Nellene's fault because she's not normal, and she won't be able to stay at home. She goes downstairs and finds her mother at the kitchen sink and says, forming the words as precisely as she possibly can, "I know you don't like my dog, but he's dead now."

Her mother turns, blinks. Her face twists into an unreadable expression. "I'm sorry, Nellene."

"I don't know what happened. He just died." It's very difficult to say this because shadows are crowding into the kitchen and the water from the faucet is whispering that Nellene is ssstupid ussseless can't even keep a dog alive and if you'd taken him to the doctor—

"Sit down," says her mother. "I'll make you breakfast."

Nellene sits, numbly, as her mother bustles at the stove. Her father comes downstairs and her mother tells him what happened—Nellene can barely make any of this out over the screaming shadows—and he says he'll bury Hodge in the backyard and does Nellene want to watch or help or be there and she shakes her head, no, she can't watch Hodge go into the ground and if she'd only taken him to the doctor, maybe—

Her mother's saying something. Talking about a cat. She was a little girl and had a cat and the cat died and she cried and Nellene realizes that her mother's relieved that Hodge is dead not just because she didn't like Hodge but because being sad when a pet dies is *normal* and she wants Nellene to be *normal*. Nellene can talk to her about being sad.

Her mother brings her pancakes and eggs and Nellene forces herself to eat them as the shadows mock her and she says "I'm sorry your cat died" and her mother starts crying and Nellene knows it's not because of the cat. It's because Nellene said something *normal*.

Her father comes in and says he's finished burying Hodge and does Nellene want to come outside and pray and Nellene doesn't, she doesn't believe in prayer, but she has to act *normal* and keep her parents happy so she goes outside and stands with her hands clasped in front of the mound of dirt and her mother even comes out and pats her shoulder and the shadows are bad, bad and Nellene doesn't know if she'll be able to get back into the house and she turns around to face the back door but it's blocked by shadows whispering awful things, horrible things, telling her she murdered Hodge, it's her fault Hodge is dead, she never deserved a dog at all and her mother's saying "Are you all right?" and her father's saying "Of course she's not all right her dog's dead" and then Nellene hears Hodge bark.

Hodge!

But it can't be Hodge because Hodge is dead but she looks down and there's Hodge with his three legs and his weird patchy skin and she can't smell him but she's never been able to smell shadows either and she wants to touch him, the way she touched him in the park that first time to make sure he was real, but she's so afraid he isn't but she also knows he can't be and Hodge

Hodge

Hodge runs towards the shadows blocking the back door, and they scatter like smoke or autumn leaves in a pile when you jumped in them when you were a kid, and then Hodge runs back to her barking and she can tell her parents can't hear him and Hodge leads her to the back door and she walks through it and into the kitchen and Hodge is at her side and she can feel the heft of him and her parents follow her and she sits down at the kitchen table again and she's still crying and her parents are talking.

"We'll get you another dog," says her father and her mother says "oh honey" and pats her hair and Nellene doesn't want another dog and she doesn't need another dog because Hodge is *right there* and she wants to tell them what a good dog he is even if he used to stink, and she wants to tell them he came back to help her because that's how much he loves her, and she wants to tell them how relieved she is that he still loves her even though she never took him to the doctor. But she can't say any of that because then she'd have to tell them about the shadows and then they'd know she's sick again, she's not *normal*, and they'd take her to the hospital, and now it's even more important for her to stay off the meds because if she takes them she could lose Hodge all over again, lose him forever this time, and she knows that other people will never accept her, not really, but that's all right as long as she can keep Hodge and he can keep the shadows from overwhelming her, and now if she keeps him she can keep him forever and for the rest of her life it will be just her and Hodge but that's okay.

"Oh honey" says her mother and pats her hair again and says "it's so hard to lose a pet" and Nellene looks down at Hodge who's vigorously licking his crotch and she looks up at her mother who's making soft noises and her father who's shaking his head, and she knows what she needs to tell them.

"I'm fine," she says.

*There's a venerable ballad tradition of women disguising them-
selves as men to go off on adventures, and an equally venerable
tradition of fantasists writing their own versions of the trope.
This is another of my older pieces; its composition dates from
the mid-1990s, when the gender and sexual politics of the story
would have seemed much more daring than they do today. I'm
delighted that those elements now barely raise an eyebrow.*

# HOMECOMING

**T**HE SEA IS a crazy whore. That's what Granny Crimson always said, in the village where I was born. Stay on land, she said, stay to shore, farm and grow and provide for your families, eh, lads. You'll get nowt from that strumpet Ocean, na, na, she'll take everything you have, life and riches and beauty, and leave you barren and dead, washed up broken on the rocks, a thing for the crabs to eat. She'll do that every time, the sea will. Stay to shore, lads, and sow your seed here, on good sweet earth and in good sweet women, true sweethearts and honest wives.

Granny Crimson was no one's granny. She was our village madwoman, a small bent hag as crazed as she said the sea was. We all knew her story. On a warm spring morning when she was still young and beautiful, her own true sweetheart had taken the road south out of our village and set sail from the great city at the end of that road. Because he had never returned, she had never loved again, or married, or birthed babes. She had grown old long before her time, gray-haired and black-hearted and twisted around the kernel of her grief, not knowing if James was dead or had found another, knowing only that he had stopped sending letters and never come back.

One of his shipmates had come back instead, a stranger knocking at her door on a bitter winter's dusk ten years after James had kissed her goodbye. The stranger, Robert, told her that he had been a friend of James. He asked if he could come inside.

They had been whaling in the northernmost seas, Robert said, standing stiff and shivering in front of Granny Crimson's hearth. She had gathered her wits enough to offer him a seat, but he refused it. Hearing the story so many years later, we all wondered what he must have made of her, already so different from the lovely maiden James had courted.

The hold was almost full of oil, Robert said; soon they would have turned homeward again, but a great storm had blown them off course, to a scoured island surrounded by jagged rocks, and from those rocks came singing, plaintive and powerful—lullabies and promises of heart's delight. No one could see the singers, but most of the men jumped from the deck, following their yearnings, and drowned.

"I was James' friend," Robert said. "He talked of you often, aye, and how he planned to marry you, too. I knew he would have wanted me to come see you, to tell you what happened. I'm sorry it took me so long."

"And you?" Granny raged at him. "They all jumped but you, you the only one pure enough to resist the salt strumpets! Aye, you're a monk, I suppose?" She cursed him, drove him out. Her mind shattered that night. She could, we all thought, have dealt with James' death by illness or accident; she could even have survived the news that he had taken another woman to wife. As much as she'd mourned him, as much as she'd already shrunk into the knotted creature of my childhood, those normal fates might finally have offered healing. But James had been snatched from her by false voices, an ending that held no peace.

And so on quiet spring nights, when the road glowed in moonlight and the young men told fantastic sea stories and gazed longingly south, Granny Crimson told anyone who would listen about the horrible whore who had ruined her life, that salt strumpet with her wanton waves.

I never saw her cry, not once. Back then, I did not pity her. I scoffed at her along with the young men yearning for the sea, and dreamed with them, too, and dared tell no one but Gareth and his mother Jenny about any of it. Of all the folk in our village, only Gareth and Jenny never told me that I must grow into a good woman and marry and raise babies. In my thirteenth year, when I grew into a thin woman with big feet and no bosom and elbows as awkward as a boy's, only Gareth never mocked me, and only Jenny ever told me I was beautiful.

She was the village wise woman. Some called her a witch, but since everyone went to her for herbs and poultices, for fortunes and charms and comfort—and since she was far too prudent to twist her knowledge into gossip—no harm befell her. She had midwived me and attended my mother's deathbed, when I was still a baby. Whenever my father came home raging with ale, it was Jenny I ran to for supper and a quiet place to sleep. On the good nights, when only she and Gareth were there, I crawled into her lap and pretended she was my mother.

"Why can't I stay here?" I often asked her.

"Why, you can, child. You're staying here now, aren't you?"

"Always. I mean stay here forever. Why can't I do that?"

"Because no one ever stays anywhere forever, except the grave."

"Oh, you know what I mean! Jenny, why do you always act as if you don't understand me? I'm asking you plain questions, not riddles!"

She always sighed, when I got into those moods—which I did at least once every evening I spent with her—and stroked my hair, and looked sad. "Yes, I know you're asking me plain questions, and I'm answering them as plainly as I can. Your father's house isn't forever either, child. When he grows too crazed for comfort you can come here, and when you're older you can go somewhere else, as I know you dream of doing."

"When I'm older! That's years and years from now—"

"Not hardly that long. Why, you're older now than you were—"

"Before I spoke. Yes, all right, I know, but I'm not old enough to go to sea and I couldn't even if I were, because I'm a girl. That's not what I'm talking about. I want to live here now, all the time, Jenny. Why can't I? Why can't you be my mother, and Gareth my brother? You found him and took him in; everyone knows that, but you're still his mother. So why can't you take me in?"

"Because to be your mother I would have to marry your father, child, which nothing on earth could convince me to do. And to take you in while he lives I would have to take you away from him, which would be a terrible thing, a hateful, hurtful thing, after everything else he's lost. And because if Gareth was your brother you might find it harder to be his friend, and he needs you as a friend, and you him. No, Peg. You may use this as your haven as often as you wish, but it is not your home. Now go dream with Gareth, child, while I get supper. That will make you happy for a little while."

There was no asking her questions when she spoke like that, firm and decided, with no playfulness or riddling at all. Sometimes I tried to talk to Gareth about what she meant, although his answers made me no happier than hers did.

"She says I wouldn't be your friend anymore, but of course I would! I'll always be your friend."

"Brothers and sisters fight. That's what she means. Like Luke and Lizbeth, always pulling each other's hair and that. Quarreling."

"I'd never quarrel with you, Gareth!"

"You're quarreling now, aren't you?"

"Not like Luke and Lizbeth! And why does she care so much about my father? All he ever does is get drunk. Doesn't she love me more than him? How could anyone want to live with him?"

"Aye, she loves you. That's why. I asked her once. She said it was bad enough you'd lost a mother; she didn't want you to throw away a father before you knew better."

"He's throwing himself away."

Gareth shrugged. "I'm just telling you what she said. Anyway, if I had a father I'd keep him, drunk or not. You're lucky to have a father."

"You're lucky to have a mother!"

"You get more care from my mother than I get from your father."

"No one gets anything from my father!"

He laughed. "Na, Peg. You're quarreling again. And I've seen him be gentle with you. He'll miss you, when we go to sea. I have no father who'll miss me."

My yearning for escape was a thorn in my heart. "I can't go to sea, Gareth. I'm a girl."

"Na, don't talk like that! You've heard the ballads of girls who become drummers or cabin boys."

"Those are only songs. And anyway, even in the songs they always run away to be with their sweethearts, and I don't want a sweetheart. Sweethearts are for people like Lizbeth." Lizbeth was the prettiest girl in the village, and she knew it. All the boys mooned over her, even Gareth, who usually had more sense. He said he didn't, but I could tell he did. Whenever he saw her his eyes became yearning and silly.

"They're true songs, though. I've heard sailors who come through here tell stories like that."

"Oh, aye! And stories of mermaids and magic fish and great beasts with golden scales who rise up out of the ocean!"

"And treasure," Gareth said with a sigh. "And pirates. And whirlwinds that swallow whole ships. And islands so beautiful no one sickens there, or dies." And we'd be off, dreaming together, telling each other tales even wilder than the ones told by the infrequent travelers who graced our road. We passed whole evenings telling such stories. Those were the good nights at Jenny's house.

On the bad ones, Granny Crimson was there, too. She had lost her own house to fire, not long after Robert came. Because she was our village madwoman, she belonged to all of us, and everyone took turns caring for her. In the warm seasons she stayed in barns and haylofts, sleeping under borrowed blankets and eating scraps, as the pigs and dogs did. But in the winter she would have frozen and died outdoors, and everyone knew it; in the winter she had to come inside. In the winter, when it came to actually taking Granny Crimson into a parlor or kitchen, most of the village wives' charity froze as hard as the water in their basins. Jenny and Father Timothy, our priest, were the only ones who would help her then, and on any cold or wet or windy night she could be found in one or another of their houses.

Those were some of the worst hours of my life, I think, those bitter winter dusks when my father came home screaming and stinking of ale, when I ran to Jenny for comfort only to find Granny Crimson there, sitting by the fire, rocking while she raved about the wickedness of the wanton sea that seduced young men away from their sweethearts and killed them. The sea she railed against was the only dream I had. I had not seen it, then, and believed I never would, because I was a girl who must stay at home. On nights like that, the warm south seas of the stories seemed more impossible than magic and miracles, and I despaired that anything in my life would ever be less miserable than it was then.

Jenny had her hands full tending to Granny Crimson on those nights, trying to coax sane conversation from her, trying to interest her in spinning or knitting or kneading dough, anything to help her forget for a moment the bitter theme of her life. And so it fell to Gareth to comfort me as best he could.

"You mustn't listen to her, Peg. She's a crazy old woman, and everyone knows it. Why, what does she know of the ocean? She's neither seen nor sailed on it."

"Neither have we."

"Oh, Peg, but we've met people who have! That peddler with the shells, last month, and the fellow just off a whaler, the month before that, and Lizbeth says that her uncle's best friend—"

"Married a mermaid," I said savagely. Damn Lizbeth, who would always be happy staying in the village, raising babies and trading tales! "How do we know any of it's true? It could all be just a peddler's pack of lies."

He shook his head impatiently. "You *saw* the shells! You held them to your ear and heard the sea! Do you doubt that?"

I closed my eyes against stinging tears. I had been entranced by the whorled shapes of the shells, smitten with their delicate colors and their strange music. But I could not afford to buy them, not even one, and the peddler had taken them away again. That chilly afternoon when I stood in the road by the stubble of our wheat field, holding a shell to my ear, was as close to the sea as I would ever get.

I felt Gareth's hand on my shoulder and shrugged it away. I hated crying. Crying was what girls did when they stayed at home.

"I'm sorry I couldn't buy you a shell, Peg. I wanted to."

"No one could have bought them. They were dearer than gold or jewels or—or blood." Gareth touched my hand and I said, "Stop it. Save that silliness for Lizbeth."

"All right," he said quietly, and took his hand away. "If you want me to, I will."

I wiped away more traitorous tears and said, "Don't be like that."

"I'm only being the same way you are."

The hurt in his voice stung me as much as the disappearing shells had, although I wouldn't have admitted it then, to him or to myself. I sniffled and said stiffly, "I'm sorry, Gareth. I didn't mean to hurt your feelings. I didn't. It's just—if we're sweethearts you'll go to sea, and I'll stay here and cry myself to sleep every night, and then you'll die and I'll turn into Granny Crimson."

"Oh," he said with a laugh, sounding cheerful again. "And if we aren't sweethearts, you won't miss me at all?"

"What? No, that's not—"

"Peg, listen to me. You'll never turn into Granny Crimson. You have too much sense, even if I did die, and I have no intention of dying. People come back from the sea all the time, or how would we be able to hold shells and listen to whaling stories? The sea kills some, but so do bucking horses and burning barns and lightning. Granny Crimson's just a daft old woman. Why does she frighten you so?"

Because she reminded me of my father, and of the parts of my father I saw in myself, what I felt I was doomed to become. But that fear ran too deep for me to speak, lest it come true. "When you go," I said instead, "will you promise to come back?" The sailor lads in the ballads always promised, and most of them indeed returned, even if only as ghosts or after so many years that their sweethearts no longer knew them. But this was no song. This was cold, bitter life.

"We'll go together," said Gareth, "and your father will cry his heart out with missing you, and when we come back his joy will make him a better man, and we'll build him a beautiful house with our riches from the voyage."

"And we'll live happily ever after," I said, as the wind howled around the chimney and Granny Crimson howled in front of the hearth and my heart howled within me. It occurred to me, on such evenings, that Gareth's ability to flee into dreams was second only to my father's. Of course I would choose such a fool as my best friend, aye, and probably fall in love with him, too, and pine away to my own death when he perished on the waves. It was my fate.

Whether my evenings with Jenny and Gareth were full of dreams or nightmares, the warmth of our fantastical south seas or the chill of Granny Crimson's grief, the following mornings were always the same. Without fail, my father woke up sick and groaning, remembering nothing of his ravings from the night before, and without fail he came to Jenny for tea to settle his stomach. He always seemed surprised to find me there.

"Peg," he'd say, blinking at me with bleary eyes, one heavy hand reaching to tousle my hair, "what's my little mouse doing here, eh? You were up before me this morning, and thought to come here and bring me home my tea?"

"She came here last night," Jenny always said, mildly enough, and always my father's eyes flashed. I took that look for anger, then;

only later did I realize it was fear and shame. For years I thought Jenny had put a charm on him, a charm to protect me, because he never said anything else about where I had spent the night, or punished me for fleeing his tantrums.

"Did she?" he always said instead. "And what medicine have you for my gut, Jenny?"

"An end to ale," she'd answer, and hand him his tea. And then they'd discuss crops or weather or how many of the mares had foaled, and he'd take me back home with him and I'd help him clean the barn and tend to the animals; I'd cook and bake and wash, and he'd help me—oh, he worked, I can't say otherwise—until the dark came. And always after dark he took his lantern and went to the inn, and always he came back howling, tossing chairs in his rage. And so I spent the days with my father, and the nights with Jenny and Gareth.

So went the years until I came to be fifteen. Lizbeth, grown luscious, was courted by ceaseless suitors. I was pole-thin, brown, calloused from work, a girl who wore trousers in the fields and wanted no lovers, only the sea wind in her hair. My body's longings were urgent, but I had hands practiced at milking cows and doing dishes, and I set them to my pleasure as surely as my toil. Gareth confessed once, blushing, that he did the same. "For Jenny says it's rolling in the hay gets the girls with child, and how could I make some girl a mother and leave her behind?"

He tried to kiss me, several times, but I'd not allow it. I dreamed of him, often and vividly, but not as often as I dreamt of the sea. "If I must stay behind," I told him one evening in early autumn as we fed the horses, "that will only make it worse, and if I go with you— well, then, it wouldn't do. I must act the part of a man. We must be comrades, Gareth, not sweethearts."

"Jenny says they're not as different as people think."

"Oh, aye, and everyone *else* says that Jenny isn't married because she refuses to flirt, because she speaks her mind too plainly."

"They're scared of how much she knows," he said, and smiled.

"She knows you're going to sea, Peg. She knew before I did. She told me when we were wee bairns that you and I would go to sea together. She dreamt it."

My heart jumped. "Oh, aye. And why tell me this now?"

"Because I'm leaving soon, Peg. Next week. And we must get ready."

The world tilted as if I were already on a ship, and my ears rang. "Next week? So soon? You never said— "

"I'm saying now, Peg, and when's the last time you looked so happy?"


"Do you understand what it means?" Jenny said. "You must let no one know you're a woman. No one at all except Gareth, who already knows. Do you hear me? And Gareth, you must treat her only as your friend, and you must never, ever tell anyone else her secret."

"Aye," Gareth said, laughing, "or the captain will propose marriage to her, as happens in all the ballads, and we know our Peg will never marry."

"The captain might do a great deal worse than that, and so might his men."

"They would be so angry?" Gareth said, frowning.

"They would be so lustful," Jenny said bluntly. "Women on land die at the hands of sailors, when they come ashore crazed from months without whores or sweethearts. You must both promise me upon your parents' graves to hide Peg's sex as if your lives depended upon it, which they may."

"My sex is not so difficult to hide," I said quietly. I had as few curves as the broom I used to sweep my father's kitchen; I would never look like Lizbeth.

"It may be more difficult than you think. A ship is much smaller than this village, child, and how shy can sailors be about their bodies? They mustn't see your breasts, Peg, and you mustn't piss or shit when anyone is watching, and you must hide from everyone your monthly bleeding, and you must pretend to shave every day. If you're wise, you'll take a northern voyage where everyone goes about bundled in furs to the nose."

"We wanted warmth," I said. "The south seas."

"Where the sailors surely strip to the waist," Jenny said, "and you would be done for."

"We could say she—he—has an old war wound and is shy about showing it," Gareth put in.

Jenny snorted. "And who's to say sailors don't brandish their war wounds as eagerly as young girls show off their ribbons at a fair? Better to avoid curiosity than to excite it."

"Why not just make me a man?" I asked impatiently. "You're a witch. You can do that, can't you?"

Jenny went very still before she spoke. "I do not know if I am a witch, and if you love me you will not bandy that word about, Margaret. I know some things about herbs and simples; I know what plants can do for the body, and for the heart, and sometimes I can see a little way into the future, as you can see the next signpost on a foggy road. But I have no charms of power, nor do I want them. Do you understand me?"

"No," I said. "You cured our pigs when they were ill; that's power. You knew I'd go to sea with Gareth before I did; that's power. When Widow Brown nearly died of a broken heart you made her live again; that's power—"

"Power to heal, to make things how they should be, how God wants them to be, child. That is how I use my gifts, and that is why Father Timothy and I are friends, and why I have not been stoned or burned or drowned. I have no charms for falseness, nor would I use them if I did. I do not deal in disguises; that is the Devil's work. God meant you to be a woman, and a woman you will stay."

"An' she were meant to be a woman, she wouldna have this lust for the sea," a voice said behind us. I turned. It was Granny Crimson, who had come in while were arguing. I did not know how long she had been there.

I had thought myself safe from her at least until the first hard frost. "Why are you here, Granny? You can sleep in a loft tonight, can't you? It's warm enough."

"Peg," Jenny said with a frown, "don't be unkind. Granny—"

"Have meself a cough," Granny Crimson said. "Came for some o' your special chest tea, and company, and talk. Wrong with that?"

"Nothing," Jenny said. "But you should not eavesdrop."

Granny Crimson sniffed "In this village? Everyone eavesdrops. Give her the boy-charm, Jenny. Ye can't keep her from going. Give her the boy-charm to keep her alive on the ship, if not on the sea."

"She is no boy," Jenny said evenly. "She is a woman."

"Oh, child, we're all both things, don't you know that? Some more than t'other. That Lizbeth, she's nearly all girl, and her brother nearly all boy, aye, they divided it evenly. This Gareth, bless 'im, has a touch of the lass in 'im, what makes him so gentle and kind. And Peggy's got a right healthy dose of boy, aye, keeps her searching the horizon. No wickedness to let it out. More wickedness to keep it under. Let the sailors see that side of 'er, as we see this."

"You ask me to deceive," Jenny said. She suddenly looked very tired.

"Deceive? Is it deceit to help her so she'll not be raped or killed? What foolishness!"

"I thought you hated the sea," I said, staring in wonder. I hadn't thought her capable of conversation, let alone sense.

"An' so I do," said Granny Crimson, "an' always will. What care you for my feelings? No more than he did, who left me so long ago, although he said he loved me. You two have never lied about that, at least. Let them go, Jenny. Give her the boy-charm and send them to their doom, like those that went before."

I had expected the boy-charm to be some foul concoction, a mixture of noxious herbs and dried bits of dead animal, but to my mingled relief and disappointment it was only a small leather pouch, drab and musty, that hung about my neck on a strong braided cord. "You must always keep it on," Jenny said, dropping the thing over my head. "That should be easy enough. Sailors are a superstitious lot, or so I hear; tell them it's a good-luck token, and you'll be right enough."

"Don't you have to *say* something?" I asked her. I had imagined an incantation or ritual, chanting and candles.

Jenny sighed. "No, Peg, although I will if you want me to." She waved her fingers. "Poof, you're a boy. Is that better?"

"No," I said. "I feel just the same." I examined my arms, my hands. Nothing had changed. I was no hairier or stronger or fiercer than before. "Do I *look* different?" I asked Gareth.

"You look like a wooden puppet," Gareth said with a laugh, "twirling to try to see yourself."

Jenny nodded. "Stop twitching, Peg. You look the same to me, but I know you too well. The charm works on strangers, not on friends."

"If I don't feel any different, how can I know if it's working?"

Granny Crimson shook her head impatiently. "Na, child, it's not to change you. It just makes folk see the boy-part that's already there, like I said. Makes 'em think that's the whole of it, as simple folk always do."

"What will I call her?" Gareth asked.

"Him," Jenny said, frowning.

"No—I mean—Peg, what's your name?"

"Her name's Will," Granny Crimson said, and for a moment I almost thought I saw a smile. "She has a stout will, this one does, and she will do it her way or not at all. William Stout, eh, lad?"

"Aye," I said, and wondered if I sounded like a man.

And so I became William Stout. We set off not an hour after that, following the road south, our packs on our backs. I had long known that men's clothing was more comfortable than women's, and it was a joyous thing to wear it without apology or excuse, fearing no pointing fingers.

We walked five miles that day, and a carter drove us another five, and by nightfall we had reached a little inn in a town neither of us had ever seen. Now ten miles seems like nothing to me, but then it was farther than I had ever gone or thought to go, and when the innkeeper accepted me as a journeyman without challenge I could have crowed for joy. That was the only reason we spent some of our meager store of money there, to test my new name.

Thereafter, as we journeyed further south, we slept as Granny Crimson did during the warm weather, in haylofts and by the sides of roads. Gareth coached me on men's ways, and I learned to swagger and to curse and even to flirt with maids on their way to market. I never did learn to piss by the side of the road; I was too afraid of being discovered, although Gareth offered to carve a wooden funnel in the shape of a prick for me.

"You'll need it on shipboard," he warned me, and I told him that maybe on shipboard I would, but on the road I preferred to learn to hold my bladder, thank you. He began carving the prick for me anyway, and it became a great joke between us. He told me that mine would be larger than his, and I said, aye, but where would I put it when I didn't need it, and what would I do with it when the wood began to reek of piss? "Why, you'll stow it in your pants and jump in the sea to clean it when it smells," he told me cheerfully, "the same as sailors do with their real ones."

And so we went on, blithe and fearless, true comrades. The weather was glorious, as if the very season blessed our adventure, and by the time we reached the Great Port I was as brown and coarse and unwashed a journeyman as you'd ever hope to meet.

The port! What a mass of filth and brawl and humanity that city is, as dirty and snarled and reeking as a tangled fishing net. The towns we saw had been growing ever larger as we traveled south, but none of them had prepared me for the city. Too much of what I saw there saddened me: drunks lying in the streets, and canker-ridden whores leaning against lightpoles for strength, poor things, and horses beaten merely for being weary of their work, as who wouldn't be in that festering place? The cityfolk I saw made my father, with all his strange moods, seem like a simple man. Gareth and I felt simple there, too, simple and frightened and alone, for all we'd been happy on the road.

We spent two weeks there before finding berths on the good ship *Charity*, and in those two weeks I think I grew older than I had in the previous two years. Whatever the boy-charm did to disguise me as a rough and ready man, the city and its docks did more. That place taught me to love the sea more than ever my girlhood dreams did.

The sea is not a whore, for she is free and joyous, but she is a woman. She obeys the moon, as women do, and her depths contain both treasures and horrors, and men try to bend her to their will and rarely succeed, no matter how much money they spend in the attempt. The sea does as she wishes, and anyone who would be her lover must be her partner, not her master.

Ships are women, too, but far tamer. The *Charity* was her own little world, smaller by far than our village. I learned to love her confines as much as I'd hated those of home, for on shipboard I could never forget the immensity that surrounded us, and that would kill us in minutes without the fragile shelter of decks and sails. I learned to love the sound of wind in the rigging, the slap of waves against the hull; I learned to love climbing the swaying mast, for from its heights I could look out on the ocean and on the horizon, those two vast powers from which the crow's nest kept me safe, as it did from the tiny deck below.

I learned all manner of shipboard chores. I swabbed decks and spliced rope and mended sails, patched the hull and painted the railings, peeled potatoes and chopped onions, and never complained at the drudgery. I grew browner even than I had on the road, and strong and happy and free.

And safe. The other sailors were far more modest than Jenny had feared, and avoided the sight of my body as I avoided the sight of theirs. They were kind, hard-working men: Tom Kincaid, the cook, who whistled jigs and always smelled of grease, and Jack Simpson, simple Jack who was afraid of the dark and who didn't know many words, but who cried when the ship's cat Mabel lost part of an ear to a rat—although she won the battle—and who nursed her back to health again until she was scarcely good for ratting, wishing only to tag about after him wherever he went. And Gully O'Shaughnessy, who taught me twenty different kinds of knots and whittled whenever he had free time. He carved wood or cork or bone, anything to hand; he made animals and tiny ships and clever boxes, and always he talked of his sweetheart Fiona back home, how when he'd grown rich from voyaging, he'd go back and marry her. And always when he said so, I thought of Granny Crimson, and hoped Gully's tale might end happily.

There were many others even among the common sailors, let alone the officers. But those three, with Gareth, were the ones I came to love, and they were the ones, at last, who taught me the most. I learned more from them than from all the foreign wonders I had left home to seek: silks of every shade and texture, pungent spices, trees and fruit and flowers in colors I could not have imagined, and seas turned every color too, under foreign skies. Without my companions, all those marvels would soon enough have grown dull, and without them I would not have weathered that stranger, sadder wonder at the end.

The world we made together is gone now. Silk and cinnamon do not bring it back to me as clearly as the smell of potatoes frying with onions, or the purr of a cat, or the feel of a knot beneath my fingers. And that in itself is proof of how the voyage changed me, who set out only wanting to see anything new and different.

There is one evening I think of often. Gareth and I had helped Tom peel potatoes and wash pots afterwards, and he had given us some extra bread, and we had carried it up on deck, to sit with Gully as he whittled in the warm, soft air. Jack was there, too, splicing line as notch-eared Mabel purred in his lap. It was a breezy night with a nearly full moon, the blazing star-road stretched across the sky above us. We were off the coast of the hot southern lands, as far from home, we thought, as we would get. Soon we would turn around and begin heading north, stopping in ports along the way for water, for trade and news and the occasional precious piece of mail.

Gully was carving a piece of ivory he'd bought at our last port. "What are you making?" I asked.

"A rose," he said, and showed me his work, the pale petals emerging from the bone as if they truly grew there. "A flower to send to Fiona, to show her I love her." His voice was rough, and he coughed, a rumble in his throat and chest. A malady had been sweeping the ship, a nasty thing of phlegm and sneezes, for all we were in a hot climate.

"Shall I help you write another letter to her?" Gareth asked. Gully couldn't read; nor could many of the other men on board. Nor would Gareth and I have been able to, maybe, if Jenny hadn't taught us. My father had asked her once why a woman needed to read, and she'd said, "To go places other than home, when she's stuck in the house caring for the likes of you, Vincent." And he'd laughed, because her own voice had been laughing and kind, and he had said nothing about my reading after that.

Gareth and I were both in demand among the other sailors. In what free time we had, we did a brisk trade writing letters in exchange for extra bits of food, or a coin or two, or simply goodwill. And in truth I'd have done that work for nothing; it was a blessing to hear the men's voices soften as they composed messages for parents and wives and sweethearts, children, neighbors. "I love you," they said. "I miss you." And, even at the farthest point of our voyage, always they said, "I'll be home soon, as soon as I can. Wait for me."

Gareth and I had both helped Gully write letters to Fiona. You'd have thought she was a goddess, the way he praised her golden hair and blue eyes. We noticed, though, that he shared no memories of things they'd done together, nor of talks they'd had. We wondered if she was truly his sweetheart or if he only wanted her to be, and our doubts deepened when he got no letters back from her.

As much time as we spent writing letters, we spent even more reading aloud to those who had received them and couldn't read for themselves. The parents and wives and sweethearts, children and neighbors, all sent messages; one sailor even got a note from his dog, written in his daughter's hand. The mail was months old by the time we got it, and doubtless some letters arrived at ports after we had sailed again. That was Gully's hope, since nothing had come from Fiona, although he'd carefully told her as many of our ports as he knew or could guess before we left.

"Na," Gully told Gareth now, "no need to write another letter. I figure she needs more than words. I figure this flower'll be better." Gareth and I exchanged a glance; I was sure now, as I knew he was, that Gully sent his letters to woo Fiona, and not to continue a love affair already begun.

We heard footsteps behind us and turned to find Tom standing there, holding a steaming bowl. "She's a hard heart who doesn't value all you give her, Gully."

Gully looked up, frowning. "She's busy, that's all. She said before I left I should come back for her." He coughed and bent over his work again, and I saw him blushing in the moonlight. "We— she gave me a kiss, even. Many kisses. She wanted to give me more than that, but I was afraid o' gettin' her with child, and me away at sea and all." He looked around at all of us, his eyes fierce. "I guess you think me soft."

"Soft," Jack said, and laughed, and winked at me, and rubbed Mabel's ears. "Part of yer soft as my Mabel's fur, eh?"

Gully's blush deepened, but Tom smiled and said, "Some might take that as an insult, Jack, but we know you don't mean it that way."

He glanced at the rest of us, his face a warning. There was no need. We all knew Jack was simple, and meant no offense. "For myself, Gully, I think it uncommon kind of you not to risk making a baby afore you left."

"She said I must na love her," Gully said. "She said it weren't her time to make a baby, and anyway there were ways to keep from getting with child."

There were, at that. I'd seen Jenny make up potions, heard her counseling the other young women of the village. She'd given me a bag of herbs before I left. "If you're forced, Peg, make this into tea and drink it. You'll get sick, but if a baby's started, it will stop." But her expression had been grim, and I'd thought of the tales I'd heard of young women who drank such things and sickened and died. It seemed to me I'd be safer risking a child. If it came to that, my secret would already be discovered, anyway.

By now in the voyage, although I still kept my modesty and my false name, I'd stopped worrying. Jenny's fears had been unfounded; perhaps there were ships as brutal as she said, but this wasn't one of them.

"'Twas love as stopped you," Tom told Gully, but there was an odd note in his voice. "And even if you were . . . soft"—and here Jack let out a guffaw, startling the cat, who leaped out of his lap— "that's no shame, is it? No shame not to stir when the time's not right. Or the person."

"She's right!" Gully's voice was fierce now. "I love her, always have, since we were mere bits of things!"

"Be calm," Tom said. "I meant no harm. Here, Gully. I brought you some soup for that cough. It will soothe your throat."

Gully put down his carving tools and took the steaming bowl. "Thankee, Tom. That's kind of you." He tipped the bowl to drink, and swallowed. "It's good."

"I'm glad," Tom said. "Did Fiona make you soup, back home?"

Gully's face tightened into a glare again, and he'd have spoken, except that a fit of coughing silenced him. I took the bowl so his shaking hands wouldn't spill it. "Enough," he managed, finally, and took the soup back from me. "I'll drink your soup, friend, but you're not to mock my love."

"Wasn't mocking. Just asking a question. I'm sure she's a fine cook."

Gareth, frowning, said, "Well, Tom, and what of you? Leave off questioning poor Gully. What of your own love life?"

Tom gave him a keen glance. "Oh, I think you know."

"If I knew, why would I ask?"

Tom chuckled. "And how should I know that? William Stout, you know him better than I. Why would he ask?" He winked at me and nodded to the others. "I'll be off to my berth now. Breakfast comes early. Gully, come see me anytime, if only to bring the bowl back. I always like having you about."

"Thankee, Tom. It's fine soup. Good night."

Tom left, and after a few minutes Gully did, too, taking his tools and the empty bowl with him. Mabel had heard some noise and slunk off, her eyes narrowed and her body low to the deck; Jack went off in search of her. "She's after something with a long tail, just you watch. I best make sure she's not hurt again."

That left me and Gareth on deck. "That was odd," I said. "All that with Tom and Gully."

"Aye."

"Why did he say that to me? Do you think he knows?"

Gareth shrugged. "He knows we're friends. That's all it has to be, Will." He always called me Will, now; it was safer. But for the first time, it irked me. For a moment, to my surprise, I found myself searingly jealous of Fiona, whose name Gully murmured so many times each day, as if by itself it were a charm against loneliness.

I was homesick, that was all; homesick at last, at the farthest point of the voyage. Tomorrow we would reach the southernmost port and take on supplies to begin the trip home, and after that each day would bring me closer to Jenny, and rooms with real furniture, and a bed that didn't roll and heave while I slept.

\*

We made port in a place with palm trees and chittering monkeys and subtle scents. Gareth and I strolled in the market there, and when I found myself eyeing a brilliant, billowing gauze skirt—because I was hot in trousers, and suddenly yearned to feel air against my legs—Gareth haggled with the merchant and bought it. "It's for my sister at home," he said, and turned to me with a smile. "She'll like it, don't you think?"

"She will," I said, trying to match his jesting tone, and when Gareth roared with laughter, I realized I'd made a pun on my false name. But I was in a sour mood, sullen and skittish at the same time—it was the heat, I told myself, this infernal heavy damp—and when we were far from the stall and from prying eyes, I said, "So is that what I am now? Your sister?"

Gareth gave me a startled look, his eyes brightening. "Would you be more, then?"

The heat was a cobra around my chest and neck, strangling me. "I'd be somewhere cool! I'd be somewhere I can think! I'd be somewhere I don't have to pretend and wear this damnable clothing! I'd be—"

"Ah," Gareth said, and for a moment I was afraid I'd wounded him, but his face was still hopeful. "Soon enough. We're turning homewards now."

And we were, and when we got back on shipboard everyone seemed lighter, happier; the very ropes strained at the moorings, eager to be off. Everyone seemed more cheerful except Gully, who came to us ashen and trembling. "I've a letter from Fiona at last," he said, "but it's so short. I'm afraid—I don't know what it says—"

He held up an envelope, addressed in a large, careful hand. I wondered if Fiona had written it herself, or asked or paid someone else to do it for her. "Give it here," Gareth said quietly.

Inside was a single piece of paper. I looked over Gareth's shoulder as he unfolded it. "Dear Gully, I am married to Cobb the blacksmith now and have a little boy but I wish you a good life. Your friend, Fiona."

"Is it bad news?" Gully said. "Is she all right?"

"She's fine," Gareth said gently.

We told him. "A child," he said, the words wooden. "A child already, and we've scarce been gone nine months. She never loved me, then."

Even in his own tales, she'd never claimed to. She'd only wanted a farewell romp, a diversion. I couldn't blame her—who knew better than I how confining life in a village could be, how welcome any escape, however momentary?—but I ached for him. "Gully," I said, "she's happy, and you must be happy, too. You must find someone who'll match your love and return it."

"Who?" he said. "How?" And then he wept, that great strong man, sobbing openly as our shipmates scurried to and fro.

But we had work to do, all of us, and I knew that work was the best thing for Gully now. It would take his mind off Fiona; it would give his body something useful to do. All of us worked very hard for the rest of the day, and we set sail that evening, and not until late in the night was there a moment to be still, to think.

It had been a long day, a tiring day. Usually I'd have gone straight to my bunk, but we were still trapped in that infernal heat. So I took myself topside and curled up on my usual coil of rope, wondering if anyone else would join me.

After a while, Tom did. "There you are," he said, and passed me something, a glowing dimness in the moonlight.

It was Gully's ivory flower. "He gave it to you?"

"If only he had! I found him about to toss it into the sea, and I took it from him. I told him it was a beautiful thing that should go to someone who'd value it, and I valued it; aye, and valued him too, more than Fiona ever could. He'd not hear me."

"He just found out. He only got the letter this forenoon. He's not himself."

"She never loved him." Tom's voice was tired, disgusted. "You and Gareth know that as well as I do. He was spinning fancies in his head, trying to fool himself about what he really is, mayhap."

I shook my head. I was weary from all that work, and tangled in my own temper. "And what's that, Tom?"

He went very still. "Don't toy with me. What you are, Will; what Gareth is, too. What you two are together." I blinked. Here was a riddle, for I was a girl in disguise, but Gareth wasn't, and neither, I was sure, was Gully. But Tom was still talking, not waiting for my answer. "I've seen the way you two look at each other. I've seen you together. Folk say sailors make do with each other for lack of women on board, but you and I and Gareth know—aye, and many others—that some of us weren't made for women any more than fowl are made for fish, whatever the preachers say."

I blinked again, taking this in. I had seen things, surely, heard ruttings in the dark belowdecks; and that was bodies meeting their needs, no matter, but Tom was talking of something else, something deeper. "You love him," I said.

Tom snorted. "You'd not known it afore? Aye, more than he loves his Fiona, who is only a fancy and a dream, and him fooling himself, mayhap. You're a clever lad, and loyal to your own mate. Help me, Will. How do I make him see me?"

His voice was anguished, and I was at a loss. Jenny would have known just what to tell him, but Jenny was thousands of miles away. I thought of all the times we had sat on deck of an evening, all the hints Tom had dropped, plain as noon to me now, and Gully had not heard them. "You need to wait, I think." I spoke slowly. "Wait and watch, and keep doing as you have been, and whenever he speaks of Fiona, remind him somehow that you're here instead. Keep his flower for him."

"Aye," Tom said, and smiled, and reached to grip my arm, no caress but a hearty squeeze. I was all muscle then, with no fear that he'd discover my secret. "Thank you, Will. Indeed you're wise."

Was I wise? I realized as I said the words that I was only telling him what Gareth had been doing, all these long years—kind, patient Gareth, whom I'd spurned and pushed away and snapped at in the market that morning—and suddenly I knew my own heart fully at last, and felt it beating as if with great wings within me. I would speak to Gareth as soon as I could. I would tell him, and thank him, and say I was sorry for having been so blind. We had watch together the next morning. I would go belowdecks now, to my berth near his, and listen to his even breathing as he slept, and in the morning I would tell him what I knew and how I felt.

But before morning came I woke to a great pitching and rolling, to bells and alarms and shouts both above and below. I scrambled out of my bunk, checked Gareth's—he was not there—and made my way above, making out snatches of news as I went. A big storm, sudden, as none had seen coming, and we'd been blown off course and were taking on water, and the anchor had torn loose, and one mast was broken, and at least one man overboard. I felt a sickening fear, then. Gareth. But no, it was Simon the boatswain, whom I'd barely known, although God keep him and all who loved him, and then I was past that bit of talk, climbing above into hell.

The rain pelted down and the wind roared and feet pounded, and the deck bucked like a wild thing and then fell away as we toppled into the troughs of waves. The men up top had lashed themselves to the ship with rope around their waists, but I saw that at least one was dead, lolling in his bonds, drowned when a wave drenched the deck and he could not free himself. I would not secure myself so.

How long we were in that chaos I cannot say. I bailed and patched leaks and clung to whatever I could find as we heaved and rolled, as the waves broke over us. And through it all, fear for Gareth flashed like lightning, for I had not seen him in the roiling maelstrom. And then another wave would come, huge and jagged and crashing, and I would be able to think only of myself.

I swallowed so much seawater in those hours that my lips and throat grew parched with salt. In any second of calm I turned my face upward to the pelting rain, to let fresh water wash away the brine. "The sea is a crazy whore," Granny Crimson had said, and I remembered hearing one of the men—Peter, I think, who hauled pallets and crates and anything heavy that needed moving—saying to a friend that he missed the taste of his sweetheart's other lips, salty as the sea. The other sailor had laughed, and I had blushed and hoped they would not notice.

The sea was indeed crazy in that tempest, although not whorishly. As wanton as she was—pouring herself over all of us, drenching everything, sweeping away anything not firmly fixed—she did it without thought of payment, unless line and sails and mast were payment, the very ship itself and all our lives.

For when the storm at last began to lose force, we knew not where we were. Farther south, someone said, off a strange coast of high green mountains and waterfalls plunging straight into the ocean, the shoreline jagged with terrible rocks. We were drifting toward them, aye, helpless to stop ourselves. We could neither sail nor steer, and although the wind was calmer, those rocks would still stave in the bruised body of the *Charity*, already broken and leaking.

Carried helpless toward that doom, we heard, all of us who were left—for perhaps a third of the crew was already dead by then—a soft and pleasing sound. Above and through the wind it came, sad and soothing at the same time, a song of longing whose words I could not make out. It came from the rocks, and when I peered at them I saw beckoning shapes and vague unearthly forms: the curve of an arm, a delicate hand, all made of swirling spray.

All of us who were left gathered at the rails, drawn by the sound. I did not see Gareth, but Gully was there, and Jack and all the others—I wondered then, fleetingly, if poor Mabel were still alive—and the wind had picked up again and was blowing us toward the phantoms, and the voices came ever clearer. I heard Jenny offering me tea, saying, "There, there, Peg, it will be all right," and I longed to cry on her shoulder.

Around me the men, like people dreaming, murmured names,

"Mother!" and "Frances!" and "my dear Jane!"

"Sally!" called Paul, our bosun, "Sally, Sally, I'm coming!" and over the rail he went, although I gasped and called and would have clutched at him had I been close enough. Too far, too far.

The wind picked up again, driving the broken *Charity* faster toward those fatal rocks, and the voices grew louder. "Mabel?" called Jack. "Don't you move! Don't you chase no rats! You stay there; I'll not let you drown!" And he too was gone.

I heard snatches of Jenny's voice, of my father's, of Granny Crimson's, even. I heard the voices of home. And then, stronger than the others, Gareth's. "Peg, do you love me? Will you say it at last? Come to me now, and tell me."

My heart lurched. He was out there; he wanted me, and I wanted him, and if I could just reach him, then—

"Will!" That was Gareth's voice, again, but it was behind me, not out on the water. "Will," he said, and I turned, weeping.

"I thought you—I heard you—I was going to jump, Gareth."

He hugged me, a crushing embrace, but before he could speak I heard someone else nearby. "Fiona! Fiona! I'm coming!"

"No!" I broke free of Gareth's arms and ran toward Gully, fighting the wind, sliding on the slick deck. Other men were going over the side now, calling out to the rocks as they jumped, but the phantoms had no more hold on me. "Gully, no! Fiona's not out there! Gully, look at me! Stop! Gareth, help me!"

I was next to Gully now, and then Gareth was, too, and I heard Tom's voice call "Gully!" and thought, good, they're safe—but then I saw Tom standing next to the rail, straining to see out into the heaving spray. "Gully! I'm coming!"

Tom heard Gully's voice on the wind. He must have thought that Gully had already gone overboard, and was finally calling him.

I grabbed Gully and shook him; I'd have done the same to Tom had I been close enough. "For God's sake, Gully, it's here, the love you want! It's right here, you silly fool! Gareth, help me!"

Gully was not a small man; it took all of our strength to drag him toward Tom. "Tom!" I called. "Gully's right here! Look!" And then to Gully, fiercely, my throat aching from screaming over the wind, "Say you love him! Tell him you love him, tell him he's your heart's desire, tell him the soup he made for you when you were sick tasted like no other soup in the world! That's what they want, those sirens, that's what they miss, and it's what you miss, too. But you have it, Gully. Right here, right now. You don't need a woman for that. You don't need Fiona who doesn't love you! Tom's pining for you, Gully, it's you he's yearned for all along, and only you can save him, can't you see that?"

I was wild, and Gully kept fighting us, pulling toward the voices. I couldn't tell if he'd heard me, over the wind and the waves and the sirens. Through the spray I saw Tom starting to climb over the rail, and Gareth let go of Gully to grab Tom instead, and I knew I couldn't hold Gully by myself.

"Gully," I said, despairing, "he loves you. Tom loves you."

What finally made him hear me? I'll never know, but I'll never forget the moment when I saw him, at last, see Tom: that start of recognition, the glimmer of fear when you realize that someone you love is going to die.

He broke away from me. He ran to Tom and helped Gareth pull him back from the rail. He held Tom and cradled him there in the wet, both of them sinking to the deck, and I saw his lips move against Tom's ear, and Tom stopped fighting, stopped trying to move, relaxed into Gully's lap. He reached for Gully's hand, and Gully took his, and kissed it, and pressed it to his heart.

In the end, only we four were left, cast onto the shores of that island. Somehow we made it through the rocks, clinging to planks as the ship broke up. I remember nothing but huge roarings and churnings and terror that I would die as I clung and kicked. And then nothing, and then waking up in blessed sunlight on a rough beach, all my skin scraped and bruised and the boy-charm gone, vanished into the waves.

"I wasn't tempted," Gareth said, much later. We four had found a freshwater spring on the island, and mussels, and they kept us alive until we could signal a passing frigate. She bore us to the next port, where Gully and Tom found berths on a ship heading even farther south, to the cold places where the great icebergs groan and heave. But Gareth and I took passage north. I called myself Will Stout, as before, and no one questioned me, and I knew that Granny Crimson was right. The charm had only made more visible what was already within me.

"I wasn't tempted, not even for a moment," Gareth said. "I knew you were right there, my own Peg, on the ship with me. What could they offer me, those wicked sirens?"

"Not wicked," I said. "Just lonely." The sirens, I believed now, were the ghosts of those who had died in shipwrecks. Grieving, they sang of home, their call a summons to anyone bereft or misplaced. I do not think all or even most of them were women. Whoever they were, they were just trying to go home themselves when they were dashed against the rocks, and now they will stay there forever, singing the comfort of the hearth, the beauty of bread and blankets and clean fresh wool; and, more powerfully still, singing welcome, and belonging, and love.

Gareth and I went home a safer way, and there were wonders, too, on that voyage. All I will say of them is that you should see them yourself, if only once in your life, because home is so much sweeter after time abroad. Gareth and I retraced our steps, making landfall in the great city and walking back to our village along the same roads we had used before. It was spring now, the air warm and fragrant, the trees bursting with that first fresh green, calves and lambs and foals gamboling in fields as we passed. We went home, and in a lovely blue dusk we walked up the main street of our village, and Jenny came flying to meet us, weeping with joy, for she had dreamed our return. And there was tea and fresh bread and a roast chicken and pie waiting at Jenny's house, and we shared it with my father and with Granny Crimson.

My father had aged, and my heart broke to see him. He was nearly blind now, but he knew my voice, and wept when he heard it. "Peg. You've come back, my own girl. I feared you were gone forever. Feared I'd lost you, like your ma." He stank of whiskey and his words were blurred, but now I felt only pity for him.

"I'm not lost," I told him. "I'm right here." I had some inkling, then, of what it must have been like for him after my mother died, for everyone said he had truly loved her. She was dissolved into an ocean he could not sail, not yet, except by leaping over rails that, for my sake, perhaps, he avoided. He drowned himself in drink instead. Jenny and Gareth and I were the only home he had left, and I wished I had known it before.

If my father had changed while we were gone, become more broken, Granny Crimson was much the same. "So ye've tangled wi' the whore," she said, eyes feral and glaring. "Ye've sailed the strumpet, the seducer—"

"Granny," I said. "You were wrong, about the sea and the sirens. When James died, it was your voice he heard on the wind, your voice he followed. He died trying to come home to you." But she did not hear me, and perhaps it was as well. If her anger at the sea for killing him had instead become anger at her own voice for luring him to his death, what then? Perhaps she would have grown quieter, but surely she'd have grown no more sane. I wondered then about Robert, who had come to tell her of James' death. Whom had he loved on board; who had made him immune to the sirens?

Gareth and I, having had our fill of salt spray and hardtack, took up farming. I wear skirts in hot weather and trousers in cold, and Gareth loves me no matter what I wear. He tells everyone I saved his life, on the ship, but he saved mine, too. If I'd stayed in our village I'd have died of loneliness, as surely as he'd have done had he been without me in the storm while the sirens sang.

We haven't had any babies, though we've certainly made enough chances for them. But I can play with other people's children, and if we can't grow bairns we can grow crops, and when we tire of that, we can have adventures. Gareth's learning the lute, and I've begun to sing—not like the sirens, no one can sing like that unless they're dead and wailing—but tunefully enough. In a few years, after my father's gone, we might strike out and try our hand as traveling minstrels. The sirens taught us that it doesn't much matter where we are, as long as it's together.

*I've always wondered how it would feel to be the last person stricken by some horrible illness before a cure was developed: the last polio patient before the Salk vaccine, or the family of the last person to die of cancer before (one fervently hopes) we find more effective treatments for that hideous illness. Even if you rejoiced in the discovery for other people, it would have to hurt that it had come too late for you and your loved ones.*

# WEATHER

**K**ERRY AND **F**RANK were taking out the recycling first thing Tuesday morning when Dan Rappaport came driving by in his pickup. He'd called them with the bad news half an hour ago, so he was the last person Frank had expected to see outside the house.

"The pass is closed," Dan said, his breath steaming through the open cab window. Late April, and it was that cold. There'd been a hard frost overnight, even down here in Reno. The daffodils and tulips had just started to bloom, and now they were going to die. Damn freaky weather.

Up higher, it was snow: Truckee and Donner Pass were socked in. Frank could see the weather even from here, even from the front yard of the tiny house he and Kerry had bought the summer she was pregnant with Alison. Their first house, and back then they'd expected to move sometime, but they never had. It was a cozy house, just right for a couple.

They'd need cozy today. Frank could see the clouds blanketing the mountains to the west, 1-80 crossing the Calfifornia border twelve miles away. There might be snow left in those clouds when they got down to the valley, or not. Frank hoped not. He didn't want to have to shovel the driveway. Losing everything bright in the backyard was bad enough.

Kerry put down her side of the recycling bin, forcing Frank to put his down, too. All those empty wine bottles get heavy. "Now, Dan," she said, as if she were scolding one of the dogs for chewing on the couch cushions. "Come on now. It'll be open again in a few hours. It never stays closed very long." And that was true, but it could be open and still be nasty driving, dangerous, even if you weren't in a truck so old it should have been in a museum somewhere. Stretches of I-80 were still two lanes in either direction, twisty-turny, with winds that could blow a car off the road in a storm. Nobody tried to drive over the mountains in bad weather except the long-haul truckers with the really big rigs, and nobody with any sense wanted to jockey with them on a slick road.

Dan had never had much sense. "I don't have a few hours," he said. His hands were clenched on the steering wheel, and he sounded like he'd already been hitting the beer, even though Frank couldn't smell anything: all that old anger rising up in a wave, the way booze makes it do. "Rosie could already be gone. This is it: hours, the doctors say." He'd already said that on the phone, told them how Sandra's sister had only called him this morning, given him hardly any notice at all.

"They know you'll get to talk to her later," Kerry said. "You have all the time in the world. It's wonderful, Dan. You're so lucky." Kerry's voice caught, the way it usually only did late at night when she'd been working on the wine and typing nonsense on her laptop. Time to change the subject.

"At least the ski resorts'll be happy," Frank said, thinking about what a dry winter it had been. Kerry gave him that look that meant, *shut up, you fool*, and he remembered that Dan's ex—the latest one, number four or five—had run off with a ski instructor. That was five years ago. There should be a statute of limitations about how long you had to avoid talking about things. Frank had enough trouble keeping track of his own life, let alone everyone else's too. Kerry was the opposite: couldn't remember what she did last night, not when she'd been sitting up with the wine and the computer, but she never forgot anything that happened to anyone else, especially if it was tragic.

"Dan," she said, "come inside and eat some breakfast with us. We'll listen to the radio, and as soon as the pass opens you can be on your way, all right? Come on. We've got fresh coffee, and I'll make some eggs and bacon. How's that sound?"

"I have to get over there," Dan said, and Kerry reached out and patted his arm through the window. "I could've driven over last night, a few days ago, I should've, I knew it was bad but I didn't know she had so little time left, no one told me—"

"You didn't have a place to stay," Kerry said gently. And he couldn't afford the time off work, but Frank wasn't going to say that. Dan worked in the dump north of town, taking old cars apart and putting them back together, and he only had that job because his boss took pity on him.

"Come on in," Frank said. "No sense starting out until the pass opens. You won't buy yourself any time if you head up now: you'll just have to sit it out somewhere higher. Do it with us over some hot coffee, Dan." If they let him go when he was this upset, he'd head to a 7-Eleven for a sixpack sure enough, or to a bar, which would be even worse. The booze was another good reason for him not to be driving all the way to Sacramento in lousy weather, and also, Frank suspected, why neither his ex-wife number two or any of her people wanted to put him up, even if he was Rosie's father. He didn't need to be drinking now, and he didn't need to be spending his gas money, which God only knew how he'd scrounged up to begin with, with a gallon costing what it did.

Dan looked away, out the windshield, and cleared his throat. "I shouldn't be bothering you. Shouldn't even have driven by here. Fact is, I feel awfully funny—"

"Don't you mind that," Kerry said, a little too quickly. "We're happy for you, Dan, happy for you and Rosie. We couldn't be happier. It's a blessing, so don't you give it another thought. Come have some eggs." Her voice was wobbling again. Frank knew better than to say that he wasn't happy for Dan, that what was happening to Dan was no different at all from what had happened to them. But maybe Dan knew that. Maybe that was why he'd come by the house. He must have known it, or he wouldn't have been so worried about being late.

So Dan followed them inside. He and Kerry sat at the kitchen table while Frank cooked. Usually Kerry cooked, because she was a lot better at it than Frank was, but he could do simple breakfast stuff fine, and Kerry was better at letting people cry at her. She liked to talk about sad stuff. Frank didn't.

Dan poured his heart out while Frank fried up a bunch of eggs and bacon and the radio droned on about the storm. "That fucking asshole Sandra's married to now doesn't want me there at all. I'm not sure Sandra does either, to tell you the truth. That's probably why her sister called; I always got on with her okay. Leah said she wanted me to know, like Sandra and the asshole didn't want me to know. I got the feeling they didn't even know she was calling me. Shit."

"Rosie's your daughter," Kerry said. "You have a right to be there."

Even with his back to the table, Frank could hear Dan gulping coffee. Outside, a few flakes of snow swirled down into the yard. Frank couldn't see the mountains at all. "I know I do," Dan said. "She's out of it now. Don't respond to nobody, that's what Leah said. Said the hospice nurse doesn't know why she's hung on this long. They hang on to wait for people, sometimes. To give them a chance to get there. That's why Leah called me."

"So you can drive over," Kerry said. "Tell her it's all right to go. That's what we had to do with Alison. They tell you to say that. They tell you to tell them it's okay to leave, even when it's breaking your heart, because having them leave is the last thing you want." Her voice had gotten thick. "You're so lucky she'll be translated, Dan."

When she said that, Frank was moving hot bacon from the frying pan to a bunch of paper towels, to drain the grease. But the pan was still hot enough to spit at him, and he got burned. "Dammit!" he said, and heard two chairs scrape. When he turned around, Dan and Kerry were both staring at him. Dan looked worried; Kerry looked mad. "I burned myself," Frank said. "On the grease. That's all. Bacon'll be ready in a minute. Eggs are ready now. We've got more coffee."

They knew there was more coffee. Frank knew he was talking too much, even if there was nothing more to his outburst than burning himself, and Kerry's eyes narrowed a little more, until he could tell she was ready to spit the way the grease had. "What?" he said, hoping they weren't about to have a fight in front of Dan. But when Kerry looked like that, there was no way around it except to plow right through whatever was eating at her.

"It's real, Frank. Translation. You should be happy for Rosie. And for Dan."

"I burned myself on the grease, Kerry. That's all. And Dan doesn't need to listen to us fight about this." Frank looked at Dan. "And no matter how real it is, somebody needing it at Rosie's age is nothing to be happy about." Dan nodded, and Kerry looked away, and Frank turned back to the food, feeling like maybe he'd danced his way around the fight after all. But when he turned back towards the table, a platter of eggs in one hand and a plate of bacon in the other, Kerry had started to cry, which she normally did only really late at night. That was usually Frank's cue to go to bed, but he couldn't do that at eight in the morning.

So he just stood there, holding the food and trying to hold his temper. After Alison died, they'd heard all the numbers and clichés. How many marriages break up after the death of a child. How you have to keep talking to each other to make sure that doesn't happen. How losing a kid is so hard because it violates the order of nature: children are supposed to bury their parents, not the other way around. The counselors at the hospital told Kerry and Frank all of that; most of their friends didn't say anything. The counselors had warned them about that, too, how people avoid the subject.

Which maybe was why Dan had come to them. He knew Kerry wouldn't avoid it, anyway. "You," she said, and she sounded drunk, even though it was only eight in the morning and she hadn't been drunk ten minutes ago. "You. You never. You never want to talk about it."

"I talk about Alison all the time," Frank told her, as gently as he could. He wanted to slam the food down and go into the backyard to cover the daffodils: they'd just come up, but he could see snow starting to come down. He had to stay here, though. Because of Dan. "Come on, Ker. You know I talk about her. Remember yesterday? We were driving to the store and we saw that bright-pink Camaro, and I said, 'Alison would have loved that car.' And you said that yeah, she would have. Remember? It was only yesterday."

"*Translation*. You never want to talk about translation."

Frank's wrists were starting to ache. He put the plates down on the table. "We should eat this stuff before it gets cold." But Kerry's chin was quivering. She wasn't going to let him change the subject. "Ker, we should maybe talk about this when Dan isn't here. Okay?" What in the world was she thinking? She knew damn well how Frank felt, and he knew how she felt, which was exactly why they didn't talk about it. There was no point. It would only upset both of them.

"It's okay," Dan said. "It is. Really. I—I know people feel different ways about it. I don't know how I feel yet. I'll have to wait and see. I won't have an opinion until I've talked to her. Until she's online. Then I can see if it really sounds like her."

"It will," Kerry said. "It will, I go to the translation boards all the time and read about people who've been talking to their dead, and they all say the messages are real, they have to be, because they say things no one else could know. Just yesterday there was a guy who heard from his dad and his dad told him to look in a certain box in the attic, and—"

Ouija boards. People had been talking to imaginary ghosts as long as there were people. Now they did it with computers, was all. Frank wondered if Kerry would still have been so obsessed with translation if it had come around in time for Alison, if she hadn't died six months before the first dead person went online, not that they'd have been able to afford it anyway.

There was nothing to do but tune her out, the way he always did. He turned up the volume on the Weather Channel. "Frank," Kerry said. "You're interrupting."

"Listen," Frank said. It was easing off a little, the radio said. The highway might open again within an hour. And right then he decided. "Eat up, Dan. I'm driving you. My truck's better than yours, and you shouldn't drive when you're upset, especially in tricky weather."

Frank felt rather than saw Kerry shaking her head. "No. It's dangerous up there!" Her voice bubbled with panic. "Even if the road opens again, it's safer to stay down here. Dan, you've got your phone. She'll call you."

"I have to try to see her," Dan said. "I have to. You understand, don't you?"

Kerry shook her head again. "Frank, no. I don't want you driving up there. I can't lose you, too." But she knew him; she could read him. She'd started crying again, but she said, "I'll fix a thermos of coffee."


The snow got thicker as they climbed, and the sparse traffic slowed and then finally stopped a few miles short of the first Truckee exit. Dan, sitting with his hands clenched on his knees, had said quietly, "Hey, thanks," when they got into the truck, and Frank had nodded, and that was all they'd said. The only voice in the truck was the droning National Weather Service guy talking about the storm. It was peaceful, after Kerry's yammering.

Frank had been driving very slowly. He trusted himself and his truck, which had a full tank of gas and new snow tires and could have gotten through just about anything short of an avalanche, but he didn't trust the other idiots on the road. When they had to stop, he unscrewed the thermos of coffee and poured himself a cup. "You want some?"

Dan shook his head. "No thanks." He stared straight ahead, peering through the windshield as if he could see all the way to Sacramento. There was nothing to look at but snow. Normally they would have had a gorgeous view of the mountains all around them and the Truckee to their left, real picture postcard stuff, but not today.

Frank saw somebody bundled in a parka trudging between the lanes, knocking on windows. "This can't be good," he said.

"Damn fool will get killed when things start moving."

But it was a cop. They didn't take chances. Frank rolled down his window, and bitter stinging snow blew into the cab. "Morning, officer."

It was a woman, CHP. "There's a spinout up there. Bad ice. Road's closed again, will be for a while. We're advising everyone to take the shoulder to the next exit and turn around." Sure enough, Frank saw the SUV ahead of them pulling onto the shoulder.

Dan groaned, and Frank shook his head. "Thank you, ma'am, but we have to stay on the road. We wouldn't be out here otherwise."

"All right, then, but I hope you're okay with sitting for a while."

Frank closed the window again and cranked up the heater a little more. "Don't burn up all your gas," Dan said.

"I'll get more when we're moving again."

Dan shook his head. "Snow in April." But the mountains got snow in April every year, at least one big storm. Reno natives still talked about the year there'd been snow on July 4. At altitude, there was no such thing as predictable weather.

Frank shifted in his seat; one ass cheek was already going numb. "You sure you don't want some coffee?"

"Yeah, I'm sure! My nerves are bad enough as it is." Dan sounded angry, and Frank swallowed his own anger and didn't say anything. I'm doing you a favor, dammit. He was tired of getting snapped at because other people couldn't deal with reality. But he was doing himself a favor too, using Dan's situation to get away from Kerry. Maybe he had it coming.

So they sat there, staring out at the snow, and finally Dan said, "I'm sorry. I was short with you. I—"

"Forget it," Frank said. "How about some music?"

"Whatever you want," Dan said, in that tone that meant *I don't really want this but I owe you so I'll put up with it*. Frank reached into the back for the box of CDs—old reliable tech—and riffled through it. The Beatles sang about missing people too much, and the Doors were too weird and depressing, the last thing Dan needed now. Finally Frank picked out Best of the Big Bands. That ought to be innocuous enough.

They were staring out at the swirling snow and listening to the Andrews Sisters singing "The Boogie Woogie Bugle Boy of Company B" when Dan's cellphone rang. Dan groaned, and Frank turned off the music. "It's probably just Leah giving you an update," he said. "Or a telemarketer." But he didn't believe that himself, and he saw Dan's hands shaking as they fumbled with the phone. He heard Dan's hoarse breathing, the hiss of snow on the windshield, the shrilling phone.

And then silence as Dan answered. "Yes? Hello?"

There was a long pause. In the bleak light from the storm, Frank saw Dan's face grow slack and stricken. Frank had never met Rosie, but knowing that she must be dead, he felt the same sucker-punch to the gut he'd felt when Alison died, that moment of numbness when the world stopped.

"Baby?" Dan said. "Rosie? Is that really you?"

No, Frank thought. No, it's not. Goddammit—

"Rosie, are you okay now? I'm so sorry I didn't get there in time. I wanted to say goodbye. I'm so sorry. I tried. We're on the road. We're stuck in snow." He was sobbing now in great heaving gasps.

Frank looked away from him. The voice on the other end would be saying that it was okay, that everything was forgiven. Kerry told him those syrupy stories all the time, the miracles of posthumous reconciliation people had always paid big money for, and now the price tag had gone up. At least Dan wasn't paying for it. Sandra and the assholes were the suckers there.

Dan fell into silence, chin quivering, and then said, "I know. I know I wasn't. I'm sorry." Frank saw him shudder. "I'm here now. I'm here. You can always call me. I love you. I'm sorry you hurt so much at the end. Yes, call your friends now. I'll talk to you soon."

He hung up, fumbling almost as much as he had when he answered the phone, his hands shaking as if he were outside in the cold, not here in the truck with a hot thermos of coffee and the heater blasting. He cleared his throat. "I told her I was sorry I wasn't there. She said, 'Daddy, you've never been there.'" His voice cracked. Frank stared straight ahead, out into the snow. Jesus.

Next to him, he heard Dan unscrewing the thermos, heard the sound of the liquid pouring into the cup. "I deserved that." Dan's voice was quiet, remote. "What she said."

Frank shifted in his seat again. He had a sudden sharp memory of yelling at Alison when she was a little thing, three or four, when she'd been racing around the house and had run into him and her Barbie doll had jammed into his stomach like a bayonet. He'd had a bruise for two weeks, but the memory of her face when he screamed at her had lasted a lot longer. He swallowed. "Do they get over things? Or are they stuck like that forever, mad at whatever they were mad at when they died?" That had to be anybody's idea of hell.

"I don't know." Dan's words were thin, frayed. "I don't know how I can make it up to her now, except by talking to her whenever she wants to talk. I can't go back and get to her seventh birthday party, that time I was out drinking. I can't go back and fight less with Sandra. I just—well, I can tell Rosie how sorry I am about all of that. Hope she knows I mean it."

"Yeah. What do you want to do now, Dan? I'll still drive you to Sacramento, if you need to see—"

"Her dead body? No." Dan shook his head, a slow heavy movement like a bear shaking off the weight of winter. "Not in this stuff. You've been awfully kind. I'll try to get to the funeral, but that won't be for a few days, anyway. The highway ought to be open by then." His voice splintered again. "I just wish I'd gotten to hug her one last time, you know?"

Frank nodded, and eased the truck carefully onto the shoulder, and headed for the exit.

It didn't take long to get back to the house. Frank pulled into the driveway, and they both got out, and Dan said, "I'll be heading home now. You go on in and tell Kerry what happened. I'm not up to it."

"If you need anything—"

"Yeah. I'll let you know. Thanks, Frank." Dan nodded and headed back to his own truck, and Frank went into the house. Kerry, sitting at the kitchen table doing a crossword puzzle, looked up when he came through the door. He saw the relief on her face, saw her exhale. And then she frowned.

"What happened?"

"The highway's still closed. Rosie's dead. She called Dan." He pulled out another chair and sat down, suddenly exhausted. "You're right, Kerry. It's real."

Her eyes filled with tears. She reached for his hand. "I'm glad you know that now."

He did know, but he knew other things, too. He knew that it didn't make any difference, that even if your dead child called you from cyberspace, you still regretted what you hadn't been able to do for her. He wouldn't miss Alison any less if she'd been translated, not even if she'd been one of the syrupy ghosts. Maybe he'd miss her more.

But that wasn't anything he could say to Kerry, who needed whatever comfort she could get. So he stood up and went to the window. There were icicles hanging from the roof. The daffodils and tulips definitely weren't going to make it.

He heard Kerry's chair scraping against the linoleum, felt her come up behind him. "Honey, there will be flowers again next year."

"I know there will."

He stood there, looking out, remembering the day they'd planted the bulbs, mixing the soil with Alison's ashes. She'd loved flowers.

*Like "Hhasalin," this story was years in the writing. I've met any number of people who are adored by their family and friends, but who can't perceive or absorb that love because they're encased in self-loathing. I've often wished there were some straightforward way to pierce that armor, although certainly the procedure would be perilous.*

# HIDEOUS FLOWERPOTS

L ATER, LAUREN WILL realize that the shame started when she was very small, although she's never able to pinpoint the moment when the joy of making things transformed into crushing anxiety about not making them well enough, when delight gave way to disappointment, when disappointment deepened to disgust.

There was no one moment when that happened, but there is a very precise moment when it begins to end. At 10:08 on the morning of Monday, February 9, 2015, a woman wearing jeans and an embroidered jacket—a garment Lauren's merciless eye instantly pegs as a thrift-store purchase—walks hesitantly to Lauren's empty desk. Lauren, who's just poured herself a cup of coffee from the break room and is standing next to a set of minimalist sculptures, swooping wire and optic fiber, waits, wondering what this person wants. She isn't looking at the art, and she's clutching a tote bag with a cartoon cat on it. Lauren feels her lip curling.

The newcomer, craning her head to scan the gallery, fixes on another woman—this one older, wearing a stylish but faded denim dress and Dansko clogs as she contemplates a wall of abstract paintings—and says, "Do you work here?"

"No," says the older woman, her voice musical and bemused. She gestures with her chin to Lauren. "I believe she does, though."

And then, raising her voice to address Lauren directly, "You do, don't you?"

"Why, yes!" Lauren says, using her flutiest tones to disguise her irritation. She doesn't just work here; she owns the place. She makes her way to her desk. "May I help you?" Maybe this stranger just wants to use the bathroom.

The newcomer swallows. "I'm an artist, and I'm hoping to place some of my pieces in galleries."

Lauren bares her teeth, not even caring if it looks like a smile. "How lovely. Have your agent contact me, please."

"Oh no," the woman says with a nervous laugh, "I don't have an agent." She reaches into the bag and pulls out something complicated and chaotic, an assemblage of wood and string. Lauren squints—if her eyes were lasers, the object would vaporize—as the woman shakes the stick, releasing a cascade of twined wool. It looks like very bad macrame. There are rocks tied into it. Also feathers. Lauren feels her face twitching. She's seized with such physical revulsion that she almost can't speak.

But she does. "Many people," she says coldly, "believe that they're artists who aren't."

The woman in front of her pales, opens her mouth, closes it again, and flees. The woman in denim, who has been staring with one eyebrow arched, walks briskly to Lauren's desk.


Six weeks later, seven women wait in a living room. It is a perfectly ordinary room with sofas, chairs, a coffee table, a television, and bookshelves. Magazines, knickknacks, and dishes of candy and nuts dot various tables. Someone's knitting lies on the floor next to the love seat, which is upholstered in pastel flowers.

The women look ordinary, too: you would not be able to pick them out in the supermarket, in the dentist's office, at a PTA meeting. The youngest is in her early thirties, the oldest in her sixties. Most wear no makeup, although some sport nail polish. They wear jeans or casual skirts, interesting jewelry, colorful sweaters and jackets. They have serious, thoughtful faces with laugh lines, sun lines, worry lines. Many of them wear glasses. All of them would call each other beautiful.

Some are married and some are not. Some are widowed, divorced, living with male or female partners. Some have children and some do not. All of them have long, painful, passionate stories about how they came to this house, this room, these other women, and nearly all of them would cry while they told you their stories, and some would apologize for crying, although they know they do not need to apologize, although they know that their fierce need to find a place where they do not need to apologize is part of what brought them to this house, this room, these other women.

One of them is crying now. The others sit quietly; the two women on either side of her pat her shoulder, rub her back, hand her tissues. The woman who is crying gestures to the center of the room and says, "I know it's *necessary*. I know there are times when it's the only thing that works. I just can't stand it."

"No," the woman to her right agrees, "you can't stand it. You couldn't stand it. That's why it's necessary. Marianne—"

"I know," Marianne says, wiping her eyes furiously. "I know all that. I already said so. I wouldn't be here otherwise, now would I?"

Marianne is tall and dark, with long, competent hands and flowing hair graying at the temples. Elena, the woman to her right, is shorter, both rounder and squarer, older and white-haired. We've met her before, wearing Dansko clogs in Lauren's gallery. A third woman speaks now, from across the room. Her name is Penelope. She never allows anyone to call her Penny, because that was what her first husband called her. Her first husband hit her. Her second husband is a good man, a kind and decent man, but it still frightens Penelope how much work she had to do to feel worthy of him, to accept what he offered her. She came here five years ago; she is the newest woman in the living room, except for Lauren, who isn't here yet, who is the reason the others are waiting.

Penelope loves her complicated, demanding grant-writing job, and she loves her serene and accepting new husband, and she loves the other women in this room. She loves them as much as she loves air or water or her own skin, her fine mind and fragile bones. The depth of her love for them is precisely the depth of her hatred for the object in the center of the room, the object Marianne has been protesting so fiercely, the object that saved Penelope's life and may (Marianne will be the first to admit) have saved Marianne's sanity.

To be more precise, there is a collection of objects in the center of the room. One is a massage table, comfortably padded. Attached to it are heavy institutional restraints, designed to be humane, not to cause pain or restrict circulation. On the table is a fleece blindfold of the type sold in travel stores for people who have difficulty sleeping on airplanes. On top of the blindfold is a length of apparently unremarkable cloth measuring tape, frayed and limp and neatly folded, which Elena bought at a garage sale many years ago. Blankets are heaped at the foot of the table, and there is a rubber bit folded inside one of the blankets. Without the bit, the women strapped to that table might bite their tongues.

"We all hate it," Penelope says. "She'll hate it, too. But she agreed. She agreed to try, even though she doesn't think it will work, even though she can't imagine how it *could* work."

"If she could imagine that," says Elena, "it wouldn't be necessary, now would it?"

The other women in the living room, who have been listening quietly to this conversation, nod and grimace.

Marianne sniffles and swipes at her face again. "She's late. Maybe she backed out. Maybe she's not coming. I hope she thought better of it. I hope—"

Elena shakes her head. "Do you really hope that?"

Marianne, sighing, looks down at her hands, clenched now in her lap. No, of course she doesn't, or she wouldn't be here. She closes her eyes, and Elena puts an arm around her and hugs. Both of them know that what Marianne really hates, even more than the table itself, is the fact that sometimes the procedure performed there—which has to be performed all too often, which has had to be performed on almost all of them, but which is performed only as a last resort—does not work.

Lauren sits in a snarl of traffic, a mile away from the living room, and fumes. She should have ridden her bike. She wanted to save her energy for the procedure, which would terrify her except that she does not believe that it can possibly work. She does not believe that it can possibly work, but it terrifies her anyway. She does not believe that it will work and she cannot believe that she is doing this. She is a rational, successful, competent woman. She is sane and strong and healthy. She is not the kind of woman who sits in a circle with other women, weeping. She feels utter contempt for women like that, and she feels utter contempt for herself for feeling contempt for women like that, and she is ready to scream because the cars ahead of her haven't budged for the last fifteen minutes.

Lauren is forty-three. She has a dual doctorate in Art History and Arts Administration, and she runs a very successful gallery, purchased with her inheritance from her parents. She has curated celebrated shows, displayed award-winning work, presided over the beginnings of influential careers. Famous painters and sculptors are indebted to her; aspiring artists speak her name with a combination of awe and terror.

Lauren has money, satisfying work, and influence. She has a busy social life attending parties and events at other galleries. She has many acquaintances, but few friends. The last time she had a lover was five years ago. He was an art critic, cultured and considerate, who left her for a trendy painter he met at Lauren's gallery. He never hit Lauren. No one has ever hit her. (Did you think that being hit was the only way for women to arrive in Elena's living room, in any place like Elena's living room?)

Lauren would have thought so, once. She abhors violence, but she also feels utter contempt for women who allow themselves to be hit, as Penelope did. She feels contempt for any woman who has starved herself, as Sally once did, or cocooned herself in too much food, as Christine did, or spent years in therapy whining about her family of origin, like Marianne. Lauren has no patience with weakness, her own or anyone else's. Her parents taught her this lesson very early. Don't cry; only weak people cry. If you've hurt yourself, get a band-aid and go on. Never whine: nobody wants to listen to it. Learn to stand on your own two feet. Be ambitious. Make your family proud. Whatever's worth doing is worth doing better than anyone else. Lauren admires strong, competent women who have made their way in the world, as she herself has. Most of the women in Elena's living room do not fall into that category.

The only woman in Elena's living room whom Lauren can stand, even a little bit, is Elena herself. Lauren admires women who tell the truth, even when the truth is expensive. She admires women who are serene and perceptive and transparent. She admires women who can be gentle without being weak; she knows this quality when she sees it, although she has never acquired it herself. It arouses a kind of wonder in her—although she can barely admit this to herself, let alone anyone else—because whenever she allows herself to be gentle, she feels weak, and then feels utter self-contempt.

And so, six weeks ago, she found herself stunned when the woman wearing the clogs walked up to her, after the woman with the macrame had left, and looked her in the eye, and asked quietly, "When's the last time you made something?"

"Excuse me?"

"When's the last time you made something? Out of paint or clay or yarn or wood. Out of dirt and seeds, even. Do you garden?" Lauren felt her face becoming as immobile as stone, and the woman in the clogs laughed. "Oh, I'm sorry. I'm being rude. I'm Elena." She stuck out her hand for Lauren to shake. Lauren ignored it.

"Excuse me." Lauren put her coffee down on her desk. Her hands had begun to quiver, a tremor she hoped wasn't visible, and she didn't want to spill hot liquid on the fine wood. "None of this is your business. I display the best work by contemporary artists. The woman who just left—"

"Isn't an artist," Elena said. "You told her that, very clearly. Good for you for not getting her hopes up, I guess. I didn't like her work, either, but look, everybody's an artist, whether other people like their work or not. Being an artist just means that you make things. I'm wondering when you forgot that."

"I never knew it. Excuse me: I have work to do."

"You never knew it? Not ever? Not even when you were a kid? Remember when we were in kindergarten and everybody made stuff and brought it home and our mothers put it up on the fridge? Thanksgiving turkeys made from handprints? Did you make those? Did your mother put them up in the kitchen? Or maybe she framed them and put them on her desk. My grandmother did that."

"Excuse me," Lauren said. She turned and walked away, into the back office. She closed the door and sat there, head pounding, for ten minutes, wishing the office door had a window so she could make sure Elena had left. You're hiding from a New Age flake, she told herself. You own this gallery. You're the boss here. There's valuable work in the gallery, and someone could walk in and steal all of it while you're hiding from the nut job. Maybe that's what this is really about. Maybe it's an elaborate scam.

Get up, she told herself. Go out there. If she's still there, tell her to leave, and if she doesn't, call the police.

She heaved herself upright and opened the office door. Elena was still there, standing primly in front of Lauren's desk with her hands clasped in front of her. When Lauren marched up to her, she waved one of Lauren's business cards and said, "Lauren, I'm sorry I upset you."

"Thank you. You need to leave now."

"I'll leave soon, I promise. But there's something I need to say first." She looked Lauren in the eye again and said, very gently, "You loathe yourself. You're filled with fury and fear and hatred.

They're consuming you from within, like acid. You want to be an artist instead of just displaying other people's art, but you won't let yourself, because you're afraid you won't be good enough at it: not good enough to have your work exhibited, not good enough to be in a gallery like this. You're afraid of being the kind of artist people like you look down on."

Lauren, wearing fashionable linen and one-of-a-kind silver jewelry, had begun to tremble with rage. When Elena concluded her collection of outrageous sentences, Lauren unclenched her jaw and opened her mouth. "You have no right to speak this way to me. I'm calling the police now."

That was what she fully intended to say. What she heard herself saying instead, as the floor swayed beneath her, was, "How do you know that?" Shame engulfed her like a tsunami; she opened her mouth again to deny what she'd just said, but before she could speak, she was shaken by a string of small memories.

Her mother, when she was ten, taking all of her artwork off the fridge and throwing it away. *You're a big girl now. Things like this are for babies.*

Her teacher in a high school drawing class, when she asked for help with the shading on a still life, looking down at her sketchpad and snorting, *You need help with more than that!*

A college Art History classmate rolling his eyes at a student exhibit of crazy quilts, which Lauren loved because they reminded her of her grandmother. *This is art? I can buy nicer blankets at Target.*

"I know because I used to be like you," Elena said. "I used to live in dread of not being good enough, except in my case it had to do with cooking. I was a restaurant critic who never cooked for anyone else, because I might burn the beans or make a slightly runny sauce, because I'd never be good enough at it to be a top chef. Now I throw a dinner party every month. That's why I can see your longing. Don't worry: other people can't see it, at least not from a distance. You're fooling them just fine. Lauren, I can help you."

"I don't need help. Especially from a deranged, impossibly rude stranger!"

That was what she intended to say, although she also wanted to ask, "And are you a *good* cook?" But she didn't say that, either. What she said instead was, "How?"

That was how Lauren found herself, unbelievably, in Elena's living room, in a circle of weeping, whining women, weak women who have banded together in a sodden clump to help each other overcome problems Lauren has never permitted herself to have. She despises them. She despises the outrageous things they say to her. She despises their claims that they love her, that she is their sister, that she is a wonderful person. They cannot know this, because she has not permitted them to know her.

The people she has permitted to know her, even a little bit, have sooner or later all gone away. She is highly intelligent, and she studies art for a living. She recognizes a pattern when she sees one.

Every time she leaves Elena's living room, she vows that she will never return, but each week she has found herself going back, always convinced that she has found some way to show these inane women that what they are doing is ridiculous. Now, stomach knotted with fear of the procedure, she sits fuming in her fashionable BMW and runs again through her list of arguments—or, more properly, her list of variations on three primary arguments—which, somehow, Elena's pathetic friends always find ways to counter.

"I don't need to be here," she'd told them last time. "I'm successful and wealthy and educated. I've never been raped or beaten or abandoned or impoverished or hungry, or infertile when I didn't want to be, or pregnant when I didn't want to be. I've never suffered from an eating disorder or an autoimmune disorder or a mental illness. My only problem is that I can't paint."

"You *can* paint," Elena says. "You won't let yourself."

Lauren ignores her. "Really, I'm ridiculously privileged."

"Yes," said Christine, all the weak women nodding as one. "That's all true. You're very lucky. So why are you so unhappy, and so angry?" And Lauren found herself gaping, unable to answer.

So she'd made the same argument from the other direction. "Have you noticed that everybody here looks alike? We're all white. We're able-bodied. We have decent incomes, even if some of you"— she said this very carefully, so they wouldn't hear the contempt she couldn't keep herself from feeling—"didn't for a long time. Doesn't all this strike you as awfully self-involved? Don't you think there are more important places to put your energy? Why aren't you working to help women in Africa or Afghanistan? Why aren't you working to help women of color in this country who live in the inner cities in dire poverty? Doesn't this little gathering seem like a parody of middle-class white feminism?

"And what about men? Shouldn't there be some men here? Plenty of men feel inadequate, too; my God, look at all those missiles and penis cars! Isn't all this, this suburban bourgeois separatism, isn't it awfully exclusionary?"

The weak women had sighed and nodded, and Sally had said, "Yes, that's all true. All those women and men are important, and of course we want to help them, and some of us do help them, however we can. But that doesn't mean that we aren't important, too."

Elena had said, very gently, "Lauren, remember the woman you insulted in the gallery? *Many people think they're artists who aren't,* you said. You killed a tiny piece of her soul when you said that, just like your mother and your teacher and your classmate killed tiny pieces of yours. Look, there are no laws against soul-murder. Society would look a hell of a lot different if there were. I can't even imagine that; I wish I could. But what you did to that woman in the gallery counts. It was one sentence, a small cut. If you add them all up, it might as well be a machete. And we're the only court for that you'll find."

Lauren bristled. "Artists need criticism!"

"Of course they do, but it has to be constructive. So no, we aren't doing this just for you. We're doing this for all the people you won't hurt any more if this works. Think of it as a public-health project.

Think of it as our guerilla movement against consumerist celebrity culture. Think of it as saving the world, one person at a time."

Aha! Lauren, her face flaming, had pounced, driven into her third argument, her core objection. "You've just made a liar of yourself! You say you love me, but that's just middle-class woo-woo New Age feminist claptrap. You don't love me. You can't; you don't even like me. You've just told me I'm a toxic bitch."

"I don't think that's exactly what I said." Elena's voice was mild. "Even if I did, it wouldn't mean we didn't love you. All of us know about feeling like we're not enough. We know how that creates cruelty, and we know how to fix it. We have a way to do that. It isn't fun, but it's worked for a lot of us."

"No," Lauren said. "I have no interest in making the world safer for bad macrame." She got up and went home. She spent the rest of the evening pinned to her bed by a migraine, and most of the next morning vomiting, and the remainder of the week gripped by anxiety so severe she could hardly move. And finally she decided, all right, let them try this ridiculous thing. It couldn't possibly work. If it didn't work, she'd be free, and she'd never have to go to Elena's hideous living room and talk to those whiny, weepy women again.

Which is why she now sits fuming in her BMW, which hasn't moved for twenty minutes. She rolls down the window and leans out to try to find the source of the obstacle, but the traffic stretches too far in front of her. She looks in her purse for her phone, to call Elena, and realizes that she left it at home. And suddenly she's gripped by fear again, terror that when at last she gets to Elena's house it will be empty, that the whiny, weepy women will all have left, that they—they, the utterly pathetic!—will scorn her as a coward and a breaker of commitments.

Moving as jerkily as someone in a silent movie, she finds herself turning off her car and getting out, locking the door of the BMW and walking away from the traffic jam, squaring her shoulders as she treks the two miles to Elena's house, where she has promised to go through some utterly ridiculous woo-woo New Age piece of self-empowerment feminist claptrap involving (bile rises in Lauren's throat, nausea vying with hysterical laughter) a massage table and, and—a thought so preposterous and horrifying that Lauren can hardly form it at all—a magical measuring tape.


Elena found the measuring tape at a garage sale where she was looking for flowerpots. Elena collects flowerpots; she plants things in them and gives them to her friends when they are sick or lonely or happy or have just moved or have just gotten married or have just gotten divorced or have just had either a wonderful or a terrible day. Elena is famous for her flowerpots, although in fact they're not her flowerpots at all. The entire point is that they're found flowerpots, and each one comes with a story which Elena and her friends can't know but like to invent. Elena calls them midlife flowerpots, and she favors the kind, so often found at garage sales, which have been handmade or hand-decorated, often by children who paint them or plaster them with sequins or stickers or macaroni, usually in preschool craft projects, and then give them to their mothers, who oooh and aaaah over them for a little while before quietly relegating them to the attic or the basement. They inevitably find their way into garage sales.

This was the third sale Elena had been to that morning. At the first, she found a flowerpot covered with bedraggled yarn pom-poms; at the second, she found a squat clay flowerpot in the shape of some amorphous animal with an improbably long neck and improbably short, stubby legs. The animal was covered in crooked Day-Glo stripes and wore an expression of wide-eyed panic, as if horrified at the notion that it had been exiled to a garage sale.

These are exquisite midlife flowerpots, and since Elena is a great believer in the power of the number three, she has high expectations for this third garage sale.

But the only flowerpots she finds are plain, mass-produced clay ones stacked neatly on a table. The cheerful woman running the garage sale, who bustles about managing children and dogs and shoppers, calls over her shoulder to Elena, "Oh, you can *have* those! Are you a gardener? I tried to grow flowers and it didn't work! I have a black thumb!"

Elena smiles and nods her thanks, but she has no intention of taking the flowerpots. These aren't midlife flowerpots; they have had no visible life at all. They are embryonic flowerpots, neonatal flowerpots. Someone else will take them, and maybe they will wind up as craft projects for bored children with strings and beads and glue, or a bored housewife trying to master acrylic paints or découpage. Elena may encounter these flowerpots at some other garage sale, several years from now, but they aren't ready for her yet.

Disappointed but philosophical, she turns away and begins browsing the other items on the tables: a ragtag collection of paperback books smelling of mildew; a plastic globe on which half of North America has peeled away, as if ravaged by some cosmic catastrophe; a pair of squat salt-and-pepper shakers which are supposed to look like mushrooms but bear an uncanny resemblance to penises. Elena chuckles and picks them up, since they'll make a perfect house-warming gift for her friends Chad and Brad, who have just bought a dilapidated Victorian they intend to renovate. The salt-and-pepper shakers are an acceptable consolation for the lack of mature flowerpots.

Elena turns to ask the bustling mother how much her find will cost—she expects to be charged a dollar, but knows she will probably be able to bargain that down to fifty cents, or even a quarter—but as she does so, her eye catches on something else: a folded, slightly frayed fabric tape lying on the table. Frowning, Elena picks it up and discovers that it's a measuring tape, the yellow kind with black markings, so worn that the numbers are hardly visible. This measuring tape has gotten a lot of use. The bustling mother must be a seamstress.

The mistress of the garage sale sees Elena holding the measuring tape and the salt-and-pepper shakers. "Oh, aren't those cute," she says with a huge laugh, gesturing at the shakers. "I love those, but I'm just not comfortable having them on the table with kids around."

"Ah," says Elena, making an effort not to roll her eyes. "Well, I'm going to give them to friends who don't have kids. How much?"

"A dollar," says the matron.

"Fifty cents," says Elena.

"Done. Oh, honey, you don't want that tape." The woman pulls it deftly out of Elena's hand and tosses it into a nearby trash can. "I shouldn't even have put it out here; I don't know what I was thinking. It's broken."

"Broken?" Elena asks. How can a measuring tape be broken?

She expects the matron to explain that the measuring tape is too worn, too old and limp—although this is precisely the state of most items that wind up in garage sales, and recycling such objects is what garage sales are for—but instead, the woman says, "It doesn't work right. Never has. It . . . measures funny."

"Funny how?" Elena asks. This tape has seen a lot of use for something that doesn't work right.

The other woman scratches her nose. "It's a little hard to explain. My daughter picked this up at a garage sale around the block when she wanted to learn to sew—she was only in second grade, you know, but already handy—and, well, she had this teensy little piece of leopard-print cloth that she wanted to use to make an outfit for her Barbie, because she wanted to do Tarzan-Ken and Jane-Barbie, and I told her, 'Darling, it isn't *big* enough.' The fabric was only, what, two inches square. No way could it cover a Barbie. It wouldn't even have made a Barbie bikini. But she went upstairs to her room and brought the tape and the fabric back down and said, 'Look, Mama, now it's big enough,' and I'll be darned if she wasn't holding a much bigger piece of leopard print, and I swear we didn't have any more in the house, because I'd used the original cloth to make a duvet cover for my aunt, and that was the last little piece I had. It was just weird. And then this other time she found a box of doll clothing in the attic, old stuff from when I was a kid, and there was a little cowboy outfit she wanted her Barbie to wear—she was into Calamity-Jane-Barbie at that point—but it was too big because it had been made for a bigger doll, and I said, 'Sweetheart, it's too *big*,' and she went and got that tape and marched right back up to the attic and came down again and the cowboy outfit had shrunk. It was just the right size for the Barbie. I mean, how weird can you get?"

"That sounds," Elena says carefully, "as if it could be, well, very *useful*. I'm surprised your daughter didn't want to keep it." I'm surprised you didn't want to keep it, she thinks.

The matron laughs. "Oh, she stopped sewing pretty soon after that, took up baton-twirling instead and put away all her sewing things. That was years ago. She's in college now. I just found that old tape in a box, but I don't even know why I put it out here. I mean, I wouldn't feel right having someone buy that thing. It's too freaky. Like something out of *Alice in Wonderland*, you know, one pill makes you larger and one pill makes you small. Too much like drugs."

Elena hadn't thought of drugs or *Alice in Wonderland*; she'd thought of other stories: of the Three Bears, for instance, in which one chair was too big and one chair was too small and one chair was just right. "But just think what you could do with it!" she says. "All your clothing would always fit. Furniture would always go where you wanted it to; no more buying a bookcase that's an inch too wide for that empty corner. Maybe you could use it to stretch food for unexpected company." Elena thinks of loaves and fishes, and wonders just how long this tape has been traveling from one garage sale to another. "Just imagine—"

"I don't like to imagine," the woman says. Her voice is light, but her gaze has gone suddenly steely. "I like things the way they are. I like the world to behave the way it's supposed to. There's enough weirdness out there: I don't need to be bringing it into my own house. Do you still want those salt-and-pepper shakers?"

Elena pays her fifty cents, and the woman walks away. Elena lingers to scan the nearest box of mildewed paperbacks: world almanacs, manuals on goldfish care, biographies of famous businessmen. This woman's daughter once played make-believe, as all children do, but Elena has a strong hunch that the mother doesn't read fiction.

On her way back to her car, Elena scoops the magical measuring tape out of the garbage can. She's dizzy, and her heart is pounding as hard as if she's just stolen the Hope Diamond.

Lauren walks into the living room forty minutes late. She's sweaty and breathing hard; her fists are clenched. When she arrives, the other women in the living room beam and exclaim in joy and relief—"Lauren, where were you, we were worried, we were afraid you weren't coming!"—and Elena gives her a big glass of cold water. Lauren stands in the middle of the room (but not too near the massage table), gasping like a fish, clutching the glass. She hates this place. She loathes these women, and at the same time she's relieved almost to tears (tears! Lauren! Lauren who never cries!) by the fact that they're still here, that they waited for her.

"I was stuck in traffic," she says. "There was an accident. Traffic was backed up; I couldn't even see the accident from my car. I couldn't tell what had happened until I walked past it."

"You *walked*?" says Penelope. "Where's your car?"

Lauren feels herself reddening. "I locked it and left it there. I walked away from it." She tries to say this very crisply, as if people abandon BMWs all the time.

"You parked it?" Elena asks.

"Um, well, no. I couldn't park; I was hemmed in. So—"

"You left it in the middle of the street," Elena says, and Lauren nods, trying to look nonchalant, feeling utterly wretched. Elena shakes her head. "Oh, my dear."

Marianne covers her mouth, and Christine squints. Sally says,

"Okay, give me your keys and tell me where the car is. Marianne and I will drive there, and I'll drive your car back here, if it hasn't been towed."

"Oh, it's probably still stuck in the traffic jam," Lauren says, waving her hand airily. She feels as if she's trapped in a particularly bad high school play.

"Keys, please," Sally says, and Lauren gives them to her and tells her where the car is, and Marianne and Sally leave, and Elena steers Lauren to a dropsical overstuffed chair with bright pink daisies all over it.

"Sit down, dear. Catch your breath and drink some more water."

Lauren sits. She drinks. She allows herself to look at the massage table, and feels her toes curling in terror. She thinks that maybe she doesn't need to do this. She thinks that maybe she does believe now that somehow these dreadful women love her, or at least that they think they do, since they waited for her when she was forty minutes late and were visibly happy when she arrived, since two of them have gone to retrieve her ridiculously abandoned car. She finds, to her horror, that she has begun to weep. She has become a weeping woman. She puts her head on her knees and rocks, wishing she were invisible. Someone is rubbing her shoulder. Lauren is more ashamed than she has ever been in her life. "I'm sorry," she says. "I'm horrible." Oh, God. She's whining. She's become a whining woman in Elena's living room. She feels like she's going to die.

"You're not horrible," Elena says vehemently. "You are not horrible." And another hand, or maybe the same one, strokes Lauren's hair, and she finds herself pulling away in unreasoning panic. Now she wants to run. Every atom in her body has been seized with the impulse to flee: away from her shame, away from these women who witnessed it, away from their appalling kindness.

"I have to go," she says. The panic is building: she can hardly form words. She gets up, trembling. "I left something on the stove. I'm expecting a delivery. I have to wash my hair. I—"

"You feel like you're going to die," Elena says. She puts a hand on Lauren's arm. "You're not going to die. You're fine. This is why we have to use the massage table, so people don't run away, so they can't run away. Because everyone wants to." The other women in the room are nodding; some are weeping. "It's all right. Please. We aren't going to hurt you. We aren't even going to touch you, once you're strapped down. We've explained this. We just—need you not to run away. You need not to run away. Because if you run away, you'll keep hurting other people the way you've been hurt, and you'll keep hurting yourself."

"I have to go to the bathroom," Lauren says, in a voice as small as a child's. She flees into Elena's fluffy pink-and-white bathroom and pees and washes her hands and brushes her hair out of her eyes, and when the panic has subsided a little bit, she squares her shoulders and marches back into the living room. She's an adult. She's in control again. She's not going to let a bunch of whiny weeping women (*but Lauren, you were weeping, too, a minute ago*) show her up as a coward. She'll go through their ridiculous ritual, and nothing will happen (*a magical measuring tape! Please!*), and then she'll go home and she'll never, ever have to come here again.

So, swallowing nausea, she resolutely lies down on the massage table (*it's not so bad; just pretend you're at the dentist*) and allows Elena and Christine to strap her down. The straps are padded and comfortable. The table's padded and comfortable. Lauren feels herself relaxing, especially when they put the soft fleece blindfold over her eyes and cover her with a blanket. The rubber bit is a little disconcerting, but never mind. She'll have a nice nap, and nothing will happen.

"We're picking up the tape now," Elena says, and Lauren feels herself grimacing. Elena has told her all about the tape, which can somehow (*ha! ha!*) read the intentions of the people who hold it, and which uses their thoughts to . . . to alter, the way a seamstress alters, whatever it is they're thinking about. This tiny piece of leopard-skin fabric is just the right size for my Barbie. This overly large Calamity-Jane outfit is just the right size for my Barbie, or maybe my Barbie is now the right size for the outfit. The bookcase is the right size for this corner. This carpet will stretch to cover that scuffed spot on the floor.

Lauren is talented and fascinating and good enough, more than good enough, savvy and hardworking, and her many professional accomplishments are still wonderful, and her cruelties toward herself and others are forgiven because she didn't know better then and she's trying to do better now, and the universe *loves* her and always will, and everyone in this room *loves* her—

Elena discovered a long time ago that when the tape is used on people, they can feel the thoughts of whomever is holding it. The women standing in a circle around the table are all holding the tape, and now the front door opens and closes, and two more women are holding the tape, because Sally and Marianne have returned from rescuing Lauren's BMW.

—and of course Lauren has made mistakes but it's all right, everyone makes mistakes, and of course she's not perfect but that's all right, too, because no one is perfect, and if she creates paintings or pottery that aren't gallery-worthy it doesn't matter, because the point is the joy of making them, and ultimately what matters is that Lauren's vibrant and fierce and alive, and the universe *loves* her—

Lauren screams. She can't stand it. She's drowning; she's going to die; she'll be obliterated. She thrashes, bucking against the comfortable padded straps, trying to rock back and forth (but the massage table is bolted to the floor to keep it from being knocked onto its side), desperate to get away, to flee this utterly overwhelming, all-encompassing love, this pitiless compassion. She howls in pain and terror, and the women holding the tape clutch it a little tighter, and keep loving her.

All of them are weeping. They know how frightened she is, because they were that frightened, too. And they know that they have to keep loving her through her fear, and through their own.

This love is a discipline, because it has to be honest. It has to be real. And so each of the women holding the tape focuses very hard on whatever she genuinely loves about Lauren. Sally loves how Lauren always says exactly what she means. Marianne loves the curve of Lauren's cheek, which is like a child's. Elena loves Lauren's passion for her work. Penelope loves Lauren's fierce courage in continuing to come here even when she so clearly hates it—so many other women have walked away—and Christine loves Lauren's laughter, which comes all too rarely but always sounds like a bubbling spring in a desert.

Each of the women thinks doggedly about what she loves about Lauren as Lauren thrashes against the restraints, her face covered in tears and spit and snot. She is a raging animal now, fighting the trap that holds her.

It takes a long time. Lauren is very strong. But at last, her screams faded to a keening whimper, she stops pulling against the restraints, and, shuddering, allows herself to know, to become lost in, the knowledge that the universe loves her, that these pathetic, weak, weeping women love her, that becoming a sane and conscious adult means learning to love herself. She realizes dimly that she is still alive, and she begins to weep: not in fear now, but in helpless, hiccupping gratitude.

Elena, who has learned to recognize each stage of this process, nods at the other women, who let go of the tape. Most of them collapse back onto their chairs and sofas. They are panting, exhausted. Their hands have cramped from clutching the tape. The tape itself is a wrinkled, damp mass, soaked with sweat and tears, and the women numbly stretch it out on the floor to dry. They reach for tissues; they reach for each other.

Elena and Marianne get up and move on rubbery legs toward the spent Lauren. They undo the restraints and remove the bit and blindfold and gently chafe her wrists and ankles; they coax her to sit up, to move to an ottoman where she can stretch out in comfort. They give her a lavender-scented pillow and cover her with two warm fleece blankets, and then Elena, sitting cross-legged on the floor next to the ottoman, sings a lullaby—hoarsely, her voice choked with phlegm and weariness—until Lauren falls asleep.

Lauren wakes up an hour or two later. Every muscle in her body hurts, and although she slept very deeply, she is still exhausted, as if fighting off the effects of anesthesia. It takes her a few moments to remember where she is and what happened, and then she takes a deep, shuddering breath and sits up. The living room is dark; the shades have been drawn, and no lights are on. She sees two women talking quietly on the couch, but they seem a million miles away. She blinks.

"How do you feel?" someone says, and she turns to find Elena still sitting cross-legged on the floor next to the ottoman. "Do you want something to drink? There's a pot of tea in the kitchen."

"Tea, please," Lauren says. Her voice sounds rusty. She longs for warmth and caffeine, for something to clear her head. She remembers that Elena asked another question, and says, "I don't know how I feel. No, I do know how I feel. I feel hungover."

"Yes. That's normal." Elena starts to get up, but Lauren puts out a hand.

"Wait. I need, I don't, I thought I was going to die."

"Yes." Elena's voice is calm. "That's normal, too. But you didn't. No one ever has."

Lauren pulls the blankets around herself more tightly. "Why did I think that? That I was going to die?"

"You have to answer that yourself. Let me go get your tea," Elena says, and Lauren sits and thinks as furiously as she can with her hungover brain while Elena moves about in the kitchen. The two women on the couch (Penelope? Marianne? Lauren can barely make them out in the dimness) are still talking, but they haven't acknowledged Lauren at all, and somehow Lauren knows that this is because they are giving her privacy.

Elena comes back. In one hand she holds a mug of tea; in the other she holds a flowerpot. The flowerpot is made of green plastic decorated with peacock feathers, yellow smiley-face stickers, and calcified gummy worms. Elena hands Lauren the mug and puts the flowerpot on the floor next to the ottoman. Lauren peers at the flowerpot. "What's that for?"

"It's a gift. It's for you. I buy them at garage sales to give to my friends. I suspect that this one was made by a very young child, probably for Mother's Day."

"Ah," Lauren says. She wraps her hands around the mug, clinging to the warmth. "Thank you." She knows that before her adventure with the massage table and the magical measuring tape, she would have found this object hideous beyond description, and she still does, but now she also treasures it as a discarded gift which has been reclaimed and re-honored. She finds, in fact, that she dare not think too much about the hideous flowerpot, or she will begin to weep again. Her metamorphosis into Weeping Woman appears to be complete.

"When you feel strong enough," Elena says, "you should go home and get some rest, start fitting all this into your everyday life."

"Everyday life," Lauren echoes. She feels fear coiling in her stomach, and blinks, tasting bile, and says, "Oh. I think . . . I think I know why I thought I was going to die."

Elena makes a quiet inquiring sound, like a cat. Lauren discovers that she is about to be swamped by tears again. She swallows them sternly, and says around the lump in her throat, "Exhibits. Openings. Hard work. I did all that stuff to prove myself, to make sure other people knew I existed. To make them love me."

Elena offers another encouraging, wordless mew. *Yes? Go on?*

"But now I know—you forced me to know—that I don't have to do any of that. To be loved, I mean." Lauren shakes her head, and swallows some tea to get rid of the taste of battery acid and mothballs. She thinks bleakly how banal she has become. Today Elena's massage table, tomorrow Oprah. Somehow she can't summon the scathing self-hatred she had to work so hard to keep at bay before.

It's probably just because she's so tired. "But losing the way you prove you existed feels like, uh, not existing." And sounds like a bad fortune cookie, she thinks bleakly.

Elena nods, making a vague noise of approval, and Lauren sighs. "So that's it? I'm okay now? I'm on a . . . a what, a guaranteed psychological minimum income, and everything's easy from now on? It's all love and flowerpots?"

"Oh no," Elena says sadly. "No one ever said that." Lauren looks across the room at the two women talking quietly on the couch, and it occurs to her that everyone else who was in the living room today had her own adventures with the massage table and the measuring tape years ago, and yet still returns to Elena's house every week. And she thinks that can't all be gratitude, or even a steely determination to continue making the world safe for bad macrame.

She drags her mind back to before the massage table, to her earliest afternoons with the whiny, weeping women. She remembers how much she despised them, and she remembers why: not simply because they wept so easily and used the word love so much, but because they fretted about getting their work done, about producing successful pasta and PTA minutes and piano recitals. At the time, Lauren thought their projects trivial; now she wonders why, if the women were so secure in the love of the universe, they still fretted about outcomes. Surely the love of the universe, which extends itself to bitterly unhappy women and singularly hideous flowerpots, can also encompass limp pasta and badly played pianos.

And then she realizes, with a chill, why everyday life is about to become newly challenging.

"If I'm not curating exhibits and discovering new artists because I need to be loved," she asks Elena carefully, "what's my motivation? Why should I do that stuff at all? If it's not about being loved—"

"Ah," Elena says. "There, you've got it. That's the rub. No, Lauren, it's no longer about being loved. It's about being loving. It's about, well, reversing the polarity."

"I think that's going to be hard," Lauren says, and knows that
*hard* doesn't even begin to cover it. She doesn't think she's ever felt
for anyone what the universe, what the women in this living room,
feel for her. She realizes now, with stabbing grief, how deficient she
is and has been, how cramped and stunted her soul has become. The
mothball-and-acid taste of fear floods her mouth again; she thinks
that maybe she will die after all. "Elena, I have no idea how to do
that. How to reverse the polarity. I don't even know where to start."

"You'll learn, just like the rest of us," Elena says, and stands up,
and puts the hideous flowerpot very gently on Lauren's lap.

*I spent over ten years as a spiritual-care volunteer—a lay chaplain, essentially—in an emergency room. Those four hours a week literally changed my life, prompting me to switch careers from university teaching to social work. The ER was so fascinating not only because of the stories I was privileged to hear, but also because staff constantly had to juggle the real, pressing requirements of hospital policy against the needs of patients. If you meet healthcare personnel who seem burned out, that conflict is likely much of the reason why.*

# REMOTE PRESENCE

A S USUAL, WIN was late to work. Since he hadn't had time to eat breakfast at home, he arrived at his office—tucked into the old wing of the hospital, now a maze of ancient files and obscure personnel—clutching a styrofoam vat of cafeteria coffee, a donut balanced atop it. He wore jeans and hiking boots and a wrinkled pinstripe dress shirt, from which his ID badge hung crookedly. "Winston Z, MDiv, LCSW, BCC," it read. In the badge photo, he was smiling. That had been a long time ago.

If he'd known that his boss would be waiting for him, he would have ironed the shirt. If he'd known that her boss would be waiting, he would have called in sick.

He'd been looking down at the donut as he approached his office, which meant he had no chance to duck down a stairwell. They'd already seen him. As soon as he looked up, his boss Sara—Director of Social Services—shook her head. Sara's boss Roxanne, one of a seemingly infinite number of Vice Presidents of Regulatory Affairs, narrowed her eyes and glared. Both of them wore elegant suits and understated jewelry. Roxanne's hair, tastefully highlighted and cut in sculptural angles, probably cost more to maintain than Win's car.

Win did his best to smile. "Good morning. How nice that you're here to help me get into my office. Hold these?" He handed his coffee and donut to Roxanne, whose expression didn't change.

Sara cleared her throat. Win unlocked the door to his windowless cubby and ushered them inside. "As you can see, there's only room for my desk and one chair in here. One of us can sit and the other two can perch. Shall we draw straws?" He heard the thin edge of panic in his voice. He was sure they did, too.

They all remained standing, and Roxanne didn't waste any time. She put the coffee and donut on his desk and said, "The JCAHO inspection begins tomorrow."

"I'm aware of that." He doubted that anyone in the building wasn't; they'd all been barraged with memos, briefings, drills, obsessive reorganization of records, and streamlining of databases. Every three years, the Joint Commission on Accreditation of Healthcare Organizations conducted a weeklong on-site accreditation survey of each hospital in the country. The survey was thorough, merciless, and struck apocalyptic terror into hospital administrators.

Roxanne blew out a sharp breath. "We can't have revenants in the building. That's one of the requirements."

"Yes, I know."

"We also can't have nonfunctional equipment in work areas."

"Understood."

"Which means we can't have a ghost wandering the halls in a telepresence unit. That's a valuable piece of hardware—"

"Which wasn't working," he said. Of course Roxanne only cared about the expensive hardware.

"If it wasn't working, it should have been repaired or returned, not possessed! And don't tell me you didn't know about it. For one thing, you've already admitted that you do. And for another, the ghost was delighted to tell me all about nice Reverend Winston who lets her visit patients. What were you thinking?"

Win swallowed. Of course Maisie would talk. She loved being the house ghost—or would have if she'd realized she was dead—and she didn't know she was doing anything wrong.

Because she wasn't. But that wouldn't cut it with Roxanne. "She needs time to transition," he said. Roxanne snorted, her eyebrows rising into her perfect hairline.

"No. She doesn't. She needs to be discharged from that machine and exorcised from the hospital, and it needs to happen by tomorrow at 8 a.m. when the JCAHO team shows up. Are we clear?"

"Yes, ma'am."

Roxanne left. Sara stayed. She cleared her throat again, and Win saw that she'd been biting her nails. "So," he said, "she left you with the dirty work of firing me?"

"Nobody's firing you. Not until after the JCAHO inspection, anyway. They require us to have spiritual care, and you're our chaplain."

JCAHO mandated that each hospital have a chaplain. It didn't specify a patient-to-chaplain ratio. Level One trauma centers, like the one where Win had trained, had to have spiritual-care coverage 24/7. Level One trauma centers had on-call schedules and twenty-four-hour shifts and hordes of sleep-deprived chaplain interns, nearly as overwhelmed and bleary-eyed as their medical counterparts, who comforted the survivors of multi-auto pileups at 4 a.m.

This was a midsized regional medical center that couldn't afford trauma certification. When he first took the job, ten years ago, Win had thought it would be calmer. Now, as much as he'd hated the stress of his intern year, he looked back on those twelve months with the fierce yearning of combat veterans deprived of the camaraderie of the front. "Yes," he said. "I'm the chaplain. For a 400-bed hospital with at least four times that many staff, not to mention families and other visitors. And the occasional ghost. We've talked about this."

"Yes. We have. Everyone who works for me is stretched too thin. I do what I can. You aren't helping anybody by being stupid." Sara glared almost as fiercely as Roxanne had, and Win's knees buckled. He sat down in his desk chair, hard, and reached for the donut.

"Look, can we discuss this after I eat my breakfast?"

Sara sighed and perched on the desk. "No. But we can discuss it while you eat your breakfast. Win, please. Just tell me what you thought you were doing."

He looked away from her, at the place where a window would have been if he'd had one. "I was doing my job. I was providing spiritual care."

Like most events in Win's workday, it started with a beeping pager. This one summoned him to the ER, where a scowling charge nurse looked up from her computer and said, "Oh, good, you're here. We've got a ghost problem."

"Down here? That's unusual." Five years ago, an ICU in Illinois had suffered a poltergeist outbreak. That unhappy spirit had specialized in bursting blood transfusion bags and kinking IV lines, resulting in five lawsuits, three graphic novels, a movie, a spinoff TV series, and the JCAHO mandate that every hospital needed a chaplain certified in social work and exorcisms.

JCAHO had overreacted. There weren't many ghosts of any kind in most hospitals. Hospitals weren't places where patients wanted to linger, either when they were alive or after they died. In the decade Win had worked here, there'd been only two ghosts: a neonate whose ectoplasmic wailing set off every alarm in the NICU, and an old man on the medical-surgical floor who'd died after a routine hernia operation and refused to leave his bed until his estranged son visited.

Being a hospital exorcist was like being a vet or a pediatrician; the families were harder to deal with than the patients. Ghosts needed love the way the living needed food. Love gave them the energy to move on. The souls of the dying either had to be freed by the living who loved them, or welcomed by the loving dead.

The NICU preemie, abandoned at the hospital by an adolescent mother the staff suspected was a sex-trafficking victim, had neither. Navigating a minefield of confidentiality rules, Win finally asked the parents in the hospital's infant-loss support group to help with a releasing ritual. The NICU quieted down, and the parents took comfort in putting their grief to tangible use. Sara had been pleased. "Win-win, Win."

The old man's case ended more bleakly. His son wouldn't come to the hospital until Billing began charging him for the unusable bed. When he finally appeared, Win conducted an exhausting counseling session—using a Ouija board, since he wasn't sensitive enough to hear ghosts directly—which uncovered good reasons for the estrangement. The son finally dredged up a grudgingly good memory of a childhood fishing trip; on the other side, the patient's wife supplied a single positive story about their honeymoon fifty years before. All of that was barely enough to budge the old man's spirit out of the hospital.

If ghosts were rare elsewhere in the hospital, they were especially unusual in the ER. Most patients didn't die down here. If they weren't DOA in the ambulance, ER staff put them on ventilators and sent them up to ICU. Ghosts craved attention, and there was too much background noise in the ER: crying babies, overhead announcements paging doctors or requesting EKGs, static-laden radio reports from ambulances. Today the noise was coming from a screamer, a few doors from the nursing station and probably drunk, bellowing "Get me the fuck out of here!"

"So what's this ghost doing?" Win asked the charge nurse. "How did you find out about it?"

"We've been having trouble with Room 32. Climate-control problems, computer glitches. It's creating traffic issues; we need that space. We thought it was wiring, had a call in to Engineering, but then Anita from Registration saw the ghost, and Vinod from Phlebotomy did, too. I guess they're both sensitives. How can sensitives even work here?"

It was a good question. Empathy drew most people to the hospital, but too much could drive you mad. Win hadn't met many sensitives among doctors and nurses—too much direct patient contact, he guessed—but there were a surprising number elsewhere.

He knew a food-service worker who talked matter-of-factly about calling her daughter and saying, "You need to get that ankle looked at; I think it's more than a sprain," when her daughter hadn't even told her about the injury. When Win asked her how she could stand working in the hospital, she'd laughed. "Oh, honey, there's pain everywhere. At least here people are trying to do something about it."

"I'll need to talk to Anita and Vinod," Win said. "And anyone who took care of the patient, if possible. Do we know who this ghost is? Do we have records?"

"Yep. Her records are all that will show up on the monitor in that room. Maisie Plymouth, died down here of a stroke at age eighty-nine, in the ER at least once a month before that with various vague complaints. I didn't know her well—I'm too new—but lots of other people did." The nurse waved over an EMT. "Hey, Dave, you knew Maisie, right?"

The EMT, who sported complicated tattoos and towered over Win—most male ER personnel struck him as people you wouldn't want to meet in a dark alley, unless you were having a heart attack at the time—grimaced and nodded. "Maisie. Oh, God. Sure I knew her. Begging your pardon, Reverend."

"No apology necessary," Win said. Clearly there was a story here.

Over the next few hours, he ferreted it out. The records showed that Maisie Plymouth had no next-of-kin or healthcare proxy. Her last residence had been one of the shabbier nursing homes in town. He talked to a social worker who confirmed that Maisie was very lonely, but said that efforts to strengthen her support systems hadn't worked. "She wouldn't even come out of her room at the nursing home. Her doc put her on antidepressants, but they didn't help. She needed people."

He talked to Dave, who—between cleaning wounds and splinting fractures—confirmed that Maisie's greatest medical need seemed to be human contact. "She just wanted to talk, you know? She said everybody in the nursing home was too old. They scared her, and the staff was overworked and had no time to sit with her.

As if we do, right? But I'd chat with her when I had a few seconds, and when I had to take care of someone else, she'd grab my hand and start to cry. And then she had the stroke. She was in Room 32 because all the critical-care bays were full, and we were jammed in there with her and a shitload of equipment, and finally there was something wrong that we could treat, except we couldn't, and her left side was paralyzed and she was struggling to talk. I think she was saying, 'I can't move.' Whatever it was, she said it over and over, and we tried to understand her and couldn't, and we tried to help her and couldn't, and she died." Dave shook his head. "Maisie. Oh, God." This time, he didn't apologize.

Win talked to Anita and Vinod, kind and serious young people—university students working their way through school—who reported that Maisie's ghost just sat in the room, smiled and waved, and wanted to talk. What were they studying? Did they like gardening? Did they have cats? Maisie had had a cat, before she went into the nursing home. Maisie missed her cat.

Win thought immediately of the therapy dogs who came to the hospital. "What about dogs? Does she like dogs?"

Anita shook her head. "No. I asked her. She's scared of dogs. One bit her when she was little."

Damn. Cats weren't allowed in the hospital, because too many people were allergic. So much for that easy fix.

Maisie was trapped by too little love. Well, of course she was. She was a ghost. Dave, who clearly cared about her, might be able to help, but he was busy with a heart-attack patient who'd just come in. So Win trudged upstairs, dug his Ouija board out of his desk drawer, and went down to the ER again. If he could get Maisie out of the room, the charge nurse would be happy, and Win and Dave could take their time with the releasing ritual.

There were quicker ways to do it. Win had been taught emergency methods, techniques that had nothing to do with love. Those procedures were what most people thought of when they heard the word "exorcism." They were brutal and violent and terrifying for the ghosts. Win was glad he'd never had to use them. He didn't plan to start now.

As he walked into the ER, he passed a CNA pulling a tele-presence unit—a wheeled flatscreen with a mic, speakers, and webcam—out of a room. Win knew the things saved the hospital money; a lot of neurologists used them to assess ER patients from their own offices, and some psychiatrists did too. They gave Win the creeps. Hospital patients needed people, not robots.

"You have to pull that?" he asked the CNA. "Doesn't it move on its own?"

"If somebody's controlling it, yeah." The CNA pointed to a toggle switch labeled "Wheel Lock" in red letters. "As long as the manual lock's off. But we can't get an internet connection on this one. Gotta send it back."

Well then, they'd just have to have a flesh-and-blood person talk to patients. What a shame. Win continued down the hall to Room 32, where he set up his Ouija board.

It was slow going. Maisie seemed happy he was there; he could feel her as a bubbly benevolence in the room. But she thought the Ouija board was some sort of Scrabble game, and all he got from her was random words.

She'd just spelled out "xi, x on triple letter" when Win remembered the telepresence unit. The computer monitor here was already displaying her records, so she was comfortable with electronics. The unit in the hall was broken. The hospital wouldn't approve of using it to house a ghost, but it would just be for a little while.

No one stopped him as he flipped off the wheel lock and rolled the ungainly thing into Room 32. He turned on the monitor and said, "Maisie? Here's a window for you. If you look through this window, I'll be able to see you. I'd like that."

Nothing happened for a few seconds. Then the screen start-ed to flicker, grainy pixels swirling into a face. Maisie Plymouth, white-haired and plump-cheeked, looked like the Platonic ideal of a grandmother. Her mouth moved, but Win couldn't hear anything.

He turned up the volume, and a soft, tremulous voice said, "Do you have a cat?"

"No," Win said. "I don't. Anita told me you miss your cat."

Maisie smiled. "Anita's a nice girl. And that young fellow, Vinny? The one with the needles?"

"Vinod," Win said. "Your friend Dave is here, too, but he's busy. Maisie, would you like to take a walk now?"

The pixels brightened. "Oh, yes! I haven't been able to do that in a long time! But what's your name?"

"I'm the chaplain. My name's Win, short for Winston. Let's go for that walk, shall we?"

The walk was nearly as slow as the Ouija board had been. Maisie knew all the staff. She greeted everyone. To their credit, they took the apparition on the screen in stride. "Hey, Maisie, how you doing? Nice to see you. How are you feeling now?"

"Oh, I'm fine. I feel so much better!"

"That's wonderful!" came a voice at Win's elbow. He turned to find the charge nurse, whose badge, he now saw, read Karen. "Maisie, I'm so glad you're feeling well. We hope you can leave the hospital soon."

"Oh," Maisie said. Her smile vanished; the pixels darkened. "But where will I go?"

Win and Karen looked at each other. "We're just going to discuss that," Win said. "Maisie, let me talk to this lady for a minute. I'll be right back."

He and Karen walked a few feet away. He had no idea what kind of hearing range Maisie had. "Okay, so she's out of Room 32."

Karen laughed. "Obviously. Nice work."

"So you have the bed back. But I think getting her to leave the machine will be harder. I'd like Dave to help; of everyone here, he seems the fondest of her. Is he still working on that cardiac patient?"

"No. That patient's up in ICU. Dave went home. He just finished a ten-day run of shifts, and now he's off five. Do you want me to call him back in?"

EMTs worked twelve hours at a stretch, and while working in the hospital was probably less stressful than being an ambulance paramedic, Win couldn't imagine where they got the energy. Working ten of those in a row was incomprehensible. "I really hope that won't be necessary. Let me go talk to her a bit more, see if there's anybody she loves who's already gone and might help out. She must have had family at some point. Parents, if nothing else."

"Okay. I'm here until seven. Keep me posted."

Win glanced at his watch. It was almost five: time for him to leave. He was on salary, such as it was. No overtime. But he'd chat with Maisie a bit and come up with some kind of game plan. He didn't think she'd do too much damage overnight.

He turned back to where the telepresence unit had been. It was gone. He realized in a moment of panic that he hadn't turned on the wheel lock.

Then he realized something else. The drunk down the hallway had stopped screaming. Win walked to the room; just outside the door, he heard the drunk say, "Yeah, my mom has a cat."

Win looked inside. Sure enough, there was the telepresence unit. The guy in the bed—an adolescent, acned and scowling—looked up and said, "Is it okay if I keep talking to this lady?"

Win swallowed. "Sure." He walked into the room to face the screen; Maisie was smiling, and he felt her kindness like heat from a tiny sun. No wonder the kid had calmed down.

The kid's face bristled with piercings. His T-shirt read "Eat Shit and Die" in neon letters. "She told me she likes to visit people but can't walk very well."

"Ah," Win said, nodding. That was one way of putting it.

"That's pretty cool, that she can use this gizmo to talk to people. My granny needs one. She's in a wheelchair."

"What's your granny's name?" Maisie asked. "Does she live near you? She's lucky, to have a grandson like you."

Win looked at his watch. "Maisie, when you're done here, I need to talk to you." He looked at the kid. "I hope you feel better."

Then he went back outside and told Karen, "You know, I don't want to bother Dave. I really think I can handle it on my own."

That night, eating dinner in his tiny kitchen, he talked to the bobblehead Jesus who stood between his salt and pepper shakers. He'd had the toy since his first semester in seminary. He'd been pious and certain then; now he was neither. His approach to faith was "Use what works," and all he knew for sure was that love trumped law. Jesus had said that, but so had a lot of other people. All the major traditions said it, when they weren't being hijacked by politicians and other fanatics.

He no longer read his Bible every day, and he could go for months without going to church, but he still liked his bobblehead Jesus. It had brown skin, which made it more historically accurate than most other depictions of Jesus, and its bobbing head conveyed expressions ranging from alarm to resignation to encouragement.

Just now, it seemed bemused, but Win supposed he was, too. "So I took her up to my office and settled her down in front of sixteen hours of training videos for chaplaincy volunteers. She should be safe there. The door's locked, and the telepresence unit doesn't have anything like hands." He licked pork-chop grease off his fingers. "I don't know if this is what you would have done or not, but they won't give me student chaplains because that program costs money and we aren't a trauma center, so it's not mandated. They won't give me volunteers because some candy-striper in Chicago got clobbered by an old guy with a cane and sued, so now any volunteer is a liability issue. Maisie needs to talk to people, and she definitely helped with that kid in the ER. And if it doesn't work out, I'll call Dave and we'll do the releasing ritual, which I guess we'll have to do anyway, at some point."

The bobblehead Jesus, its face painted with a serene smile, jiggled noncommittally. Do the work, Win imagined it saying. Your job's to visit sick people who are frightened and lonely. Love trumps law. It's easier to ask forgiveness than permission.

He slept well that night.

The next morning he woke up earlier than usual, made himself a nice breakfast, and still got to work half an hour early. His office door was open. In front of it sat a mop and bucket.

Housekeeping. Of course they'd come in to clean the office, and they had keys. How could he not have thought of that?

Win told himself to calm down. He knew all the housekeepers. He liked all the housekeepers. Most were Hispanic or Filipina, and almost all were Catholic, and when they weren't cleaning up one mess or another, they paid very close attention to patients. The housekeepers were part of what he'd come to see as his secret army, all the staff who weren't strictly required to take care of patients but did anyway. A housekeeper would pass him in the hall and say, "Father, that poor lady in 722, you should go see her"—they all addressed him as a Catholic priest, even though he was a Methodist minister—or someone from Security would alert him to a distraught family member who might be calmed down by prayer, or someone from Admitting or Engineering would tell him about something they'd seen that he might be able to help with.

Administrators got most of the money at the hospital. Doctors and nurses got all the TV shows. But none of what they did would be possible without everyone else, the vast support structure that kept the place running. Laundry, lab, the medical library: all of them were essential. The hospital was almost as complex an organism as the human bodies it tended.

Approaching his office, he heard voices: his TV saying something about existential crisis, and Maisie saying something about catnip, and a softer voice, Spanish-accented, saying, "Here is my kitty. Can you see her?" He peered inside to find a housekeeper named Luz, one of his favorites, holding her phone up to the flatscreen. "That is Tulip when she was a baby. Here she is now. Look how fat she's gotten!"

"Good morning," Win said, and Luz turned, smiling. Luz was

a sensitive. She wouldn't have needed the telepresence unit. She'd helped calm down the ghost of the old man so Win could talk to him. Too many people, even after they'd died, were scared of chaplains. Tiny women with mops didn't scare anybody, although Win often thought they really ran the hospital.

"Good morning, Father. We've been visiting."

"Yes, I can see that." He reached out to stop the video, which was droning on about the dying process. Did Maisie remember that? "Thank you, Luz." He added her to his list of people who might be able to help release Maisie. But not now. Not yet. No hurry.

"You're welcome," Luz said, and left.

"Maisie, did you enjoy the videos?"

"Oh, yes. But I liked talking to that nice lady more."

"I'm sure you did. Would you like to talk to some more people?"


Sara, leaning on the edge of his desk, bit back a groan. "That was—when?"

"A week ago. Dave should have been back by now, but he got called out of town. A sick aunt, Karen said."

"No, Win. This has nothing to do with Dave, and you know it. If you'd been doing your job, Maisie would be gone by now. You're exploiting her."

Sara's voice was cold, and Win winced. Any hope of keeping his job evaporated. "I think that's a little harsh. She and the patients both benefit—"

"You benefit. Maybe patients do. Maisie doesn't. She needs to go wherever she's going. You're keeping her here."

"I don't think so. She doesn't know—"

"Then it's your job to tell her. Today. Right now. In fact, I'll come with you."

She didn't trust him. He supposed he didn't blame her. He suspected he had Maisie, plus the JCAHO inspection, to thank for the

fact that he wasn't being escorted out of the building by security. They
needed him to fix the problem he'd created. He gulped the remains
of his coffee, now gone cold, and followed Sara out of his office. He
felt jittery and defensive, which he recognized, clinically, as evidence
of guilt. Was he exploiting Maisie? The idea horrified him. Surely he
was giving a lonely soul purpose and company after too long without
both. But Sara was right. Maisie couldn't have chosen freely to visit
patients this way unless she understood where she was, and why.

"Do you know where she is?" Sara, three steps ahead of him,
didn't even turn around to ask.

"Probably ER. That's still her favorite place. That or post-op."

Sara gave the elevator button a vicious jab. "Post-op," she said
to the button. "Wonderful. All we need is somebody coming out
of anesthesia and being terrified—"

"Sara, you haven't met her. She's about as terrifying as the
Beanie Babies in the gift shop."

"That's not the—"

A beeper went off, sudden and shrill. This time, Sara did look at
Win. "Is that yours or mine?"

It was hers. She dialed her cellphone. "This is Sara. You paged
me? Right. Yes. Okay. I'll be right there."

She hung up and glared at Win. "Urgent ethics consult." Win
suppressed the urge to say, *A lot of that going around.* It wasn't funny, even to him. Especially to him. "I have to go. The minute I'm
through there, I'll head down to the ER. I'd better find that telepresence unit vacated."

"Of course," Win said. Saved by the beeper. "I'm going to
take the B elevators. They're faster." They were, but walking to the
other elevator bank would also get him away from Sara.

He took the long way to the ER, through the waiting room,
which was jammed with howling children, flu patients coughing
behind surgical masks, and people vomiting into blue plastic barf
bags. In the ER proper, he was met with a wave of stench, sweet
festering rot. A doctor with two dabs of Vicks Vaporub under her

nostrils hurried by, shaking her head, and said, "You picked the *wrong* time to come through here." He knew the smell: gangrene, messenger of death or amputation, the ancient enemy of soldiers, diabetics, and the homeless.

Trying to breathe shallowly through his mouth, his breakfast threatening to come back up anyway, he made his way to the charge desk. His gut clenched when he saw Karen—someone else who'd lecture him, no doubt—but she only nodded and gave him a sympathetic grimace.

"So the jig's up, eh? Sara just called down here. I'm sorry. We've enjoyed having Maisie around, now that we have the bed back again. She's our ER mascot."

"Thanks. Do you know where she is?"

"Follow your nose. Homeless guy, losing his foot as soon as an OR opens up. Maisie's keeping him company. She's the only one down here who doesn't mind the smell."

"No," Win said, "she wouldn't. Do you have any more Vicks?" The stuff didn't cut the reek entirely, but it helped.

Somebody had cleaned up the homeless patient: gotten him out of whatever he'd been wearing, into the ER shower and a gown. His foot was uncovered. Win couldn't look at it. The telepresence unit stood next to the bed. "We were talking about how sad it is when you can't walk anymore," Maisie said.

Bile burned Win's throat. "I'm sorry this is happening to you," he told the patient.

"Yeah. Trench foot, that's what the doc said. Because, well, you can't take your shoes off on the street, if you have any, because they'll be stolen. I got a blister, and it got worse. So here we are."

"He doesn't know where he'll go," Maisie said. "Afterward. He's scared."

"People at the hospital will help you," said Win. "You'll get rehab and social services."

"That's what they told me, yeah. A group home or something. I don't like those places."

Win looked at Maisie, whose face was furrowed into a frown, and said, "We help people find places to go when they leave here. That's part of what the hospital is for." He took a breath. "No one can stay here forever."

"I want to keep talking to Joe," Maisie said. "Until the surgeons come. We were talking about our favorite places to walk. We both love the river: the people in little boats, and the babies and birds."

Joe said, "I'm scared."

"It's scary," Win said. He felt helpless, which was nothing new. He couldn't imagine losing a limb.

"She's making me less scared. She can stay, right? Until they come? I mean, I know there are all kinds of other people here who need her. But I think surgery will come soon. They're just finishing up another operation, the nurse said."

What would Sara do, if she were here? Win wished he had a video of this conversation to show her: Maisie, being terrifying. He thought of Roxanne. He thought of Karen, saying, "We like having her around." He thought of the bobblehead Jesus.

Love trumped law.

If Sara wanted Maisie out of this room, Sara would have to kick her out herself.

"Maisie, you can stay until surgery comes for Joe, but then I have to talk to you, all right? It's very important. Ask Karen to page me. Will you promise to do that?"

"I promise." She looked frightened now, and the warmth from the monitor faded as if blocked by clouds. "Did I do something wrong?"

"No, you didn't, but please have Karen page me."

He told Karen what was happening. He left the ER, washed his face and hands in the restroom, and then went to the cafeteria. He felt utterly drained, the donut and coffee a lifetime ago. Halfway through a Caesar salad, he got Karen's page.

He took Maisie upstairs to his office, put the "In meeting, do not disturb" sign on his door, and sat down at his desk. Never had he been more conscious of the closeness of the space. He found himself leaning into the monitor, as if to absorb Maisie's glow, and forced himself to back off. He had no right to demand comfort of her. "Maisie, do you know where you are?"

"At the hospital."

"Yes. Do you remember coming here? Can you tell me what happened?"

The face on the screen blurred a moment; when it refocused, it was tracked with tears. "I came here and everything went away. And then I was back, but I was in that little room. The nice young people talked to me. Then you came, and I could leave the little room."

"Yes," Win said. "Tell me about going away."

Maisie was quiet for a very long time. "I was lonely. There was no one else there. Only people very far away. They couldn't see me. I didn't know how to get to where they were."

Win rubbed his eyes. "Who were the other people? Were any of them people you knew? Your parents, maybe, or friends?"

"I don't know. They were too far away. I tried to call, but they couldn't hear me. I like being here. I like talking to people."

"I know you do. Maisie, before you went away, what's the last thing you remember?"

Her face blurred again, pulsed, sharpened. "Tubes? Tubes and needles? They were putting a tube down my throat. Is that right?"

"It's not a test. I'm just trying to help you understand what happened." Chaplains were trained not to use euphemisms. Call things what they are: Alarming rest results. Terminal diagnosis. Death. "Maisie, you died."

"I did?" Her nose wrinkled; she looked for a moment as if she might giggle, and the flow of joy from the monitor strengthened a little. "But I'm not dead now. I'm right here."

Win breathed in, treasuring air that didn't smell like gangrene. "Your spirit is here. Your body died. You're in a machine. It's a screen on wheels that doctors use when they can't see patients in person. I invited you into the machine so you could leave the little room, but now it's time to leave the hospital."

"I don't understand."

"Maisie, some people are coming to inspect the hospital tomorrow. They get upset if spirits are still here who shouldn't be."

Maisie's image wobbled. "Please don't make me leave. I like talking to the people here. The people here like to talk to me."

"Yes, they do."

"Don't make me leave. I was lonely there. Why do I have to go?"

Because of my job, which I've surely already lost. Because of stupid rules. Because it isn't fair. "Because it's time for you to go somewhere else," Win said. "It's time to join those other people. You'll like talking to them, too. You won't be lonely anymore." He had no idea if that was true. He certainly hoped so. "We all have to make that journey, Maisie. This is your time."

"I don't want to. Please don't make me."

"No, I'm not going to make you." He couldn't stand the idea of using the emergency techniques on her. But if he didn't, Sara or Roxanne might call in someone who would. "Other people might, though. It will be much easier if you leave on your own."

The tears were back. "I don't know how."

Win looked at his watch. Two o'clock. Technically, he had three more hours of work. He wondered when he'd get home tonight.

"I can't leave," Maisie said. "I told Joe I'd visit him after his operation."

Joe wouldn't be alert enough for a visit until tomorrow at the earliest. "Someday you'll see him again," Win said, "and I'll visit him. I'll tell him you wanted to say good-bye. Now, Maisie, I want you to remember someone you loved very much. Imagine that person at the end of a long tunnel. Can you do that?"

"There's no one," she said, and then the intercom crackled with a Code Blue in ICU. Someone had stopped breathing, or gone into cardiac arrest. A moment later, a beeper went off: definitely his.

"I have to go," he said. He wasn't grateful for the beeper this time. "Please stay here. Don't talk to anyone. Can you do that?"

"What did I do wrong?"

"Nothing. I did something wrong, not you."

His beeper went off again, shrill and imperious. Maisie said, "Will you come back soon?"

"As soon as I can, I promise."

As soon as he could wasn't very soon. The ICU patient survived, but her husband asked Win to stay during a long discussion with her doctors, who clearly didn't expect her to live much longer. The husband kept turning to Win and asking, "God will produce a miracle if we pray hard enough, won't He?"

God wasn't a vending machine. "We pray for best possible outcomes," Win said, feeling the familiar ache of futility. In this case, the best possible outcome was a quick, merciful death, with viable organs donated to people in desperate need. But the husband wasn't ready for that conversation, and might never be.

Win lied about having another meeting and wished the husband well. He had to get back to Maisie, but he needed a break.

He headed up to the nursery. The place had one of the tightest security protocols in the hospital, but as the chaplain, he got buzzed in right away.

The nurse who'd let him in frowned. "We didn't call you, did we?"

"Nope. I'm here for myself."

He looked at babies for a while. The mewling bundles always made him feel better. They were hope, the future, the best news the hospital offered. Fortified, he headed back to his office. Maisie was still there, although he didn't see how she could have gotten out. The bigger danger was that Sara or Roxanne might have come by and discovered her.

"I have to visit Joe," she said.

"Maisie—"

"I promised. He's lonely."

Win looked at his watch: 4:20. "He may not be able to talk yet."

"I know."

"If I let you see him, will you let me help you leave?"

"I promised."

Which wasn't an answer. He rubbed his eyes. "Okay. We'll look in on him, but then we're coming back here."

Heavily drugged and still unconscious, Joe lay in a thicket of IVs. His roommate, closest to the door, was asleep. Maisie had rolled docilely along next to Win as they went in, but now she shot forward to station herself by Joe's bed. As unsensitive as Win was, he felt the backrush of her joy. "Let me stay until he wakes up. Please?"

"No. He may not wake up until tomorrow. You need to be gone by then." It was as brutal as Win had allowed himself to be with her.

"I'm not ready! I don't know where to go! I told him I'd visit him."

"You're visiting him now."

"He doesn't know that. Please? I'll stay in your office until tomorrow. I'll be good."

He looked at her fine-wrinkled face on the monitor. He wasn't going to get her out of the hospital by tomorrow, not without using force, but he couldn't put back her in his office, either. It was amazing he'd avoided Sara and Roxanne for the entire afternoon, but they were probably dealing with inspection crises in other parts of the hospital. He couldn't be the only brushfire.

He thought furiously for a few seconds. "Okay, Maisie. I have a nice quiet place for you, all right? For overnight."

"Where?"

It was one of the storage closets near his office. Maisie followed him inside; he pushed her against the wall, behind a bunch of brooms. "I'm sorry, but I have to make sure you stay here." He flipped on the wheel lock, and then he turned off her voice. "If anyone comes in, don't let them see you. They might hurt you."

She looked terrified. She started mouthing something. "If you won't leave," he told her, "this is the only option. I'm sorry. Truly I am." Feeling wretched, he turned off the monitor. Even so, he felt her yearning for contact, but he must be imagining it. The machine was off.

He went outside, into sweet fresh air with birds and sunshine and children in the park across the street. He'd left work a few minutes early. He didn't care. He walked through the park, intensely glad that he was still alive and whole, even if he'd very soon be unemployed, and then he headed back to his car to go home.

He couldn't sleep that night. He'd gone over his finances after dinner. He had enough money to last three months, if he was careful. He could put the word out to local clergy, talk to people at other hospitals, maybe call some of the area nonprofits.

He yearned to get out of this game entirely, do something low-wage and physical. Construction. A warehouse job. But those were young men's games, and he was no longer young. If he was lucky, he'd wind up at Home Depot helping people pick paint or carpet or drill bits.

Worrying, he stared into the dark until the sky outside his bedroom window lightened. All hope of sleep gone, he got up to make coffee. His eyes felt coated with sand. This was not the best condition in which to withstand a JCAHO inspection, or anything else the hospital was likely to throw at him.

He sat at his table as the face of the bobblehead Jesus wiggled back and forth, caught in some turbulence Win couldn't feel. He had a brief fantasy of trying to get Maisie out of the telepresence unit and into the plastic statue, but he wouldn't be able to talk to her there. She'd be even unhappier than she was now, and he had to keep her hidden for another week. Dave would be back soon, and Win had Luz, but he couldn't risk a releasing ritual—which took time, and required space—until the inspectors were gone.

Some theologian, required reading in seminary, had said the

essence of Christianity was that if you didn't love, you were dead, and if you did love, the ruling powers would kill you. As a student, Win had found the idea shockingly cynical. Now it seemed like the bleakest realism.

He drained his coffee and stood on legs that felt like styrofoam. Time to shower.

The JCAHO inspectors looked like Secret Service agents. Male or female, they wore white shirts and dark suits and carried clipboards; Win was surprised they didn't sport sunglasses and earpieces. He spotted a set of them, moving purposefully down the long hallway that led to the ER, as he entered the hospital.

Sweating, he ducked into the lab waiting room, where a receptionist yawned and nodded in greeting. The inspectors hadn't seen him. He told himself he was being ridiculous. They didn't know him and weren't looking for him.

Roxanne did and was. He found her waiting outside his office. Her usually flawless hair looked like something had been chewing on it. He wondered where Sara was, and was surprised when Roxanne gave him a faint smile. "You look as tired as I feel."

Win suspected there was a lot of that going around. "Sorry to hear it."

"I'm just here to make sure the situation's been resolved."

Win couldn't bring himself to lie. "She won't be bothering anyone."

"Well, that's evasive."

No flies on Roxanne. Win felt his face tightening. "It's the best answer I can give you."

He expected her to start yelling, to fire him then and there, to whip out her cellphone and call an outside exorcist. Instead, she sagged. "Win, I know you think I'm the enemy. I'm not. If we lose our accreditation, we lose our federal funding, and if we lose our federal funding, the hospital closes, and if the hospital closes, this community loses 400 beds. None of us can let that happen."

"I know." Win's precarious self-regard crumbled a little more. "I've done the best I could. I couldn't bear to do an emergency exorcism. That's a forceful eviction, and she's lonely and in pain. She needs a releasing ritual, but I didn't have the time or manpower."

"You knew about the inspection. You knew you had a deadline."

Win looked away. "I didn't think things would get so complicated."

"You didn't expect to be found out." Roxanne's voice was tired and even. "All right. Where is she now?"

He led her to the storage closet. "I turned everything off. She's behind a bunch of brooms. Do they inspect closets?"

"They inspect everything," Roxanne said, as Win flipped on the light. "Where did you say she was? Behind those brooms?"

Win felt his bones go hollow. "She was behind those brooms, yes."

Roxanne turned to stare at him. "Win—"

"I have no idea how she could have gotten out! I don't even know who might have found her—oh."

"Oh?"

"Luz. One of the housekeepers. Maybe. She cleans this part of the building, and she's a sensitive."

"So she'd have heard the ghost even with the tech disabled." This time, Roxanne did take out her cellphone. "We need to page housekeeper Luz, please. Would you ask her to come to the chaplain's office?"

How often did housekeepers hear themselves paged by name? Luz would be terrified. Win hoped she had nothing to do with this. Surely she needed her job even more than he needed his.

She was waiting for them when they got back to Win's office. When she saw them, she raised her chin. "Are you looking for Maisie?"

"Yes," Win said, relief mixed with fear. "Do you know—"

"That was terrible," Luz said, her words thick with contempt.

"Terrible!" Win had thought no one was scared of tiny ladies with mops. He'd been wrong. "Locking her up like that! She was crying, Father. She kept saying, 'I can't move. I can't move.' How could you?"

Win remembered Dave's anguish. *Her left side was paralyzed and she was struggling to talk. I think she was saying, "I can't move."* His face burned. He had no self-defense to offer. Luz was right.

He deserved to lose his job.

"You let her out?" said Roxanne.

"Of course I let her out! But first I checked to see if Joe in 374 was awake, because that was where she wanted to go. And he was, and I pray to God that poor man's all right."

"Is she still there?" Win said. There was sure to be a JCAHO team in post-op.

"I have no idea. I've had work to do. I still have work to do, keeping everything spotless for your precious inspectors!" She came a few steps closer, her eyes narrowing. "And if they think Maisie is dirt, *fuck* their rules. We've been marked down before and passed reinspection. I've been here longer than either of you. I know."

She straightened her back and swept down the hall, pushing her mop and bucket in front of her. Win looked at Roxanne. "She has a point."

"She might, except that they're extra jumpy about the ghost issue because of the Illinois lawsuits. If there's an investigation, it will be clear we didn't take appropriate steps. Did she say 374?"

"I think so. Why?"

"There was a code in 374 forty minutes ago. You didn't hear it?"

"I wasn't here yet." Win looked at his beeper: nothing. "No one paged me."

"Luz said she hopes he's all right. That must have been what she meant. Okay, let's go."

Win hurried to keep up with her. He hoped Roxanne had misheard the room number. He hoped Luz had simply been wishing someone well after the traumatic loss of a limb. "Would the inspectors observe a code?"

"I hope not. I hope they'd let the code team work instead of putting them under extra pressure. But really, who knows?"

When the elevator doors opened on the third floor, they saw the JCAHO team, a clump of black at the nurse's station. "They're auditing charts," Roxanne said quietly. "Good. That should keep them busy for a while."

Win peered down the hall. He didn't see the hive of people and equipment that always spilled into the hallway during a code. Whatever had happened, it was over. He had to fight not to turn and look at the inspection team as he and Roxanne walked by the nurse's station. It felt like trying to escape the notice of a grizzly bear.

Safely past, Win and Roxanne glanced at each other. They'd become conspirators, but he knew she wasn't really on his side. She'd throw him under the bus as soon as this fiasco was over.

Almost there: 368, 370, 372. Throat tightening, Win walked into 374. The telepresence unit stood next to the window. Maisie frowned down at Joe in the bed, but the other half of the room was empty. The first bed had been replaced with a jumble of EKG tickertape, latex gloves, and tubing. "Ah," said Roxanne. "So the other patient coded. He must be in ICU, and they haven't brought back the bed."

What had Joe made of the code? Had he even been aware of it? Win walked over to look at him. Joe was too still. His monitor showed low BP, irregular heartbeat. A tech at the nursing station would be tracking all that.

Someone else hurried into the room: Luz. Win felt like he'd fallen into one of those movies where only three people live in LA or New York; the hospital staff seemed to have narrowed to him, Luz, and Roxanne. "They didn't clean," Luz said, "the code team, and the inspectors are coming! We have to get this straightened up. You—" She pointed to Roxanne. "—you stand out there and if they come down the hall, do something, talk to them. Give me time to clean! And you, Father, you stay out of my way!"

Gladly. Win circled the bed and fell back against the wall, next to Maisie. She was saying something, pleading. "Joe, where are you going? Please don't go away."

Win's mouth fell open. He closed it again. Joe was dying. Joe was on his way out.

Go, he thought. Take her with you. Please go. He was afraid to speak. He didn't want to distract her.

If Joe coded, the room would be crammed full of medical staff again within a minute. They'd bring Joe back, and Joe would bring Maisie back. Dammit.

Win didn't want Joe to die. Did he?

Luz swept furiously, muttering something in Spanish. Win heard Roxanne, outside the room. "I'm sorry you're here when we're so short on beds, but I'm sure we're not the first hospital you've inspected with that problem."

On the telepresence screen, Maisie's frown had been replaced by a shy smile. "Oh! Yes, I see it now. It looks like a long way." There was a pause, and then, "Do you know how to get there? It's so far. But I'll go with you, if you know."

Win's pulse skipped as the heartbeat on the monitor gyrated into the uncontrolled twitching of v-fib. Alarms began ringing. He heard the Code Blue on the intercom and squeezed himself into a corner, pulling the telepresence unit with him, as people in scrubs hurtled into position around the bed. Luz was gone; in all the frenzy, the JCAHO team surely wouldn't scold anyone for the trash still on the floor. And with luck, they'd stay outside.

The telepresence screen showed the back of Maisie's head, her bird's nest of white hair, dwindling, surrounded by swirling darkness. He still felt her signature cheer, but it was receding. He wondered if the JCAHO team included sensitives. He'd be surprised if it didn't.

A nurse was doing CPR, and the doorway was completely

blocked by medical staff maneuvering equipment, handing IV bags and clipboards and syringes over each other's heads. "Halt CPR," someone said—a doctor—and Win heard "Clear!" and smelled the frying flesh that always followed the shock from the paddles. Joe's ribs would already be broken from the compressions. All the medical personnel Win knew wanted "Do Not Resuscitate" tattooed on their chests.

At least there was no room in here for the JCAHO team. On the monitor, Maisie was still dwindling, but more slowly than Win would have liked.

"Clear!" said the doctor, and there was another burning reek and then, "Hey, he's looking better."

Maisie turned forward again. "Joe, where are you going? Didn't you just say you saw your mother?"

Win cringed, but no one had heard her over the discussion of cardiac rhythms and blood values. He reached out and turned off the sound. Maisie didn't seem to notice. Instead she smiled and turned around again. "Crap," said the doctor. "Lost him. Okay, here we go. Clear!"

Again the reek, but this time, Maisie didn't turn around.

The team kept working. Maisie was still receding, fragmenting into isolated pixels. But Win could feel her, however faintly. And then he became aware that the frantic activity around the bed had stopped.

"Does anyone want to continue?" the doctor said.

Silence and shaking heads. One of the nurses said quietly, "This guy's a train wreck."

"Bad room today," said a tech.

The doctor sighed. "Yeah, okay. Thanks, everybody. Time of death, 10:15 a.m."

Win looked at the telepresence screen. It still showed pulsing pixels. He'd turned off the sound, but he was afraid to turn off the unit completely, afraid that would somehow make Maisie panic and rush back. Afraid she'd feel trapped again, instead of freed.

The code team was leaving and the JCAHO team was coming in, although Win had no idea what they planned to inspect. Joe's charred body? He heard Roxanne, still in the hall. "I'd really like to show you those statistics from last quarter!"

They ignored her. Win took a deep breath, pulled the telepresence unit to face the wall, and stepped out of his corner to face the team. "I'm the chaplain. I'd like to pray over this patient, please. Can you give us a few minutes?"

"Yes, of course, we'll wait outside," said one of the black suits. Roxanne, peering into the room, gave Win an unreadable look.

Win put one hand on the corpse's forehead and offered a heartfelt, if formulaic, prayer for the repose of Joe's soul, speaking more loudly than usual so the group in the hallway would hear him. Moving into the Lord's Prayer, which he could have recited under general anesthesia, he reached out with one hand to tilt the telepresence screen towards him. Swirling stars, still. He could just barely feel Maisie.

He finished the Lord's Prayer. He started offering a blessing, but the inspectors thought he was done. They were trooping back through the door.

Win closed his eyes and shoved the screen wallward again. He had to keep them from looking at it. How? What was the right thing to do here, the loving thing, his final stand in this job?

I'm not the enemy, Roxanne had said, and he supposed JCA-HO wasn't the enemy either. All of them were just trying to keep hospitals open and safe.

Stupid rules were the enemy.

Win squared his shoulders. "I'm the chaplain here. I really would have preferred to pray with this patient when he was still alive, when he might have taken some comfort in it. I didn't get to do that because I'm the only chaplain in this hospital." He paused; they stared at him impassively, but at least they were looking at him and not at the unit facing the wall. "You guys don't mandate anything close to adequate spiritual-care coverage. Patients who aren't in trauma centers still need spiritual care. All our staff—doctors and nurses and techs, even housekeeping—do what they can. But we need more chaplains." He looked at their faces, at Roxanne's face. He saw no reaction. "Will you think about that when you revise your guidelines? Or should I make a formal request? I could go through my professional organization, but you're here now, and I know you appreciate efficiency."

They squinted. He didn't think almighty JCAHO teams were used to hearing complaints about their procedures during inspections. Then one of the inspectors blinked. "What's a remote-presence unit doing here?"

Win wondered if they could see him sweating. "I don't know. It was here when I got here." The inspector walked to the unit and turned it around. Win's stomach lurched, but the screen was completely dark. Win saw nothing. He felt nothing: no benevolence or joy or comfort or desire to comfort, no warmth.

A dizzying rush of certainty gave way to a bolus of tears in his throat. Maisie was gone. The crisis was resolved. He'd probably still lose his job, but the hospital wouldn't get dinged by JCAHO. A burden of guilt he hadn't even realized he was carrying fell away.

Grief replaced it. He hadn't been able to tell Maisie that he was sorry, that he knew how cruel he'd been. He wondered if he would have been able to resist the urge to rationalize, to protest that he'd only been trying to protect her. Would she have understood that?

A fine job he'd done of being loving.

The inspector was still frowning at the telepresence unit. "It's on. Can someone tell me why?"

"We'll certainly find out," Roxanne said. She marched to the bed and rang the call bell. A nurse showed up almost instantly: Welcome to inspection week. Roxanne said crisply, "Can you tell us why there's a telepresence unit here?"

The nurse gave all of them a dazzling smile. "One of the surgeons was called away to another hospital, but he checked on this patient via remote. That was just before the first code, and staff's been too busy to put the unit away. I'll do that now." She turned off the unit and pushed it out the door. Win saw Roxanne exhale.

"Will you think about what I said?" Win was talking as much to Roxanne as to the inspectors. "This patient deserved more spiritual support than we could offer. So do all our other patients, and their families."

"We'll take it under advisement," said one of the suits. What had he expected? There'd be no official response to anything, including Win's employment status, until at least the end of the week.

Time to go. The team members around the door parted for him. Unsure if he was crying for Maisie or Joe or himself, Win wiped his face on his sleeve. The hallway was very quiet. A few feet from the room, Luz leaned against the wall with her mop and pail beside her, and as he passed, she gave him a small, fierce nod. "Don't worry, Father. They need you."

*I have a deep fondness for 12-Step groups; Alcoholics Anonymous saved my mother's life (I have her permission to say so), and some of my happiest childhood memories are of attending open meetings with her, eating cake and cookies and listening to stories that always had happy endings. But very few writers can resist an intriguing coincidence, and when I realized that Alien Abductees shared the same initials, I started wondering what else the two groups might have in common.*

# RECOVERIES

SO HERE'S THE thing. You're scared shitless, because you know something heavy's going down tonight, and you may be the only one who can stop it, but that will be dangerous in ways you can't stand to think about. Your friend Vanessa—your best and oldest friend—is all about patterns, and today's a doozy. It's her twenty-eighth birthday, and also the tenth anniversary of her parents' disappearance, and also her first anniversary of sobriety or anyway of not drinking, and also—not at all coincidentally—the day when, at midnight, her parole will end.

Vanessa plans to drink again no later than thirty seconds after twelve. You can see it in her scowl; you can smell it on her. You know that her AA sponsor, Minta, knows it too. Vanessa hasn't said so, of course, but this isn't Minta's first rodeo with angry alkies, and it's not your first rodeo with Vanessa.

So Minta, who has the kind of money you and Vanessa can only dream about, invites both of you out to dinner, her treat, to celebrate Vanessa's birthday. She chooses a trendy vegan place on the Upper West Side that serves neither alcohol nor anything that Vanessa, who always calls herself the ultimate carnivore because her parents were exactly the opposite, would ever want to eat. You're the vegan; animal products do very bad things to you. If Vanessa had her way, she'd be at a steakhouse tearing into a filet mignon. With scotch.

The restaurant's all glass and chrome and blond wood, and the patrons are self-consciously beautiful: men with neatly trimmed beards and Birkenstocks, women with black pencil skirts and Tevas, everybody wearing that expression that says, *I work out more than you do, and I'm more enlightened, and I have more money.* A side salad costs half your weekly food budget.

"Vanessa, you want to drink right now, don't you?" Minta swirls her fork to capture a clump of sprouts, as if they're spaghetti. She has to shout to be heard, even across the tiny table, and you think this has to be some kind of breach of anonymity, but it's doubtful anyone at the other tables can hear, or would care if they could. They're probably all in twelve-step groups too.

"I always want to drink." Vanessa pokes cautiously at her own dish, a tofu stir-fry with unidentifiable vegetables. You're choking down one of those exorbitant salads, another in an endless series of meals that won't satisfy you, that will give you only enough to keep going. As soon as you've absorbed what you need, you'll lose the rest in the bathroom. "I know I'm supposed to be over it by now."

"Some people never get over it. Dry drunk's better than wet drunk, girl. Take what you can get. Anyway, a year is about when most people fall off the cloud-nine newly sober high."

"Which I never had."

Minta laughs. "Maybe you have something to look forward to, then. Vanessa, you have to admit that this is better than where you were a year ago." You nod vigorously around one of the recalcitrant lettuce leaves.

A year ago, on her twenty-seventh birthday, Vanessa woke up in a jail cell with a bandaged head, the great-grandmother of all hangovers, and no memory of the night before. Her boyfriend was pressing assault charges because she'd thrown dishes at him. The judge gave her a year's probation with mandatory AA meetings. "Flying saucers," Vanessa says now, and you wince. "This is another anniversary, you know."

Minta nods. "I know. But don't use it as an excuse to drink."

You swallow the lump of lettuce, wondering how long it will stay down. "How often have we talked about this?" you ask Vanessa. "It's not like they were there for you even before they left."

Vanessa's nostrils flare, and her gaze goes steely. "I want dessert." Alcohol converts to sugar in the bloodstream; for the past year, sugar has been Vanessa's drug of choice. She's put on seventeen pounds.

"Cake at the meeting." Minta checks her watch. "In half an hour."

Vanessa groans. "No. Please? Let me go home. Kat will keep me safe."

"Meeting. I know Kat is the world's best roommate, but you need to be with your tribe right now. It's not fair to dump all of this on Kat."

You and Vanessa are each other's tribe, or at least the closest either of you has ever found. You gnaw more lettuce. "Is it an open meeting? I'll come, you want."

Vanessa grimaces. "Why would you want to sit through one of those?" You've told her that you love meetings, all those stories of misery and rebirth—stories about how to be human—but Vanessa's always and only bored. "Hell, Kat, why are you here? Why do you even put up with me?"

You wonder that yourself, but you don't feel like feeding Vanessa's endless hunger for sympathy, and you need to lay the groundwork for what you may need to do later. Your backpack, with its secret weapon, hangs on the back of your chair. "I was abandoned too, Van, remember? And I'm not exactly easy to live with either."

After everything fell apart a year ago—Vanessa's boyfriend fleeing in a storm of fury and boxes—you packed up your tiny tenement apartment and moved your books and your ragged collection of all-black clothing into Vanessa's minute condo. You even fork over a chunk of rent when you can, although the place is paid for from the sale of Vanessa's old house; or, more properly, from the sale of the three-acre lot it sits on, which is as desirable now—to beautiful people with BMWs—as it was isolated and inconvenient when you and Vanessa were kids. For all her rage and self-pity and endless self-sabotage, Vanessa has never complained about your own oddities: the green shakes and protein powders crowding the fridge and counters, the fad-diet books piled everywhere next to stacks of anthropology and folklore, the hours you spend puking in the bathroom.

You know Minta thinks you have an eating disorder. She has no idea.

On Vanessa's fourteenth birthday, she tells her parents she won't go to AA meetings with them anymore. She won't know anything about the First Step for another thirteen years: this AA stands for Alien Abductees. Vanessa's parents are notably humor deprived, and this is about as close to a joke as they ever get. Anything normal people consider funny just makes them stare in bafflement. Their weirdness might be taken as evidence that they really have been kidnapped by aliens, but Vanessa thinks they're just jerks. You aren't so sure.

They bought their house, on its bucolic three acres, when Vanessa was seven, right after her father inherited a shitload of money from her grandfather, who'd invested in oil. Vanessa thinks it's the worst thing that ever happened to them. That's when they dragged her out of the suburbs, away from birthday parties and swimming pools and sleepovers. She tells you long, involved stories about these things, about cake and ice cream and balloons, diving boards and giggling in sleeping bags. She's as nostalgic as the elderly people one of your former foster families made you visit in nursing homes.

Vanessa's parents bought the house both because it was cheap and because this area is an epicenter of supernormal activity, a hotbed of chakras and auras, hippies and get-rich-quick gurus. Everybody's got some secret to eternal life; the entire county's awash in crystals, cleansing enemas, and detox diets. Vanessa's back porch looks out over a meadow, facing away from town and any risk of light pollution. Every night, in all weather, her parents go outside to hold hands and stare up at the heavens with the other AAs, nearly as diverse and improbable a group as the one Vanessa will be court-ordered to join as an adult. Either people come to her parents' house or her parents go to someone else's. They don't talk much. They all know each other's stories, because it's the same story: the searing light, the levitation, the anal probes. Denial and government coverups. Massive conspiracies. The only ideological differences revolve around whether the aliens are benevolent or evil, but this bunch believes that the abductions enlightened them, that even the anal probes are healing interventions.

You aren't so sure about that, either.

Vanessa's parents have always made her attend these gatherings, but this morning—after they sang "Happy Birthday" and gave her a hundred bucks, because they never ask her what she wants and don't have a clue what she likes—she told them she's had enough. If aliens come, let them walk upstairs and knock on her bedroom door while she's doing homework. If they can fly across the universe, they can find their way into the house.

She tells you about this while you sit on your log in the woods, where you come to have important conversations. "They didn't yell at me," Vanessa says, and you laugh. Vanessa's biggest complaint about her parents is that they never yell at her.

"Let me guess," you say. "Your mom told you that everything you need to know is already inside you." This is wisdom Vanessa's mother claims to have gotten from the aliens, but it never helps. It just makes Vanessa feel crazier. You know how much she hates her mother's hushed, reverent Abductee Voice, how much she hates not having chores or a curfew, like the kids at school. As far as either of you can tell, Vanessa has no special New Age knowledge of how to talk to boys or solve algebra problems or write English papers. Her parents have delegated their parental responsibilities to the aliens, who don't seem to be coming.

Because the house is so far from the nearest school district, your social life is each other. Getting to school means a forty-five minute bus ride each morning. It's not a school bus—there aren't enough other kids out here for the district to send one—but an ancient county commuter bus. You know Vanessa's ashamed for other kids to meet her parents or see her house, which is full of star charts and posters about ley lines and magical pyramids. You—the girl who lives up the road with her seventh set of foster parents—are Vanessa's only friend out here. She doesn't have to be ashamed of her parents with you, although you know she's ashamed of you at school, where the two of you ignore each other. Vanessa tries to ingratiate herself with the cool kids, which never works because they can smell her desperation. You hang out with the other geeks and nerds, the kids who are as fascinated as you are with those new personal computers none of you can afford. Your crowd talks about Commodores the way the cool kids talk about Corvettes.

You've only recently started going to school again, after years of homeschooling. You don't do well with doctors, which means you don't do well with immunizations. You've gone through six previous foster families because whenever they tried to take you to the doctor, you ran away. The current set is lenient about rules, willing to lie to CPS and the social workers. They've cooked up a deal with a local doctor who forges immunization records, and supplies pain pills to your foster mom, in return for a modest cut of what the state pays to people who take in particularly difficult foster children.

"Difficult?" Vanessa says when you tell her this. "You're a total brainiac and goody-two-shoes. All the teachers love you. Anyway, maybe you should see a real doctor about that eating problem."

"I hate doctors, Van. I'm scared of them."

"That was when you were a baby. How can you even remember it? And they won't give you shots if they think you've already had them."

"I'm good," you say.

You and Vanessa are both fourteen, but you look older—or, rather, look so odd that no one's quite sure how old you are—and the latest foster dad just scored a fake driver's license for you "because in the old days, kids were driving when they were twelve" and he doesn't want to bother taking you places. The evening of Vanessa's birthday, while her parents and the other AAs stare up into cloud cover, the two of you drive the twenty miles to the mall and split the birthday money. You buy a book of fairy tales and a pricy computer programming manual at Barnes & Noble. Vanessa, in her endless quest to get a rise out of her parents, buys makeup and sexy clothing and pigs out on burgers and fries and ice cream at the food court while you nibble a fruit salad. You get about halfway through it before you have to rush to the restroom.

The two of you stay at the mall, window browsing and people watching, until it closes at ten. On the way home, Vanessa asks you to stop at a 7-Eleven and buy some beer. "We still have money, and I've never had beer. Do you think my parents will notice if I come home drunk?"

"No." This plan strikes you as fifty-eight kinds of terrible. "Don't get drunk just to be rebellious, Van. That's stupid. You already bought all that slutwear."

Vanessa pouts. "That feels like playing dress-up. Beer's real. And you've got the ID. I'll drink while you drive, so we'll be safe."

"You're not supposed to drink in the car. Open-bottle laws." You swallow panic. You don't think the police have any records from all those foster families, but who knows? "Vanessa, I really can't afford trouble with cops."

Vanessa scowls. "Do you have to take the fun out of everything?"

"I drove you out here, didn't I?"

"Come on, Kat. It's my birthday. All the kids at school drink."

"Not the ones I know."

"The ones you know are freaks." She's angry enough to be mean now. Then her voice softens into wheedling, and she says, "It's, like, an initiation rite. You're into those, right? Like all that folklore crap you read?"

She's not going to let you talk her out of it. "Okay," you say. If she can tell how miserable you are, she doesn't care.

You go inside, and Vanessa picks out a sixpack. "You could buy a single bottle," you say, and she pouts again.

"It's my *birthday*."

The guy behind the counter squints hard, but shrugs at your fake ID and lets you pay. Back out in the car, you check the road for cops, and then—coast clear—Vanessa uses her house key as a bottle opener and sips, narrating like this is some kind of nature documentary. "It's fizzy. Kinda yeasty. It tastes okay, but I'm not feeling anything." She finishes the first beer, too quickly, and reaches for another.

Halfway through the second bottle, she lets out a whoop. "Peace! Joy! All's well with the world! Kat, you gotta try this." Giggling, she props the bottle between her legs and reaches to hug you. "Best. Birthday. Ever."

Your hands are clenched on the wheel, and your stomach's threatening to empty again even though there's nothing left in it. "Vanessa, don't do that when I'm driving!"

Vanessa frowns. You never snap at her. But she's drunk and magnanimous. "Aw, poor Kat. You feel left out. You gotta have some beer too! Three of these are for you."

"I'm driving." You stare straight ahead, your entire body aching with anger and hunger and loneliness.

"Well, when we get home. We'll sit on the log."

She sips her third beer all the way home. You see her eyeing the other three and know she's trying to save some for you. At her parents' house, you turn off the headlights and cut the engine to coast to a gentle stop—although Vanessa's parents probably aren't here, and wouldn't pay attention if they were—and then you grab the flashlight from the glove box, and Vanessa grabs the remaining beer, and you make your way into the woods. Vanessa has to lean on you even though it's a clear path; you walk it a lot, and so do deer and stray dogs and the raccoons who raid the trash.

The log's in a glade, eerie in moonlight. You hear owls, wind rustling in the trees. Vanessa thumps down on the log, and you fold yourself cross-legged on the damp ground. Vanessa laughs. "Man, you look skinny. You look like a stick insect with huge eyes. Why do you look so sad, Kat?"

"I'm just tired. Okay. Give me that."

Vanessa opens the fourth bottle for herself. "You'll only need two, because you're so skinny." You doubt you'll get that far. She gives you the fifth bottle and sighs at the sixth, alone in its cardboard case. "Gotta get more."

"I don't think that's a good idea." You carefully remove the top, sniff at the opening, and take the tiniest of sips. "Ugh."

Vanessa laughs. "Drink more! Drink enough for it to work!"

Anger surges in you. You're tired of being bossed around, tired of being used, tired of being careful. You make a face, hold your nose, and chug down the entire bottle. Vanessa blinks. "Damn! How'd you do that? I want to be able to do that."

And then she stares at you. You watch your hand, resting on your knee, turn green and mottled, feel your limbs assuming strange, painful shapes. Your vision has changed, which means your eyes probably have too. You're acutely aware of every small rustle in the woods, every heartbeat, the warm smell of Vanessa's flesh a few feet away. Hunger grips your entire body. It's hard to think clearly.

But you do. You force yourself to. You shove your green, serrated fingers down your throat and turn to vomit the beer into the darkness of the woods. Your hands resume their old shape; your vision's normal again. You shove the bottle back at Vanessa, although it's almost empty, and tell her, "I don't want any more."


The AA meeting's a blur, permeated with the smell of coffee combined with church-basement mildew that Vanessa always says should be packaged as AA Air Freshener. Hang one in your car and voila, instant meeting. The first speaker's a dreary drunkalogue, listing every bar he ever went to. Vanessa, who's heaped a paper plate with cookies and cake—sheet cake slathered with frosting, so sweet that you wonder how even she can eat the stuff—keeps her head bent over her food. The second speaker's a sarcastic marketing exec who wears chunky silver jewelry and curses every other word. She gets the room roaring; you laugh so hard your face hurts. You whisper to Vanessa, "This is better than cable. I should come to meetings with you more often."

Vanessa scowls. You wonder if she's heard a word the woman's said. "This is fucking field research for you, isn't it?"

You took courses from the Electronic University Network, paid for with your programming and graphic-arts skills. You couldn't go to a real college, because you'd have needed immunizations there, too, and the crooked doctor was in prison by then. You took every class you could afford in computer science and anthropology. You aced all of them, and Vanessa—who never went to college at all, who may have gotten through high school only because she was having a very suspect relationship with her math teacher—resents the hell out of it.

But she's right. This is field research.

The advertising exec is telling a hilarious story about one of her blackouts. That's one of the AA staples, like vomiting and DTs. All alkies worth their salt have blackouts, periods of amnesia from which they emerge to discover that they've done horrible things. Vanessa's had a ton herself. Identify, don't compare, people always say at meetings, and on this point, you know that Vanessa's happy to comply. She hates blackouts. She hates not knowing what she's done.

The morning after Vanessa's fourteenth birthday, you wake up with a pounding headache and stabbing dread. You changed; you barely kept yourself from doing more. Vanessa will never talk to you again. She must hate you now.

You stagger into the bathroom, where you empty the contents of your stomach. The foster parents have left for work. You're alone. You think about running away, but you've done that so often that the idea exhausts you. You think about telling Vanessa that she was just seeing things, but that's dishonest and would make you a terrible friend. You think about not going to school, but that's delaying the inevitable. You have to have the conversation sometime.

You spend so much time dithering that you almost miss the bus. You usually get to the bus stop long before Vanessa does, but today you race to hop on just as the bus is leaving. You grab a seat near the front, only to hear Vanessa calling you. "Hey! Hey, Kat, I saved a seat for you."

You hesitate, and she calls again. "Kat?" She's crying. Vanessa hates crying. She hardly ever cries. In a flash you're beside her, thinking that she must be terrified of you now, that she must be very brave to have called you over. You feel a surge of affection for her. Courage isn't Vanessa's strong suit.

She sobs and hiccups, and you wonder if she's still drunk. "Kat, what did I do? I did something awful, right? Last night? And that's why you tried to ignore me?"

You blink. You hand her a tissue. What *she* did last night isn't the issue. You can't look at her. "You got drunk, Vanessa," and then, "You scared me." You think that if she remembers what happened, maybe she'll blame herself for scaring you, and as soon as you think this, you feel abject shame. Yes, she bullied you into drinking, but you're the one who pulled the idiotic stunt of chugging the entire bottle.

She sniffles. "Look, Kat, you have to tell me what happened. I don't, I can't, I don't remember everything. I mean, I remember sitting in the car with the beer, drinking it. And I remember starting to walk into the woods. That's all."

You draw in a long breath and look at Vanessa, finally. "Really? That's all you remember?"

It's Vanessa's turn to look away. "Yeah. That's all. So what did I do?"

"Nothing," you say, dizzy with relief. "Nothing bad. You just got drunk. Are you okay? Are you sick? You don't look so good." But you're the one who's shaking. The idiotic stunt could have— should have—broken everything wide open, but it didn't. You got away with it. You vow to yourself, then and there, that you'll never do anything like that again.

At this meeting, as at every one you've ever been to, people talk about their blackouts with shame and terror: learning third-hand about humiliating scenes at parties, about insults shouted at soulmates and damage done to children who'll be paying for a lifetime of therapy to get over it. Or not learning, never learning. Losing that time forever.

Most of Vanessa's own blackouts appear to have been sordid messes filled with shattered dishes and anonymous sexual encounters. You know she picked up chlamydia and herpes during those adventures, and she told you once, with a sigh, that she can't say for sure there was nothing anal.

But you also know she wants to forget most of the previous year, and you can tell, from how she's staring at the clock, that she'd love to lose the three hours until her parole's over. There's a bar near the apartment. It's open until two, which will leave plenty of time for disaster if she gets there at midnight.

A group from the meeting always goes out for coffee afterwards. Minta pressures Vanessa to come tonight, and you tell them you're happy to tag along. "More fieldwork," you tease Vanessa, but you and Minta both know it's more than that. After all of you leave the diner, handling Van will be up to you. Minta, who's a fierce and confrontational sponsor, is also a firm believer in the First Step. Ultimately, she's powerless over Vanessa.

She's told you that you are, too. She's told you that you and

Vanessa are badly codependent, that you need to get to meetings of your own. The meetings you really need, you can't find.

A few weeks after the beer incident, your health teacher begins a substance abuse unit. This is one of the few classes you share with Vanessa, because most of yours are Honors and none of hers are. "We're going to talk about drinking today," the teacher says, and everybody snickers. School drug education is completely lame, a set of horror stories in which people who party always wind up dying with their heads in toilets.

Vanessa, sitting across the room and trying to impress a football player, isn't paying attention. You're the only one who is. The teacher puts a list of alcoholism red flags up on the board. Family history. Craving. Drinking until you're sick. Going to places where you know there will be booze. Blackouts.

Blackouts. Despite the unspoken rule of ignoring each other in this building, you glance at Vanessa. She's looking back at you, wide-eyed. Maybe she's recognized herself in this list. Maybe she'll avoid beer from now on.

After class, Vanessa catches your eye again and ducks into a stairwell. You follow her. "Blackouts!" she says, and, "Alcoholism's genetic! Kat, my parents? And the AAs? They were all just drunk! That's why they have those memories of seeing weird shit and losing time. Aliens are their version of doing embarrassing things at parties! There aren't any aliens at all!"

She's desperate for any connection to her parents; you know that. But even for Vanessa, this is nuts. You shake your head. "Um, Van, have you ever seen your parents drink? Or any of those people? You're the one who drinks." And has blackouts, although that's so obvious you don't want to point it out.

"Of course I haven't seen them drink, but that's the point! That's why they don't! What I thought was my parents' joke about AA wasn't really a joke at all! The other AA is where they should be, but it's too embarrassing, so instead they invented the story about aliens and started their own group to stargaze, instead of doing whatever drunks do at those meetings."

Vanessa clings to this theory for years, while you bury yourself in academic tomes about folklore. You develop your own ideas. You believe that changeling stories, all those tales about goblins and faeries left in cradles, about human babies spirited away and returned only years later if at all, are the earlier versions of alien abduction stories. Lost time. Elf Hill. Exotic beings with overly large eyes and pointed ears. Being returned to the wrong place with your clothing on backwards. People have been telling stories like that as long as there have been people.

You're looking for your parents, too.

Vanessa scoffs at your theory as much as you scoff at hers. "Do changeling stories have anal probes?" She asks you this one summer evening when you're both seventeen, sitting on the log in the forest while you watch Vanessa down a sixpack. You haven't repeated your own mistake, but you come out here with her to keep an eye on her.

"No anal probes. Sex, though. Tam Lin was basically a sex slave to the Queene of Faerie."

"I don't believe in UFOs," Vanessa says. Neither do you. You don't believe aliens are coming back; you want to find aliens who are already here, passing. You gaze into the darkness between the trees, listening to the tiny night rustlings, yearning for kin.

Vanessa shakes her head. "Seriously, Kat? You don't think that if there were green pointy-eared kids around, somebody would have noticed? Those stories are just how people explained kids who were born sick or disabled."

"They'd have to be able to blend in," you say quietly.

"Then how would you find them? Nah, it's all nonsense. Everybody who went through that shit, with elves or grays or whatever, was just high. My parents must have been lushes in their youth and turned their blackouts into fairy tales; if you can't remember, that means you were sucked up into a flying saucer and anal-probed. If they'd been born earlier, they would have been sucked into fairy-land, and they'd be spending their time peering at fake photos and tromping around in the woods instead of gazing up at the sky. Either way, they won't find anything."

She's slurring by now, badly. Alcohol's a disinhibitor. Drinking usually makes Vanessa smarter, or anyway more willing to say smart things, until she falls off the cliff of incoherence. You'd tell her that the mere existence of the stories is its own evidence, but she becomes abruptly and violently ill, and when you get her back to the house she falls asleep, and the next morning she doesn't remember the conversation.


The after-meeting gang crowds into a diner booth and orders milkshakes and burgers and coffee. You buy Vanessa an ice cream sundae for her birthday, and she thanks you, but she barely touches it. She checks her watch every two seconds. People chat about their holiday plans, the nightmare of dealing with family, the stress of the first sober Christmas. You dig in your backpack for a legal pad and pretend to research a folklore paper. They're all fascinated, flattered that you're writing an ethnography of twelve-step culture. You tell them that you're focusing on how they used drinking to fit in when they drank, and how they use the program to fit in now. You're looking at definitions of belonging. What did that look like in childhood, and during the drinking years, and in sobriety?

Since AAs love nothing better than to talk about themselves, you get more material than you could possibly use even if this weren't just a ruse to keep Vanessa in the diner. You scribble furious faux-notes as Vanessa takes slow, deliberate bites of her sundae and fidgets with her watch. She only snaps to attention, frowning, when one of the AAs—a thin brunette who teaches yoga—says, "My parents left me when I was a kid, and after that I never felt like I fit in anywhere." There's a collective sigh. Everyone, including you, can identify with that one.

*

On Vanessa's eighteenth birthday, you buy her dinner at a barbeque place in the city. She chows down on ribs; you, as usual, choke down a salad. You're living in a tiny, decrepit loft, working at a graphic-design firm and taking online classes. Vanessa's doing temp work and brooding about her latest boyfriend. You're tired of listening to her obsess about him—he's as much of a loser as all the others, and why can't she see it?—so you try to distract her with stories about the jerks in your office and the tribal initiation rites you're studying in your anthropology class. You have a complicated theory about how photocopying at work serves the same function as vision quests in certain Native American tribes, but Vanessa, who's on her fourth beer, isn't even pretending to follow this.

After dinner, you take her to the Italian bakery across the street for dessert, and then you go home, claiming a work deadline instead of admitting that you can no longer stand to be around Van when she's drunk. You know she plans to hook up with the boyfriend, a bouncer at an East Village club who *only* likes her when she's drunk.

She calls you the following afternoon, static crackling on the line from upstate, and tells you everything that's happened. Over the years, she'll retell the story obsessively, repeating it until it's hardened into a translucent amulet, her identity in amber.

After you left, she called Tom but got only his answering machine. "I'm coming over," she told him, and on the way she bought a quart of gin because she intended to get well and truly hammered in the company of somebody who'd drink with her. But he'd already started drinking with somebody else; when he answered the door, Vanessa saw the half-naked blonde behind him, and she cursed him and ran out of there.

And wound up on the street, on her birthday, with nothing to show for it but a bottle of gin and the aftertaste of cannoli, and it was dark and raining and she thought about finding a bar, but she was out of money and too tired for the buy-me-a-drink-for-sex hustle.

There was nowhere to go but home, so she did: dug out the return bus ticket she hadn't planned to use until the next morning and headed ten blocks up, to the huge glass and steel bus station with its kiosks and filthy restrooms and bays full of humming behemoth vehicles, and got on one of them for the two-hour ride upstate. Her parents and the other AAs would be stargazing, even in the rain, but she was pretty sure they'd have left her a card and some cash, the standard birthday gift. She'd go up to her room. She'd listen to music and drink gin. Tomorrow she'd wake up with an awful hangover, but she'd have the birthday money. She'd figure something out. She'd find a new guy.

She went home. Nobody was there. They were undoubtedly stargazing at somebody else's house. A card and a thick envelope sat on the kitchen counter—sometimes her parents gave her, like, a few hundred dollar bills—but she didn't even touch them. She went upstairs and drank until she passed out.

The next morning, her parents still weren't home, which was weird. Wearing her old plaid robe, Vanessa made herself coffee and, yawning, opened the card, a photo of some galaxy or other. Inside she saw her mother's handwriting. "Goodbye sweet girl you are of age now and we are going home. Love." They'd both signed it.

Goodbye? Vanessa squinted at it, blinked, and then reached for the fat envelope. The bills weren't singles; they were hundreds. Her parents, she'd later learn, had left her the entire contents of their bank account.

She made phone calls. She interrogated the other AAs. Where were her parents? When were they coming back? She was met with gasps of awe. They'd finally done it! They'd finally ascended! They'd been talking about it, saying they thought it was close! "Oh honey," said one woman, "they aren't coming back. They've been picked up. They've been recovered. You should be excited for them."

At which point, hysterical and ranting, she called you. "This can't be happening!" You were glad that she was upstate, that she wasn't in the same room, because you were nearly as upset as she was, and you couldn't tell her why.

"You're right," you said, your throat tight. "It can't be happening. It's nuts. You just have to look for them, Van."

A few months later, the cops gave up. Vanessa hired private investigators, who also gave up. Her parents had never been smart enough to pull off a WITSEC-level disappearance.

Vanessa already felt abandoned by her parents, and when it was clear that they weren't coming back, she set about filling the black hole of her life with booze. You, meanwhile, were going through your own agony, which you couldn't share with Vanessa. You couldn't share it with anyone at all.

The aliens had picked up Vanessa's parents and left you here, again. Alone.

The coffee-shop group finally disbands. It's 11:00. Minta suggests a late movie, but Vanessa pleads headache and says she just wants to go home. "Don't worry," you tell Minta. "I'm not going to let her do anything dumb."

You mean it.

Until that horrible night ten years ago, you hung out with Vanessa not just because she was the only other kid in your neighborhood, but because she, or rather her parents, might have helped you find your people. You have no idea why, aside from sheer habit, you've put up with her since then. If you ever went to a therapist—which you'll never do—that would be your presenting issue.

You and Vanessa take the subway downtown. The closer you get to your stop, the twitchier she gets.

"Van," you say, over the rumble of the number 1 train, "You're not going to do anything dumb. Right? You're not going to throw away this entire year?"

She turns and glares at you. "This year? This year of feeling shitty and just wanting to drink and block everything out? This year of feeling like I don't fit in anywhere, like you and Minta are watching everything I do and just waiting for me to screw up?"

She goes on like this for another minute or so. She's on such a roll that you wonder if she's already managed to sneak a drink. But you don't smell it, and you can always smell it.

You wait for her to wind down, and then you say, "Van. Come on. You want to block everything out? You hate blackouts. You know you do."

"Yeah, well. Now I want them. The less I have to remember, the less it hurts."

"You hated being in jail. You hated being on probation."

"That won't happen again."

"How do you know that? You can't know that."

Vanessa waves her hand dismissively; she can't know, but she doesn't care. She just wants to feel the booze sliding down her throat. She's ruled by her craving. You know the feeling. There's nothing you can say, and the train's at your stop anyway. The two of you get out and trudge up the stairs, Vanessa a few feet ahead of you because she's so much taller. You glance at your watch: 11:30.

In the apartment, you ease off your backpack as Vanessa hurls herself into her bedroom and slams the door. You hear her rattling through her closet, hear bureau drawers opening and closing. When she comes out again, she's wearing a slinky red dress and high heels.

"It's 11:45," she says. "It will take me five minutes to walk to the bar. So I guess I have to listen to you lecture me for another ten minutes, right?"

"Right," you say, and hold up the can of beer you've been lugging around in your backpack all day. Vanessa blinks, clearly startled. She forces a smile. You're her surrogate parent now; she's relying on you for the disapproval she could never get from her actual parents. You wonder why you've never realized this before.

She stares at the beer. "Is that for me, Kat?" Her voice is shaky. "You shouldn't have."

"I didn't," you tell her, and pop the tab and down the can in one gulp, the same way you did on that night in the woods fourteen years ago. Vanessa gapes.

"Kat?"

Alcohol's a disinhibitor. You let go, unclench, and watch yourself reflected in the apartment windows. You're seeing what she sees. Your limbs turn green and knobbed; your signature black cotton clothing distorts because now it's draped over too many joints; your eyes expand, huge and faceted. That's as far as it's ever gone before, but tonight, hoping you'll still be able to call it back, you let it go a little further. You grow mandibles. Your hands become claws.

"You're not drunk yet," you tell her, forcing English words through this new anatomy. Each syllable blends with clicks and chirps. You hope she can understand you. "You're really seeing this. It happened on your fourteenth birthday too, when I chugged that beer, and I was so relieved when you didn't remember it, because I was afraid you'd hate me if I showed you that you were wrong about your parents. Aliens are real. I don't know if I'm the same kind who picked them up. I don't even know if that's really what happened to them. But it's certainly possible, okay? They weren't telling those stories to hide drinking, and you don't have to drink to feel connected to them."

Vanessa, who sat down very suddenly on the couch at the beginning of this speech, whimpers. You take a step closer, every part of your body screaming in pain, yearning to transform further. You don't let it.

This is the hardest thing you've ever done.

"Now you know why I'm so fascinated by changeling stories. You think you don't fit in? Cry me a river. I'd give anything to have a group like you do. I'd give anything to be able to say, 'My name's Kat, and I'm an extraterrestrial who got left here by my parents and left behind again when they picked up my best friend's parents and couldn't bother with me.' You think you've got abandonment issues, Vanessa? Get in line."

You take another step, and Van shrinks into the back of the couch. "And you know why I'd love a group like that, aside from the fact that I'm horribly lonely? You know why I always eat salad and fucking protein powder even though they make me sick and I hate them? You know why they make me sick? They make me sick because you aren't the ultimate carnivore, Vanessa. I am. I've wanted meat every second I've been aware, and not just any meat. Not cow meat. Human flesh. You. My parents must have loved me, because they left me somewhere with lots and lots of food. And the whole time you've known me, I've never let myself eat it."

A third step. Vanessa's eyes are almost as big as yours now. She fumbles in her bag for her phone, and you force yourself to start turning back. "Van," you say, and she looks up. "Van, I'm changing back. I'm going to be the Kat you've always known. Don't call anybody, okay? I'm not going to eat anybody, and I don't want to be dissected. That's why I never told your parents or the others what I was. I didn't want them to worship me. I didn't want them to put me in a lab. I didn't want to eat them."

She blinks. You force yourself back into fully human form, or as fully human as your form gets. You know she'll never look at you the same way again. You know there's no going back from what you've just done. You take a deep breath. "So, listen, you think you have trouble with your cravings? Well, so do I, and I have a lot less support than you do, and I've stayed vegan one lousy second at a time because I don't want to hurt people who've tried to help me, because this is where I live. Okay? If I can stay abstinent, so can you. But if you drink, I will too. We both fall off the wagon together. Deal?" You see her swallow. "So do the right thing, Van, because now there's a lot more at stake than your individual life. For all you know, you could be saving the entire planet."

She nods jerkily. The beer's churning in your stomach. "I have to throw up now," you say. "Excuse me." You run into the bathroom, certain that you'll be left behind again, that Vanessa's fled the apartment, that she's calling someone even now—as you heave and puke—and that you'll live the rest of your life, however long that is, as a science experiment.

But when you emerge from the bathroom, she's waiting for you, standing with crossed arms, and once again you're amazed by her courage. "You must have done it sometime," she says. "Eaten, the, you know, meat. The whole time I've known you, you said, but you must have before that. Or you wouldn't know. Would you?" Sometimes Van's smart even when she's not drunk. You look away, and she says, "Fair's fair. You know everything about me."

You stare out the window over her left shoulder. "The first pediatrician. And that foster mother. And the nurse in the room. Of course the exam turned up abnormalities, so I acted in self-defense. I was just a baby. It's a pretty famous unsolved case: four people, three adults and an infant, missing from a clinic, never seen again. You can find it if you do an internet search."

Vanessa shakes her head. "If you were just a baby, how—"

"I grew. That's what eating meat does. I was a baby and then after I ate I was what I am now, more or less. I haven't changed much the whole time you've known me, right?" She shakes her head. "Yeah, so. I got into the hall—no one saw me leave the room—and then I just walked out of the building. I used the money from my foster mother's wallet to hop a bus east." You look back at her. "I have no idea what I'd turn into if I ate more."

"Vanished," she says, her voice tight. "No bodies?" You can't answer. All that blood and bone and flesh; you ate it all. Not a speck of any of those three people was left in the room. Vanessa shudders. "My parents vanished. Do you think—"

"I don't know," you tell her, although you've thought about it. "I don't think so, Van. I mean, they'd had some kind of contact before that, right? They knew it was coming. We don't warn our meals."

Vanessa lets out a long breath. After a moment she says, "Well,

I hope you're right, even though I figured they had to be dead." And then, cautiously, "It wasn't you, right?"

You recoil. "God no! No, Vanessa! I was the same before and after your parents disappeared, right? I'd have changed."

She nods, seems to accept this. "Do you think they came in a spaceship, or—"

"I don't know. I figure if it or they were still here, if they were meat-eaters like me, we'd have heard a bunch of horror stories. More missing people. So maybe a spaceship, if they were meat-eaters. Either way, they wanted nothing to do with me."

"Shit," Vanessa says. "That hurts. I'm sorry."

"I'm not. I mean, I kind of am. I was. But now I'm glad. Because I like people." You're embarrassed, but it's true. Those sincere alkies at the meeting, the geeky students in your classes, the checker at the grocery store who frets over how thin you are and keeps asking you whether you have a warm winter coat. Vanessa. "It sounds corny, but I love you guys. I don't want to eat any of you. I just want to go native, even if I have to live on salad and throw up all the time. I just want to belong."

You realize, right then, why you still hang out with Vanessa. You want to save someone, to be the hero instead of the monster. And maybe you want to give her the chance to be a hero, too. You swallow. "You'll help me, right?"

A tear slides down her cheek. "Hell, Kat. I've never helped anybody. But I will if I can."


That was years ago. So far, both of you have kept your promises, one lousy second at a time.

*This is one of the three new stories I wrote for this book. It's a response to "Windows," because like many people, I hate not knowing what happens to characters. In this piece I've answered one question and left another hanging; I hope readers won't be angry about that. Actually, the stories collected here contain a lot of not knowing, because I think most of us spend our lives swimming through mystery without really being aware of it. But there's a difference between not knowing and refusing to accept what's already known. This story plays with that idea, too*

# WISHBONE

'M DELIGHTED THAT you're interviewing me. Please don't be nervous, and please stop calling me Oldest Among Us. My name's Mandy. What's yours?

Gallia-of-Forby-Creche? What do people call you? Gal. I like that. How old are you? Thirteen. Ninety years younger than I am.

A lottery! That's fitting. I won a lottery to be on this ship, and you won a lottery to be the student in your creche to interview me. What do you want to know?

What do I miss most about Earth? Oh, Gal. I miss all the things you've only seen images of: the redwoods and the ocean and the animals, wild animals, not the ones we raise on the ship for food, but animals who belong only to themselves and lead their own lives. I miss how those things could surprise you, be danger-ous, even: I miss how they smelled and tasted and felt against your skin, even then when Earth was dying, because no still or holo can capture that.

And I miss—oh! I miss all the things I can't miss, the things I didn't know enough to pay attention to at the time. I was too stupid to realize that I was going to be staring at stars for the rest of my life, that I should spend my last few months on Earth soaking in sunsets and mountains and oceans and forests, not that any of them were in great shape at that point. I was only nineteen when we set out, not much older than you are now, and I was so busy spinning dreams about space and the stars, so impatient to be *off*, that I didn't take enough time to appreciate what I was leaving. Not that I could have stockpiled everything, anyway; you can't possibly imagine how large a world is when you've spent your life on a ship.

You've already heard all this, I'm sure. For as long as I've been the only remaining Earthborn on the ship—twelve years now—someone interviews me every Fire Festival. They always ask that question, and I always say the same thing. But it hits harder this year. I may not live to see another, and of course I won't live to see NewEarth, if we get there. Neither will you. Neither will anyone else, not for generations.

I'm so sad for you. You'll never get to see a world.

Do I miss people who stayed on Earth? Yes, of course. For a long time I missed my parents, especially after the fire cut off our comms, but I know they're dead by now. I'm sad for everyone who had to stay behind, but we have people here. We have each other. We don't have redwoods, or the ocean.

Yes, a lot of people ask me what it was like to know who your parents were. I was lucky; my parents were wonderful. After the fire, not being able to talk to them was agonizing, and that lasted for a long time, and then for another long time I found myself almost happy about it. Without comms, I could pretend Earth was okay, that somehow they'd found a way to save the planet and themselves. I could tell myself that maybe there were still people who looked up at the stars and wondered about us the way I wondered about them. As long as we couldn't talk to them, I'd never know for sure. I could imagine whatever I wanted.

But I've gotten away from your question, haven't I? My parents were wonderful, but other people had horrible parents. And I think—you must know this, must have learned it—that the two pregnant women who died in the fire were the most deeply mourned of all, because they took so much hope with them. That's when we switched to in vivo, to the artificial wombs and creches: not just because putting those things at the core of the ship made them easier to protect, but because that way no one but the geneticists would know who was whose child. Even the two pregnant women who survived wanted their babies raised communally. Everyone thought it was wiser. This way, we're all your family. I hope that's how it works for you, that you know how loved you are, by all of us. You're our future, even more literally than children were on Earth.

No, Gal, you don't need to be afraid to ask the next question. I think I know what it is. I'll ask it for you. How do I feel about the Unearthers? Is that what you were going to ask?

Yes. I thought so.

And I'm going to answer honestly, and that means I'm going to talk for a while, so brace yourself.

So. I'm the last person on this ship who remembers Earth, and soon I'll be dead, and there are already people denying that the planet I was born on, the one that sent all of us on this journey to find another like it, even existed. It doesn't matter that we have thousands of hours of footage, plus stills and holos and the artifacts people brought from Earth. The Unearthers think it's all faked. Logic doesn't work on them. Asking where they think we came from if we're not from Earth doesn't work, either. They say we've always been here, as if generation ships just pop into existence.

Talking to them about Earth doesn't work. They say I'm a propaganda agent or brainwashed or demented, even though I've passed all the annual neurocog exams. I can remember strings of words. I can draw an airlock. I can count backwards from 100 by sevens. What I can't do is convince a bunch of idiots that we didn't evolve in space—how could we have?—and that what we left is worth trying to find again.

And yes, I know they're a minority. But I'm afraid that in another generation or two, they won't be. And right now, they're trying to erase *me*, Gal. I *remember* the fire. I remember what it felt like to lose contact with Earth so soon after we'd left, just a few years. You can't imagine, of course you can't, that was seventy-four years ago and you weren't born yet. Now the Fire Festival's about heroism and survival and overcoming adversity, but early on it was about danger, and loss, and grief. People *died.* I knew them. You only know their names, if that.

And being erased isn't even the worst part of it. The most terrifying thing is that the Unearthers are doing *exactly what landed us here in the first place.* Earth became unlivable because people refused to honor history and evidence. There were flat-Earthers and anti-vaxxers and Holocaust deniers and climate-change deniers, so *of course* there are now Unearthers. What did we think would happen? How could we have expected anything else? And why didn't the original planners foresee this? They drew up contingency plans for hull breaches and life-system failures and first contact with aliens, but they forgot about stupidity.

That's more of an answer than you expected, isn't it? You probably only understood a third of it. You look frightened, Gal. I'm sorry. But you *should* be frightened. You and your friends need to make sure the Unearthers don't win. They aren't a joke. They're dangerous. You need to remember that I was real, that the place I came from was real, that we evolved to live on a planet, not in a ship.

Have you ever heard of a man named Erik Erikson? He was a famous psychologist, back on Earth. He studied human development, and he believed that in each life stage, there was a conflict to resolve. For you, in adolescence, it's group identity versus alienation. That's one reason creches are so important; they give you a group to belong to. My conflict, in late old age—later than most people ever reached, in Erikson's time!—is immortality versus extinction. And it's funny, because that's the task facing the entire ship now. If we make it to NewEarth, we'll have a chance to start over, to do better. If the Unearthers win and decide that we just need to rove around the universe mining asteroids, or whatever their damnfool plan is, then we're doomed. We can live in this ship for a long time, but not forever. It wasn't designed for that.

One more question, Gal, because I'm getting tired.

What was my artifact? I'll show you. I have it right here. No, mine isn't part of the artifact display; it won't go there until I die. But maybe it won't go there at all. I think I'll give it to you instead. Not many people look at the artifact displays anymore, all those gew-gaws from Earth that don't mean anything apart from the stories attached to them: the buttons and pictures and dolls, the tiny nonuseful heirlooms, one each, we were allowed to bring.

Yes, it's a bone. It's a kind of bone called a wishbone, from a chicken. The chickens here have them too, but here anything that isn't eaten gets recycled. I brought this because we used to play a silly game with them. If one person grabs one end and someone else grabs the second and they pull, the break usually isn't even. There's more bone on one side than the other. So before they pull, each person makes a wish, and the wish made by the person who gets more of the bone will come true.

What's that? Yes, exactly. Both people can't have their wish granted. It's a zero-sum game. One person wins. The other loses.

Why would we do that to each other? Bless you, child. Yes, I am crying, a little, because if you can ask that, this experiment worked. The idea of competition really is foreign to you. We created a collectivist society.

Of course, whether the wishes come true really has nothing to do with the chicken bone. But in my family we always broke the wishbone when we ate a chicken. Before the lottery results were announced, my parents wished that I'd stay on Earth; I wished that I'd leave. I won, the wishbone game and the lottery both. It worked that time: coincidence. Before I left, my mother gave me this wishbone and said, "Don't break it. Keep it whole. Work towards a future where nothing needs to be broken for people to get what they need, and where no one's success cancels anyone else's."

Imagination: that's the key. You can't imagine playing games that would hurt people. We couldn't have built the generation ship without being able to imagine NewEarth. The Unearthers think OldEarth never existed because they can't imagine it, even with the holos and the footage and the artifacts. And they're afraid of what they don't know, the way people always have been. Can we imagine a future where nothing needs to be broken? I don't know. I hope so.

Yes, Gal, I am tired. But before you leave, it's my turn to ask you a question.

Do you believe in Earth? Yes? What makes you believe, when you've never seen it?

Ha! Who *would* make up a wishbone, or giraffes, or penguins? Well, people with imagination can make up amazing things. But you're right: even if they never existed—and giraffes and penguins did, I promise you, just like this wishbone does—they should have. A future where things like that can exist again, along with things we can't even imagine now, is worth working for.

Here, Gal. Here's my wishbone. When you're very old, give it to someone else. Tell them my story. Tell them zero-sum games don't work. Tell them to keep the wishbone whole. We can have space *and* a world, this time: if we're smart, and if we're kind, and if we remember where we came from.

# ACKNOWLEDGEMENTS

I AM DEEPLY GRATEFUL to all of my editors, especially the ones who bought the previously published stories in this volume. Thank you for making me a better writer and for giving my voice a wider audience. Thanks also to all the readers who've taken the time to comment on my stories or to share what my work has meant to them. That kind of feedback means more than you can know; it's what keeps writers going.

This book would not exist without the following people:

Kevin Finegan, who unknowingly inspired me to try to publish a second story collection.

Jo Walton, brilliant writer and fierce friend, who has always championed my work and hounded me about getting more of it into the world, and who—at the San Jose Worldcon in 2018—literally grabbed my elbow and marched me into the dealers room to talk to editors about publishing this book.

Jacob Weisman, who introduced me to Patrick Swenson.

Patrick Swenson, who has been every writer's dream of an editor, and who designed such a beautiful volume that I dance inside whenever I look at it.

And, finally and always, my husband Gary Meyer, who reads everything I write before anyone else does, and keeps me in fabulous home-cooked food and clean laundry, and always has more faith in me than I have in myself.

# ABOUT THE AUTHOR

SUSAN PALWICK has published four novels with Tor Books and a previous story collection, *The Fate of Mice*, with Tachyon Publications. Her fiction has been honored with a Crawford Award from the International Association for the Fantastic in the Arts, an Alex Award from the American Library Association, and a Silver Pen Award from the Nevada Writers Hall of Fame, and has also been nominated for the World Fantasy Award and the Mythopoeic Award. Her poetry publications include a collection of sonnets from Texas A&M University Press. After retiring from twenty years as an English professor at the University of Nevada, Reno, Susan recently earned her Master of Social Work degree, also from UNR. She and her husband live with their three cats in the foothills of the Sierra Nevada.

# PUBLICATION HISTORY

"Windows" originally appeared in *Asimov's* (2014); reprinted in *Best American Science Fiction and Fantasy*, ed Adams and Hill (2015) | "The Shining Hills" originally appeared in *Lightspeed* (2017) | "Ash" originally appeared in *The Magazine of Fantasy & Science Fiction* (2016) | "Cucumber Gravy" originally appeared in *SciFiction* (2001); reprinted in *Lightspeed* (2011) | "Hhasalin" originally appeared in *The Magazine of Fantasy & Science Fiction* (2013) | "Sanctuary" originally appeared in *Eclipse Online* (2013) | "City of Enemies" is previously unpublished and appears here for the first time | "Lucite" originally appeared in *Asimov's* (2016) | "Hodge" is previously unpublished and appears here for the first time | "Homecoming" originally appeared at *Tor.com* (2013) "Weather" originally appeared in *Clarkesworld* (2014); reprinted in *The Year's Best Science Fiction*, ed Dozois (2014) | "Hideous Flowerpots" originally appeared in *The Magazine of Fantasy & Science Fiction* (2018) | "Remote Presence" originally appeared in *Lightspeed* (2017) | "Recoveries" originally appeared at *Tor.com* (2018) | "Wishbone" is previously unpublished and appears here for the first time.

# OTHER TITLES FROM FAIRWOOD PRESS

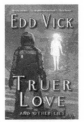

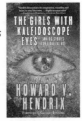
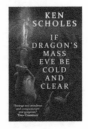

9 781933 846842